THE IDOL

THE
IDOL

ROBERT MERLE

Translated from the French by
Barbara Bray

COLLINS HARVILL
8 Grafton Street, London W1
1989

COLLINS HARVILL
William Collins Sons and Co. Ltd
London . Glasgow . Sydney . Auckland
Toronto . Johannesburg

BRITISH LIBRARY CATALOGUING IN PUBLICATION DATA

Merle, Robert
The Idol
I. Title
843'.912 [F]

ISBN 0-00-271345-4

Published in France by Librairie Plon, Paris
under the title *L'Idole*

First published in Great Britain
by Collins Harvill 1989
© Librairie Plon 1987
English translation © William Collins Sons & Co. Ltd 1989

Photoset in Monophoto Van Dijck
by Servis Filmsetting Limited
Printed and bound in Great Britain by
Hartnolls Limited, Bodmin, Cornwall

FOREWORD

I made the acquaintance of Signora Vittoria Peretti forty years ago, when I was translating Webster's brilliant but uneven play on the subject, written in a language that makes Shakespeare's seem clear as crystal.

It was only ten years later, reading Stendhal's *Chroniques italiennes*, that I realised how horribly unfair Webster's account of Vittoria was. Of course he may have been misinformed, but how, when the mere facts present her as an obvious victim, could he have blackened her name to the point of calling her *The White Devil*? The suggestion is that in her the beauty of the flesh concealed a diabolical soul. A good example of Puritan misogyny! The poor woman is persecuted and imprisoned, and it's all her fault.

Stendhal's story consists of some thirty pages, but is not the original work some say it is — rather it is a literal translation of an old chronicle that must have attracted him because of his predilection for strong passions and energetic characters.

In 1957 I wrote a short story based on the chronicle, but on reflection it left me dissatisfied. It took me some time, though, to realise why.

Vittoria was good, intelligent, cultivated and generous. It wasn't for these virtues, however, that she was idolised, but because of the way female beauty was overvalued in a male-dominated society — an error of judgment even more dangerous for its object than for morality itself.

In our day Vittoria would have been some kind of star, and the worst that would have happened to her, though that's pathetic enough, would have been to lose her admirers as she grew old. But in the sixteenth century her life was quite different. She was sold in marriage to a man she didn't love. Her virtue was fiercely guarded. She was kept in seclusion twice, and even, for a few months, imprisoned in the Castel Sant'Angelo. She was spied on, kept under surveillance, betrayed by her confessor. Her reputation was publicly tarnished. A Pope annulled her second marriage.

In short, she was a woman alone against a whole society, and to make her fate comprehensible one must obviously recreate its archaic, brutal and vindictive setting. It was precisely this that seemed to me to be lacking in the story I wrote in 1957. It was too linear. It described what happened, but neglected the background necessary to explain why.

When I conceived the idea of the present novel I thought at first I could simply rewrite my earlier attempt.

But this proved impossible. I soon saw I had to undo everything and start again, to revise and expand my research, and while using the same theme, give it a much broader and more imaginative treatment, with new or newly-conceived protagonists, a fuller background of other characters, and a narrative style that would bring out the extreme complexity of the situation with which Vittoria had to contend.

When my researches were complete I went to Lake Garda, and was moved by the sight of the place where Vittoria spent her last summer of happiness, in 1585. Its name is different now, but the four centuries that have passed over it since have done it no harm except to darken its stones. It is quite unlike a Venetian villa as it stands, rough and austere, beside the water. When I saw it, even the great magnolia trees on the jetty did nothing to lighten the atmosphere, especially as at that time of the year their petals were falling one by one on to the ripples of the misty lake. The air was balmy, but the place was melancholy.

Not a tile was missing from the palace itself. How sad to think that houses live so much longer than the men who build them. I would have preferred it to be the other way round: to have found nothing but fallen pillars strewn on the ground, and Vittoria herself sitting on the ruins amid her long tresses, rewarding me with a grateful look for having told her story fairly and with compassion.

1

Monsignor Rossellino (il bello muto)⋆

Five years ago – to be precise, on December 5th 1572 at seven in the morning – as I was going up the steps leading to the Vatican, I tripped and fell; my neck struck the edge of a stair, the blow crushed my larynx, and I would have died there and then of asphyxiation if a barber-surgeon who happened to be there hadn't opened my throat with a small pair of scissors. The wound healed, but the accident left me dumb.

In those days there were no more than ten barber-surgeons in Rome, and I concluded that if Providence had put one of the cleverest of them in my way so early in the morning it must have been because Providence itself deliberately intended the barely credible series of events that affected my life from then on: my fall, the crushing of my larynx, the barber's intervention, my dumbness, and my meeting with Cardinal Montalto.

Before the accident I'd been one of the most brilliant preachers in the Eternal City. All the nobility of Rome flocked to my sermons, which brought me not only fame but also the favour of the most exalted ladies. They would often invite me to their palaces, set exquisite dishes before me and generally make much of me, asking nothing in return but that I speak to them with my usual fire of the pains of hell or the bliss of heaven. Whichever I depicted, it gave them great pleasure, and I was foolish enough to take pride in supplying it.

I was then twenty-eight. According to the women in my family – and

⋆ The handsome mute

7

everyone knows how that visceral sex (*tota mulier in ventre*)★ loves to chatter – I was quite good-looking. And although my behaviour was virtuous, I did rather glory in my flesh, conscious that the charms of my corporeal frame greatly enhanced those of my eloquence.

In the summer months the Contessa V. liked to sit under an ancient tree in her garden, surrounded by her friends, and listen to me. I remember how when I described – vividly but with proper restraint – the tortures of the damned, little drops of perspiration would break out on her lovely brow, gasps would escape from her parted lips and her graceful neck would suddenly flush. It was as if she enjoyed yielding up her little body to the demons' cruelties. As I spun out my description her agitation increased, and this so affected me that I would embellish my account with further details which I cannot now call to mind without shame.

After my throat had been carved up and my fine deep voice had fallen silent, I realised that a snake had been lying stretched out along one of the branches under which I used to preach, just waiting for the right moment to drop between the Contessa and me like a dreadful bond.

It was a fig tree, and though it bore leaves it was barren.

I concluded that the same divine hand that had withered the fig tree in the Gospel had taken away my voice to prevent me from falling into sin – and the sin of my weak flesh was perhaps not the worst. I was just considering retiring into a monastery for the rest of my life when I received a terse note from Cardinal Montalto asking me to call on him in his palace.

I imagine Felice Peretti, who had received his cardinal's hat two years before, had chosen the name Montalto to reflect both the loftiness of his ambitions and the ruggedness of his character. I trembled as I drew near the terrible cardinal's palace, though the building itself was modest and bare. I knew that as Grand Inquisitor in Venice he had fallen upon the immorality of the clergy with fire and sword; his austerity had made him so universally hated that the priests had finally leagued together against him and prevailed upon the Senate to expel him from the Most Serene Republic.

★ All of a woman is in her belly.

He now lived in such seclusion that until now I had never set eyes on him. And, to tell the truth, I was disappointed at first. At that time Rome was full of magnificent prelates, of whom Pope Gregory XIII was undoubtedly the finest: he was then seventy years old but held himself very erect; agile and graceful in his movements, he could vault into the saddle like a youth.

Cardinal Montalto was of no more than medium height, and although he wasn't a hunchback as some spiteful people claimed, he gave that impression with his large shaggy head sunk between massive shoulders. I say his head was large because it struck me as out of proportion to the rest of his body, and it was shaggy because as a former Franciscan he wore his hair and beard long: both were dishevelled and carelessly trimmed. This gave him a rough appearance that was very unusual in Rome, where most prelates looked like pebbles worn smooth and shiny by rubbing together in the tides.

A large nose, thin lips, projecting chin, bushy black eyebrows (in contrast to his pepper-and-salt hair and beard), and beneath them deep-set black eyes, very bright and piercing, added to the strength but scarcely to the attractiveness of a countenance which, were it not for my profound respect for His Eminence, I might best describe as savage.

He was ill-favoured, fallen from favour, and I expected no favours from him. Even so I was surprised by the roughness of his manner and the imperious curtness of his words.

"Rossellino," he said, not replying to my dumbshow of civilities, "sit down at that little table. Yes, there – sit down. In front of you there's a pen, ink, paper, a lighted candle and a brass tray. Why the candle? To burn your answers as soon as you've written them. Why the tray? To hold the ashes. Now write! And no hypocrisy, please! And still less any clerical jargon! Just the truth pure and simple! If the truth ever is pure. And if you lie even once I'll have you shown the door. Are you ready?"

This opening terrified me. I took the goose-quill in my trembling hand, dipped it in the ink and waited. The answers that follow were written on little squares of paper. As soon as I'd written what I had to say on one of them the cardinal, who was standing behind me, took or rather snatched it from my hands, glanced at it, and immediately burned it in the candle flame.

"Are you chaste?"

"Yes, Your Eminence."

"Leave out 'Your Eminence.' It slows down the writing. Have you ever been tempted not to be?"

"Yes."

"Where, when and with whom?"

"In Contessa V.'s garden, before I fell down on the Vatican steps."

"Explain."

"I was describing the torments of the damned to the Contessa. It disturbed her. Her agitation disturbed me."

"Have you seen the Contessa again?"

"Not since my accident."

"How do you see your accident?"

"As a decree of Providence. My fall saved me from falling. I realised the vanity of the life I was leading and that my fine voice was just a snare. And I was the first to be caught in it."

"Well said! What do you plan to do now?"

"Bury myself in a monastery."

"Ill reasoned! You're a secular priest. Stay in the world. Serve the Church."

"Is that possible?"

"Of course. What do you consider the ills that beset the State?"

"Anarchy, corruption, contempt for the law, and the fact that bandits, titled or otherwise, go unpunished."

"And the ills of the Church?"

"Immorality, the craving for riches and display, simony, absenteeism among the bishops, and the use of excommunication for non-religious purposes."

"*Bene, bene, bene*. But complaining about abuses isn't enough. They must be remedied."

"Can I remedy them?"

"You can't, but I can. Do you want to help me?"

"Is that possible, when I'm dumb?"

"Yes. For that very reason."

With his implacable black eyes riveted on mine, Montalto was silent long enough to convey all the implications of what he'd said. I wrote: "I offer my devotion, loyalty and silence to Your Eminence *ad majorem gloriam Dei et Ecclesiae*".

"*Bene*. You shall be my chief secretary. Listen, Rossellino, I didn't inherit a fortune. I don't buy and sell preferment. Unlike a lot of other cardinals, I don't receive an allowance from Philip II of Spain for selling him my vote in the conclave. So you won't be paid much."

"That doesn't matter."

"*Bene*. What do you think of the present Pope?"

Then, as I hesitated, Montalto glared at me and shouted: "Answer! Answer at once! Say what you think!"

I wrote: "It's a great sin for a priest to have a natural child. For a Pope it's a scandal. It's an even greater scandal when he makes his natural son the governor of Rome."

Montalto tore the square of paper out of my hands, burned it in the candle flame and said curtly: "Go on."

"The Pope is indolent and won't go to any trouble. He'll never lift a finger to remedy abuses. All he cares about are the arts, the splendour of his court and his collection of jewellery."

Montalto read the piece of paper, set light to it, and for once watched it burn on the brass tray. A half-smile played over his thin lips, though I noticed at once it did nothing to soften his savage countenance.

"Where do you live?"

I wrote: "With an elderly aunt on the Appian Way."

"I wager she spoils you outrageously."

"Yes, she does."

"Women have two ways of weakening a man: food and the flesh. You will come and live here, Rossellino. You will sleep in an unheated room. And you'll eat with me and like me – poorly and scantily."

"I shall regard it as a very great honour, Your Eminence."

"*Bene*. No fine phrases. You may go. I'll see you tomorrow."

And that was how I became chief secretary to Cardinal Montalto. As soon as Gregory XIII heard of it he jested about it for a week.

"*Il bello muto*" – as he called me – "must have committed some very great sins when he still had his voice, otherwise he wouldn't have undertaken the awful penance of living in Montalto's hovel, sharing his meagre rations and putting up with his temper. As for Montalto, he's pulled off a typical monkish trick and got himself a secretary who couldn't be more discreet."

Giulietta Accoramboni

I was born in Gubbio, Umbria, where my father and his brother Bernardo made and sold majolica plates and dishes. As everyone knows, the glaze used on these wares was imported from Majorca by Arab craftsmen: it produces a very clear white base that takes colours very well. However, the colours only retained their brightness because of a varnish invented by the painter Giorgio Andreoli, from whom in his old age the two brothers bought his factory, which was also in Gubbio.

Majolica ware, famous not only in Italy but also in France, Austria and all the rest of Europe, usually has a carefully painted head of a man or a woman in the middle and is surrounded by a border illustrating allegorical themes. I remember seeing one on a wall in my uncle Bernardo's house; it depicted the haughty profile of his wife Tarquinia: the worthy folk of Gubbio called her *la superba*, both because of her physical attractions and on account of her overbearing character.

The allusion to the last king of ancient Rome did not displease my aunt. In her youth she had dreamed of marrying into the nobility, and sometimes, looking at the ducal palace opposite her house in Gubbio, she found herself regretting that she'd become the wife of a rich merchant when her beauty might have opened other doors.

The plate bearing her portrait met with a peculiar fate. One day, during a furious argument between Tarquinia and her son Marcello, he rushed towards her in a blind rage, his hands outstretched as if to strangle her. But at the last moment, frightened by the enormity of the crime he was about to commit, he deflected his wrath on to the majolica portrait, wrenched it from the wall and smashed it to pieces on the floor.

Perhaps I ought to explain why I was there in my uncle's house to be the witness of this symbolical murder. In the summer of 1570 there were a few cases of plague in Gubbio, so Tarquinia decided to leave the city and retire to her house in the country with her three children, her husband and me. My being of the party is no proof of my aunt's affection for me, but rather of mine for her daughter Vittoria. She and I were playmates and, being three years her senior, I was also to some extent her mentor.

Uncle Bernardo had some scruples about leaving my father alone in charge of the majolica factory at a time when to stay in Gubbio meant risking one's life. But having spent his whole life deferring to *la superba* out of a characteristic mixture of kindness and indolence, he couldn't bring himself to oppose her even when justice and brotherly love demanded it.

True, his cowardice saved his life. But at what cost! The plague that ravaged Gubbio carried off my mother and father, my brothers and sisters, and most of the factory hands. Bernardo's sensitive and somewhat torpid nature gradually succumbed beneath the weight of his grief. The factory, too, was in a bad way. It was hard to replace the Spanish-Arab workmen who had died in the plague, and my uncle, though a very good artist, lacked my father's business talent.

This was the moment Tarquinia decided to move to Rome, so as to marry off Vittoria in accordance with her own ambitions. I saw poor Bernardo begging and praying her when he should have been giving orders. In the end, as usual, he gave in. And he and his younger son Flaminio stayed on in Gubbio, struggling to derive from majolica the money Tarquinia needed to rent a fine palace in Rome, in the Piazza dei Rusticucci near St Peter's. Here she at once began to keep open house.

Marcello, who was not interested in majolica or indeed in any other kind of work, accompanied his mother to Rome, where he set up as a nobleman, wearing dagger and sword, learning to fence, and making high-ranking but shady friends who doted on his equivocal good looks. He also cultivated the friendship of a rich widow old enough to be his mother. With her, as with his mother, he often quarrelled, mainly about the money he borrowed from her. Strangely enough, no one in Rome ventured to doubt that he really was a nobleman. Of course, he was exceedingly pugnacious, and a disagreeable look was enough to make his sword fly from its scabbard. And there was no shortage of pseudo-noblemen in the Eternal City.

This brief sketch is enough to show that my uncle Bernardo's family was divided equally between angels and devils. The angels worked in Gubbio. The devils spent money like water in Rome. To tell the truth, Vittoria was neither angel nor devil but a bit of both. As for me, I didn't really count, and this didn't change even when, just before he died, Bernardo adopted me. The reason *la superba* didn't object to this was that it posed no threat to her own children: Bernardo by now had nothing but debts.

As I am about the only person in the family with an ounce of commonsense, I think I'm the best one to describe Vittoria – I won't say without prejudice one way or the other, because I love her. But I refuse to join in the idolatry that surrounds her on all sides. I have a rational love for her, even though she herself is so lacking in reason.

On the diabolical side Vittoria inherited from *la superba* her passionate temperament, her unyielding character, and, for those who know her well, her touchy pride. She also inherited Tarquinia's beauty; but in this respect she greatly surpasses her mother. For the goodness that comes to her from her father, and from him alone, gives her eyes, her delicately curved lips and her smooth features a very engaging sweetness. The inside has affected the outside. I predict that her face will age well, whereas time has made Tarquinia's grim and inhuman.

Vittoria is tall, comely and imposing. Her big blue eyes are fringed with black lashes thick as leaves on a tree. And, incredible as it may sound, when she undoes her silky blonde curls she has only to tilt her head back and her hair touches the ground. In Gubbio she couldn't appear in the street without everybody, young and old, coming up to her and saying respectfully: "*Col suo permesso, signorina,*"[*] and reverently touching the golden fleece with the tips of their fingers.

When she's naked she can hide her whole body with her hair, but it takes so much looking after, it is so heavy, gives her so many headaches, and so often even makes her overbalance if she turns too quickly that she frequently talks of having it cut off, at least to waist length. I'm the only one who finds this a sensible idea: it plunges all the rest of the Rusticucci palace, servants included, into such consternation, draws such screeches from Tarquinia, and so obviously pains Bernardo when he brings us the gold he's managed to scrape together in Gubbio, that out of sheer kindness Vittoria resigns herself to remaining a slave to her own beauty.

She was fully developed at eleven, and at thirteen was already almost

[*] With your permission, miss.

what she is today: a woman made to rule over the world and over men. Whenever anyone from Rome strayed as far as Gubbio and asked disdainfully what there was to see in our little town, some would say the ducal palace, others the palace of the Council, but the wisest answered "Vittoria Accoramboni". And if the visitor had the good fortune to see her in the street, he would return to the city of the Popes full of extravagant praise for our *Bellissima*.

That was what we called her in Gubbio: the adjective *bellissima* was as inseparable from her name as *serenissima* was from that of the Venetian Republic.

Vittoria's hair was washed every week on Tuesday and Saturday. This rite involved our whole domestic staff: the men to keep up a good fire, bring buckets of hot water to fill a wooden bath, drain out the dirty water by means of a tap in the bottom of the tub, replenish the hot water, and so on; the women to soap the long masses of hair with the necessary care. Meanwhile Vittoria, sitting on a stool by one end of the bath, the back of her neck resting on a little cushion on the edge and the whole length of her tresses in the water, would read Petrarch's sonnets, sometimes aloud.

I think she got into the habit partly so as not to be deafened by the chatter of the maids crowding round her, and partly because she adored poetry. Tarquinia had seen to it that she received the education of a queen in all respects. She even knew Latin.

Since towels alone were not enough to dry such a long and luxuriant mane, they had to be supplemented by a fire or, if the weather was fine, by the sun. The latter, according to Tarquinia, had the additional advantage of heightening the golden tints. So on fine days Vittoria would be conducted with some ceremony to a south-facing balcony and installed on a chair, two maids holding her hair up like a train so that it shouldn't touch the ground on the way. As soon as their mistress was seated they spread the great lengths of golden silk on a specially built rack, like choice fruit left to ripen.

This ritual was carried out at the beginning of the afternoon, and as the people of Gubbio knew of it, every idle stroller would make for my uncle Bernardo's house on the appointed days in the hope of catching a distant glimpse of Vittoria's hair absorbing gold from the sun.

The same custom continued in Rome after we moved to the

Rusticucci palace, but as Tarquinia by now put more emphasis on decorum, it was no longer carried out magnanimously in public, as it had been in our own little town, but unseen, in an inner courtyard.

The open-house policy Tarquinia initiated at such expense on her arrival in Rome didn't produce the expected results. A number of gentlemen, young and old, handsome and ugly, frequented the Rusticucci palace, but while Vittoria attracted them, her father's indigence did not. It was all very well to marry a merchant's daughter and enter a family without kin or connections, but in that case the merchant must be rich! In this case, however, he had nothing but debts, and these cast a shadow over Vittoria's dazzling beauty. Moreover, the daughter herself was proud and learned and didn't suffer fools gladly. She would have been more popular if her mind had been more humdrum and her character less haughty.

For two years Tarquinia kept her daughter on display without receiving an offer, despite all the real or alleged suitors who swarmed around her like flies round a drop of honey. To tell the truth, the least alluring of the swains did make a few timid overtures, but Tarquinia, while not actually turning him down, didn't encourage him, saying equivocally that her daughter, just turned sixteen, was still very young to marry. Although Francesco Peretti was the nephew of a cardinal, *la superba* considered his nobility too slight and his fortune too unremarkable. In her early days in Rome nothing less than a prince would have satisfied her. But for some time now she would have made do with a marquis or a count. However, she found Peretti's offer merely comical and rash, and she considered it was very good of her to treat him so politely, merely meeting a semi-request with a semi-refusal.

On April 15th 1573 an event occurred that Tarquinia might have expected if she'd paid as much attention to other people as she did to her own ambitions: my uncle Bernardo died. He'd never forgiven himself for leaving my father alone in Gubbio during the plague. The decline of the majolica factory, Tarquinia's move to Rome, the absence of his beloved daughter, her mother's unceasing demands for money and the debts he'd incurred to meet them – all these had seemed to him a punishment from God. And instead of struggling against his misfortunes he had only longed for them to crush him altogether.

The news was brought one day on the stroke of noon by Flaminio, who had ridden in haste from Gubbio alone and without an escort. We were taking our midday meal when he appeared, covered in mud, still wearing his boots, his hair dishevelled, his doublet undone, and tears streaming down his cheeks. As soon as he saw Tarquinia he went over to her with outstretched arms as it to seek refuge in her bosom, crying out in a voice of desperation: "Father is dead! We are ruined!"

Tarquinia stood up, white as chalk, and went towards him. But instead of taking him in her arms she frowned, put her hand over his mouth and whispered furiously into his ear: "Are you mad, saying we're ruined in front of the servants? Do you want the whole of Rome to know it by tomorrow?"

"Oh mother, mother, mother!" cried Vittoria, her voice rising as she spoke. And unable to say more, she rose from the table and ran from the room, her long hair streaming behind her.

"Giulietta," said Tarquinia, without batting an eyelid, "go and see she doesn't play her usual trick and shut herself up in her room. I wish to see her this evening."

I too rose, astonished at her coolness.

"My son," she went on, turning to Flaminio, "just look at you! Half undressed and covered with mud! Go and tidy yourself up in your apartments and I'll see you there in about an hour. We have things to talk about."

To join Vittoria in her room I had to go through the whole house, where every corner was already loud with the servants' laments. Of course, Bernardo was a good master, and some of them might be afraid of losing their jobs if the household's style of living were cut back. But they also wept out of decorum, out of popular politeness, the common people's desire to show us they shared our grief. The maids in particular mourned with alacrity: they had made a speciality out of births, marriages and deaths and were always ready to join in with the appropriate emotions.

At the foot of the stairs I passed Marcello, magnificently dressed in a doublet of pale yellow satin, with a dagger at his side. He caught me by the arm and said: "I've just arrived from Amalfi. What's the meaning of these tears? No one can speak to tell me what's the matter. Do you know?"

"Your father's dead."

"Oh!" he said.

But his large black eyes remained dry and his handsome face was expressionless.

"Well," he said at last, "it was only to be expected. Why did he make himself a slave and beast of burden to that virago? Where's Vittoria?"

"In her room. I'm just going to her."

"Good," he said, his upper lip curling in an ironic smile. "Have a good cry together! There's pleasure in tears. As for me, I can't stand moaning and groaning, and I'm going to shut myself up in my room. I'll only come out to tell Tarquinia what I think she ought to do now that — largely thanks to her — our ruin is complete."

"Tell me now!" said Tarquinia haughtily, appearing between us. "But do it in my room, away from other ears. No, don't leave us, Giulietta. Your good sense will come in useful."

As she spoke she took Marcello's arm as if to lead him away, but he threw her off violently.

"Don't touch me!" he hissed. "You know I hate being touched!"

"Even by Vittoria?" said Tarquinia harshly.

"Especially by her!" said Marcello, his handsome face distorted in sudden fury. "I've known it for a long time — women are octopuses. Nothing but tentacles and suckers. And Vittoria's no exception!"

Tarquinia said nothing for as long as it took to open the door of her room and usher Marcello and me in. Then she shot the bolt, turned to Marcello, and said with spurious mildness as she fixed him with her cold blue eye: "How strange, Marcello! I'd have thought Vittoria was an exception, and that there was a soft spot for her in your heart of stone."

"The heart of stone I inherited from you, Madam!" said Marcello, with an angry glare. "Apparently the death of the man who sweated blood for you in Gubbio doesn't bring one tear to your beautiful bright eyes."

"Nor to yours!"

"Mother! Mother!" I said (for as uncle Bernardo had adopted me I was obliged to call her that whether I liked it or not). "Forgive me, but there's no point in my staying if you are going to quarrel."

"You're right, Giulietta," agreed Tarquinia, casting me a disdainful

18

look nonetheless. "You're the only one here with any commonsense! Well, Marcello, since you have an opinion on what's to be done, let's hear it!"

Marcello went and stood by the window with his hands on his hips, perhaps to put his face in shadow and make it less easy to read. And perhaps too, since he was a born actor with an instinctive sense of theatre, to present an elegant silhouette against the window frame.

"I'd like to point out," said he, "that my advice is purely disinterested. Since I don't cost you a penny, mother, I am not affected by our imminent ruin."

"Which shows that Margherita Sorghini's tentacles and suckers are good for something at least," said Tarquinia scornfully. "They keep you in food and clothing."

"Yes," said Marcello. "And now that you've spat your venom on the lady whose friend I am —"

"A very expensive friend," said Tarquinia.

"— As I was saying, this is my advice. Sell the workshop in Gubbio as soon and as profitably as possible. That will pay your debts."

"Only some of them," said Tarquinia.

"Perhaps. You should know. Then, marry off Vittoria, also as soon and as profitably as possible."

"Do you think I need you to reach those conclusions?"

"In that case," said Marcello with a sneer, "I wager you have a few fine suitors up your ample sleeves."

"Only one who's declared himself," said Tarquinia with a sigh. "Francesco Peretti."

"Peretti! Good Lord, that wretched fellow! Minor nobility, little fortune and less wit!"

"But he's a cardinal's nephew, and the Cardinal has adopted him; he's given him his name and treats him like a son. He'll inherit the Cardinal's fortune."

"Some fortune!" said Marcello, throwing up his hands. "Montalto lives in the barest palace in Rome, his coach is a wreck and his horses, which he feeds no better than he feeds himself, are so skinny they can scarcely walk. If they weren't held up by the shafts they'd collapse! And Montalto's so absurdly virtuous he's refused the allowance that Philip II wanted to make him. A fine cardinal! And a fine heir!"

"I know, I know," answered Tarquinia, frowning. "But what can I do? I haven't had time to find anyone better."

"In other words," said Marcello wryly, "Bernardo died too soon for you."

As he spoke he folded his arms theatrically over his chest. But Tarquinia saw neither the affectation nor the irony, any more than she had realised the unseemliness of what she herself had just said. As for me, I was amazed by the blatant cynicism of both mother and son. But I couldn't help seeing that, though each was devilish enough, Marcello for all his airs was the shrewder and less insensitive of the two.

"Well, what do you think, Giulietta?" said Tarquinia condescendingly.

She looked down on me, partly because of my position as a poor adopted niece, partly – literally – because of my small stature, and partly because my mere prettiness couldn't compete with the majestic beauty of the women of her own family. However, she did show me the kind of respect people like her reluctantly grant to those around them with virtues they themselves lack and take no trouble to acquire.

"What do I think about the marriage, or what do I think about Francesco Peretti?" I answered after a moment.

"Both."

"Well, I quite like Francesco. There's nothing brilliant about him, of course, but he's gentle and refined, and does have a certain courage and dignity."

"And what about the marriage?" asked Marcello, looking at me intently.

"From what point of view?"

"Vittoria's."

"Francesco will do anything she wants, so she won't be unhappy."

"And what about Peretti himself?"

"He's too good a man to be happy living with an Accoramboni."

Marcello burst out laughing.

"But you're an Accoramboni yourself, Giulietta!" he said.

"So I know what I'm talking about."

At that he laughed more heartily still.

20

"Hush!" said Tarquinia, hissing like a dozen snakes. "Marcello, how can you roar with laughter on the day of your father's death! What will the servants think if they hear you?"

"They'll think I'm crazy, and they'll be right. We're all crazy in this house. All except Giulietta. My father was a coward whose wife made him tremble! Flaminio is a prize idiot, the dupe of his own pious play-acting! My mother's a gorgon —"

"And Marcello's a pimp!" said Tarquinia harshly.

Although the light was behind him, I saw or thought I saw Marcello turn pale.

"Madam," he said tonelessly, "if you were a man I'd already have put two inches of steel in your chest!"

Despite the melodramatic language, this was no pretence. As he spoke, his hand trembled on the hilt of his dagger, and I got the distinct impression he was restraining a furious impulse to have done with his mother once and for all. I sprang forward and placed myself between the two of them, as I'd done more than once already since I'd entered this unruly family. They carried every passion to excess.

As I pushed Marcello back with both my hands against his chest, I could feel him trembling in every limb in an effort to stifle his fury. He didn't even see me. His black eyes seemed to dart thunderbolts at Tarquinia over my head.

"Marcello!" I cried. "Please!"

He saw me at last and relaxed, and the shadow of a smile — a genuine smile for once — appeared on his face. Perhaps he remembered how, as a child, I'd sometimes intervened between him and his mother and received blows meant for him.

"You're a good girl, Giulietta," he said. His voice was low and breathless, and as he spoke he gripped my arms with both hands. Then, as if more surprised than anyone else at this gesture, he pushed me away.

"As I see you both agree with me," said Tarquinia without a trace of irony, and evidently blind to the danger she'd just been in, or unmoved by it, "I shall inform Vittoria at once of my plans concerning Peretti."

"At once?" I said indignantly.

"You won't do anything of the kind, mother!" cried Marcello. "I'll find a way to prevent you. I'll camp outside Vittoria's door if necessary.

You can see her tomorrow. At least have the decency to give her a day and a night to weep."

He swiftly left the room, and when soon afterwards I went to his sister's apartments on the first floor, I found him in the little antechamber that sometimes served as Caterina Acquaviva's bedroom.

He was lying full-length on a *divano-letto* where Caterina often spent the night to be within call. It was quite big enough for Caterina, but so small for Marcello that his feet protruded over the end. The daylight, entering through a little south-facing window, fell on his saturnine face, and as I went in he was toying with his dagger — a childish but disturbing game it seemed to me — and trying to catch the sunbeams on its naked blade.

As I entered the antechamber Caterina came out of Vittoria's room. Closing the door carefully behind her, she told me Vittoria had been asking for me and had just sent her to look for me.

Caterina Acquaviva was as fresh and lively as her name — dark-haired and plump, with a wonderfully smooth olive complexion and large innocent eyes. When she looked over my shoulder and saw Marcello lying on her couch she blushed. Her brown bosom, left half uncovered by a low square neckline, began to heave, and in a tender voice she couldn't keep from trembling she said: "Signor Marcello, you'd be more comfortable if I took off your boots."

"If you like," he answered indifferently; he did not apologise for occupying her couch or vouchsafe her so much as a glance.

I found Vittoria sitting by the window with her long tresses tossed behind her over a high-backed chair, the ends reaching the floor. Her hands lay clasped in her lap. She wasn't weeping. She was just staring into space.

"Oh, Giulietta!" she murmured. "I'm glad to see you. You at least loved our poor father. Oh, how badly we treated him!"

"You have nothing to reproach yourself with," I said after a moment's silence. "It wasn't you who decided to leave Gubbio and come to Rome."

"But it was because of me we came!" she cried. "And you know how much I've enjoyed living here. Poor father, slaving away in Gubbio while we were amusing ourselves in Rome . . ."

I made no answer, for it was true. And it was true too that Vittoria had sometimes seemed to forget Bernardo even existed. I remember it was at this precise moment I first asked myself whether Vittoria's dazzling beauty was as great a gift from heaven as everyone said..

To break the continuing silence I asked: "Vittoria, tell me truthfully – would you rather be alone?"

"No, stay. I thought I heard Marcello's voice outside. Is he back from Amalfi? What is he doing here?"

"Guarding you. He's sworn to stop Tarquinia coming in."

She heaved a sigh and leaned her head to one side. "Thank him for me. Tell him he can come in and see me if he likes."

I left her and went into the little room outside, closing the door behind me before I spoke to Marcello. There was a heavy curtain over the door, and I didn't want Vittoria to hear. I knew only too well how Marcello would take his sister's disguised request.

He hadn't moved from the couch or sheathed his dagger. He'd put it down on the little bedside table and seemed to sleeping. This allowed Caterina, sitting cross-legged on a cushion on the floor with her back against the wall, to contemplate his features without fear of rebuff.

As soon as I appeared she stood up guiltily, but I told her to sit down again – Vittoria didn't need her for the moment. I spoke softly so as not to wake Marcello. I was just wondering whether I should speak to him when the younger brother, Flaminio, glided into the room, as quietly as he did everything.

Flaminio was a kind of smaller, paler replica of Vittoria. His short fair curly hair grew in a halo around his head, and his pale blue eyes gave a subtle cast to his otherwise rather insipid countenance. In my opinion he was so pious he ought to have taken religious orders long ago. Then he'd have escaped both the family quarrels and the exhausting work at the majolica factory. Better still, he would with time have made a very pretty little monsignore, adored by the ladies of his congregation as he already was by all the maids in the Rusticucci palace, with the exception of Caterina. She had other aspirations.

Flaminio, though he'd made no more noise than a mouse, didn't have time to open his lips. Marcello leaped up and had him by the throat in one bound. I realised then that he'd only been pretending to sleep, to escape Caterina's dumb adoration. But this time I didn't intervene: Flaminio

23

was in no danger. As he never returned a blow, Marcello considered it beneath his dignity to strike him.

"What are you doing here?" said Marcello, through clenched teeth, though his voice was low. "Who sent you? Answer! Who sent you? Tarquinia? What message did she send? Answer me, you envoy of the devil!"

"But I haven't got any message," replied Flaminio in the gentle lilting voice that always surprised me, though I never found it all that convincing as it was not incompatible with pious falsehoods.

"Well, what are you here for?" said Marcello, without either relaxing his grip or raising his voice. He was probably afraid of attracting Vittoria's attention, knowing she always protected her younger brother.

"I want to see Vittoria," faltered Flaminio.

"She can't see anyone," growled Marcello, with a furtive glance at Vittoria's door, as if afraid she might open it and give him the lie. "Not anyone," he repeated. "And I'm here to keep everyone away. So be off before I throw you out!"

And, still holding him by the throat, he opened the door leading out on to the gallery and shoved him through it. Perhaps I should explain that the Rusticucci palace was built round a square courtyard with cool trees and a pool in the middle. The open gallery I've just mentioned ran right round the first floor, benefiting from the sun or shade of the courtyard according to the time of day.

"Marcello," I said as soon as he'd shut the door, "what you said isn't quite true. Vittoria told me to tell you you can go in and see her if you wish."

Joy was so swiftly succeeded by coldness on his face that I doubted if I'd really seen it. He lay or rather threw himself down on Caterina's little bed, shut his eyes, and said: "No. I don't want to. I've no use for the tears and sighs, the upturned eyes and all the other mumbo jumbo women go in for. Tell her I'm tired after my journey, and sleeping."

That night after I'd gone to my own room I had a strange dream. I call it strange because dreams are usually vague and shapeless, whereas this one surprised me by its coherence and the clarity of the words uttered in it. So strongly did they imprint themselves on my mind that when I thought about it next day I could scarcely believe I hadn't really heard them.

I was alone in a huge, magnificent room with precious rugs covering the floor and the walls, which were lined with divans on all four sides. In the middle stood a low octagonal table of fragant cedar, covered with fine oriental carving but bare except for a big shallow dish in which some strong but to me unfamiliar perfumes were burning. There were no other furnishings but the rugs, the divans and the table. The huge door was also of cedar, studded with iron, and had a barred spy-hole in it. I knew, without trying it, that it was locked.

The room was well lit by a single window, opening like a door, that let in the morning sun. The window was protected outside by a wrought-iron grille, through which I could see a beautiful garden full of flowers. In the middle of the garden stood a big golden cage full of brightly coloured birds, singing. I'd have liked to go nearer, but the grille was bolted.

As I stood there looking at the cage I saw that more birds, just like those inside the cage, were fluttering around it, apparently as eager to get in as the others were to get out. Just like us, I thought: we long to be united with the one we love, yet after the bonds are forged we come to find them too heavy.

But though this thought passed through my mind it didn't make me sad. I was a prisoner too, because I couldn't push aside the grille or open the heavy cedar door. But as I watched the birds fluttering in the cage I felt as light and happy as if I might at any moment do the same. And I really was light, for I wore neither stifling bodice nor heavy farthingale. I was naked beneath a long, loose saffron-yellow robe with a low neck, made of soft, clinging material that left my limbs delightfully free. Catching sight of myself in a long Venetian mirror on the wall, I went over, and was surprised to see I was taller and, what is more, prettier than I had been the day before. It seemed to me any man who saw me must love me. I twirled round and danced on tiptoe about the room, my arms outstretched so that my wide sleeves were like wings. Everything felt like a caress: the folds of my gown, the warm breeze from the garden that I could feel through it, the perfumes burning in the bowl, the carpet deep and soft beneath my feet.

Suddenly, to my great displeasure, I found I was not, as I'd thought, alone in the room. Vittoria and Caterina were there, both dressed in long robes like mine but in different colours, Vittoria in pink and Caterina in purple.

I noticed with annoyance that the colours suited them. But it was their attitude that increased the sudden dislike I felt for both of them.

Caterina was sitting on the carpet, her dark head resting on the edge of a divan. She had let the wide opening of her robe slip down, showing a plump shoulder and more than half revealing her dark and perfect breasts. Her black eyes, which looked huge and very bright, were fixed expectantly on the heavy nail-studded door.

As for Vittoria, sitting primly on one of the divans, I had at first no criticism to make of her demeanour. But when I looked more closely at her face it seemed to me less beautiful than usual, and I saw on it an expression of duplicity which I had never observed before and which her attitude was soon to confirm. For, standing up, she said nonchalantly, as if to herself: "This gown is much too hot. And since we're alone I'm going to take it off. My hair will be enough to cover me."

And she took off her robe and stretched out on a divan, arranging her hair so as to conceal her bosom and belly. Then she gave a little sigh and shut her eyes, as if getting ready to go to sleep. But I wasn't taken in: I could see her lids were admitting a slit of light, and that she too was watching the door. I don't know which I hated more at that moment, Caterina's immodesty or Vittoria's hypocritical propriety.

I resolved to be irreproachable and shame them both. I sat down on a divan with my legs close together, crossing my arms over my chest to hold the unseemly low neckline in place. After a while I noticed that the divan I had chosen quite at random was just opposite the door. I decided to make up for this by keeping my head turned resolutely to the right, as if I was looking out at the garden through the grille. After a moment I was pleased to notice that in this position I would be showing my better profile to any visitor entering through the door. I remember that far from feeling guilty at having this involuntary advantage, I regarded it as a reward bestowed by Providence for my modesty.

Caterina let out a stifled cry, and by following the direction of her head I could see what had upset her. A face had just appeared in the spy-hole in the door, though its features were not clearly visible because of the bars. Its black eyes, however, were quite plain, as were the dazzling looks it darted at each of us in turn, quite transfixing me.

I could see out of the corner of my eye that Vittoria, try as she might to seem impassive, was staring into space in such a way as to bring out the beauty of her glance. As for Caterina, with her breast heaving, her mouth half open and her head rolling to and fro on the edge of the divan, she seemed to be seething in some infernal cauldron.

The nail-studded door swung ponderously open and Marcello appeared. None of us showed the slightest surprise. He was wearing a long robe of Titian red and his dagger hung from a golden belt around his waist. He locked the door behind him, removed the key and held it up to us in a theatrical gesture, then strode over and threw it out through the grille into the garden. That done, he went back into the middle of the room, paced slowly round the low table, looked at us one after the other and said, with an ironical curl of the lip: "Now you're in my power, my doves, and you won't escape me."

I rose up from the divan on which I was so modestly seated, walked over to him boldly, and said: "But you're a prisoner too, Marcello — you've thrown away the key."

"Very sensible, Giulietta," he answered with a smile. "You might say I'm just as much your prisoner as all of you are mine. But it's not really so. I am free. And here" — drawing his dagger — "is the instrument of my freedom."

And, twisting and turning the dagger in his hands so that the blade caught the light, he tried to reflect it successively on Vittoria, Caterina and myself.

"Do you mean you intend to take your own life, Marcello?"

"Yes. But not without taking all yours first."

"But why?"

"What's the point of living," said Marcello, "when in the end we all die?"

Suddenly Vittoria opened her blue eyes wide, threw aside her hair (at the risk of revealing her breasts, or more probably intending to do so), propped herself on one elbow, and said: "Why me, Marcello?"

"Life," he answered in a low, weary voice, "is a deceitful and cruel game. Women are but fleshly snares. Whoever comes within reach of their tentacles succumbs and dies. I prefer to kill myself, and

27

you with me."

I was furious with Vittoria for trying to attract Marcello's attention. To recapture it for myself, while at the same time showing him how docile I was, I went over close enough to touch him and put both hands on his chest, saying sweetly: "May it be as you wish, Marcello. Kill us if you must, only tell me which of us you're going to kill first."

"You, of course, Giulietta," said he, his eyes smiling, "because you're such a good girl."

Then I woke up. And I don't know why, but when I realised where and who I was I began to think of my dead family. And my life seemed so horribly empty that I began to weep.

But I finally grew tired of weeping. I dried my eyes, struck the flint and lit my candle, then went and looked at myself in the little Venetian mirror – a smaller version of the one in my dream. For some time I stood scrutinising my reflection, as if it could tell me something about myself that I didn't already know. Strangely enough, I felt different, though I couldn't have said whether the change was for the better or the worse.

I felt uneasy. How was it my dream had made Marcello into a kind of hero when in reality, despite my old affection for him, I regarded him as unscrupulous, lazy, violent and corrupt? And why had the same dream so unfairly depicted Vittoria as a monster of hypocrisy, even suggesting a sort of incestuous attraction for her brother of which I knew she was entirely innocent?

I went back to bed, blew out the candle, and lay for a long while with my eyes wide open in the dark. I didn't even try to sleep: I knew I wouldn't succeed. Although I wasn't responsible for the vagaries of my dream, I felt guilty at having harboured such ungenerous feelings about Vittoria, even in my sleep. I began to have doubts about myself. Was I really, after all, the good, "reasonable" Giulietta, the very embodiment of commonsense, that everybody took me for?

2

His Eminence Cardinal Cherubi

Two years after Gregory XIII came to the Papal throne I became vicar-general to His Eminence Cardinal Montalto. But the honour – if such it was – didn't last long. A year later, in May 1573 to be exact, the Cardinal dismissed me from his employ with his customary discourtesy.

As certain far from charitable rumours circulated in Rome on my fall from favour, I should like to explain here – with the simplicity of heart that is, so to speak, *nutrimentum spiritus* – the reason why it came about, a reason so trivial that in future it will be a subject of astonishment to all men of intelligence. The fact that a woman – Signorina Vittoria Accoramboni – was if not the cause at least the occasion of it, can only add to their stupefaction.

I don't know that I can be suspected of bitterness or resentment on the subject, for my sudden dismissal, though so painful at the time, soon turned out to be a blessing in disguise.

As soon as His Holiness Pope Gregory XIII heard that His Eminence had put me back on the shelf – or "sent me back to my gondolas", to use the contemptuous expression the Cardinal himself didn't shrink from employing – he spread his protecting wing over me and, taking the Cardinal at his word, recommended me to the Patriarch of Venice. The Patriarch took me into his service the more readily as I was myself a Venetian, and because the Pope dropped the hint that he intended one day to make me a cardinal.

This prospect particularly pleased the Patriarch because he cherished papal ambitions himself, and thought that by taking me in he'd be making a friend who might one day vote for him in the conclave, when the amiable soul of Gregory XIII was summoned home by its Creator. In fact, when the time came, he didn't get my vote. Alas, there was nothing I could do about it! And some still remember with weeping and gnashing of teeth the man who *was* elected.

I now regard the time I spent with His Eminence Cardinal Montalto — something less than a year — as a sort of earthly Purgatory into which I was plunged for the expiation of my sins. For while the Cardinal really was remarkable in point of intelligence and energy and for the austerity of his life, God forgive me for thinking it would have been better for those around him if he'd had a bit less virtue and a bit more gentleness. And this applies even to such utterly devoted servants as *il bello muto*, his secretary, and to objects of his special affection like his adopted son, Francesco Peretti.

But it can't be denied that he did show some kindness to both those two. He went to the trouble of inventing a sign language in which the former could communicate with his master more quickly than in writing. And he did his best, or thought he did, to ensure Francesco's happiness. But absolute submission to his tyrannical temper was the price both had to pay, and to pay a hundred times over, for his favours.

Certainly the Cardinal's virtue was without flaw or weakness. But there is such a thing as too much excellence. *Tutior est locus in terra quam turribus altis*: the earth is safer than the top of a tower. You don't have so far to fall. In all humility, it may be that my virtues are small in the sight of God, and I'm not ashamed to admit that if Montalto's disfavour brought me the favour of His Holiness, it was less on account of my own merits than because of Gregory XIII's hostility towards His Eminence.

In Rome, everything is known and nothing is said. As I wasn't a Roman I might have remained ignorant for ever of the reasons for this aversion if Cardinal de' Medici hadn't mentioned it to me one day. His powerful and illustrious family made him so invulnerable he could afford to tell the truth from time to time, even in the Vatican.

According to Cardinal de' Medici — I'm transcribing his veiled allusions into plain language — His Holiness disliked Montalto first because he suspected him of wanting to succeed him; secondly because the Cardinal was a Franciscan (the Pope, like the people of Rome, regarded friars as hypocrites); and thirdly because the asceticism of the

Cardinal's life seemed an implicit reproach to his own.

Be that as it may, from the first day Gregory XIII sat on the supreme throne he rigorously refused to include Montalto in his government, and despite the great abilities even his enemies admitted he possessed, never entrusted him with any post. Worse, he seemed to ignore his very existence.

As His Eminence's vicar-general – albeit of recent appointment – I was one of the first to notice a great change in his appearance. I can't say whether he was grieved at his undeserved lack of favour or if his extreme austerity had undermined his robust health: he never complained. But suddenly he seemed bowed with age, his bright black eyes grew dull, at least in public, and he started to move about on crutches, as if his crooked though strong legs had all at once refused to serve him. He rarely spoke, and as soon as he did open his mouth he was racked by a painful cough. And he, who had been so quick-tempered, so haughty, so impatient of other people's opinions, was now regarded by the other cardinals as a paragon of humility.

By the cardinals, but not by the Pope: his antipathy towards Montalto remained unchanged. His entourage even had the greatest difficulty in persuading him that out of respect for Montalto's crutches he ought to exempt him from kneeling when he approached the papal throne. When people praised the invalid's unfailing gentleness towards his peers, the Pope said drily: "I've seen a lot of things in my long life, but I've never seen an eagle change into a dove."

And to tell the truth, once the Cardinal was back in his own palace – and he seldom left it – I never saw his powerful talons or curved beak offer his familiars or servants the smallest vestige of an olive branch. His cough didn't prevent him from scolding, nor did his crutches stop him appearing wherever he was least expected. I don't know whether he was as moribund as he looked, but neither his suspicion nor his tyranny ever relaxed.

He gave further proof of these qualities as soon as he learned that Francesco Peretti was aspiring to the hand of the beautiful Vittoria Accoramboni. From the very day he heard about it he started to collect information about her and her family. He acquired – and I know how, though I don't know through whom – the services of a chambermaid in the Rusticucci palace who, by a fortunate coincidence, came like him from Grottammare in the Marches. The girl didn't betray her mistress for money, but because the Cardinal was in a position to help her relations, who earned a precarious living as fisher-folk in Grottammare. His Eminence also won the Roman priest Racasi over to his cause: Racasi was Vittoria's and her mother's confessor. I didn't know the details of the inquiry, but I did know its result, for the Cardinal called me in at the last minute to consult me – I had relations in Gubbio, where the Accorambonis came from. But I could only confirm what he already knew: Vittoria had the reputation of being beautiful, kind and virtuous, but her brother Marcello was a good-for-nothing and her other brother an incompetent. Her mother was an ambitious woman seeking a wealthy match for her daughter. The majolica factory in Gubbio was up for sale, and, worse, the family hadn't a penny left to bless themselves with.

"In short," said the Cardinal bluntly, "these people are getting too big for their boots. I'll wager they're just living off their debts. The Rusticucci palace is just a hollow shell. That's not the kind of family I want to marry Francesco into."

At that moment poor Francesco Peretti, who was allowed to come and go freely in his adoptive father's apartments, entered the room. Hearing what had just been said he was as petrified as if he'd heard his own death warrant. He turned extremely pale, threw himself at the Cardinal's feet, and stammered, though not without some vehemence: "Father! Father! You crucify me! I can't live without Vittoria! She's a most exceptional woman, as distinguished for her virtues as for her charms. Of course I'm not blind to her origins. But is she to be condemned for the faults of her family, when she herself doesn't share them? Oh, father – in fairness to me and to her I implore you: see her and listen to her before you banish her from my life!"

I must confess I was surprised by both the force and the skill of his plea. Like everyone else in Rome I regarded Francesco Peretti as a naïve, amiable, but somewhat unintelligent and unambitious young man; in fact, rather spineless. I now saw that when driven by strong emotion he was capable not only of courage – and one needed that to confront the formidable Montalto – but also of wit. For he had appealed to the quality the Cardinal prized above all in others and in himself: the sense of fairness.

I could see the Cardinal himself was as surprised as anyone to find that the son he still regarded as a child might be a man. But at first he said nothing.

His Eminence was very calculating, and never made an unpremeditated answer. He dragged himself on his crutches over to the window looking out on the courtyard, and stood there silent for some time with his back to Francesco. It was then I noticed how the use of crutches added to his deformity, making his neck sink deeper between his shoulders. Taking the unwieldiness of his body together with the fierce and heavy countenance that seemed drawn downwards by a large nose and a projecting jaw, you had to admit Montalto had little reason to glory in the flesh. Come to think of it, perhaps that was one of the reasons why Gregory XIII, who though over seventy was still a very handsome man, disliked him so much.

There were four people in the room just then: the Cardinal, standing by the window with his back to the rest of us; Francesco Peretti, rising from his knees and gazing at his uncle as if his life depended on him; *il bello muto*, silent and still as a cat; and myself – very curious, to tell the truth, as to what His Eminence would decide to do, and uncertain whether his natural inflexibility or his love of justice would prevail.

However, when he turned round he spoke not to Francesco but to *il bello muto*.

"Rossellino," he grumbled, "I see there are some withered heads among the geraniums in the middle of the courtyard. That is not as it should be. Tell the gardener to cut off the dead ones."

By way of reply *il bello muto* raised his eyebrows and made a sign with his right hand which I only understood because of Montalto's brusque answer: "Yes, now. Once a thing's decided upon it shouldn't be put off."

Then he looked at Francesco Peretti. "Go and bring Vittoria to me, Francesco."

"What?" said Francesco, dumbfounded. "Now?"

"Yes, now. It's only fair I should see and hear her."

Montalto, like all great politicians, had a talent for showmanship. (In my opinion that may have accounted for his crutches: I occasionally wondered if he really needed them). I could see that while giving in to Francesco he was trying at the same time, by this sudden summons, to

33

preserve his reputation for inflexibility. The gesture was effective but superfluous: he could just as well have waited till next day to see Vittoria. But that would have been to procrastinate, and the master, magisterial even when he yielded, was giving us a lesson in morality: just as *il bello muto* should fly to see to the dead geraniums, so Francesco should hasten to fetch Vittoria. It escaped no one that there was something regal about Montalto's impatience.

I've often thought that if, when Vittoria arrived, I'd asked His Eminence for permission to retire, seeing that the interview was a family matter which didn't concern me, I might have avoided my subsequent sudden fall from grace. But as I've said, I now have reason to bless the curiosity that made me stay, eyes and ears agog. While her beauty was famous all over Italy, Vittoria, being as yet unmarried, went out rarely except to go to Mass, and even then she wore a mask and a long cloak that concealed her figure. So I'd never really seen, still less heard her, and had no means of guessing how the maiden would stand up to the Minotaur.

Like St Augustine, I weathered various storms in my youth, and they left me, like Gregory XIII, with a son. But after I rose to the purple I put away such faults, and Providence decreed that age should come to the aid of my virtue. Not I that I proclaim, with the poet Terence, *Deleo omnes dehinc ex animo mulieres*: henceforth I banish all women from my mind. On the contrary. Debarred from more intimate dealings, I delight still in their beauty. And as I'm now moved by merely aesthetic considerations, I've become infinitely more exacting in my appraisal of their charms than when I was swept along on the surges of the blood.

That's why, when told in advance that some Roman lady is beautiful, I'm often disappointed when I see her and her imperfections leap to the eye. But this didn't happen when Vittoria appeared in Montalto's dilapidated palace and absolutely lit up our ancient dwelling.

I was surprised how tall she was, and how graceful too, as she showed by the way she knelt before the Cardinal's chair, her large hooped skirts making a charming frame around her slim waist and her long hair falling down in a truly regal train. As she kissed His Eminence's hand she still retained the modest, sober yet proud air that struck me so forcibly at that first encounter. I could only see her profile from where I stood, so I moved noiselessly behind the Cardinal's chair to see her from the front. But from any angle her features were perfection itself. And when, after touching Montalto's ring with her lips, she looked up, I was dazzled by the light of her great blue eyes. I say "light" and not "brilliance" because, although they were brilliant too, I believe their radiance came as much from her beautiful soul as from themselves. I couldn't say whether some rays of that beauty managed to pierce Montalto's thick skin — or perhaps I should say his armour. But the fact is that when he spoke to her his glance was less fierce and his voice less harsh than before. "Please sit down, Signorina," he said, almost courteously.

She did so, after sweeping her golden mane round in front of her so as not to sit on it. As she draped her hair over her knees she inadvertently attracted the Cardinal's attention to this typically feminine adornment, which as such must have struck him as reprehensible, for he frowned and said with his usual bluntness: "Couldn't you put your hair up instead of displaying it like a flag?"

Vittoria, seeming not to notice his rudeness, answered calmly: "I've tried, but it's so heavy it makes me overbalance."

"Cut it off then!" said Montalto, his black eyes suddenly flashing.

"I wish I could," said Vittoria with the same unfailing sweetness. "It's a great nuisance to me. But I can't. My mother has categorically forbidden it."

"*Dos est magna parentium virtus*"*, said Montalto sardonically, with a significant glance at me and a reference to Tarquinia's reputation.

I was just about to reply with a faint smile when I thought I saw Vittoria turn pale, and wondered whether she might have understood the Cardinal's meaning even though he had shrouded it in Latin.

A silence ensued, disagreeable to everyone, including Francesco Peretti, who stood behind Vittoria's chair much less in control of himself than she was, blushing and paling alternately and fixing his wan eyes anxiously upon his uncle. As for *il bello muto*, he kept looking from his master to Vittoria in astonishment. Not insensible himself to feminine charm (it was said that before his accident he entertained the warmest possible sentiments for Contessa V.), he was probably wondering why the Cardinal had begun by picking a quarrel with Vittoria over her

---

* The virtue of parents is a great dowry.

35

wonderful tresses. Perhaps, like me, he was remembering that Mary Magdalen had dried Christ's feet with her long hair and that Our Lord, far from telling her to cut it off, had accepted her homage with His customary gentleness.

There wasn't a trace of softness to be seen at that moment on Montalto's fearsome mask. After the slight relaxation at the start, when he'd seemed surprised by Vittoria's beauty and dignity, his face had suddenly soured. The discussion about her hair seemed to have roused the latent misogyny so frequent in celibate priests that one wonders if they've been as deserving as they claim in remaining chaste.

Be that as it may, Vittoria's cause seemed lost before it was even pleaded, for Montalto turned to *il bello muto* (perhaps he was vexed with me for not answering his quip about Tarquinia) and spoke again in Latin: "*In vero formosa est. Sed rara est adeo concordia formae atque pudicitiae.*"*

Il bello muto, who in spite of his unbounded veneration for the Cardinal didn't always agree with what he said, raised his eyebrows and looked at his master doubtfully, as if wondering whether his malicious quotation was really apt. *Il bello muto* had a great advantage over all Montalto's other servants: as he could only express his disagreement in signs, it was easier for His Eminence to forgive him for it.

For my own part, though I was extremely shocked by the Cardinal's quotation from Juvenal, for in my view nothing about Vittoria's reputation or behaviour justified it, I put on a neutral expression, not wishing to expose myself again to Montalto's displeasure. As for poor Francesco, who would have been furious if he'd understood Latin, he sensed that something was going on. His pale eyes darted like anxious little animals from one to another of them, as if begging for an explanation of Montalto's words and the silence that had followed them.

The silence was broken by Vittoria. Looking up with the reserved yet proud expression that had already impressed me, she fixed her luminous eyes on the Cardinal and said mildly: "*Reverendissime pater, Juvenalis errat. Mihi concordia est.*"†

"What?" cried Montalto in amazement. "Do you understand Latin, Vittoria?"

* She really is beautiful. But beauty and chastity rarely go together.
† Most reverend father, Juvenal is mistaken. In me they do go together.

36

"Yes, Your Eminence," she said simply, without any attempt at showing off or rubbing it in.

The Cardinal said nothing, and there was another silence, this time very different from the first. Although his fixed expression remained impenetrable, I thought he must be revising his opinions. It was hard for him now to conclude that because Vittoria's hair was long her ideas were short and her brain light.

But Montalto's austerity derived from the strictness of his principles and not from any barrenness in his nature. He loved beautiful gardens and fine sculpture, and his secular learning was as extensive as his religious scholarship. As for women, although he suspected that souls were in danger from their femininity —his misogyny had its origin in theology — he wasn't insensitive to their beauty. But he would have liked them to be like flowers: colourful but tethered to the ground — and, thank Heaven, dumb. He'd also have liked them to wither after a few days, so that one wouldn't have time to get attached to them. At first, like *il bello muto* and myself, he was overwhelmed by the radiance of Vittoria's appearance, but then his principles reasserted themselves and he imagined the chaos that such incomparable beauty could bring upon the State. He was already thinking of separating her from his nephew for ever when she proved to him that she was a human being worthy of respect: she could speak Latin and had read Juvenal.

I'm reporting what I took to be the rapid evolution of the Cardinal's attitude towards Vittoria, but I don't blame him for being harsh with her at first. I deplore it of course, but there was plenty of precedent. Our Holy Mother the Church has not always been kind to the more charming half of the human race. And let me recall here that it wasn't until the Council of Mâcon in the ninth century — and then only by a small majority — that the bishops accepted that the *gentil sesso* possesses a soul.

Montalto, forgetting the suspect length of her hair and the snakes that the Devil had no doubt hidden in it, now saw that Vittoria possessed not only a soul but also a mind. He started questioning her in Latin, and was obviously pleased that she understood so quickly and replied so well.

"Vittoria," he said, "you must have had a good teacher, to have read Juvenal."

37

"An excellent teacher, Your Eminence. He was kind, pious and learned. He was a Franciscan friar."

And knowing His Eminence belonged to the same order, she gave him a smile in which a touch of badinage mingled with a truly filial benevolence.

I must confess that smile enchanted me as much by its subtlety as by the kindheartedness it revealed. I saw in a flash that Vittoria had already forgiven Montalto for his unkind remarks, and asked nothing better than to look on him as if he were the father she no longer had. I could tell His Eminence must have had the same impression, for his fierce black eyes softened and he said more gently: "And how was it this friar was so fond of Juvenal?"

"He despised the morals of our own age and admired Juvenal because he criticised the morals of his."

"And did this friar introduce you to Italian literature too?"

"Yes, Your Eminence. He made me read Dante, Petrarch, Boccaccio and Ariosto."

"And which did you like the best?"

"Dante because of his imagination, but most of all Petrarch, for his sweetness."

"But not Boccaccio?"

"No, Your Eminence. I don't like Boccaccio at all."

Vittoria said this with some emphasis, and Montalto smiled.

"What has he done to you that you dislike him so much?"

"My tutor made me read his *Corbaccio*."★

At this we all laughed heartily — the Cardinal, *il bello muto* and myself. Francesco, whose learning was confined to a smattering of law, merely smiled, not because he'd read *Il Corbaccio*, but because he saw that ice had been succeeded by sunshine, giving life and warmth back to his love.

"So you don't care for Boccaccio's satire against women?" said Montalto.

"No, Your Eminence," Vittoria replied. "I think it's cruel and unfair."

"Well," said the Cardinal affably, "to get your revenge on your friar

★ The Riding Crop

38

you ought to have read Ariosto on the religious orders."

"But I did," cried Vittoria. "My tutor recommended it."

Montalto clasped his hands together and started to laugh.

"Splendid! A friar with a sense of fair play! And one who could make fun of himself. Vittoria, since you love Petrarch for his sweetness, please recite the sonnet you find the most moving."

"Gladly, Your Eminence," said Vittoria.

Unfortunately I can't remember which sonnet it was, but I do remember the voice in which she recited it: a voice at once so soft and vibrant that I cannot do it justice by any comparison with birds or the most crystalline of bells. The voice, the diction, the play of her features and the expression in her great blue eyes all combined to create a unique moment; it delights me just to think of it even now. Montalto beckoned *il bello muto* to him and with his help stood up, supported on his crutches. He looked at Vittoria for some time, then, with a gentleness I'd never heard in his voice before, said: "Vittoria, when you are married . . ."

"What, father?" cried Francesco, transported with happiness.

But Montalto waved him away as if he'd been a fly, and went on: "Vittoria, when you are married I should be glad if your domestic duties left you time to come and read to a sick old man now and then."

"Oh, father, I'd be very happy too!" cried Vittoria, throwing herself at his feet in an access of affection and goodwill.

And indeed, when she left the Cardinal's palace, Vittoria had several reasons to be glad. She might have parodied Julius Caesar and said, "I came, he saw, I conquered." Yet I wasn't sure that her victory, one of whose effects was to save her family and herself from want, really pleased her all that much in her heart of hearts. I'd noticed that throughout her interview with the Cardinal she hadn't looked at Francesco once.

True, she was very young, and it's possible that at that stage in her life she prized the marriage more highly than she did the mate.

But the most surprising thing of all about that encounter was what Montalto said afterwards – words that were indirectly to have such an enormous influence on my life, for the worse at first and later for the better.

As soon as Vittoria had left the room, seeming suddenly to empty it of warmth and light, His Eminence dragged himself over to the window. He stood there with his back to us watching Vittoria as, escorted by Francesco, she crossed the courtyard, passing by the bed of geraniums he'd ordered *il bello muto* to have put in order. Then, turning painfully to face us – for it was difficult to manoeuvre that heavy frame on its crutches – he shook his head several times and exclaimed: "How could anyone see her and not love her? Hear and not adore her?"

"Just so, Your Eminence," said I. And I made some excuse to leave the room, so anxious was I that he shouldn't see how flabbergasted and, why not admit it, amused I was by what he'd said.

Now as ill luck – or, as it turned out, good luck – would have it, the following day I had to go and see the Pope in the Vatican, and I found His Holiness very morose, though I'm sure he had no reason to be, as he was in perfect health and living a life quite free from care. But about once a month Gregory XIII would be overcome with melancholy. This black mood was all the more dreaded by his entourage because while it lasted he would often make decisions extremely detrimental to the State, and when he recovered he refused, with the quiet obstinacy of the weak, to rescind them.

Finding him thus depressed, with the people of his court doing all they could to distract him, I thought to cheer him up by telling him about the interview that had taken place between Montalto and Vittoria the previous day. At first he listened with rather a sour expresssion, but when I came to to the memorable remarks with which the scene had ended he cried: "What? What? Cherubi, did you hear properly? Did Montalto really say that? Are you sure?"

"I could hardly believe my ears, Your Holiness, but yes, he did say it."

"What?" cried Gregory XIII, suddenly forgetting his hypochondria and roaring with laughter. "Montalto said, 'How could anyone see her and not love her? Hear and not adore her?'? Oh, Cherubi, she must be a very beautiful girl to have struck a spark of humanity from that old wreck!"

And he put his hands on his little fat belly and laughed till the tears ran down his cheeks. He made little jokes to his courtiers on the subject for all the rest of that day.

And on the next day Montalto gave me the sack and "sent me back to my gondolas".

40

Although I'm only a chambermaid and of low birth – my father's a fisherman in Grottammare, and his only possession is his boat – I do know how to behave and I'm not uneducated. I can read, and even write a little. And to whom do I owe it all but to Signora Vittoria Accoramboni, who had the infinite patience to teach me though she was very young herself at the time? She was just the same age as me – sixteen – when I entered her service. Anyway, she never treated me as a *cameriera*, but rather as a companion and confidante, and she went to a lot of trouble to knock the rustic corners off me. And as a result, when I go to see my family in Grottammare, my mother finds fault with me:

"Just look at you now! A real signorina! Can't eat unless you use a fork! You even bring one with you from Rome, and keep it in a case, like a jewel! *Ma che modi sono questi!*★ A fork, *Madonna santa*! It's only natural to use one to shift the muck, because that stinks! But a fork to put a perfectly good piece of conger eel in your mouth – caught this morning by your own father, and cooked by your own mamma! I tell you, Caterina – you insult your father! You insult your mother! And you insult God! A fork, *Dio mio*! An invention of the devil! The fingers God gave you aren't good enough for you, little fool that you are! And as if that cursed fork isn't enough, what's this I hear? You know how to read and write? And you're proud of it, shameless hussy! *Madonna*! you're ruined! What man's going to want anything to do with you after this?"

My mamma's quite right about husbands. The last time I went to see my parents in Grottammare, Giovanni looked very grumpy – and he had held me so close on my sixteenth birthday! I intimidate him, and he doesn't like it – after all, I'm only a woman, in other words nothing. And when he plants a couple of smacking kisses on this mere woman's cheek she can hardly bear the smell of him. I ask you: how could I ever live with a man who reeks of fish when in the palazzo Rusticucci I'm used to mixing with perfumed gentlemen with a sparkle to them? Not to mention the handsomest of them all, whose name I can't bring myself to utter, so little has he any eyes for me. Even though I'm so pretty.

Of course, I'm not as tall and beautiful as Vittoria, but I'm not

★ What a way to carry on!

41

unattractive either: dark, with black eyes and an olive complexion. And I don't mind saying that when it comes to bosoms there's no one in petticoats who can rival mine for size, plumpness, firmness and colour. That's why I wear low square necks – to show it off, no matter what Giulietta Accoramboni says. She accuses me of immodesty and trying to lead men on by showing bits of my bare skin. Jesus! She can afford to be a prude – she's got about as much tit as my elbow! She could show all she's got without attracting anyone! As far as I'm concerned, it doesn't make any difference whether I'm covered up or not. I don't go around with a bare arse, as far as I know, yet there isn't a man in the house whose eyes I can't feel on me like a warm shower when I wiggle past him. Oh yes, there is one, alas! The only one I'd like to like me. The world is badly organised, as my father says, when he comes home from the sea without having caught a single fish. As for that fish of mine, I don't know what nets you'd need to catch him.

To return to the Signora, she's always been so kind to me, so trusting and generous, that my heart is bound to hers with links of steel. To say I love her is putting it mildly. If you want to know the truth, I'd die for her if her life was in danger. I'd even – and may Our Lady forgive me for such impious words – I'd even kill for her. The fact is, my life with her is a paradise. I see her, hear her, serve her. And she, that lovely woman, forgets her rank and beauty and talks to me like a friend – to me, just a little worm beneath her feet!

The last time I went to Grottammare I told my mother, and only her, how His Eminence Cardinal Montalto had got my confessor to have me report on Vittoria. My mother grabbed hold of me, called me wicked and ungrateful, and beat me. May God forgive the poor ignorant woman! It was only for her and father that I agreed to do it. The little cottage they live in by the sea is rented to them for next to nothing by the parish priest of Grottammare. And how could a parish priest resist a powerful cardinal to whom he owes his living? Anyway, why all the fuss, or as my father, who's a Tuscan, would say, the stink? Vittoria's as virtuous as she is kind. What could I say of her but good?

Not that Vittoria dislikes men. She likes them as much as I do. But unlike your humble servant she's too proud not to be chaste. Before she married Signor Peretti I was the only one who knew whom she liked and whom she disliked among men that used to come to the Rusticucci palace. But she was distant and dignified with all of them, and never betrayed the slightest partiality. How I wish I had such self-control! I, who can't see the object of my adoration without going red and white and all of a flutter! I'm like a volcano in eruption, sending out lava in all directions. Vittoria's as calm as a volcano that's extinct. But watch out: inside the crater it's still seething.

I take good care not to say anything like this in my reports to His Eminence. I record only actions, and they are irreproachable. As for thoughts, let Vittoria's confessor guess what they are and sort them out for himself! But it takes a clever man to see into a woman's heart: she can't always understand it herself!

It was six years ago that necessity forced Vittoria to marry Francesco Peretti, who I know has nothing in common with the sort of husband she'd dreamed of. Not that, like Tarquinia, she'd set her heart on a prince or a duke. No, what she'd have liked is a hero! If you ask me, she's stuffed her head too full of tales of chivalry! Signor Peretti is too sensitive and considerate to make it a bad marriage. But nobody could say it's a good one. Vittoria still goes on dreaming, without realising that what's permissible in a girl is not permissible in a wife. As for Signor Peretti, what do you think a husband must feel like when he's only occasionally tolerated in his wife's bedroom, and when after six years of marriage he still hasn't given her a child? But maybe that isn't even his fault. Who knows?

If you want my opinion, Signor Peretti is too timid and doesn't know how to show off his own good points. One evening in November, coming back from Vespers with his mother Camilla and myself, he was set upon in a narrow alley by three bandits who tried to rob him. He immediately drew his sword and faced up to them, wounding two of them, driving all three away, and getting a flesh wound in the arm. And what do you think he did when he got back to the palace? He made me swear on my medal of the Virgin Mary that I wouldn't mention the matter to Vittoria: he said he didn't want to worry her! And that was a prize opportunity for him to cover himself with a bit of glory in Vittoria's eyes, since she's got such a high opinion of heroes. Poor Signor Peretti! He's so awkward I feel quite sorry for him. I wouldn't like to speak ill of my own sex but, if you ask me,

43

it doesn't do to treat them too gently. Nor to implore them for the favour of spending a night with them.

But Signor Peretti is like his mother Camilla – gentle and kind. When I heard she was coming to live with us in the Rusticucci palace I could tell just from looking at her delicate sweet face which of the two old women was going to get the better of the other. Not that *la superba* is horrible to Camilla. It's just that the Perettis aren't made of stern enough stuff to stand up to the Accorambonis. It's not accident that swifts win out over swallows: they've got bigger beaks, stronger and more sharply curved. I'm just telling you things as I see them, with my own little natural commonsense.

Still, Signor Peretti has been very kind to my family. He helped them a lot when my father damaged his boat on the rocks a couple of years back. And he's very lenient with my brother, Domenico. I'm ashamed to tell you that Domenico is a bandit. But as everyone knows, in this unfortunate country there's a scallywag in most families, even amongst the nobility. And unfortunately for me the Accorambonis are no exception.

To get back to Domenico, he's ten years older than I am, and the only left-handed one among all my eight brothers and sisters. When he was a boy my father used to beat the living daylights out of him to make him use his right hand "like a Christian". But it didn't do any good. Domenico even crosses himself in church with his left hand. This worried our parish priest, who thought it was a mark of the devil and used to warn my mother when she went to confession that if Domenico didn't mend his ways he had little chance of salvation.

But Domenico didn't mend his ways, and instead of calling him by his real name, which after all was that of a saint, people in Grottammare got into the habit of calling him *il mancino*, the left-handed one. Nicknames aren't unusual in Grottammare, but people didn't say *il mancino* in the same way as they might have said *il zoppo*, the lame one, or *il cieco*, the blind one. Everyone knew that to be blind was a misfortune, but to be left-handed was, as the priest said, a mark of the devil.

As Domenico did everything with the wrong hand it didn't surprise anyone that he turned out badly. He quarrelled with my father when he was eighteen, and took to the road as a bandit. However, when he was broke or ill he always came and took refuge at home in Grottammare: my father would never speak to or even look at him, but he didn't forbid my mother to feed and look after him. Everyone in Grottammare would know he was there, but no police officer would ever have been foolish enough to try to come to our place and arrest him. He'd have had to deal with my father and my other four brothers, and, if the row went on long enough, with the other master fishermen.

Il mancino was also banished from Rome for his misdeeds. But sometimes he slipped into the city at night, and then, at my earnest request, Signor Peretti would grant him his hospitality and protection. This was extremely good of him, for when the Bargello heard about it at the Corte* he read him a lecture that ended as follows: "Signor Peretti, you are nursing a viper in your bosom, and some day or other it will bite you."

"It's in the nature of a snake to bite," said Peretti, smiling. "It can't help it."

"As you like," said the Bargello. "Don't say I didn't warn you."

But a few weeks later the Bargello himself rescinded my brother's banishment. For my part, I confess I'm always glad to see *il mancino*, even if he is a bandit. He's older than I am, as I've said, and I like him best of all my five brothers.

When I was a little girl it was a great honour and joy for me to sleep in the same bed with him. I remember how, after the candle had been blown out, he used to stroke me gently on my chest and tummy, and drop little kisses on my neck. These caresses sent delicious shivers down my spine. But when I got older my mother wouldn't let me go on sleeping with each of my brothers in turn, as I used to do, and made me share a bed with my two elder sisters. They were two great sluts already, and didn't treat me nearly so nicely.

Il mancino has black hair and a swarthy complexion. He's on the small side, but slim and wiry and very strong. He leans a bit to one side as he walks, and moves as silently as a cat. He speaks softly and his black eyes are soft too, especially when they rest on me. But when he's angry his eyes grow suddenly harsh: one glance is enough to make me want to sink

---

* The *Corte* was the Papal police, the *Bargello* its commandant.

45

through the floor. But I tremble then with pleasure as well as fear. That's girls for you: raving mad, and as bad as one another. Rank has nothing to do with it. Signora Vittoria spends all her time dreaming of her heroes, and my head is full of bad lads — my brother *il mancino*, and the other whose name I won't say.

Marcello Accoramboni

It was on July 15th 1580, at noon, that I stabbed Recanati, and I had good reason for doing so even though other people thought it was pointless.

I'd made up my mind to kill him two and a half months before. But I hadn't looked for him, I hadn't lain in wait for him. I'd decided to leave it to chance. And if chance hadn't brought him so miraculously within reach of my dagger before July 30th I'd have given the whole thing up.

I'd settled on July 30th as the last date for his execution. After that I'd have let the chatterbox off. Why July 30th? Just for fun. As the only thing I had against him was words, I wanted chance to decide for me whether he deserved to live or die. In short, I wanted to give him a chance of saving his miserable skin. In the same spirit I sent him a message by *il mancino* to say, unless he wanted me to make him eat his words, he should keep out of my way. But the idiot only laughed! The saying is right: "Those fate wants to destroy, she first makes blind."

I could have said that in Latin once, when I was learning Latin, with Vittoria, from a Franciscan friar. But I've forgotten it all now. She, of course, remembers everything.

We're so different and yet so alike, she and I. I was born an hour after she was. I've been told the priest who baptised us took a very poor view of twins, especially when they weren't of the same sex. He thought it unwholesome for a boy and a girl to be close together in the same womb, and told Tarquinia one of us would probably be an idiot or die in infancy. Neither of us died, and no one has ever taken me for an idiot. But I've always thought, and still do, that Vittoria is really the only one of us who's really intelligent. As for the soul, that's even more unevenly divided. There's only one soul between us, and she's got it. All I have are instincts.

As I was very swarthy and Vittoria was famous all over Gubbio for her golden mane – twice a week our little town paid more or less public homage to it – I always thought, as a child, that I must be ugly. And I was glad of it, and quite happy to live hidden at Vittoria's feet. But as I grew older I realised that women's eyes, all women's eyes, were always feasting on my face. And when I got to be a man it was worse still: they started to cling to me like octopuses. Their eyes and smiles and cloying words all got me down. I found them all the more horrifying because between Vittoria and me, though we were very fond of one another, there had always been the strictest reserve. We'd been as close as it's possible to be before we were born, but now as if by common accord we kept our bodies more utterly apart than any ordinary brother and sister – so much so that I can't remember ever kissing her, or even touching her with the tips of my fingers.

It would be foolish to conclude that I hate the female body. To put it bluntly, I quite like entering it, and get gratification from crushing its softness with my muscles and my weight. But that's not enough for the sex with tentacles – they have to love me, tell me about it, cling on to me. I can't bear that devouring sort of love. To me it's an insult compared with the distant, noble, disembodied affection I feel for Vittoria.

As for Recanati, here's how the whole thing came about. On July 15th at midday, not far from Santa Maria della Corte in Rome, I caught sight of Recanati riding alone in his carriage. He was lolling back on the cushions and glancing with great complacency at the passers-by on either side, not so much to observe them as to make sure they observed him in all his luxury. And indeed the vehicle he was riding in was a splendid affair, beautifully carved and gilded and drawn by four magnificent chestnuts whose golden manes streamed in the wind as they sped along. I was daydreaming in the sun at the time, and had forgotten all about Recanati. But seeing him suddenly like that, so arrogant and sure of himself and so near (the street was a very narrow one), I felt a new surge of hatred for him. Our eyes met, though only for a moment, because of the speed at which his carriage was travelling. But I darted him a furious glance, to which the craven wretch replied with a scornful smile, confident in the speed of his horses. He drove by. I trembled with rage, my hand on my dagger. It was only two short weeks till the end I'd set to my vendetta.

For a moment I thought of running after him, but apart from the fact that his carriage was moving so fast, it would have been beneath my dignity. I walked on, head bowed, trembling at the knees, gasping for breath, and stifling my impotent rage as best I could.

It was then that chance – I don't like to call it Providence – came to my aid. A heavy waggon drawn by six big horses and full, as I learned later, of stone carvings being delivered to the Vatican, suddenly got in the way of the carriage. Recanati's horses pulled up short, a collision was avoided, and the incident would have been over in a few seconds if the drivers – they're an irascible lot – hadn't started exchanging insults. These were followed by lashes with their whips, after which the two combatants dismounted and began to fight. Great din and confusion ensued, with the passers-by taking sides.

I was a little way off, but though my heart beat faster I deliberately walked on at the same steady pace, still leaving chance to decide whether the carriage should or should not move forward and Recanati be left within my reach when I arrived at the spot.

It was as if the thing had been planned from all eternity. The waggon was blocking the carriage's path, the chestnuts were whinnying and pawing the ground but couldn't get on, the crowd had eyes for nothing but the two brawling drivers. The way was clear.

Coolly, taking my time, I climbed on to the running board. With my left hand I seized Recanati by the throat and with my right, not uttering a word, put the point of my dagger to his heart. He recognised me and turned pale. His eyes rolled in their sockets with terror. Sweat started out on his brow. He couldn't speak. He just shook his head several times, trying to say "no."

I felt great disgust then for what I was about to do. Not because it was murder, but because Recanati was a coward. The sweat was streaming down his cheeks now: my left hand, holding him by the throat, was all wet. I'm sure I wasn't gripping him so tightly he couldn't speak – it was just terror that silenced him and made him hang limp as a rag doll in my grasp. Worse still, his cowardice made him give off an unbearable smell, and what with that and my left hand being sticky with his sweat I felt so nauseated I nearly gave up and spared the wretch's life. I felt more like an executioner than an avenger. I hesitated a second or two. But how could I

48

abandon my vendetta then without seeming a coward myself, in my own eyes? It was fear, really, that drove me on: fear of losing my self-respect.

I pressed on my dagger and was amazed at how easily it sank into Recanati's body. There seemed to be no effort on my part: it was as if he'd been made of dough. I'd never have believed it was so easy to kill a man.

As for Recanati himself, he shuddered, grimaced, and he gave a couple of gasps as if desperately seeking for air. That was all. Then he sank back on the cushions, his eyes staring. I pulled out my dagger, wiped it on his doublet and put it back in its sheath. Then I stepped down off the running board and looked around me. The drivers were still fighting, the crowd still shouting encouragement, and it looked as if no one had noticed what had been happening in the carriage.

I strolled off without a backward glance and walked to Margherita Sorghini's house. I didn't feel anything, except some difficulty in walking and breathing because of the heat — and also a kind of sad astonishment when I remembered how easily my sharp blade had pierced Recanati's heart.

The maid told me Margherita had just taken her midday bath and was resting on the "little terrace". It wasn't as small as all that. It had a view over the whole of Rome, and possessed an original feature in the form of a large tent that stood in the middle — a sort of canopy with white linen curtains around it that could be drawn to keep out the wind or the sun. Margherita was lying inside it, naked, on a huge couch, white to match the curtains. When I came in she propped herself up on one elbow and looked at me inquiringly. She could see from my face that something unusual had happened.

I signed to her not to ask questions, and noticing the bath of cold water in which she liked to cool herself in the hot weather, I stripped off my clothes and plunged in it up to the neck. I felt as if the clear water was cleansing me of my crime. Overhead, on the white top of the tent, I could see the shadows of the swifts as they swooped like arrows in all directions, uttering their shrill cries. Although I believe in neither God nor the Devil, I was sure I'd committed a great sin. And yet what I felt at that moment, strangely mingled with the sense of well-being that came from the coolness of the water and the shadows of the swifts, was not remorse but great disappointment. Recanati's murder meant nothing to

49

me. For it to be satisfactory he'd have had to know he was dead. I'd blown out a candle, and the candle wasn't even aware it was extinguished. I felt Margherita's eyes on me and frowned, and she at once looked away. As with all women – except Vittoria – there's something of the octopus about Margherita. But because she's twice my age and scared to death of losing me, I've managed to train her. Apart from love-making – and it's I who decide on that – she refrains from touching me and putting her arms round me, and from stifling me with all the thousand little wiles with which women usually try to ensnare us.

I got out of the tub, drew aside the curtain of the tent, and went out into the harsh sunlight, blinking and breathing in the pleasant bitter smell of the geraniums that grew around the edge of the roof. The tiles were so hot I kept hopping from one foot to the other. When the last drop of water had evaporated and my shoulders and the back of my neck were beginning to burn, I went back into the tent. Margherita, who must have been watching me through a chink in the curtains, shut her eyes just in time. Her jet-black tresses and olive complexion, the dark rings on her breasts and dark pubic hair all attracted me. Little wrinkles scored her eyelids, her breasts were heavy, and her ripening beauty looked already on the point of fading. But I loved her in her decline and in the slavery I'd reduced her to, though I suspected she still managed to retain the upper hand.

I stood by the bed and looked at her: she didn't dare open her eyes. That's how I liked her – defenceless, abandoned, docile. Without a word I fell on her and possessed her. After a while I felt her disobeying my rules and making little surreptitious movements with her hips in order to attain her own pleasure. But I was too far beyond words, too carried away by the inevitability of my orgasm. I came, and she let out one little cry. A swift seemed to answer her, overhead.

I slid off the bed on to the mat that covered the floor of the tent, not wishing to prolong the contact any more than was necessary. I feel slightly guilty when I do this, as this is the rule Margherita finds it hardest to accept. Giulietta says that having made my mother an object of hatred and my sister an object of adoration, I don't know which way to turn when it comes to other women, and that I'm really afraid of them. But I don't know if in this instance I should trust to her "commonsense".

What experience has she of relations between men and women? Worse still, her judgment is clouded, because she loves me too. I should put the beastly word in inverted commas. I hate it.

Because Margherita provides me with clothes and food and lodging, everyone in Rome whispers that I fleece her. They'd say it aloud if they weren't afraid of my sword. This opinion — yet another one! — is so far from the truth that it hardly bothers me. If Recanati had said only that, I'd never have taken the trouble to kill him.

I don't ask anything of Margherita. She's the one who showers gifts on me, in the hope of binding her young lover to her. That's just where she makes a mistake: I'm already bound. Even if I found a young girl with the same charms, I wouldn't exchange my elderly mistress for her at any price.

I was sitting on the mat, covered in sweat and gradually getting my breath back. I was propped up against the bed with my neck resting on a cushion that Margherita slipped under it as soon as I leaned back. If I'd turned my head I could have seen her fingers an inch away from my hair, and I could feel she was restraining a longing to stroke it, as she does sometimes, very lightly, when I'm making love to her and she knows I'm too wrought up to stop her. I looked at her fingers. She wears lots of rings, and I sometimes put them on my own fingers and admire the stones. She'd give them to me if I asked her. And I realised, then, that it was the hand and not the face that gave away a person's age. Margherita's body was ten years younger than her face, and her face ten years younger than her hand. I leaned my head to the right and kissed it. I regretted it immediately. I felt her behind me trembling at the unaccustomed homage.

"Take your hand away," I said curtly. And went on almost at once: "I've just killed Recanati."

Margherita took her hand away and sighed, and when she spoke her voice was subdued. "I thought as much."

But as she is always, at least in appearance, punctiliously obedient, she didn't ask questions. I often wonder whether this acceptance of my rules isn't a sort of game to her, a game she plays with the utmost skill, just as she'd play the coquette with a lover who wanted her to. She didn't really need to interrogate me: her silence was a question in itself. And she knew very well that at that moment I had a great need to confide in someone. So who is it who's governed by my rules? Her or me?

"Do you want to know why?" I asked grumpily.

"Yes."

Nothing could be more correct or in accordance with my rules than that "Yes." And if it hadn't been for the suppressed quiver in her voice I might almost have thought she was laughing at me. But no. I was sure she was already calculating the difficulties – perhaps insurmountable ones – the murder was going to introduce into our relationship.

"Two and a half months ago, in La Monteverdi's salon," I said in a low voice, "some cliché-loving fool said Vittoria Peretti was beyond any doubt the most beautiful woman in Italy. Recanati was there – and you know what he's like: all show, all vanity and brag, with scarcely enough brain to tell his left hand from his right. Well, that imbecile was annoyed by the other one's praise of Vittoria, and said in his pompous conceited way: 'Yes, Vittoria's very beautiful. Too beautiful. So beautiful that one day she'll turn whore.' He hadn't seen me: I was hidden behind a palm. I threw myself on him, but people separated us. The next day I sent him a challenge, but he answered that he came from too ancient and noble a family to fight me."

"What?" said Margherita. "Noble? Him?"

"He's no more noble than I am. He refused out of sheer cowardice. And it was that that cost him his life, at least as much as the stupid impertinence that made him think I wouldn't dare stab him. When I sent him a message by *il mancino* that I was going to, he pretended to laugh."

"So what's going to happen now?" asked Margherita.

"I don't know. And I don't care. Don't ask questions. If Recanati had accepted my challenge I'd only have wounded him in the arm. He deserved what he got for being such a fool."

We heard the door on to the terrace opening, and Margherita asked, trembling: "Is that you, Maria?"

"Yes, Signora. *Il mancino* wants to see Signor Marcello. He says it's important. Very important."

"Already!" exclaimed Margherita.

She turned pale, shot me just one look, then lapsed back into silence and immobility. As for me, I felt perfectly calm and even jaunty, as if detached from my own existence. I got dressed and went down the spiral staircase to the inner courtyard, where *il mancino* was pacing back and forth as well as he could within the space available, and doing so in characteristic fashion – sidelong, and keeping his eyes skinned.

"What do you want?"

"To tell you to leave here, Signore, and go to the Rusticucci palace."

Il mancino never looked you straight in the eye when he spoke to you. He gazed at your belt, at the place your purse hung from, as if he were weighing it up in his mind.

"Why?"

At this he sighed. He was a taciturn fellow, though he prided himself on speaking good Italian and not the patois of the fisherfolk in Grottammare. His lengthy dealings with the Corte had led him to the simple conclusion that the less you say the better it is for you.

"Signora Sorghini," said he with his customary politeness," is a wealthy widow, but she lacks influential connections. So her house isn't immune from the police. Whereas your brother-in-law is a cardinal's son, and the Bargello would think twice before searching the Rusticucci palace."

"Do you think he might want to?"

"Certainly, Signore, if you're in it."

"What do you mean?"

Il mancino looked at my purse in silence. I began to undo the strings and he suddenly became eloquent.

"This afternoon," he said, "the Bargello was questioning Maria Magdalena, the girl they call *la sorda*. But she's not really deaf, she only pretends to be because it helps her cheat her customers and make them pay more than the amount agreed in advance. Perhaps I should mention she's a whore," he added primly.

"Get to the point!" I said.

"We've got plenty of time," said *il mancino*. "The Bargello has asked for an audience with the governor about you, and there are lots of people waiting ahead of him."

"Cut it short anyway. To think I took you for a man of few words!"

"I am, Signore, but in this instance, and with your permission, I'd like to give you your money's worth. While the Bargello was questioning *la sorda* about some quarrel she'd had with a client, someone rushed into the Corte and told the Bargello he'd seen Recanati murdered, seen it with his own eyes, and knew who the murderer was. The Bargello looked very worried. He sent *la sorda* away, and she ran straight to the Mount of Olives."

"Is that where you meditate?"

"It's where I drink. It's a tavern."

"And I suppose this *sorda* is one of your friends?"

"For shame, Signore!" said *il mancino* in shocked tones. "I don't mix with such people. But *la sorda* knows the vast esteem in which I hold your lordship."

"And she gave you this information."

"She didn't give it to me, Signore. She sold it to me for fifty piastres."

"I'll give you a hundred if you'll walk in front of me and spy out the land on the way to the Rusticucci palace."

"Thank you for your bounty, Signore," said *il mancino*, "but I wasn't asking for anything. I was acting out of friendship."

"And so was I."

There was no trap waiting for me at the gate of the Rusticucci palace, so the Bargello must still have been discussing my fate with the governor. But so that the gatekeeper shouldn't see me and have some tale to tell if he was questioned, I slipped in by a small back door to which I had the key. *Il mancino* came in with me: our house had been one of his hiding places since Francesco offered him his protection.

The first person we met in the courtyard was *il mancino's* sister. She went pale and then blushed when she saw us, threw herself into her brother's arms, and jabbered to him at length in incomprehensible Grottammare patois, casting surreptitious but ardent looks at me the while. I turned my head away, but it was no use: she could still see me in profile, and my cheek felt as if it was burning. Caterina Acquaviva is undoubtedly the worst octopus of the lot. Giulietta says she's "fresh and lively, like her surname", but I see her as a furnace rather than a stream. And I don't like the way she exhibits her bosom.

I ordered her curtly to go and tell Vittoria I was here, and she swayed off in her usual manner. Amazing how proud the ugly little monkey is of her little body. I forced myself not to watch her. She'd have felt it.

I told Vittoria the whole story. She flushed when I recounted what Recanati had said about her, but that was her only reaction. When I'd finished she hurried off to repeat what I'd told her to Francesco, who immediately had his horses harnessed and went and asked an audience of the Pope.

Gregory XIII heard him out patiently. Just as he hated Montalto, so he loved his nephew, perhaps because it was obvious he was no genius.

"Since time immemorial in this country," he said, "a brother has always considered himself as much insulted as a husband by anything that seems to call his sister's honour in question. So there's some excuse for this young man. Tell him to pray and repent. That doesn't mean he is pardoned. But if he doesn't commit another murder the Corte will leave him alone."

Though it was much praised in Rome, the Pope's leniency didn't impress me: there was nothing evangelical about it. Whenever Gregory XIII didn't know what to do about something, he first tried to imagine what Montalto would have done if he'd been Pope. In this case it was quite plain: Montalto would have had me arrested, tried and hanged. Gregory XIII did the opposite, and with a pleasure I'd describe as malicious if I weren't talking about the sovereign pontiff.

3

Monsignor Rossellino (il bello muto)

Every morning and evening I thank Divine Providence which caused me to fall on the steps of the Vatican and struck me dumb, thus snatching me away from worldly success and earthly peril in order to engage me in the service of a master who may sometimes be harsh (though is he not harsh on himself?), but who works unremittingly for the glory of God and the Church.

In my view, though, it would be wrong to see Our Saviour's hand in all the hazards of life, great and small. The devil isn't so weak he plays no part in the convergences and coincidences which put souls in danger, and which God in His omnipotence allows so that He may put his creatures' virtue to the test.

I should like to relate here, for the edification of the faithful, one of the most dramatic and baneful of these coincidences, because it led astray an entire family and was the origin not only of abundant blood and tears but also of great disturbance in the State.

When my story begins, six years had passed since Francesco Peretti married Vittoria Accoramboni, and in all that time hardly a day had gone by without the wife of the Cardinal's adopted son visiting His Eminence for at least the better part of an hour. In fact, the Cardinal saw her more often than he saw Francesco, which we accounted for by the fact that Francesco was often too busy with the minor post he held at the papal court to go and see his uncle every day. No one knew exactly what Peretti's job consisted of,* though he was extremely well paid for it – if not as well as the Pope's son was for his; but even so, His Eminence would

* Peretti was in fact third chamberlain to the Pope. (Author's note)

only have had to say the word for Francesco to run and throw himself at his feet. If the Cardinal didn't say the word it was because, while he greatly loved his adopted son, he was even more greatly bored by him.

"Francesco has all the virtues," Monsignor Cherubi used to say before he was dismissed. "The only thing he lacks is charm. He hasn't read anything, seen anything, done anything or learned anything." If His Eminence had heard about this remark (which I took good care not to repeat), he would have replied that Monsignor Cherubi himself had all the charms required for a successful career but lacked certain virtues, including discretion.

His Eminence used to take his morning meal with extraordinary punctuality on the stroke of noon – and I can remember what a frugal repast it was, too, for I shared it with him – and afterwards walked for about half an hour in his garden. This involved some quite strenuous exercise because of his crutches, but it was also a relaxation, for the Cardinal took a close interest in his trees and shrubs and, in the summer, his flowers. So close indeed that for the head gardener, who accompanied him, it was the most dreaded moment of the day. Nothing escaped the Cardinal's eye: a weed, a clipped hedge out of true, an unhoed or unwatered flower-bed, a rose tree with greenfly, a stake not driven in firmly enough. Such minor imperfections in the garden vexed His Eminence almost as much as the major abuses that Gregory XIII's slackness had allowed to develop in the State.

When he had made his inspection the Cardinal would limp back to the palace, but to go to his library he had to abandon his crutches and be carried upstairs on a chair borne by a couple of hefty footmen. Then he would dictate letters to me until he drew out his watch and said with thinly disguised satisfaction: "Four o'clock. Vittoria will soon be here."

And sure enough on the stroke of four, with a punctuality I later learned greatly astonished everyone in the Rusticucci palace, his beloved niece would arrive, dressed in a high-necked gown, her radiant countenance framed in a lace collar. This austerity was deliberate. So simply was she attired that her only ornament was a single row of pearls. But how can one speak of simplicity except as a virtuous intention, when Vittoria's wonderful golden mane hung down over her shoulders and fell to the ground in a truly regal train?

So many little jokes about these daily visits had spread about the court, encouraged by the malice of Gregory XIII, that His Eminence decided early on that they should always take place in my presence. I felt an intruder between uncle and niece, however, so I used to sit out of the way at a little desk and copy a letter, as quiet as a mouse. It wasn't enough to be dumb. I tried to be invisible as well.

When Vittoria took leave of His Eminence, however, she always summoned me back into the land of the living with the most ravishing smile of farewell. The first time she noticed my presence in this way I was as amazed as if the Madonna in the picture on the Cardinal's right had stopped contemplating the infant Jesus for a moment to look at me. I trust no one will be offended by this comparison. What painter wouldn't have been happy to have Vittoria as a model for a Virgin and Child? – if she could ever have agreed to pose for such a subject, for it would have been supremely painful for a woman who was never a mother.

When Vittoria had sat down facing her uncle the conversation invariably began with the Cardinal questioning her closely about the physical and moral health of the inmates of the Rusticucci palace. Was Flaminio at last going to embrace his real vocation? Was Marcello at last going to get down to work? Why didn't he marry the rich widow he was infatuated with instead of flaunting the fact that they were living in sin? Wouldn't it be wiser for Francesco to pack *il mancino* off to the farm he'd inherited from his father in Grottammare, instead of letting him sponge on his own hospitality in Rome, spending most of his time in a tavern with a blasphemous name and making money as a pimp? How was poor Camilla's ulcer? Wouldn't it be better if she had her meals in her own room instead of exposing herself to Tarquinia's constant sarcasms? Couldn't Vittoria use her influence with her mother to stop the two old ladies fighting? Giulietta was twenty-five now: why wasn't a marriage arranged for her since she wasn't pious enough to go into a convent? He'd noticed Francesco was putting on weight. Shouldn't he take up riding and fencing again? And he'd heard that the gatekeeper drank. It was a bad enough habit in anyone, but worse still in someone whose job it was to stay wide awake and on the alert. Why didn't they dismiss him and get someone else?

And so His Eminence tried to set things to rights in the Rusticucci palace just as he did his own garden every day, and as he dreamed of doing in the State. But here as elsewhere he showed his political astuteness: he was careful not to mention Caterina Acquaviva's loose morals, because she was a valuable source of information.

There was one other subject the Cardinal never mentioned, for fear of hurting his niece, and that was the barrenness of the marriage that meant so much to him. Heaven knows he worried enough about it! Although so secretive by nature, he even spoke about it to me.

"You know, Rossellini," he said one day, though without explicitly referring to Vittoria, "it's a very bad thing for a woman not to have children, especially if she's got a lively imagination. Sooner or later she'll start thinking that perhaps some other man . . ."

Whatever she may have thought about some of them, Vittoria answered her uncle's questions skilfully and with dignity, never showing the slightest impatience. She sat with her beautiful hands resting on her hair, which she draped over her lap to avoid sitting on it — the very attitude that had so annoyed the Cardinal at their first meeting.

She was too fond of His Eminence and had too much admiration for his intelligence not to acquiesce in his speaking as head of the family, even at Francesco's expense. But she accepted it only within certain limits.

Her answers were qualified. She agreed with his suggestions concerning Flaminio, *il mancino*, the gatekeeper, and Tarquinia's role in the "fight between the old women" (as we have seen in the case of Cherubi's dismissal, the Cardinal sometimes expressed himself rather roughly). But Vittoria pleaded "her husband's authority" as an excuse not to make any decisions. She was more evasive about Giulietta. If Giulietta didn't favour either marriage or the cloister there was no way of forcing her. When it came to her twin brother, Vittoria became frankly defensive. Whose fault was it if Marcello found in La Sorghini the affection so cruelly denied him by Tarquinia in his childhood? And wasn't it obvious that in this unfortunate affair he had been the victim rather than the seducer? The liaison was certainly a scandal, but would it be any less scandalous if he married a woman old enough to be his mother, and married her for her money?

From anyone else but Vittoria His Eminence wouldn't have been able to tolerate such opposition to his own opinions. But I think he was fascinated by the combination in her of the gentle and the indomitable. I'm sure that as a Franciscan of very austere morals he'd never experienced the emotion of love such as I myself had felt for the Contessa V. before my accident. He was all the more unable to call it by its proper name because at the time he first came to know it he was a bent old man, crippled and ailing, for whom it was a great effort to get up out of a chair, hoist himself on to his crutches and walk a few steps round his garden. So how could he have given the name of love to an inclination not accompanied by any physical desire? Thus it was that the Cardinal was able to love Vittoria in all innocence, and that Vittoria was able to let him love her without fear, reassured by his cloth, his age and his state of health. To a certain extent at least she returned the exacting, jealous, uneasy and imperious affection he lavished on her. How otherwise, with her proud nature, would she have put up with his screening so strictly, through her husband, the people the Perettis were allowed to mix with? Especially as it resulted in such a contrast with the sort of life she had led before she was married, when the Rusticucci palace kept open house for everyone, respectable or otherwise, who was outstanding enough to aspire to her hand. What sacrifices she must have made in the past six years for a marriage in which she'd found neither the felicity of a deep attachment nor the happiness of motherhood!

Because of the restrictions imposed by the Cardinal there weren't twenty people in Rome who could claim the rare honour of visiting and being visited by Vittoria. It often struck me that the life of a sultan's wife was hardly more sequestered and, though nothing would have induced me to say such a thing to the Cardinal, I did think all those precautions were vain. There's no wall the Devil can't get through if he has friends within, as I know all too well.

On March 19th 1581 – a date I'm not likely to forget, as on that day His Eminence got into the most furious and unjust rage with me – Vittoria, after replying to the Cardinal's inquisition, was reading aloud in Latin from St Augustine's *Confessions*. Her uncle was interrupting her on every page to demand some comment, exactly as he'd have done with a priest, when a visitor arrived who was due at five o'clock.

I should explain that because of his hatred of pomp and ceremony (a hatred that Gregory XIII dismissed as a hypocritical affectation of simplicity), the people to whom the Cardinal had granted an audience used to present themselves at the time arranged without being preceded or announced by a majordomo, the only stipulation being that they should be absolutely punctual.

Cardinal Montalto had many visitors, including various eminent noblemen, Italian and foreign, attracted by his great experience and reputation for wisdom. To tell the truth, he used his audiences and his correspondence to win their support, and court gossip had it that he was winning himself allies in case some "great misfortune" occurred. If you'd asked the gossips "What misfortune?" you'd only have met with sealed lips, sanctimonious expressions and evasive looks, or even shrugs at so foolish a question. For apart from a victory by the Huguenot heresy there was only one great misfortune feared in the Vatican, and that was one never mentioned, though people thought about it all the time. It was the death of Gregory XIII.

This would be so much the greater a misfortune because it would raise the problem of the succession. And seeing Cardinal Montalto cultivating the friendship of the mighty, who could fail to conclude he was thinking of making a bid for it? True, when the cardinals gathered in conclave to choose a new Pope they were cut off from the outside world – so much so that their food was passed to them through a hatch, and the dishes inspected so that no messages could be smuggled in. But even so, who was so naïve as to think that the princes had no influence on the vote? Everyone knew that in a previous election the imperious Philip II of Spain had ruled out sixty-five of the seventy cardinals, leaving the conclave only five candidates, who suited him, to choose from.

Prince Paolo Giordano Orsini, Duke of Bracciano, who had an appointment with His Eminence at five o'clock on March 19th, was far from being as powerful as the King of Spain, but he did belong to a leading Italian family. And through his wife Isabella he was related to the Grand Duke of Tuscany, Francesco de' Medici, whose brother was a cardinal with considerable influence in the conclave. But not only was Bracciano rich by birth and by marriage; he had also performed great feats of valour at the Battle of Lepanto, where the Grand Turk's fleet had been destroyed by the combined navies of the Christian powers. Venice had afterwards appointed Bracciano commander of its galleys, and for the last five years he had been winning renown hunting down the Barbary pirates.

This great captain was also a man of taste and culture, open-minded, a lover of the arts, interested in everything. He was a protector of poets, and sought out the company of learned men such as His Eminence. Physically he was of good stature, but didn't appear tall because he was so broad. He had blue eyes, sandy hair, regular features, a strong round neck and a complexion weathered by his sea voyages. As the result of an arrow wound in the thigh he had got at Lepanto, he walked with a slight limp, and as if to disguise it he took long strides. But the resulting air of aggressiveness was belied by the expression of his mouth, which was tender and voluptuous.

He was a happy man who had succeeded in everything except marriage. His wife Isabella, tired of his long absences, had had an affair with a relative of his, Troilo Orsini. Troilo, horrified by his own treachery, had run away to Paris, where he thought himself safe from the vendetta sworn against him by Isabella's brother and husband. But a year later he was located in the French capital by an arquebus that Francesco de' Medici had hired to strike him down but not to kill him outright, so that its owner had time, before finishing him off with his dagger, to tell him who had ordered his death.

Isabella's adultery had, to use the expression then current, "drawn a mask" over the face of the Medicis and of Bracciano, and it was necessary for her to die too. This unwritten law, barbarous though it might be, was accepted so naturally in Italy that when Gregory XIII was told of the execution of Troilo Orsini he blandly asked: "And what have they done with the Duchess?"

But the surprising thing was they hadn't done anything. She had been shut up for five years in her castle at Bracciano, waiting for death. But death hadn't come, because her husband couldn't bring himself to kill her. He had loved her. She had given him a son, Virginio. Moreover, although he was a warrior he had no liking for blood, least of all the blood of a woman. He knew it would not add to his glory, even though custom excused and even demanded the execution of an adulteress. Is it not strange that people and princes haven't paid more heed to what Our Saviour said about such cases?: "Let him that is without sin among you cast the first stone." In our daily lives, do we really only pay lip-service to Christianity?

To return to March 19th, as soon as I saw by the clock on my little desk that it was five to five, I wrote on a piece of paper, "Your Eminence, it is time to end the interview," and went over and gave it into his hands. I emphasise that I put it into his hands and not on his lap, as he maintained afterwards. Then I went back to my seat, rather surprised that the Cardinal hadn't at once taken leave of his niece, as he usually did when I gave him a little reminder of that kind. I thought about reminding him again, but remembering he had rebuked me the day before for what he called my "excess of zeal", I decided not to. And very sorry I was I hadn't, for at five o'clock exactly, unpreceded by any majordomo – we had none – in walked Prince Orsini, Duke of Bracciano, with the long swift stride that always made him look as if he was going into the attack.

He was advancing into the room with his eyes fixed on the Cardinal and a courteous smile on his lips when he suddenly caught sight of Vittoria. He stopped dead as if dumbstruck, turned pale, and stood speechless, with his eyes riveted on her. The thick carpet covering the tiles of the study floor had muffled his steps, and Vittoria hadn't heard him come in. She went on reading from the *Confessions* in her clear, harmonious voice. As for His Eminence, he said, restraining his vexation with difficulty: "Leave us, please, Vittoria. I have to speak with Prince Orsini."

Vittoria looked up, saw Bracciano, and rose to her feet. The book fell out of her hands and on to the floor. She glanced at it in dismay, but her eyes came back to gaze at Bracciano, and she said in a tremulous voice, still looking at the Prince though her words were addressed to the Cardinal: "Forgive me for being so clumsy, father."

"It's nothing! It's nothing!" exclaimed His Eminence, his dark eyes blazing. "Rossellino will pick it up! Rossellino, see Vittoria out."

Not knowing which of the two orders I was supposed to obey first, I hesitated a moment. The Cardinal glared at me: "Well are you deaf as well as dumb? See Vittoria out!"

Vittoria seemed to emerge from her trance. She came over and kissed her uncle's hand as if in a dream, walked by the still motionless Prince with downcast eyes, and went out through the door I held open for her. I

63

caught her up at the top of the stairs, just as she was starting to descend. I noticed that the tips of her golden tresses touched each step as her feet moved down to the next. Her left hand, which she rested on the marble balustrade, was trembling. When I took leave of her at the door leading into the courtyard and her maid came forward with her mask and the great cape with which she covered her hair, she forgot to give me the gracious smile with which she usually deigned to acknowledge my existence. The maid arranged the cape over her shoulders, and before pulling up the hood Vittoria began to put on her mask. It was black, with three little brilliants between the eyes. At first she placed it on her forehead, while she fastened the ribbon at the back of her neck. As she did so she half-closed her eyes, and I could see that her lovely countenance was pale and devoid of expression. When finally she pulled the strip of velvet down over her face, it was as if she were lowering a mask of fabric over a mask of flesh.

Aziza the Wasp

I was born in Tunis, of parents people in this part of the world would describe as Moorish. When I was ten years old I was abducted in broad daylight from the medina by some brigands, who sold me to a pirate. No sooner was I aboard his ship than he set sail, intending, as I later found out, to scour the shores of the Adriatic in search of plunder. His name was Abensur, and he'd bought me not as merchandise for re-sale, but as something to beguile his idle hours during the dangerous expedition he planned.

He was a believer, and conscientious according to his lights, and when I told him I wasn't yet fully formed he swore not to deflower me until I'd become a woman. And he presented me with a little dagger, to defend myself against the advances of the crew. I was — and am still — as nimble and quick as a little monkey, and twice I used my dagger to sting a hand that tried to hold me too close. And that was why they nicknamed me the Wasp.

The breezes of the Adriatic are even more capricious than those of the Mediterranean: they can be blowing like fury one minute and die away the next. As soon as Abensur saw the Venetian galleys appear on the horizon he ordered his single-masted tartan to change tack, and it went bounding away over the waves before the wind. But after an hour the wind dropped, the boat was becalmed, and the galleys were gaining on us. When it was clear we were going to be captured, Abensur, who knew there was a price on his head, buckled on his money-belt and dived into the sea. The shores of a country called Albania were just visible in the distance. I found out afterwards that the Albanians are a fierce people and they hate the Turks, who've been trying for centuries to enslave them. And they hate the foreigners who pillage their coasts even more. But who knows? Perhaps Abensur did manage to reach land and survive. God is great!

I liked Abensur. He was both tough and gentle, like all real men. And I was longing to be a woman so that he could possess me.

The sailors on the Venetian galleys that captured us were free men, not slaves. And they soon proved it: those of our men who hadn't been killed in the boarding were put in chains, to be sold later in Venice. As for me, they diced for me. And I was won by what seemed to me the worst of the lot – a fat, stinking, one-eyed fellow with a beard, who seemed to have some kind of authority among them. As soon as I realised what had happened I tried to take to my heels, and when he made to grab me I pricked him in the arm with my little dagger. He let out a roar of rage and called on the others to help him. In the end they caught and disarmed me. The man with one eye, foaming with wrath, tore off my clothes and tied me naked to the rail in the full glare of the sun. He said he was going to leave me there to cook until nightfall, and then hand me over to the appetites of the crew. After that he would indulge his own pleasure by stabbing me.

All this he ordered to be translated into Arabic for my benefit by a very young sailor who seemed to be given more kicks than piastres by the rest of the crew. He'd hardly finished his translation when all hands were needed on deck and I was left alone in the blazing sun, my bonds cutting into my arms and legs. After a while the cabin-boy who spoke my language slipped through the rigging like an eel and came and gave me a drink. He whispered that his name was Folletto, and that he felt sorry for me because he was often beaten too. He had big black eyes in a woman's face, gentle and attractive. Looking at him more closely I realised what use he must be put to on the ship. A cabin boy on our tartan had served the same purpose. But unlike our crew, the *roumis* on the galley, instead of being grateful for his favours, repaid him with blows and contempt.

All the time my sufferings lasted, those ruffians kept coming up one by one to look at me, touch me, prod me like a sheep on sale in the market, and sneer. I tried to put a brave face on it, but as well as getting terribly scorched by the sun I was quaking inwardly, not so much at the thought of the final stroke of the dagger – I welcomed that – as at what I'd have to go through before I died. My stomach turned at the thought of those coarse, evil-smelling swine sprawling over me. More than once I fleetingly regretted not having given myself to Abensur.

But Folletto, effeminate though he might be, wasn't lacking in courage, and at the risk of his life – may the Almighty reward him! – he made his way to the stern of the galley and told the captain about what I was going through. To get to the bottom of it the captain came for'ard in person – something he never did in the ordinary way, according to Folletto. I could tell from his lofty manner and magnificent clothes that he was not only the captain of the ship but also some great emir in his own country. I thought him very handsome, with his sky-blue eyes, hair like a gold coin and shoulders wide as a door. And he was so tall my head scarcely came up to the middle of his chest. He was accompanied by a tall thin man I supposed to be the mate, and by Folletto, who translated his questions into Arabic.

"What's your name?"

"Aziza the Wasp."

"Why the Wasp?"

"Because Abensur, my master, gave me a little dagger to stick in the sailors who tried to come near me."

"You were a virgin, then?"

"I still am. Abensur never touched me."

"Who tied you up?"

"The man with one eye. He won me, gambling. I stuck my dagger in him."

The fair-haired Emir seemed to pause for thought, then spoke quietly and at some length with the mate. According to what Folletto told me,

66

the captain was from Rome, like him, and the crew were Venetian. And the emir knew Venetians too well to set them against him by acting hastily.

Finally he told Folletto to untie me, and sent the mate to find the man with one eye. My bonds had been so tight I could scarcely stand when Folletto released me. The Emir told him to give me something to drink and to help me get dressed. He kept his eyes on me all the time this was being done. I liked his eyes. Sometimes they were pale blue like the sky at dawn, sometimes – but only when he was angry – they were the blue of a steel blade.

When the man with one eye presented himself he swept off his cap to the Emir, bowed low and called him "my lord", but he spoke like a man quite sure of himself. "Your lordship knows," he said, "that when a woman is captured aboard a prize she belongs to the crew. And this one is mine. I won her at dice."

"She's a wasp. She's stung you. And she'll sting you again."

"No, she won't. I'm going to squash her."

"She won't be any good to you if you do that. Sell her to me."

"With your permission, my lord," said the man with one eye, scowling at me vindictively, "I'd rather squash her."

The fair-haired Emir turned to the mate and said: "Assemble the crew."

When all the sailors were gathered round us the Emir spoke to them: "This girl is a wasp. She has stung the man with one eye, and the man with one eye wants first to let you loose on her and then squash her. I want to buy her from him. If he agrees, I'll pay each one of you ten ducats in compensation."

When Folletto translated this to me later he explained that the Emir hadn't picked on the sum of ten ducats by chance. It was the price of a well-known harlot in Venice, where the galley would put in in three or four days' time if the wind was favourable.

The sailors acclaimed the proposal unanimously, and the man with one eye saw it was time for him to parley. If he held out he'd have both the Emir and his comrades against him.

"My lord," he said, bowing again, "as you're so generous with my mates, I'll be generous with you. If you want the wasp I'll let you have her for five hundred ducats."

"Five hundred! Deuce take it!" cried the Emir. "Your generosity costs me dear!"

He smiled, and seemed to weigh me up with his eye, scraggy little cat that I was.

"It's a heavy price," he said, "for such a light piece of goods."

The men all guffawed at this sally. All except the man with one eye. He meant to stick to his figure.

"My lord," he said, "the price of a thing depends on the pleasure the buyer expects to get from it."

"There's something in what you say, master," said the Emir. "You shall have your five hundred ducats. The mate will pay you right away."

And sure enough the mate came back soon afterwards with a big jute sack, sat down on a stool behind an upturned barrel, and paid out ten ducats to each of the crew and five hundred to the man with one eye.

I'd never seen so many gold coins in my life. I asked Folletto in a whisper why the Emir was giving away all that wealth.

"To buy you!" he said in Arabic.

"To buy me?" I answered in amazement. "Wouldn't it have been easier for him just to slit the one-eyed man's throat?"

"No, no!" laughed Folletto. "They don't do things in that way in Venice. In Venice people buy and sell."

As the Emir needed Folletto as an interpreter, he gave him the job of looking after me, and the poor boy was no longer at the mercy of the lust and brutality of the crew. On the Emir's instructions he started to teach me Italian – not the Italian of Venice, but the language as spoken in Rome, where he and the Emir came from. I made rapid progress, so passionately did I long to understand and make myself understood by my new master. Folletto told me his own name was really a nickname, and meant an elf or sprite. Nature must have made him a boy by mistake: apart from the sexual organs themselves, his body was completely feminine.

The Duke, for I must now call him by his Italian name, told me, laughing, that he would be as decent a man as Abensur the pirate, and wouldn't make love to me until I was old enough. But he did ask me to share his siesta, and seemed pleased to see from the expression in my eyes

68

that I was wild with pride and joy at his suggestion. It was very hot in his cabin and he slept naked: I was dazzled by the ample proportions of his body and the whiteness of his skin. Like marble. Later, in Italy, I saw a statue that's called the Farnese Hercules – it was just like him, and seemed to me to give off the same sense of power. God is indeed great to have put me in the bed of such a man!

Each of his thighs was as thick as my whole body, and when he stretched out his leg the muscles were like steel. I gazed in wonder at the breadth of his shoulders and at his chest, curved like a shield and adorned with a mass of short golden hair. Even when he slept the strength didn't leave his body. On the contrary. Every so often some little muscles would contract and ripple beneath the skin like waves on a calm sea. I would lie propped on my elbow and look at him, longing to run my small hand over the vast expanses of his limbs. But my adoration was mingled with such respect I didn't dare. It was hot, but that wasn't the only reason why my skin felt damp. The Adriatic swell made the ship move up and down, and it was as if my master were rocking me in his arms.

When he opened his eyes he seemed surprised at first to see me there. Then he recognised me, smiled, and seeing from my eyes what I was feeling, murmured some words in Italian which I didn't understand but which sounded sweet and musical as birdsong. Then he drew me towards him and started to caress me, and I was amazed at such gentleness and patience in one so strong. Thrills ran through my body, and I could feel myself vibrating like a viola. I was surprised to hear myself uttering little moans in time to the rhythm of his caresses. I'd never moaned or cried out when I'd stroked myself. But the pleasure my master was giving me now was infinitely stronger and more piercing. I lay with my head in the crook of his huge shoulder, passive as a doll in his large hands, and truly abandoned myself. The only notion in my head was the delightful thought that I repeated with every groan: "He is my master. I belong to him. He can do with me as he wills."

When it was over, seeing his body hadn't remained indifferent to my emotion, I stretched out my hand towards his sex, but he caught hold of my wrist and shook his head, smiling. "Not until I've possessed you," he said in Italian. As I didn't understand, he called Folletto – who was either asleep or pretending to be asleep in a little cubby-hole adjoining our cabin

– and asked him to translate. Then, still smiling, he ran his great fingers through my tangle of black curls, turned his back to me and went to sleep.

Later, when he'd dressed and gone out on deck, I asked Folletto why my master had rejected my caresses. He thought for a minute. Because of his dual nature he understood men as well as women, but he always needed a little time to sort out his own complications.

"You already feel you belong to him, just with one caress," he said. "But he won't feel you're his until he's entered you. Men think it's very important it should be their sex that makes a woman belong to them. They don't understand that women always give themselves beforehand."

"That's true, Folletto! Quite true! How is it you understand it so well?"

"Because I'm in love with the Prince too, Aziza. And when you moan in his arms it's your place I'd like to be in, not his."

This embarrassed me, so I changed the subject. "What will he do with me when he gets back to Rome? Sell me? Put me in his harem?"

Folletto began to laugh.

"The *roumis* don't have harems, Aziza," he said. "They have a lawful wife. And sometimes they take a concubine."

"What?" I said in astonishment. "*A* concubine? Just one?"

"Sometimes they have several," he said, "but one after the other."

That made me sad, for I thought that when my master got tired of me he'd get rid of me. I told Folletto of my fears.

"No," he said. "He'll keep *you*."

"Why?"

"Because you belong to him without thinking he belongs to you. So with you he doesn't have to be afraid of screams and tears, or whims and fancies, or jealous scenes and endless demands for money. For him you'll be the harbour where he can come and anchor after a storm."

When I think of it now I don't know whether what he said was meant as a prediction or a piece of advice. But I followed the advice, though it wasn't always easy, and now the prediction has come true.

A month after that conversation my body became mature, and when my period was over my master took me one day during the siesta – but so slowly, after so much preparation, in so many stages, with so many pauses, that I hardly felt it at all, only the joy and pride of being a woman when his great penis so gently and delicately filled me.

Our fleet of galleys was still sweeping the Adriatic in search of Barbary pirates, but they grew fewer and fewer, frightened off by the Prince's reputation for invincibility. When my master saw I could understand Italian he decided the time had come for him to convert me to his religion. When we put in at Venice he had a priest come on board to instruct me.

Before this *roumi* actually spoke I was rather apprehensive about what he was going to teach me. But when he said God created heaven and earth and man, and was the master of human destiny, and that we did good when we obeyed and evil when we disobeyed him, and that when they died good people went to paradise and wicked people were delivered over to the devil, I realised that Allah and the God of the *roumis* were one and the same deity, called by a different name according to whether you were born in Tunis or in Rome. And I had no more scruples about being baptised. I did wake up sometimes in the night, though, and say to myself: "Well, my poor Aziza, you're a *roumia* now! and the concubine of a *roumi*! What would they think of you in the medina, and what would your poor parents say if they knew!" And sometimes I'd cry, and sometimes I'd laugh. I cried when I thought of them, and laughed when I thought of myself.

Since we've been back in Rome there have been other women in the Prince's life, but as Folletto said, not all at once – only one after the other (that's the *roumis'* version of the harem). But he's always kept me on as his confidante and friend, and hasn't concealed anything from me about his love affairs.

But that's not to say he doesn't want my caresses any more, or I his. Every so often he sends for me through Folletto, who says with a sigh, "Go, he's asking for you." I find the Prince not lying on the bed but sitting propped up with cushions, and without saying anything I lie down between his thighs. He strokes my curly head with both hands, and gradually his legs stiffen until they imprison my body as in a vice. I like that imperious way of gripping me as if I were his mare. And I like it when his hands press my head down harder and harder in a gallop, until he lets out the hoarse groan that seems to come from the depths of his body. I feel proud that I've given him his supreme moment at the same time as he belonged to me. He gasps to get his breath back and says, "Come up here," and I cuddle up with my head on his heart and say: "Listen how hard it's beating! How strong it is! It'll never stop!" "Yes, it will," he says. "It'll stop one day."

I sense a shadow in his voice. He's thinking of the wound in his thigh, which has never healed since the Battle of Lepanto. I say again it's because the *roumi* doctors don't look after him properly! We've got two great doctors in Tunis, one an Arab and the other a Jew, and I'm sure their medicines would be better.

"But how can I go to Tunis?" he asks with a shrug. "That den of pirates! When I've hanged so many of them!"

I listen to his heart, beating less rapidly now. I'm lying curled up beside him, my head in the crook of his left shoulder. He's so broad I can hardly reach over his full chest and touch the crook of his right shoulder.

I'm sixteen now. I get enough to eat, and I have a large appetite. But I haven't got taller or fatter, and I don't weigh any more than a feather. My breasts are no bigger than pomegranates, and I've got little hard round buttocks like a boy. I really can't see what he finds to love in me, except perhaps the colour of my skin, which is olive brown, and my face with its curly hair, gazelle's eyes, little nose and big mouth.

I lie with my nose against his skin, which smells nice – it always smells nice, even when he's been sweating. I say nothing and wait. Although I'm impatient too, the waiting is delicious. I'm absolutely sure what's going to happen. Paolo's a fair man. He won't send me away until I've been satisfied too. I shut my eyes and wait with all my being.

But it sometimes happens that we quarrel, always about the same thing. I usually know how to keep quiet, but on this subject I get so cross I can't hold my tongue. "You ought to have done it five years ago! She was unfaithful to you with one of your relations! What a disgrace! And all you've done is shut her up in your castle at Bracciano! And now she gives herself to the guards, to the grooms, to the muleteers, to the scullions! Every day she dishonours you more!"

His eyes go grey as steel and he shoves me from him. "Be quiet! Go away! You're just a barbarian! How can you, a woman, tell me to kill another woman? You're no more a Christian than Francesco de' Medici is, or his brother the Cardinal, or the Pope! Francesco exhorts me to deal with Isabella 'like a gentleman'! His brother exhorts me to behave 'like a Christian'! That's what he said – 'a Christian'! What a joke! And the Pope pretends in public to be surprised I haven't yet 'cleared matters up'! But listen to me, Aziza, once and for all – I'm a soldier, not an executioner!"

I don't say anything. I just sit on the bed with my arms round my knees. I look at him sideways like a little girl who's been scolded and beaten, though he's never raised his hand against me. It always touches and amuses him when I look at him like this. He's not taken in by it, but he's a man who loves everything about women, even their wiles. "Come here, you naughty girl," he says after a moment. And I throw myself into his arms, and cuddle up against him. If only he'd suddenly want to take me now, how happy I'd be to be covered by his great body!

I'm not really bloodthirsty, and it doesn't matter to me whether he kills his wife or not. I'm Paolo's slave, not even his concubine. But it makes me furious that his wife should dishonour him. I hear what people say in various places, even in the street, and it makes me furious to hear them call such a hero a coward, even under their breath.

That last little quarrel took place before March 19th. After that, of course, things changed.

Raimondo Orsini (*il bruto*)

My brother Lodovico, Count of Oppedo, and I belong to the younger branch of the Orsini family. The head of the older branch – and thus of ours as well – is, as everyone knows, the grandissimo, bellissimo and valorosissimo Paolo Giordano Orsini, Duke of Bracciano. He reigns in his splendour in the Montegiordano palace with its four towers, just across the Tiber from the Castel Sant'Angelo. Lodovico and I have to make do with a much smaller palace with no towers nor any right of asylum.

I find it intolerable. Why shouldn't we, Orsinis too even though we do belong to the younger branch of the family, be able to give shelter and protection in our own house to anyone we like – even a highwayman –

73

without the Bargello della Corte* breaking in, hauling our guest off by the scruff of the neck, giving him a mere apology for a trial and hanging him? What true Orsini could swallow such an insult?

And Paolo Giordano has another advantage over us. Not only has he done well out of his inheritance, but he's acquired even more wealth on top of it. The five years he spent in the service of Venice brought him enormous wealth – he was allowed to keep half of all the "prizes" he took.

He's been a good kinsman to us, and not at all stingy with his piastres. But lately he's tightened the purse-strings. Last January he said to me: "Raimondo, here are ten thousand piastres for Lodovico and yourself. Now listen. They're the last you'll get – you spend money like water, and trying to bail you out is like trying to fill the Danaides' barrel." At least, I think he said the Danaides. I don't know who they are, or why on earth they tried to put wine in a barrel with holes in it.

The worst of it is, it got around that Paolo wasn't going to pay our debts any more. And from that day on we haven't been able to get any credit, not even from the Jews. So when the ten thousand piastres had gone up in smoke we had to resort to extreme measures: we sent a couple of our men to waylay travellers in the mountains of Nora. Unfortunately the wretches are brutes, and not content with robbing they often kill their victims, even when it isn't strictly necessary. It's true that I myself in my youth used to be be called *il bruto*, because I was rather free with my fists and feet, and if an affair got complicated I tended to use my dagger. But that's not fair either. My brother Lodovico is as quick on the draw as I am, but people have never called him *il bruto*, because he's got a pretty face and knows how to read and write.

I can sign my own name, and that's enough for me. I believe the sword's more useful to a gentleman than the pen. But, just the same, I've got more than my share of shrewdness, and don't let there be any mistake about it.

Paolo asked me to go and see him in the Montegiordano palace on March 28th, and he added a note saying "Please be discreet, and don't bring twenty other people with you." I was much intrigued when my secretary read that out to me.

* The chief of police

74

"Ah, Raimondo!" Paolo said, welcoming me in his great hall with his usual cordiality. "How are you? How's my great baby been managing since I weaned him?"

"Quite well."

"Quite well as far as cash is concerned, or quite well morally?"

I smiled and gave no answer, not knowing if he knew that the two bandits at large in the mountains were our men.

"You don't answer!" he said. "You don't trust me, though I'm older than you, and your kinsman! Do you take me for the Bargello? But never mind – sit down, and have a cup of this good wine. I want to ask you to do something for me."

I sat down, but he remained standing. He didn't drink either, but went on pacing back and forth in silence. Then suddenly I realised: Paolo, the great Paolo, usually so regal and sure of himself, was embarrassed.

"The thing is," he said at last, "I've decided to put an end to Isabella's scandalous existence."

"That's a change!" I said. "For five years you've been refusing to do it!"

"The reason is, Raimondo, that Isabella's sinking deeper and deeper into bad ways. Five years ago she was only an adulteress. Now she's a veritable Messalina."

I frowned. "What are you talking about, Paolo? I can't make you out! To start with, who's this Messalina?"

"A woman with an insatiable appetite for men, who gives herself to anyone, day or night."

"And where's this marvellous creature to be found?"

"Raimondo! She's been dead for centuries! She was an empress in ancient Rome."

"What's the point of talking about her if she's dead?"

Paolo didn't answer, so I thought for a moment and said: "What it amounts to, Paolo, is that for five years you refused to kill your wife, and now you've made up your mind to do it. Right – that's your business."

"No, Raimondo," he answered, looking me straight in the eye. "It's yours. I want to entrust you with the execution."

"Me?"

"Yes, you. It goes without saying that I'll reward your devotion."

75

I was silent. It was the first time the idea had entered my head, and to tell the truth I found it rather shocking.

"I thought it was the custom for the husband to kill an unfaithful wife himself," I said. "He's the one she's insulted."

"Never mind about custom. I want to go about it differently. I'll write you a note so that Isabella knows you're doing it for me."

"Yes," I said slowly. "Like that it would be all right, I suppose. But you're depriving yourself of a treat, not killing her yourself – she did give you horns."

I looked at him as I said that, and I thought he went white.

"I'm not depriving myself of any treat," he said quietly. "I loved her, remember."

After a moment I went on. "You said something about a reward."

"Twenty thousand piastres."

"I'd have thought thirty thousand."

"If you like!" he answered angrily. Then he said it again. "If you like! We're not going to haggle! That would be too sordid!"

"Listen," I said, annoyed at his tone. "It would be cheaper if you got one of your bandits to do it – one of those you shelter in your house."

"Certainly not!" he cried. "That would be unworthy of her and of me! If she doesn't die by my own hand it must at least be by the hand of another Orsini."

I thought again and said: "Paolo, you've said she's a trollop. Would you let her be treated like one . . . beforehand?"

His eyes flashed with fury. "You haven't changed, Raimondo!" he said. "You really are brutish! Who else would think of that at a time like this?"

I stood up. "If I'm brutish," I said through clenched teeth, "this brute will take his leave."

He seized me by the arm. "No, Raimondo, don't get angry – please! I need you."

And he made me sit down again.

He took a few more paces round the room and then went on: "Do what you like about Isabella. But I don't want her treated inhumanly."

"I didn't intend to. Even *il bruto* can have a heart."

He took my hands. "Oh, Raimondo – I'm sorry. I've hurt your

feelings."

"No, no," I said, hastily withdrawing my hands.

After that, not wanting to part with ruffled feelings, we talked of other matters. But I still couldn't get over what he'd said. Once again I'd come up against the family view of me as a brute and a dullard, and I didn't want to leave without demonstrating, even in veiled terms, that I wasn't stupid as he supposed.

"Paolo," I said innocently, "you've lost your secretary, I believe?"

"Lost is the word. He's become a priest."

"I've got a suggestion, if you want to replace him."

"Who?"

"Marcello Accoramboni."

Paolo looked dumbfounded. He stood there speechless, blinking. I went on with a detached air: "He's educated. He even learned Latin once."

"But how do you know all this, Raimondo?" he asked, raising his eyebrows. "Have you met him?"

"No. But I know a girl who often sees him."

"Who?"

"Caterina Acquaviva."

"Who's she?"

"Vittoria Peretti's maid."

Then he really went white. To conceal his agitation he turned his back on me and went and looked down out of the window at the huge inner courtyard. That didn't tell him anything he didn't know, I'll wager. The outlaws he gave asylum to camped there day and night, and he maintained them in the knowledge that he had only to arm them to match the power of the Pope himself.

"This girl – how well do you know her?" he asked, without turning round.

"I tumble her whenever I feel like it."

"Could you arrange for me to meet her?"

"I could, but I don't think it's a good idea."

He turned and looked at me. "Why not?"

"Her parents live in Grottammare. I suspect she's in the pay of Montalto."

77

"In that case," he said, "we'll say no more about it."

And he took me by the arm and led me to the top of the stairs. I was glad to find him so polite after I'd ferreted out his little secrets. As a matter of fact I was quite touched. My affection for him revived, and I said: "I could introduce you to Marcello Accoramboni, though."

"What? You just said you didn't know him."

"I don't. But he fraternises with *il mancino*, Caterina's brother."

"Who's *il mancino*?"

"A brigand turned pimp. He haunts a tavern called the Mount of Olives. Some say he owns it."

"You mix with some strange people, Raimondo," said Paolo with a little smile.

"So do you," I answered, "judging by those I've seen in your courtyard."

We embraced and went our separate ways without coming to any decision about Marcello. Of course, Paolo didn't really need me to introduce him, now I'd told him who *il mancino* was and where to find him.

As for Isabella, as soon as she saw me appear outside the walls of Bracciano with Alfredo my squire and my heavy escort, she realised what I'd come for. I scarcely needed to show her Paolo's note. But she received me with her usual kindness, without a trace of fear on her beautiful face. And after asking me to sit down she started to talk to me quite conversationally and with the utmost courtesy.

"Whatever you do you must thank Paolo for having let me go on living for five years after my affair with Troilo. It's much more than I'd hoped. And tell him I'm very touched that he didn't have the heart to kill me himself. Naturally, Raimondo, you're not very keen on this kind of job either. You've always had rather a soft spot for me – don't say you haven't. And I've always thought it unfair that they call you *il bruto*. Your eyes aren't the eyes of a brute. Nor are your lips."

She rose gracefully from her chair and came and kissed me on the mouth, then went and sat down again as if nothing had happened.

"And how do you propose to do it?" she asked, quite naturally.

I gulped and mumbled: "By the legal method: with a red silk cord."

"Oh no, Raimondo," she said, "not like that – please! Strangling makes people look so ugly! I don't want to look ugly even after I'm dead. No, a dagger, Raimondo — a dagger! A dagger right in the heart!"

"Whatever you say," I murmured.

"And one more little request, Raimondo," she went on, with her head a little on one side and still speaking quite conversationally. "I'd like you to give me another three days of life, please."

"To put your affairs in order?"

"Oh no!" she answered with a carefree laugh. "My affairs have been in order for five years . . . But I've noticed there are a lot of handsome fellows in your escort, starting with yourself. And you've always hankered after me, Raimondo — don't deny it."

"I'm sorry, Isabella," I said, averting my eyes. "It's all very well about me — I'm your cousin too, like Troilo. But the others — All the others — How could you have become such a . . ."

I tried to remember the name Paolo had mentioned, but I couldn't, so I said: ". . . such an insatiable woman?"

She laughed again. How beautiful she was! Those teeth, that mouth, those eyes, that forest of black hair!

But then, serious again, she said: "When Paolo and I were together we used to make love often, several times a day. He was an indefatigable lover. And he could do wonders with his mouth. I wanted to make love all the time, Raimondo — all the time. But I adored Paolo, so in the intervals I made do with thinking about him and just dreaming he was making love to me. Then he went away to fight. His absence was hell. And one evening I threw myself at Troilo's head just because he looked like his cousin. Poor Troilo, he was dying of fright, and as soon as he realised what he'd let himself in for he ran away. Then the whole world collapsed. Troilo was killed, my son was taken away from me, and I was waiting for death. And while I was waiting . . . You see, Raimondo, some people make themselves drunk with wine. And now you know what I make myself drunk with."

I spent the night with her in her room, and the next morning at dawn, when I got back to my own room, I started to cry. I couldn't see why she had to die. She was so alive.

During the morning I went to see the chaplain, and after I'd made my confession I said: "Father, you know why I'm here."

"Yes," he answered, lowering his eyes.

"But I don't want to do it until she's confessed. I don't want her to die a sinner."

The chaplain was so old his face was almost fleshless – all you could see on the bones was the thin, almost transparent skin. He was already so much like a skeleton I was almost surprised to find there were really eyes in his hollow sockets, though when you looked at them you could see they too were dead.

"But I haven't heard her confession for ages!" he said in a voice so faint you expected it to fade away completely at any moment. "What would be the use? She doesn't repent! Her only idea is to sin again!"

"So will she be damned?" I asked.

"Who knows?" he cried, throwing up his bony hands.

"Father, hear her confession, I beg you," said I. "Hear it one last time!"

"No, no, no!" he answered with a vigour that amazed me in one so old and frail. "It would be a false confession! Yet another! Even when she's kneeling in front of me with downcast eyes reciting the list of her iniquities, I can see she's still revelling in them."

He turned away, and I watched him go. I was wild with rage; if he hadn't been a priest I'd have run him through.

I had my midday meal alone with Isabella in her room.

"Give me the key, Isabella," I said, "so that I can come in whenever I wish."

She smiled. "Take it," she said. "It's in the lock. But you might not find me alone."

And with a bitter curl of the lip she added: "Thank God, I'm not often alone." But she resumed at once, lightly: "And how's Paolo? Has the wound in his thigh healed? And has he still got his little Moorish girl?"

"Yes."

"What's she like? Have you seen her?"

"Once, by accident. He keeps her out of the way. She's a kind of skinny little kitten with big eyes and a big mouth."

Isabella started to laugh, God knows why, and went on quite gaily: "There've been others as well, I'll wager."

"Plenty."

She raised her glass to her lips but didn't drink.

"Men are lucky, Raimondo. They can sleep with anybody and everybody and people don't call them harlots. And when they commit adultery, no one kills them. Still," she said, "I wouldn't not be a woman for anything. Come on, Raimondo. Hurry up! What are you waiting for? If you're not careful I'll start calling you *il bruto* myself!"

Her hand clutched mine and she pulled me out of my chair, her eyes blazing. Her couch was very low and twice as wide as an ordinary bed. The only other furniture in the room consisted of rugs and draperies and cushions. The curtains were drawn across the window because of the sun.

When I got back to my room I sent for Alfredo, my squire. He's my cousin on my mother's side, and if anyone ought to be called *il bruto* it's him rather than me. He's as strong as a bull and ruthless as a wolf. You can tell just by looking at him: he's got a muzzle rather than a face. But in his way he's devoted to me, and I'm quite fond of him. Lodovico says that's because I feel intelligent when I talk to him. But Lodovico's wrong: I never feel intelligent. I live in a sort of cloud, and I don't really understand what's going on. The mere fact of being alive puzzles me. One day I asked Paolo to explain it to me. But he only laughed.

"Alfredo," I said. "About Isabella. I'm going to do it today."

He opened his little piggy eyes wide. "But this is only the second day. You promised her three."

"Exactly. If she were still alive tomorrow morning she'd think, 'My last day has come,' and brave as she is she'd be afraid. I don't want her to be afraid. I don't want her to suffer. I want to kill her without warning, so that she doesn't even realise it."

Alfredo looked at me, intrigued. "You don't want her to be afraid," he repeated. "You don't want her to suffer. You want her to die without realising it."

"Yes."

"Why?"

"Don't ask me why. Just find out how it can be done. I'll wait for you here. I've got the key to her room."

He nodded sagely and went off, pleased that I was trusting in his cunning. I threw myself on the bed and tried to sleep, but in vain. Alfredo came back as it was getting dark.

"Now's your chance," he said. "Amin is with her."

"Who's Amin?"

"The muleteer here. A gigantic Black. She has him service her every evening."

Alfredo was holding a couple of stilettos with long thin blades.

I swallowed.

"What are the stilettos for? And why two of them?"

"One for me and one for you. When Amin's on top of her I'll stab him behind the ear. That'll kill him stone dead. Then I'll pull him off her and you can stab her in the heart. Stilettos only make a small wound and there won't be much blood."

I stood up, trembling in every limb, and downed a large glass of wine. "Come on then," I said.

"We'll have to take our shoes off first," said Alfredo.

I led the way into Isabella's room. My hands were clammy, and my heart was thumping so loudly against my ribs I was afraid everyone else would hear it. In the dark I could just make out the huge form of the Black lying on the couch, but I couldn't see Isabella. She was underneath him, letting out little childish moans. I realised she was so far gone she wouldn't be able to hear my heart beating, or anything else either.

Alfredo moved forward, but I pulled him back. I wanted the two of them to reach the height of their pleasure.

It was a long wait. The Black was panting like a bellows, the sweat streaming down between his shoulder-blades. I was fascinated by the incredible strength and speed with which his muscular buttocks moved back and forth. Isabella, invisible, groaned softly and mournfully like an infant with a fever.

Then the Black let out a single hoarse, triumphant cry, and she uttered several cries too, in a shrill crescendo. When she'd finished I gave Alfredo a shove, he leaned forward, and everything happened as he'd said it would. Isabella's face gave one convulsive twitch, she blinked, and it was all over. The room was suddenly filled with stillness and silence. The two who were still living gazed down at the two corpses.

"At least they died happy," said Alfredo with a snigger. I turned on him angrily.

"Get him out of here. Throw the body anywhere you like. Leave me on my own."

The Black was so heavy Alfredo couldn't carry him and had to haul him out of the room by the shoulders. When he'd done so I locked the door behind him and went and knelt by the bed beside Isabella. I took one of her hands in both of mine. It was still warm and supple. Tears rolled down my cheeks and I started to pray. But I felt gloomy and numb. Between repetitions of the Lord's Prayer I wondered dimly why it was so wrong for Isabella to have done what she did. When her hand had grown cold and stiff in mine I stood up and left her.

4

Marcello Accoramboni

I began to ask myself a few questions after a sudden change came over life inside the Rusticucci palace: the exits and entrances were so closely guarded, our peaceful home seemed more like a citadel under siege.

All this had an effect on the mood of the people living there. Lips were sealed as well as doors closed. Everywhere I met only with silence, tension and anxious expectation. You'd have thought that instead of being a stone's throw from St Peter's the Rusticucci palace had been transported into the heart of a brigand-infested forest, with an attack expected from one night to the next.

Peretti, who seemed to be the source of these severe measures, never mentioned them. Though usually so affable and talkative, he now spoke very little and avoided people's eyes. Vittoria was pale and practically dumb. Camilla and Tarquinia had called a halt, at least for the moment, to their verbal jousting. Flaminio spent all his time praying, and never left his room except to come and sit at meals with downcast eyes. I thought Giulietta would be the best person to approach in the circumstances, but she admitted she knew nothing, and seemed mortified that no one had thought to inform her or ask her advice about all these mysteries. The servants observed their masters, and like them remained silent.

It seemed to me, from certain indications, that even Tarquinia didn't know the reasons for the new régime. She kept darting inquiring looks at Vittoria, which the latter seemed not to notice, and judging by her increasingly imperious manner I suspected she wouldn't be able to restrain her curiosity much longer. And sure enough, one night, about an hour after the evening meal, as Vittoria was going up to her room, *la superba* also rose to her feet. From her determined air I guessed it wouldn't be long either before I stopped her. But I waited a few minutes to let them actually cross swords before I intervened.

After a suitable interval I went up the spiral staircase to the first floor and the gallery around the courtyard, lit that night by a splendid moon. Then I crept stealthily along to Vittoria's room. To reach it you have to go through a little antechamber where her maid sleeps if Vittoria isn't well.

There was no light in the antechamber, and thinking it was empty I was about to go in when I thought I heard the sound of breathing coming from inside. I held my own breath, trod even more lightly than before, and peeped inside. At first I could see nothing, but after a while, when I'd got used to the dark, I could make out Caterina, standing with her back to me and busy listening at Vittoria's door. Listening to what mother and daughter were saying to each other. If anyone asks me how I recognised Caterina when her back was turned, I can tell them plainly I recognised her by her behind.

She was listening so intently I got within reach without her noticing. Grabbing her by her hair with my left hand and clapping my right over her mouth to stop her screaming, I pulled her back into my arms and dragged her out into the gallery; she struggled and lashed out in all directions as she tried to scratch me, like a cat. She even tried to bite the hand I'd laid over her mouth. But as soon as we were out in the gallery, with the moonlight on my face, she became as meek as a lamb, gazing at me submissively and quite ready to go on leaning against me if I'd let her. But I set her roughly on her feet, and holding her at arm's length by the neck of her dress, led her to my own room, where I locked her in and told her to stay there and wait for me.

I then retraced my steps, and without pausing to knock went into Vittoria's room. She was sitting at her dressing-table looking at herself in the mirror and languidly brushing her hair. Tarquinia stood behind her, seemingly interrupted in one of her characteristic tirades. When I came in Tarquinia stood there open-mouthed, and the only word of hers I heard before she caught sight of me was "coach". From this I deduced that she was complaining about being treated like the fifth wheel of a coach, and not told anything. She'd protested about this more than once since Vittoria had got married, always employing the same comparison.

"Madam," said I with a mocking bow, "there are two people who are superfluous in this room: you and I. If, like the rest of us, you're puzzled about the new order of things in this house, apply to the person responsible – Signor Peretti, your son-in-law. Vittoria is obviously neither able nor willing to answer your questions."

"I grant you she's not willing," said Tarquinia, raising her voice, "but I doubt very much that she's unable."

"Even so, have you the power to force her?"

"She owes me an answer!" cried Tarquinia. "I'm her mother!"

"Madam," I said, bowing again, "you must see that this exaggeration is ridiculous. The fact that you're her mother doesn't give you unlimited rights over her. In particular it doesn't give you the right to force her confidence or prevent her from getting some sleep. Allow me to give you a piece of advice: Get out!"

"And who are you to give me advice?" she cried, turning on me with a look of the utmost contempt. "A murderer and a pimp!"

"Mother!" cried Vittoria. "You're only provoking him!"

"Yes, and I'll provoke him again!" shouted Tarquinia in a fury. "A murderer and a pimp! As for you," whirling round on her daughter, "you can't say anything to me when I ask you a question, but you soon find your tongue to defend this ruffian!"

"Madam," I said, "you shouldn't resort to insult so fast. Insult leads to violence, and if you don't leave this room immediately this 'ruffian' will be reluctantly obliged to throw you out!"

"Scoundrel!" she cried, drawing herself up. "Would you use violence on your own mother?"

"With pleasure," I answered, grinning.

Tarquinia's eyes glittered, but she could see from mine that I meant what I said. She gathered up the folds of her huge skirt in her hand and swept haughtily out of the room. It struck me yet again that what really annoyed me about *la superba* was not so much her obnoxious character as her love of dramatics. Especially as she couldn't act.

"I'll leave you, Vittoria," I said. "Lock your door in future if you want to avoid incursions from the fifth wheel of the coach."

In the ordinary course of events this little joke would have made her smile, but not now. I looked at her in the mirror. She seemed tired, and was brushing her hair without her usual energy. Her lovely face showed nothing, not even sadness.

"Remember, Vittoria," I said quietly "– what you want, whatever you want, that's what I want too."

I don't know why I said the words that were later to turn out so prophetic. But I'm sure I was expressing my inmost feeling. I've never thought of Vittoria and myself as being really separate.

"Thank you, Marcello. For everything."

As she spoke she looked at me in the mirror, and I looked back at her. Her face was brightly lit by the two candelabras on either side of the glass, while mine was in the shadow, so the difference in our colouring was less visible than usual and the likeness of feature and expression infinitely more striking. My heart began to thump. It was as if the secret of my life was there, and I had only to decipher it.

"Thank you, Marcello," she said again.

And she shut her eyes for a moment. It was as if a curtain had fallen on a play that would go on being acted unseen. I left her to her thoughts and went out, closing the door softly behind me.

Caterina hadn't moved from the little low chair on which I'd planted her before locking her into my room. And I noticed straight away that she'd surreptitiously undone a couple of buttons on her bodice so that the square neck showed off more of her bosom. What a fleshly snare she was, this girl! But she was her own first victim! It was plain that all she was conscious of was her own femininity. From the roots of her luxuriant hair to the calves of her legs which her short skirt more than half revealed, she was all lure, bait, lime and trap.

When I came in she stood up, half dead with fright but still making play with her large eyes, parted lips and supple body – and all with an air of feigned embarrassment, false naïvety but all too genuine willingness. If at the same time as showing me her beautiful bosom she could have shown me her pretty behind, I'll wager she'd have done it. Most astonishing of all was that though she was throwing all her sexuality in my face, she wasn't even vulgar.

As she stood there, still and inviting, I realised she was expecting to be punished, and that I'd have to punish her myself if I didn't want to have to denounce her to Peretti. He'd have dismissed her at once, and I didn't want that: Vittoria was so attached to her. She'd even taught her to read.

So I stepped forward and gave her two vigorous slaps, then got hold of her by the shoulders and shook her.

"Who pays you to spy on Vittoria?" I yelled.

A purely rhetorical question, for I didn't think she'd listened at the door for any other reason than the curiosity typical of ladies' maids or the tendency they all have to identify with their mistress.

Her answer left me speechless.

"Oh, but the Cardinal doesn't pay me," she said, the tears welling up in her eyes. "He comes from Grottammare, and I'd be afraid of harming my parents if I didn't do as he says."

I turned my back on her to hide my stupefaction, and walked over to a little table with a five-branched candelabra on it. I struck the flint and lit the candles one by one. There was a stool by the table and I sat Caterina down on it. Strangely enough, this ceremonial seemed to impress her more than the two slaps.

"Answer me. How do you get your reports to the Cardinal?"

"Indirectly. Through Father Racasi, the priest who hears my confession."

"Often?"

"Once a week. Twice, since March 19th."

This was the first time I'd heard the date mentioned, but still I showed no surprise.

"Tell me everything that happened that day," I said.

"Nothing much, apparently," she answered. "It just so happened on March 19th that as she was taking leave of the Cardinal, Vittoria met Prince Orsini. She was very affected by the encounter."

"How do you know?" I exclaimed. "Did she tell you?"

"No, that's just it," said Caterina brightly. "She didn't say anything. And usually she tells me everything. And I can see what she's been like since."

"What has she been like?"

"Lost in dreams."

If that was Vittoria's state of mind, it was easy to imagine the effect the

88

meeting might have had on the Prince. Everything was clear now, including the state of siege we'd been living in. The Cardinal must have been afraid Orsini would abduct Vittoria.

"Listen to me now, Caterina," I went on after a moment's silence. "From now on, when you make your confession to Father Racasi, you're not to say anything about Vittoria but what I tell you to say."

She answered without hesitation, her whole body starting towards me. "Signor Accoramboni, I'll do anything you want."

"Do you tell Father Racasi about your sweethearts?"

"Of course," she answered, lowering her eyes. "I don't leave out my mortal sins. I'm a good Catholic."

"Does he ask you their names?"

"No, never. Just the number of times I've committed the sin of the flesh with them."

"How many young men have you got?"

"Two," she said. I couldn't tell if her confusion was real or assumed.

"From now on you'll have only one."

"Which have I got to give up?" she said eagerly.

"Both."

She stared at me. She was only too delighted to do as I wished, but didn't yet dare understand what I meant. I signed to her to stand up, stretched out my hand, and touched the two buttons she'd undone while I was with Vittoria.

"Do you want to know," I said, "who's going to be your only sweetheart?"

"Yes," she answered, quivering from head to foot.

"You'll find out once you've finished what you started so aptly when I wasn't here."

Again she couldn't quite bring herself to understand, but then, having undone a third button without seeing me manifest any disapproval, she went on undressing with a grace that was natural and some little simperings that were not. Curiously enough, when she blushed it wasn't her brow and cheeks that coloured, but her neck and the upper part of her bosom.

As soon as she was naked I took her hand and led her over to the bed, where I signed to her to sit down. I just stood there, looking at her. She didn't say anything: she was still rather afraid of me, though her big black eyes were very eloquent. How strange women are! How incomprehensible that complete submission to their lovers that they call love! For my part, I'm both attracted and repelled by these curious animals. I don't know why, but I always feel a great impulse to punish them. Sometimes I think, "You're out of your mind, Marcello! What does it mean? What do you want to punish them *for*?"

The truth is I can never quite understand what I do. It's certain I decided to sleep with Caterina and then get her out of the Cardinal's power and make her the agent of my own designs. But what were my designs? I still didn't know, except that they included what had always been my first priority – to protect Vittoria.

But Caterina wasn't only an instrument. As I was standing there by the bed I felt not only ardent desire but also a kind of tenderness. However, as I couldn't conceal the former I decided I'd anyway hide the latter – at least, as long as I could. I don't trust octopus-women, the ones that cling on to you.

Once she was naked Caterina recovered her usual boldness. Her breath came shorter and louder, and when she saw me undo my doublet the whole way down her hand didn't hesitate to run up my trunk-hose in the opposite direction. Her fingers trembled a little as they undid the laces, but not from fear.

At evening Mass four days later in the chapel of the Rusticucci palace, Caterina was sitting behind me, in the back row. And she leaned forward and whispered in my ear that *il mancino* wanted to see me. I slipped her the key to my room, which I keep on me so that *la superba* can't poke her nose into my affairs.

"Lock him in my room and bring me back the key," I whispered. "I'll go to him in a quarter of an hour."

When I joined him, *il mancino* rose and bowed. He's short and wiry and upright, and his bows are at once respectful and proud. I like them – they make you feel that the esteem he has for you is tempered by the esteem he has for himself. Like his sister, he's lost his Grottammare patois, and he knows how to express himself: he speaks correct and even elegant Italian. He's a subtle fellow, and his meticulous politeness is intended to convey that he expects as much in return. He's been treating me recently with a tinge of courteous familiarity. He knows that though I'm neither a bandit nor a pimp, I've used my dagger in Rome in broad daylight and I live on the generosity of the Signora Sorghini.

"Sit down, Domenico," I said, returning his bow. "Would you like a drop of wine?"

"Thank you, no, Signore," he replied, bowing again. "I never drink between meals."

"And your health is all the better for it."

"Signore," he said, "if you'll allow me to come straight to the point, I have a message for you, and two bits of useful information. The message won't cost you anything, because I've already been indemnified by the person who sent it. On the other hand," lowering his eyes delicately, "the information will have to be paid for."

"Very well," I said. "Let's start with the message."

"Prince Orsini, Duke of Bracciano, would like to meet you tomorrow on the stroke of noon in a room at the Mount of Olives."

"Prince Orsini! At the Mount of Olives! In a room frequented by prostitutes!"

"It's a modest enough place, to be sure," said *il mancino*, "but easier to get into unnoticed than Montegiordano. I know the tavern quite well – plenty of respectable people just pull their hat down over their eyes and their cloak up over their nose when they go there. No one will spot the Prince."

"I'll be there. Now let's have the information."

"There are two bits of information. Perhaps you already know about the first – if it isn't public property by now, it soon will be. If it's not new to you, it's free. Otherwise it'll cost you twenty piastres. I rely on your word."

"And so you may."

"The Prince's adulterous wife, after so long a reprieve people thought it would last for ever, has been dispatched."

"When?"

"A week ago."

"You shall have your twenty piastres."

"Signore," said *il mancino*, "the second piece of information will cost you fifty."

"I'm listening."

"My sister Caterina, in obedience to some third person," he said without batting an eyelid, "has dismissed her two admirers. One of them was called Raimondo Orsini. It's a pity you didn't think to ask my sister his name, Signore – it would have saved you fifty ducats."

"It's a pity," I said drily, "that Caterina didn't think to tell me. But she's an affectionate sister, and takes care of her brother's interests."

"No, no, Signore!" cried *il mancino*. "You mustn't think that! Caterina is absolutely uncalculating. She can't see any further than the end of her nipples."

His jest both amused and convinced me. "And what's the point of this bit of information?" I asked.

"That's for you to judge," answered *il mancino*, with feline prudence.

"I'd like to know what you think."

"Before my sister broke with Raimondo, the Prince might have hoped to reach her through his cousins, and through her to enter into contact with the Signora, your sister. Now that possibility is gone."

"Well reasoned."

And on my part, unwittingly, well played. Little did I imagine when I told Caterina to dismiss her two lovers that one of them was an Orsini.

Next day on the stroke of noon, with my cloak up over my nose as *il mancino* had suggested, I went to the Mount of Olives. I didn't recognise anyone when I went in – there was such a press of people. *Il mancino*'s sight must be keener than mine, for before I saw him he whispered in my ear.

"Follow me, Signore,"

We went up a rickety wooden staircase, passing a scantily clad girl who ran down and shrieked as she went. She was pursued by a man brandishing a cutlass and also yelling. *Il mancino* tripped the man up, disarming him as he fell. Then he seized him by the collar, shoved him up against the wall, and said with a smile on his lips but a harsh look in his eyes: "Signore, squabbles between lovers are settled peacefully here. Go down and find a table and order a pitcher of wine in my name. I'll join you."

The man obeyed, gentle as a sucking lamb. "He's one of *la sorda's* customers," he explained. "I don't approve of her methods. I'm all for

92

honesty — at least, as far as possible."

He pointed out a door on the landing. "That's the place," he said. "And if you don't mind my saying so, Signore — don't be too haughty. The Orsinis are very hot-blooded."

"So am I."

I tested my sword in its scabbard, knocked once on the door, then entered abruptly, flinging the door back against the wall in case anyone had had the idea of hiding behind it. I came upon two gentlemen, one standing and the other seated, both wearing black masks. My noisy entrance had startled them. I shut the door behind me, taking care not to turn my back towards them. Then I made the briefest of bows and put my hat down on a stool so as to have my hands free if the worst came to the worst.

"Gentlemen," I said, "I am Marcello Accoramboni. Which of you is Prince Orsini?"

"I am," said the man who was standing.

The other, sitting at a table, just looked out of the window as if he weren't involved.

"Then I'd be obliged," said I, "if you'd speak to me with your face uncovered."

"I don't see any reason why I should take off my mask," said the gentleman curtly.

"The reason is, Signore, that I'm not wearing a mask myself."

"Come, come, *carissimo*," said the man at the table, "don't make it a point of honour. Take it off, since he asks you to!"

"It's a strange request! And made in a curious tone!"

"My tone," I said, "was dictated by yours."

"*Carissimo*," said the second gentleman, "take it off. It's I who am asking you this time."

The other obeyed, in a fury, and when the mask was off, his face struck me as a very pretty one were it not for an insufferable air of conceit. But the first thing I noticed was his youth. I'd seen Prince Orsini since he returned from Venice, and the person I was looking at was a good twenty years younger than he.

"Signore," said I, "you have lied to me. You are not Prince Orsini."

"I am Lodovico Orsini, Count of Oppedo," he replied loudly, "and I can't allow the first rascal who comes along to call me a liar."

"Rascal?" said I, half drawing my sword.

"A quarrel here, gentlemen? In this low tavern?" said the other man.

He rose and put a powerful arm round Lodovico's shoulders. It was plain the gesture was an affectionate one, yet at the same time it paralysed my interlocutor. I slipped my blade back in the scabbard and waited. I seemed to remember this Lodovico was Raimondo's brother, and that they were a pair of robber barons, despite their noble birth. Either this Lodovico was incredibly quarrelsome, or he bore me a grudge for depriving his brother of Caterina's favours.

"Come now, *carissimo*," went on the other gentleman, "calm yourself, please! Signor Accoramboni will think we've lured him into an ambush."

And taking him by the arm he sat him down at the table by the window, where he crouched forward with his hands clutching the edge, darting murderous looks at me that I pretended not to see.

Then the second gentleman faced me, took off his mask, and said: "I am Prince Orsini."

This time it really was he. Anyone who has ever seen him, even once, can never forget him. It's not that the Prince is especially tall. He's scarcely an inch taller than I am, but very powerfully built, broad-shouldered and barrel-chested, and his legs, in their close-fitting hose, are very muscular. His face is handsome, with strong regular features, a voluptuous mouth, large bright eyes and short curls of reddish gold, such as you see on Roman medals. His expression, while reflecting pride and authority, is also sensitive and courteous.

I was won over by his appearance, or rather I would have been if his subterfuge with Lodovico hadn't still irked me. Had he been trying to test me, to see if I was adaptable and obedient enough to do his will? If so, my reaction must certainly have undeceived him.

It didn't look like that, however. He gazed at me in silence, and the more his eyes scrutinised my face the more reasons they seemed to find to like me. But of course I soon realised that it wasn't my person that attracted him, but my resemblance to Vittoria.

"Signor Accoramboni," said the Prince with studied courtesy," I must beg you to forgive me for asking you to come here. But if it's agreeable to you I have a proposition to make."

94

"My lord," I answered, bowing, "I shall listen with the greatest interest and respect to any honest propositions your Highness chooses to make."

He must have marvellous self-control, for he scarcely raised an eyebrow at the word "honest". And yet hadn't I made it plain that if his proposals were not so he couldn't count on me to co-operate?

"I'm told, Signor Accoramboni," he went on, "that you can read and write, and that you were taught Latin."

"As far as Latin is concerned, my lord, I forgot it faster than I learned it. But it's true I can read and write, though I'm no scholar."

"I wasn't looking for a scholar," said the Prince with a smile. "I used to have one as my secretary, but the wretch has left me to become a priest. Would you like to take his place?"

It took me a full second to answer, so taken aback was I by the suggestion, coming from so lofty a personage and made so graciously.

"It would indeed be a great honour, my lord," I said with a bow. "But there are difficulties."

"What difficulties?" said the Prince, a flash of impatience in his eyes.

"It seems to me that as your Highness's secretary I would rank before all the other people in your household."

"Of course."

"But I've heard that many of them are allies and relations, belonging to the most ancient nobility."

"That is so."

"Well, I don't see these dashing gentlemen accepting someone like me, whose nobility is recent and controversial."

I said this proudly and sardonically, with my hand on my hip. Everybody in Rome knew I'd promoted myself to the aristocracy when I arrived there.

My words produced two quite opposite effects. Lodovico growled like a mastiff on a chain, but the Prince's reaction was friendly. It both tickled him and earned his respect that I should make fun of my sham nobility at the same time as I insisted that his entourage must defer to it. He burst out laughing.

"Signor Accoramboni," he said good-humouredly, "once you're my secretary no one in my house will dare make fun of you."

95

"Not even," said I, looking at Lodovico, "the Count of Oppedo?"

"Not even he," said the Prince.

"The Count of Oppedo," put in Lodovico offensively, "doesn't stab people without warning in a coach. He fights them fairly, in a duel."

"As I would have done, Signor Conte," said I," if Recanati had accepted my challenge."

"Come, *carissimo*," said the Prince, "you know that's how it happened. And Signor Accoramboni had very good reasons: Recanati had gravely insulted a member of his family in public."

"A member of his family"! How the Prince had enjoyed saying that! Yet at the same time the words disturbed him, and the image of Vittoria was superimposed upon mine. The emotion was too much for him: he clasped his hands behind his back and started to pace the little room, his eyes downcast.

"Well," he said at last, stopping in front of me, "is that the only difficulty, Signor Accoramboni?"

"I can't foretell the future," I answered, "but for the moment I see no other."

"So you accept?"

"With deference and gratitude," I said, bowing.

Lodovico growled again, not because of my words, which were irreproachable, but because of the irony with which they were uttered. As for the Prince, he raised one eyebrow and gave me a quick inquiring glance – but I had foreseen it. My eyes were already lowered and my bearing meeker than a girl's.

"As to the emoluments . . ." began the Prince.

"Please, please, my lord!" I cried, looking up, "let us not speak of them! I have made up my mind to accept no reward. The honour of serving Your Highness is enough for me."

Lodovico fumed again, and the Prince himself looked slightly ill at ease. If he didn't pay me my dependence on him would be purely nominal. But he was too shrewd to press the point.

"Signor Accoramboni doesn't need the Orsinis' money," hissed Lodovico. "He has other resources."

"Yes indeed," said I calmly. "I'm the lover of a rich widow. And I pray the Lord every day that I may retain her favours. I shouldn't like to have to turn brigand and rob defenceless travellers in the mountains."

At that the Prince laughed openly. Lodovico, white as a sheet, opened his mouth to reply, but his kinsman silenced him with a wave of the hand.

"Signor Accoramboni," he said, "I shall expect you at Montegiordano at ten o'clock on Monday. And please forgive me for asking you to meet me in this hovel. I wouldn't, in your own interests, have wanted you to be seen entering my house if you were going to reject my proposal. Now, of course, things are different."

He said all this with the utmost courtesy. I took up my hat from where I'd left it on the stool, and made the Prince a deep bow. I made another one – curt, stiff and meagre – to Lodovico, who replied with a nod.

Then I went down the rickety wooden stairs, not touching the banisters, which were black with dirt from countless hands.

I've advanced a pawn on the chessboard, but I don't know where the move will lead me in the end. I've made three enemies: Raimondo Orsini, Lodovico Orsini, and, as soon as it's known that I'm working for the Prince, Cardinal Montalto. As for the one friend I've acquired, he obviously means to use me as a tool.

We'll see about that. I like the Prince well enough, but I know he was a mercenary in the service of Venice: he's half pirate and half condottiere. In a state as weak as this one, with a Pope as spineless as the present incumbent, he must think he can do as he pleases. He'll be disappointed.

Aziza the Wasp

Ever since March 19th my master hasn't eaten or slept or gone out. He spends hours lying on a divan, dreaming, or wandering aimlessly round the palace. He hardly even goes riding. The wound in his thigh is playing up again too, and his limp has become more pronounced. He still requires my caresses, but as soon as they're over he lapses into melancholy, which is very unlike him.

Naturally I was rather jealous at first, but I managed to stifle it. I know exactly what my place is in my master's heart, in his house and in his country. My place in his heart is quite important, though there's no chance of its ever coming first. My place in his house is small. My place in his country is non-existent: who'd take any notice of a little Moorish slave bought for five hundred ducats on board a Venetian galley?

After March 19th I did my best to use the feminine art of patience with Paolo. As soon as I realised he wanted to be alone I left him, making sure that even my departure was unobtrusive. When we were together and he wanted to be silent, I didn't utter a word. When he tried, unfairly, to pick a quarrel with me – with me, Aziza the Wasp – I let my tongue lie at rest in my mouth. And when he started lauding the beauty of his beloved, he could read nothing but sympathy in the big black eyes looking into his.

And so I succeeded – not always easily – in remaining his confidante and the skinny little cat on whose head he puts his great hands when he wants me to be his.

On the evening of the day he engaged Marcello Accoramboni as his secretary – he related the interview to me in detail – I listened in amazement to the torrent of words issuing at last from his lips. He was nearly within reach of the goal, he said! He was exultant!

I could scarcely believe my ears, hearing this great captain talk such childish nonsense.

"But Paolo," I said, when after a while his eloquence flagged, "if what you say is true you haven't really won Marcello over to your cause. He's distanced himself from the gentlemen of your family: from Raimondo, from Lodovico, and even from yourself. He's insisted on having his own sham nobility recognised, just to show what a low opinion he has of yours. And by loftily refusing any salary he's emphasised how little importance he attaches to your wealth. You are in his debt, not he in yours. And you can't rely on him to help you abduct Vittoria and become her lover. Is it likely a man who stabbed Recanati to death for saying a word out of turn about his twin sister is going to help you turn her into an adulteress?"

My master's blue eyes turned greyer than the blade of his sword. He was beside himself.

"Go away, you Moorish devil!" he cried. "Go away and never let me see you again! Or else I'll tell my majordomo to sell you!"

I was very sorry he was angry but not at all intimidated by his threats. My patience, my submissiveness and my love have tied so strong a bond between us he'd find it very hard to break it. Besides, he is a just man.

And he proved it two days later.

He sent Folletto to fetch me and as usual, after showing me into the Prince's bedroom, the youth curled up in a corner and prepared, all eyes and ears, to follow our frolics. This custom dated from the days on the Venetian galley when I couldn't speak Italian and my master might need Folletto at any moment to translate what he said to me. But although my Italian was perfect now, the same arrangement had continued at Montegiordano. The Prince didn't really notice, as Folletto stayed as quiet as a mouse. But his presence did trouble me, for he'd told me he derived a kind of bitter pleasure from imagining himself in my place, giving and receiving the caresses that made me moan.

He must have been disappointed that day, though. All we did was talk.

"Aziza, my wasp," my master said, looking at me with his bright affectionate eyes, "there's really quite a large brain in that little head of yours. You were perfectly right about Marcello. Yesterday evening I wrote a long letter to Vittoria, and finding myself alone for a moment with her brother I asked him to give it to her. He turned pale, threw the letter down on the table, and said through clenched teeth: 'My lord, you insult me! Do you think I'm the sort of man to suborn my own sister?' And he drew his sword, his eyes blazing."

"Drew his sword on you! In your own house? What did you do?"

"I drew my sword too."

"Oh, master, you shouldn't have condescended! You, a prince! And he isn't even a nobleman!"

"Yes," said Paolo, "but he looked so handsome, and so like Vittoria! As I expected, the duel only lasted a minute. I just pricked him in the arm, and then called my barber to dress the wound. I was astounded that he'd had the audacity to face up to me. When the barber had gone I picked the letter up off the table and held it out to him.

"'My intentions towards Vittoria are honourable,' I said. 'But first I must find out how she feels.'

"Marcello was pale – he'd lost more blood than I'd intended – but his black eyes were as fierce as ever. He looked at me for some time, then said: 'If your intentions really are honourable I'll do my best to further them, provided Vittoria returns your feelings.' Then he took the letter and left."

When Paolo paused I stayed silent so long he grew impatient.

"Well, what do you think, my wasp?"

"I think you've promised to make Vittoria a duchess and that she's already married."

"I know that. What else?"

"I think Francesco Peretti is the son of an influential cardinal and a protégé of the present Pope. Lastly, I think that if your plan is what I believe it is, you're setting out on a highly dangerous course."

"I know that too," he said curtly. And, naked as he was, he got up from his couch and started pacing up and down like a caged tiger.

Caterina Acquaviva

After March 19th came a fortnight when for various reasons I was very unhappy. First, Vittoria didn't confide in me as she had done before. This worried me all the more because I was afraid she might have found out I was sending reports about her to the Cardinal through Father Racasi. But as after March 19th my reports didn't have anything in them, I gradually stopped fretting. As for her thoughts, no doubt they weren't the kind you tell anyone about, not even another woman, not even a confessor. *I* didn't tell Father Racasi everything! Far from it.

Another thing was the sacking of the old door-keeper at the Rusticucci palace. He was very fond of wine and women, and a girl could easily get round him by allowing him a few minor liberties — pinches and so on. But he was replaced by a grim wretch who stuck to the letter of his instructions and wouldn't let anyone in or out, man or woman, except Marcello and *il mancino*.

I was particularly upset because I couldn't get out to visit my two sweethearts, Raimondo Orsini and Silla Savelli, who'd clubbed together to rent a room nearby to meet me in — either turn and turn about or, as I preferred, both together. I'm ashamed to admit that — I'm afraid it might make people think badly of me. But how can I change my own nature? When I tell Father Racasi it's not my fault I'm made like that, he says it *is* a fault *in* me, and I must pray to God to correct me. So I pray and pray, but after a while instead of thinking about what my lips are saying I'm thinking about Raimondo and Silla.

But after March 19th, like everyone else here I lived in complete seclusion, and as far as I was concerned in such painful chastity I wondered whether in the long run I wasn't going to dry up like Giulietta and lose all my curves.

Two long weeks went by in that sad situation, and then one evening *il mancino* smuggled me a letter from Raimondo suggesting he should come and see me in the Rusticucci palace itself. He asked me to draw a map to show him how to reach me. At first I really didn't know what to answer. I thought the whole thing was very risky. Still, I longed for Raimondo's embraces so much I couldn't sleep, and I was just about to do as he said when Marcello found me listening at Vittoria's door, gave me a couple of boxes on the ear that would have felled an ox, and then made love to me. I'd been dreaming of him ever since I entered Signora Vittoria's service, so a few seconds in his arms left me in transports of happiness. I was walking on air! I had wings!

I told him all about my reports to the Cardinal and showed him Raimondo's letter.

"My dear Caterina, you're as stupid as the moon★," said Marcello. "It's more than time I took you in hand. Did you really think Raimondo wanted a map of the palace to come and see you?"

He laughed. "With your permission I'll answer that letter, through your brother."

I agreed to everything. Marcello had only to look at me for my whole being to say yes.

I don't know what answer it was he gave Raimondo, but it can't have been very agreeable, for two days later my brother brought me a furious note:

"Caterina,
You must be the vilest trollop who ever crawled on the face of the earth to have dropped two well-born gentlemen like Silla and me for the arrogant scoundrel who dictated that reply to you. But just you wait! My dagger will make him answer for his insults with his

★ See p. 106.

heart's blood. As for you – if, when you're finally let out, I ever meet you in the street, be sure I'll make lace of your innards. So you'll be punished, you whore, where you've sinned the most.

Raimondo"

This missive filled me with fear and trembling, and as soon as I could slip into Marcello's room I showed it to him, even before I undressed. He shook his head gravely.

"Caterina," he said, "did you ever take money or presents from those two?"

"Never!"

"Then they've no right to call you a whore. But the description fits them perfectly, for they live off Prince Orsini. It fits me too – I live on the generosity of Margherita Sorghini. So there are three male whores on the one hand, and on the other a respectable girl who works for her living and who, far from selling her pretty little behind, gives it away just for pleasure."

I tilted my head to one side. "Signor Marcello," I said. "Do you really think my behind is pretty?"

"It's perfect," said Marcello seriously. "I'm sure there's not its equal in the whole of Rome. Now listen to me, Caterina, and don't worry. My heart's blood is in no danger from their daggers. How could they dare kill their powerful cousin's secretary? And as for your nice little innards, sticking a stiletto where they're no longer allowed to stick something else is just an angry dream of theirs. If they really meant to do it they wouldn't have signed their name to the threat."

Marcello went on to say he thought Silla must really have written the note, as Raimondo can't read or write. But now my fears were set at rest I'd had enough talking, and started to undress. I may be a bit foolish, especially in the eyes of such an educated man as Signor Marcello, but there's one thing everyone must admit I'm good at: I always know exactly what I want.

Three days later, as I was brushing Signora Vittoria's golden hair while she sat at her mirror, Marcello came stealthily into the room, his doublet thrown over his shoulders. When he made to stop it from falling, you could see there was a bloodstained bandage on his left arm. Vittoria caught sight of it in the glass and gave a little cry, thus enabling me to conceal mine.

"It's nothing," said Marcello. "A slight accident. I was fencing with the Prince."

"Leave us, Caterina," said Vittoria.

"No no," Marcello cried. "Let her stay. I trust her completely now. She deserves it."

And he exchanged a look with me in the mirror. A flood of warmth swept right through me. Our Lady knows I've always been full of reverence and gratitude for the Signora. But what were my feelings for her now that her brother had made me his own!

I was standing behind Vittoria doing her hair and trying not to step on it. It hung straight down behind the stool she sat on and spread out on the carpet in a kind of long train that I'd carefully arranged in a coil. Behind me stood Marcello in his shirtsleeves with his doublet over his shoulders, so near me my back went hot and cold, traversed by little shivers.

In the glass I could see him feeling for something in a pocket in the armhole of his doublet. He brought out a sealed letter and put it down beside a jewel box that was standing on the dressing-table. Before he came in, the Signora had been taking out her rings one by one and cleaning them with a little sponge.

"What's this?" asked Vittoria, tonelessly.

"A letter that a great nobleman who's in love with you humbly begs you to read," said Marcello.

Vittoria turned pale and dropped the ring she had been polishing. It was a big uncut diamond set in gold, its upper half covered by a V picked out in smaller stones. Although it was quite a handsome ring I'd noticed she never wore it. According to Giulietta that was because it was a present from Signora Tarquinia. If you ask me, it was because Signora Tarquinia had given it to her just before her father died.

The ring with her initial on it rolled round twice before coming to rest an inch away from the saucer holding the sponge. Vittoria's hands gripped the edge of the dressing-table so hard I saw her fingers go white. Marcello stood behind me, motionless and silent. I could see his face in the mirror, and beneath his mine (he's a head taller than I am), and beneath mine again Vittoria's, because she was sitting down. When

Marcello put the letter down in front of her I'd stopped brushing her hair, but a couple of seconds later I went on so as not to appear curious as to whether or not she was going to read it. But I was brushing more slowly now, and making as little sound as possible, listening to her breath coming in the faintest of gasps. She was looking down at the letter like a bird at a snake, but although her face was ashen it betrayed nothing. And when I listened more carefully her breathing too seemed normal. The only real sign of emotion was the way her hands were clutching the dressing-table.

I stole a glance as Marcello's reflection. How handsome he was! Even then I couldn't help noticing and being affected by it. His eyes were riveted on Vittoria and he too seemed impassive. But I knew him, and I could tell he was as anxious as his sister by the little unconscious twitch that showed on his lower lip whenever he was nervous.

At the time it seemed to take Vittoria an age to make up her mind, but when I looked back at it later, I realised it couldn't have been more than a few seconds.

I'll tell you frankly how I felt when the Signora finally came to a decision and seized the letter, broke the seal with trembling fingers, then read the contents not once but twice. I felt hurt and disappointed. I know I'm an incorrigible manhunter myself, and need the fingers of both hands to count all my past lovers. But I haven't been married at the altar, so at least I'm not an adulteress. And if you ask me, as the Signora knew what she was going to read, she was already being unfaithful to Signor Peretti.

While she was reading, Vittoria tossed her head impatiently; I realised that my brushing was irking her and stopped with the brush in mid-air, holding my breath. I glanced again at Marcello in the mirror, but he'd moved away as if he'd lost interest in what was happening, and as only the dressing-table was lit I couldn't see him properly in the shadows. Looking back at Vittoria again I could tell how hard she was trying to remain expressionless. But although her features didn't move, she couldn't keep her face from flushing.

As soon as she'd read the letter the second time she put it to the flame of one of the candles and set it alight. Then, taking the sponge out of the saucer with her other hand, she set the letter down in its place and watched it burn. In the glass I saw Marcello came back again, but instead of standing behind me he went and perched on the edge of the dressing-table on Vittoria's right.

"And what answer am I to give," he asked with an attempt at lightness, "to the nobleman who's written to you?"

"There is no answer," said Vittoria haughtily.

At that it seemed to me the Signora was trying to have it both ways. She'd allowed herself the pleasure of reading a love letter from the man she loved, and now she was allowing herself the pleasure of acting the virtuous wife. I must say I'm not so complicated as that: when I've decided to be naughty I just go ahead. I don't try to have one foot in the camp of sin and the other in that of virtue.

Marcello gave a mocking little laugh. "Well then, Vittoria," he said, "I wish you goodnight and pleasant dreams."

As he spoke he bent over without touching or kissing her, and leaned his right hand on the dressing-table so that it was between the sponge and the ring decorated with a V. When he straightened up again the ring had gone. It was so skilfully done I could scarcely believe my eyes.

Before he left the room he brushed against my hand, which meant he wanted to see me in his room when I came off duty. I shuddered from head to foot, and felt a quiet rush of pleasure go up my legs and down my back again. That may sound silly, but it's just what I felt.

However, I didn't lose my head. So that Vittoria shouldn't suspect me, I said: "Signora, Signor Marcello has taken your ring with the V on it."

"Yes," she answered absently, "I know – I saw him. Let him keep it! It's a habit of his. When he was little he used to steal my dolls."

Then she added: "Leave me, Caterina. I need to get some sleep."

I curtseyed and went out. She didn't need to sleep at all! What she needed was to be alone with her thoughts. She might be a great lady, but I was better off than she was. My lover was only a few yards away from me. And, thank God, he wasn't a dream.

But there was one thing that bothered me, and I decided to clear it up as soon as I set foot in Marcello's room. "Signor Marcello," I said, "what am I supposed to tell Father Racasi about all this?"

"Say I brought Vittoria a letter and she burned it and said there wasn't any reply."

"So she didn't read it?"

"No."

"I'm sorry, Signor Marcello, but that's what Father Racasi calls a sin of omission."

"Have you told him the name of your new lover?"

"No."

"That's a sin of omission as well. So that makes two."

But why I found it easier to commit two than one I don't know.

Marcello Accoramboni

It took me a couple of hours to disengage myself from my little octopus's tentacles. But I like Caterina even though she *is* an octopus. She brings to the act a proletarian gaiety that Margherita lacks. And it's not true she's "as stupid as the moon".★ It's our Italian expression that's stupid. The moon is supposed to be foolish because it has such an innocent round face when it's full. But foolish it isn't, judging by the number of amorous exchanges it encourages, or even causes, in the summer by its very presence.

As a matter of fact, Caterina is quite shrewd. But — how shall I put it? — her shrewdness is limited. As *il mancino* has rightly observed, she can't see any further than the end of her nipples. In her period of painful chastity she so longed for Raimondo's embraces that it didn't occur to her for a moment the map he asked her for might be used to abduct Vittoria.

That evening after she left me, my thoughts took a more serious turn. I hadn't blown out the candle and I lay on my bed twisting the ring I'd stolen from Vittoria round and round on my little finger. "Stolen" is perhaps too strong a word. I was sure she never wore it. She disliked it: not, as Giulietta said, because it was a present from her mother, but simply because it bore witness to Tarquinia's natural bad taste and was indescribably ugly. But it lent itself to my purposes because of the V in diamonds.

I wasn't thinking in order to make up my mind. That was already done. I was just trying to understand why I'd come to that decision. What a task! I've noticed before that in a situation where you're

★ Cf. p. 101.

emotionally involved with other people, three things are each more difficult than the last: to know what you think, to know what you feel, and to know what you want. In this case the subject of my wonderings was not myself, but Vittoria. My other self.

Because our natures were so alike I'd always been able to tell, from certain signs, what was going on in Vittoria's heart. But on March 19th she severed the link between us, and I could only find out what was troubling her through Caterina, that insignificant but crucial witness. From then on I had to rely on observation instead of intuition. For it was now very important to me to know what Vittoria felt and what she wanted, even if she was doing her best to blind herself to it.

From that point of view what had just taken place in her room was extremely revealing. When I put the "letter from a great nobleman who was in love with her" down in front of her — an act highly offensive in itself, especially in a brother — what she ought to have done, without the slightest hesitation and without even touching the thing, was tell me contemptuously to take the infamous object back whence it came. But she did nothing of the sort. She did hesitate. But her hesitation was merely a pause to manipulate her conscience. From that moment on, the outcome was not in doubt.

She opened the letter. Neither curiosity nor the pleasure of being flattered played any part in her decision to do so. Vittoria, who in any case was adored by everybody, was quite above such petty vanities. She opened the letter because she loved the Prince, because she wanted to be his, and because she couldn't resist his appeal. From the moment she broke the wax seal — and how they trembled doing it, those lovely fingers! — and began to read — in front of two witnesses, what's more — she was already betraying Peretti.

When she'd read it she burned what she'd just been worshipping and said haughtily, "There is no answer!" What a farce! I caught Caterina's eye in the glass, and even she wasn't taken in. Yes, Vittoria, there was an answer to that letter, and a very explicit one: the answer lay in having read it.

But it might be that the answer wouldn't be as plain to the Prince as it was to me. So I decided to give things a shove in the right direction the following day.

Meanwhile I saw that the goal I guessed at would only be reached through plenty of blood and plenty of mud. If only Peretti hadn't been, as ill luck would have it, the son of a cardinal, and if only Prince Orsini had been friends with Gregory XIII, it would have been easy for the Pope to issue a *precetto* irrevocably annulling the marriage between Vittoria and Peretti. How many times has the present Pope made use of this reprehensible procedure for completely non-religious reasons? By this means his unfortunate adversary is "de-married" overnight from his lawful spouse – the couple live henceforward in mortal sin – and is excluded from the communion of the faithful. But here there could be no such solution. Anything that could be done would have to be done in spite of the Pope and of Montalto. In other words, in the face of both the spiritual and the temporal power of Rome.

A terrifying prospect, though for me, as I twisted Vittoria's ring round my finger in the candle-light, there was something exhilarating about it. I felt that with the tiny little prod I meant to give events just to bring Vittoria nearer to her heart's desire, I, the good-for-nothing, the scoundrel, Recanati's murderer and La Sorghini's pimp, was going to make the whole State rock on its foundations.

Next morning I presented myself at Montegiordano at the usual hour. The majordomo showed me straight into the Prince's private apartments, telling me confidentially that his master had gone out very early with a few attendants for a gallop in the Campagna. I realised this was to beguile his impatience. Instead of waiting to hear the news I was expected to bring, he'd arranged for me to do the waiting. I recognised this as one of the little political wiles by which the great ones of this world try to make you think they're as great as they're supposed to be. I went over to a sunlit window overlooking the huge courtyard, the chaotic encampment of all the people – outlaws, exiles, fugitives from papal prisons and bandits sought for by the Corte – to whom Orsini gave asylum, board and lodging so as to build up his power against the Pope.

Then suddenly the main gate opened and the Prince, at the head of his suite, galloped without slackening his pace straight through the archway and across the whole length of the courtyard. There was a terrific scramble, with the crowd first falling away on either side and then surging forward again to hail him like a returning monarch. He dismounted at the foot of the tower from which I was looking down, and I heard him limping heavily but powerfully up the stone stairs that led to his apartments.

The door, flung back hastily by a page, flew open before him, and he advanced upon me with the long aggressive stride forced on him by his limp. The swing of his broad shoulders seemed to propel him forward even faster. His Roman head, covered with the red-gold curls that made him look like a living statue, came to rest in the sunlight flooding in through the window. His breath coming in gasps, his blue eyes gazing straight at me, he spoke.

"Well?" he asked.

Without a word I took Vittoria's ring from my doublet pocket and held it out to him. He took it with a look of amazement, turned it round and round, noticed the initial picked out in diamonds. At that he turned so pale I thought he was going to faint, and stood there open-mouthed and speechless, his blue eyes glittering with all the joy welling up inside him. Then, sensing a question he was unable to put into words, I told him, adding only one word to what Vittoria had said: "My lord, there is no other answer."

5

Father Racasi

Every Friday, accompanied by my second curate, I go to the Rusticucci palace to confess Signora Camilla Peretti, Signora Tarquinia Accoramboni, Signora Vittoria Peretti, and the latter's maid, Caterina Acquaviva. My curate confesses the rest of the staff. But ever since Francesco Peretti, probably on the advice of the Cardinal, has kept his household strictly secluded, I also take my first curate with me, so that Francesco and Flaminio can make their confessions to him. As for Marcello, he's never there on Friday, and according to Tarquinia he confesses to a mendicant friar at the widow Sorghini's house.

On Saturday Cardinal Montalto, to whom I owe so much, does me the great honour of hearing my own confession, and I take the opportunity to lay before him the tricky problems I'm sometimes confronted with by the people to whom I act as spiritual adviser. His Eminence always listens very carefully, and I admire the perspicacity and subtlety with which he manages to resolve my difficulties.

The Cardinal has a reputation for austerity and even harshness, but I must say that to me he's always shown the utmost indulgence. Although there is a confessional in the oratory adjoining his study, it would be hard for him even to enter it, on crutches. So he remains sitting in his usual armchair, and I kneel at his feet. But with a consideration for which I'm very grateful, he always tells *il bello muto* to put a cushion under my knees before he leaves us.

The Cardinal is also very lenient towards the sins of which I accuse myself. True, the list has grown much shorter as the powers that led me into temptation have waned. The sin of the flesh is now as far from me in thought as it is in deed. And as for the sin of greed that took its place, that has dwindled together with the efficiency of my stomach. I sometimes think sadly that I'll only attain the saintliness I dreamed of as a child when age and illness have reduced me to a vegetable existence. But where will the merit be then?

"Peccadilloes, Racasi, mere peccadilloes!" the Cardinal said to me impatiently yesterday, shaking his terrible head. "Now let's hear your little problems . . ."

"Oh, Your Eminence!" I said, "I have had one indeed since yesterday! But it isn't a small one. One of my female penitents was sent a love letter by devious means. And she read it."

"She read it!" said the Cardinal, his black eyes looking daggers from beneath his bushy eyebrows.

"It's really more complicated than that. She says she read it. But her maid, whom I confess also, says she didn't."

"It's not complicated at all," said the Cardinal shortly. "She might have read it when the maid wasn't there."

"Yes, but the maid says it all took place in front of her, and that her mistress burned the letter without opening it."

"Then the maid's lying," said the Cardinal, frowning. "Have you told her so, and rubbed her nose in it?"

"Your Eminence," I said, hanging my head, "I could hardly do that without betraying the secret of her mistress's confession."

"True! True!" exclaimed His Eminence angrily.

He mastered his wrath, though, and I went on: "But mistress and maid both say the same about the answer that was given to the messenger. After she'd read the letter, the person it was addressed to burned it in a little saucer and told the messenger haughtily: 'There is no answer.'"

"But she had read it!" cried the Cardinal indignantly. "Did you think to ask if she'd read it twice?"

"Yes, I did, Your Eminence," said I, secretly rather pleased with my own zeal. "And unfortunately yes – she had read it twice."

"God in Heaven!" said the Cardinal. After a moment he went on: "What did she feel as she was reading it? Did you ask her?"

"Yes, Your Eminence. The penitent spoke of being in great confusion."

"Be more precise."

"She said she felt shame and remorse, but at the same time she was disturbed. I might even say tempted."

"Did she say 'tempted'?"

"No, Your Eminence. She didn't actually say the word. But I deduced it from the fact that she was disturbed."

"Don't deduce things!" cried the Cardinal. "Stick to the facts! Did she strike you as truly repentant?"

"Your Eminence," I answered, "you know what women are. Even when they're weeping for their sins they still manage to enjoy them."

"I know, I know!" said the Cardinal. "Spare me the obvious! Tell me the facts!"

"Well," I told him after a moment, "my penitent thinks she repents! She sincerely believes so."

"Sincerely! And what about you, Racasi," he thundered, "are you sincere? Or are you trying to reassure me?"

This question agitated me greatly. I was afraid that in his wrath the Cardinal might name the penitent, of whose identity he was supposed to be ignorant. Fortunately he must have realised what a terrible situation that would put me in, for he pretended to have forgotten what he'd just asked me and went on more quietly: "Anyhow, no one's conscience is ever sincere. Which of us can deny it?"

I was flattered by that "us", appealing to my experience as well as his own. But as I couldn't indulge in vanity right in the middle of my confession I just bowed my head in agreement.

"One last point, Racasi, and I'd like a straightforward answer, please. And now I'm appealing beyond the facts, to your own personal intuition. If the lover gained access to your penitent, could she, in your opinion, resist him?"

I shook my head and answered sadly, with downcast eyes: "I doubt it, Your Eminence."

"Help me up, Racasi," said the Cardinal roughly.

I rose to do so, but as soon as he'd fitted his crutches under his armpits he waved me impatiently out of the way. Then he turned his back on me and went and stood in front of a picture of the Madonna and Child that hung on the wall. He stood looking at it for some time, but, if you ask me, without seeing it. For he shook his head several times, and I heard him mutter brokenly: "Oh, my poor boy! They'll kill him!"

I felt so uncomfortable at having overheard him that I really didn't know what to do with myself. On the other hand, I couldn't leave the room without the Cardinal's leave, not to mention his absolution.

Perhaps he sensed my embarrassment, for he swung round ponderously on his crutches, transfixed me with his terrible black eyes, and ordered: "Keep your lips sealed about all this, and leave me, please."

"But Your Eminence," I stammered, "you haven't given me absolution."

If I didn't look up to the Cardinal with such gratitude and veneration I'd say no penitent was ever granted the remission of his sins faster, more absentmindedly or in more of a mumble than I was then. But His Eminence, for reasons of his own that were no business of mine, was too deeply disturbed for me to hold it against him.

Although I believe, as the Church teaches, that when a priest pronounces absolution he really does speak in God's place, "*in loco Dei*", and must be fully conscious of his extraordinary privilege in doing so, it is only too true that through care, fatigue, anxiety and human frailty in general, Christ's representative may sometimes deliver in a mechanical and routine manner the words that should each be considered and weighed with the utmost gravity. But it is very wrong for a priest to take such things lightly: confession, by allowing him to fathom the hearts and minds of the faithful, gives the Church immense power in the city of men.

I say this in all humility, without of course sitting in judgment on anyone, least of all those whom divine grace has placed far above me both in the State and in the hierarchy.

Lodovico Orsini, Count of Oppedo

That Thursday evening, knowing how Paolo hates unpunctuality, I made a great effort to be at Montegiordano on the stroke of nine.

"Ah, here you are at last!," he cried, embracing me in his usual manner – that is, clutching me in his Herculean arms and half crushing me to death on his vast chest.

"But I'm not late!" said I, disengaging myself.

"True enough!" he exclaimed in surprise, glancing at his watch. "Forgive my impatience, *carissimo*. And please stop casting those murderous looks at Marcello – you know how touchy he is. He even drew his sword on me – on me, Lodovico! – just for a word he took amiss. But enough of that! Marcello is my secretary and my friend. And I want you – do you hear, Lodovico? – I want you and him to be friends too. Give him your hand."

"What?" I cried. "Give my hand to that reptile?"

"Conte," said Marcello, drawing himself up, "you need to revise your zoology. A reptile hasn't got hands. But," he added, putting his hand on the hilt of his sword, "it can bite."

"But it won't!" cried Paolo. "Come now, Lodovico, your hand in his this instant, or I really will be angry with you."

I obeyed, and took Marcello's reluctant hand. It was cold and dry and didn't grip mine. The young buck was certainly bold enough, and held his life cheap.

"Sit down, Lodovico, and listen," Paolo went on. "I've never been so close to open war against the State. Montalto has closed his door to me, for one thing. Yes, Lodovico, he's actually done that! What an insult! Next, he's shut his niece up in the Rusticucci palace, pretending to believe I was planning to abduct her!"

"You probably would have," I said wryly.

"Certainly not!" snapped Paolo. "I've told Marcello and now I tell you: my intentions are honourable."

There were a number of things I could have said on that score, but I preferred to be silent lest I reveal my true feelings. I'd summed up the situation: Vittoria was just an unscrupulous adventuress, and Marcello a pimp. He was a pimp twice over – in living off La Sorghini, and in prostituting his own sister to crazy Paolo in the hope of plucking a duchess's coronet for her out of the mud. As for Paolo, he'd fallen right into the hands of those sinister twins – mere nobodies from a majolica factory in Gubbio! And he, a Prince Orsini, was cherishing the senseless dream of taking that harlot to him for a second duchess, forgetting that if he did so his son Virginio – an Orsini through his father and a Medici through his mother! – might find his heritage challenged by a creature born on the dunghill of the common people . . .

"Are you listening, Lodovico?" asked Paolo impatiently. "Or do I have to say the same thing a thousand times? Montalto, not content with sequestering his niece, is taking her under escort tomorrow morning at dawn to Santa Maria, and she and her family are going to be shut up in a palace there. And — listen to this, Lodovico — most of the escort is going to be made up of papal troops! The Pope himself is trying to thwart me. It's an insult — a deliberate insult to me, an Orsini! But he's mistaken if he thinks I'm going to take it lying down!"

"What do you mean to do?"

"Attack the escort."

"That's what he hopes you'll do," said I coolly. "Do you intend to attack them on the way, or at Santa Maria itself?"

"I don't know yet."

"Well, let me tell you, Paolo — neither is feasible. I know the area like the back of my hand. I went hunting there a couple of years ago."

"That's just why I sent for you," said Paolo, smiling.

"The palace there is really a fortress," I went on. "It's built on a cliff overlooking the sea, and the sea is very rough on that part of the coast. The palace is surrounded by high walls, and the only way to get to it is along a single road that leads to a huge cleft in the rocks with a drawbridge across it. The country round about is bare and arid, and it all belongs to Montalto."

"I'll attack before they get there, then," said Paolo.

"That would be much worse. The road is narrow, and runs between the sea and a range of rocky hills that are uninhabited and have no paths or tracks over them."

"Perfect!" said Paolo. "No line of retreat for the escort on either side when we attack them."

"And none for you either, Paolo."

"What do you mean?" said Paolo with a start. "Do you mean I might get beaten? But I've got enough men at Montegiordano to attack the escort five to one."

"That's not the point. You couldn't deploy them. Remember the terrain: a narrow road between inaccessible hills and the sea. And you're quite likely to be attacked yourself from the rear."

"By whom?"

"The papal army. You don't think you and a large body of men are going to set out from Montegiordano at dawn tomorrow without the Pope being informed immediately? And he'll send some of his troops after you to take you from the rear, while the rest stay in Rome and seize your palace. And mine too while they're at it."

There was a lengthy silence. Paolo strode back and forth, stooping forward with his head on one side. I knew my arguments had convinced him. So I said no more, and just let them sink in. That whore had driven him mad, but not to the point of engaging in open war with the Pope under adverse conditions and with his army dispersed. He still had a streak of reason left.

Suddenly he let out a kind of roar. "The sea, Lodovico! I'm a sailor — why didn't I think of it before?"

"The sea?" said I. "But that's a wild coast, unprotected from the open sea, without any creeks or inlets. How could an army land there?"

"An army couldn't — no. But a boat could, launched from one of my galleys out at sea."

"But the sea will be watched!"

"By day, but not at night."

"At night? With all the reefs there are along that coast? And even if the boat escapes them it'll be smashed against the cliffs."

"No, no!" cried Paolo. "There's no coast so inaccessible you can't find a place somewhere to haul a boat up out of the water."

"Suppose that's true! How do you think you'd persuade the Signora to escape with you by the same route?"

"I shan't even try! Do you think I'd let her expose herself to such dangers? But at least I'll see her! And at least," he added softly, as if to himself, "I'll be able to make sure she returns my feelings."

I was dumbfounded. I'd been sure that, to be so taken with that creature, his dealings with her must have gone much further than the first encounter at Montalto's house, which Raimondo had heard about from Caterina. So things were much worse than I'd thought. He really did love her. The devil was in the woman — she'd bewitched him!

"My lord," said Marcello suddenly. "My place too is in that boat. I claim the honour of going with you."

"Oh Marcello!" said Paolo, putting his arms round his shoulders and drawing him close, "you're a brave lad – I knew it!"

I turned my head away and pretended to be looking out into the courtyard, so shocked was I by Paolo's familiarity with the wretch. *Affè de Dio*! He was treating him like a brother-in-law already! The world had turned upside-down! And all because a scrap of skirt and a wisp of hair had struck this great prince's fancy! A man who'd already had more women than an August night has stars! What had this female got that the others lacked? She was beautiful? A cow is beautiful, but I wouldn't let even my squire marry her.

I gradually recovered my composure, and, turning to Paolo, even managed to smile.

"Well, *carissimo*, I can see you're not to be put off this crazy venture. May heaven protect you! I'll pray you don't get drowned! What an end that would be for a famous admiral!"

He laughed and embraced me, and I came away. I was smiling, but there was rage in my heart. I ran down the stairs with my fist pounding the banister and my teeth set. Oh Paolo, I thought, you don't deserve to live! You dishonour the Orsinis!

I couldn't get over his extraordinary frivolity. He'd summoned me just because he knew I was familiar with the country around Santa Maria. Apparently it hadn't occurred to him that I might be shocked by his plans concerning that loose woman. Worse still, before I dissuaded him he was quite ready to engage in open war against the Pope, though that could only end in his ruin and mine as well, and of course that of my brother. How could anyone excuse, or even comprehend, such criminal blindness?

That night I had a dream. I can't call it a nightmare, because when I woke up and thought about it I felt happy and peaceful and relieved of my fears. In my dream Paolo and the Peretti twins were at Santa Maria, being pursued by the papal army. It was night-time, and they were on a little boat trying to reach Paolo's galley out at sea. But the boat struck a reef and started to fill with water. Marcello went under first. Vittoria's voluminous skirt held her up for a while, but she too gradually sank. Only Paolo survived, but a wave swept him on to a sharp rock, which cut off his penis. As for me, I was on board the galley when he was pulled out of the water. The ship's surgeon dressed his wound, and when he'd finished and I glanced at him inquiringly he said quietly, "He's only fainted. He'll live, but he's no longer a man." I looked at Raimondo, standing beside me, and said coldly, "Thank God." When I woke up I went over the dream in my mind, then after a while got up and wrote it down. I thought it might be prophetic, and I wanted to make a sort of appointment with the future.

Giulietta Accoramboni

I now know the reason for our strict seclusion in the Rusticucci palace. And for the unbearable tension that resulted from it, for Vittoria's silence, and for the sudden departure to Santa Maria. But what pains me is that instead of finding out about it from Vittoria herself, who seems to have forgotten all the deep and time-honoured bonds between us, I owe my enlightenment to Francesco Peretti. On the Cardinal's orders he left his mother and mother-in-law behind in Rome (where no doubt the one will finally peck the other to death) and came to Santa Maria, since when, as Vittoria now refuses to speak to him, he's so isolated and desperate that he's forced to use me as a confidante.

So I know the story of the letter that was received, read and burned – a story that only takes on its full ominousness when you know the sort of man Prince Orsini is, his power in the State, his reckless love of women, and his rash and rebellious character.

Francesco was reluctant to tell me everything. The Cardinal had made him promise never to reveal to his wife that he knew about the letter – no doubt because His Eminence didn't want to give away the sources of his information, which came from Father Racasi, or Caterina Acquaviva, or perhaps both. Be that as it may, when Francesco told me about the famous letter he asked me to keep my lips sealed on the subject.

He made this request at the top of a little watch-tower we'd been exploring on the cliff. We looked down on a tiny creek far below where the waves broke on the reefs, producing masses of fleecy white foam. According to the majordomo at Santa Maria it was in the privacy of this creek that the bishop who owned the place before Montalto used to bathe. And sure enough if I leaned out I could see, despite the spray, the steps that had been hewn in the cliff for him to climb down to the little beach.

The watch-tower itself must have been built in the days when this part of the coast, inhospitable though it is, used to fear the incursions of the Barbary pirates. This explanation was reinforced by the little stone sentry-box that stood in a corner of the platform where we were standing, whipped by a strong and chilly breeze although it was already May.

"My poor Francesco" – I spoke into his ear, for we were nearly deafened by the whistling of the wind and the crash of the waves – "I don't mind promising to keep it secret. It doesn't make any difference to me. But it was wrong of you to make the Cardinal the same promise yourself. And it would be even more wrong of you to keep your word."

"Come out of the wind," he said, taking me by the hand. "I can scarcely hear you."

And he led me into the little sentry-box, where three small look-out holes had been glassed in and we were comparatively sheltered. I say comparatively because there was no door, and gusts swept inside now and then.

I repeated what I'd said before, and Francesco listened, looking both anxious and puzzled. I felt very sorry for him, for as I've said, Vittoria hadn't been speaking to him since we'd been shut up in the Rusticucci palace.

"But why?" he asked. "Why shouldn't I have promised the Cardinal not to mention the letter?"

"Because when you speak to Vittoria you won't be able to mention the wrongs she's done you, either."

He looked at me. Kindness and sincerity and practically all the other virtues were written all over that honest face. All that was missing was strength.

"*Has* she done me any wrong?" he asked doubtfully.

I was amazed to see that not only was he still faithful to a wife no longer truly faithful to him, but he also wanted to think of her as being pure as undriven snow.

"Come now, *carissimo*," I said, taking him firmly by the arm, "it was you yourself who told me: she received a love letter sent by devious means, and knowing full well who'd written it and why, she opened it."

"But she burned it!" he cried, with so innocent a surge of hope it gave my heart a wrench.

"The fact of having burned it," I said, "doesn't alter the fact of having read it. And having enjoyed reading it, presumably, since she read it twice."

"But she confessed!" said he.

"To her priest! Not to you!"

"She wouldn't have wanted to hurt me," he said, averting his eyes.

I looked at him. I was tired of seeing him cling to his illusions. It ended up annoying me, and I said, more roughly than I intended: "And I suppose it's because she doesn't want to hurt you that since March 19th she's closed her door to you?"

He flinched as if I'd struck him, blinked, disengaged his arm, and turned away, obviously ashamed to let me see his suffering. I for my part was reproaching myself for having been so brutal. But I soon deflected these reproofs on to Vittoria. How could she, usually so magnanimous, be so cruel to him? But even as I formulated them I knew my criticisms didn't ring true. I'd just been harsh to Francesco myself. It was awful to be so harsh to a man who was so kind. But he wasn't merely kind – he was soft, and it was the softness in his character which called forth that kind of response in a wife. And after all, how could you blame a wife for not being sensitive to her husband's feelings when she was married to him against her will and didn't love him?

At length Francesco turned back towards me, went and leaned against the curved wall of the tower, and said flatly: "Why do you say I was wrong to promise not to say anything to Vittoria about the letter? Wouldn't it be indelicate of me to show I know something she's chosen to conceal from me?"

For a moment I was speechless. Poor Francesco! Such scruples! And how little he knew about women! Delicacy is a virtue they value highly in a man but which they seldom practise themselves, especially when driven by passion or self-interest! And they only prize it in a man as a guarantee that he'll always treat them well, even when they no longer deserve it.

"Francesco," I said at last, "if you keep your promise and say nothing

120

about the letter you'll greatly weaken your position when the time comes for you to face up to Vittoria."

"Face up to her!" he exclaimed, wide-eyed. "The expressions you use, Giulietta! But I've never sought any quarrel with Vittoria!"

"But she'll seek one with you, and it'll be a quarrel on the grand scale, you may be sure. That's all the reward you'll get for your silence."

And I was right. It happened in my presence the following day in Vittoria's bedroom, which we were both trying to make more habitable. Francesco knocked, entered and said good-day. Then, turning to Vittoria, he asked her with unusual clumsiness if she was comfortable in her new home.

"Comfortable, sir?" she replied scornfully, fixing him with glittering eyes. "I am very *un*comfortable! Horribly uncomfortable! The walls are damp. The ceilings are mouldy. The windows don't shut properly. They had to be forced open, and the wood has swollen so much since that they won't shut again. I ask for a fire and I'm told there isn't any wood left – it will have to be sent for, and that will take time! And to crown all," she added, her voice rising, "to crown all, sir, one of my trunks was lost on the journey and I haven't anything left to wear. But what does that matter? Why should I dress myself up, and for whom? I don't see anyone. First you cloistered me in my palace in Rome, and as if that wasn't enough, you now imprison me in a wilderness."

I looked at her. She was superb in her vehemence, superb in her aroused beauty. But unfortunately she was also superb in the sense in which the word had been applied to her mother Tarquinia in Gubbio – in the sense of "arrogant".

"Madam," said Francesco in a strangled voice, "I think you know who advised that those measures be taken, and why?"

I thought the "why" would stop Vittoria or at least give her pause, but no. Her anger leaped neatly over it and attacked the "who" instead.

"Who, sir?" she cried. "Who? Who else but the Cardinal interferes in our marriage and usurps, with your consent, the rights of a husband? It's true you're not much of a husband yourself, and even less of a father."

She'd been shutting her door to him for a month and a half, and here she was reproaching him for not being adequate as a husband! The cruelty, the unfairness and – why shouldn't I say it, despite my affection for her? – the meanness of this attack paralysed Francesco and left him completely at a loss. He turned pale and almost turned on his heel and walked away. If he summoned up the courage to stay it was not so much to defend himself, still less to counter-attack, as to vindicate his uncle.

"Madam," he said shakily, "you know the Cardinal loves you like his own daughter, and you must realise that if he advised the measures you complain of he did so because he thought your honour was in peril."

"My honour, sir!" cried Vittoria. "Since when, and for what reason, has my honour been suspect? And do you think the best way to protect it is to put me in jail and have me guarded by soldiers?"

At one and the same time I admired her and was put out by her insolence. She now had the effrontery to raise the very question she hadn't dared answer before. And in the process of diabolically confusing the issues she was uttering a veiled threat. She was hinting that her present imprisonment was not the best way to preserve her virtue.

I had only to look at Francesco's honest face to know what was going on inside him. He was shrewd enough to see that Vittoria's pose of injured innocence was disingenuous. But far from holding it against her, he was embarrassed for her. He looked away from her and down at the floor. Oh Francesco, I thought angrily, now or never is the time to lose your temper, to voice your bitterness, to humble your wife's arrogance. Now's the time to speak out about the famous letter, which she opened and read and read again; which caused the delicious agitation she admitted to her confessor. And by the same token, why don't you just mention in passing that no one knows which of you is responsible for the fact that your marriage is childless?

But my hope was vain. How could a perfect gentleman like Francesco break his word to the most venerated of uncles? He stood there miserably with downcast eyes, as if he were the guilty party.

"You are silent, sir," said Vittoria. "And I think you are right. As for me, I ask you for the first and last time to stop treating me like a criminal when I am guiltless. I insist that you take me back to Rome tomorrow."

I looked at Francesco. He seemed to be angered at last by her use of the word "guiltless", but over the years she'd gained the upper hand so firmly that he was incapable of voicing his grievances. When he broke his silence he didn't even speak sharply; merely with regret: "Madam, that is not possible."

And with an awkward bow he left. Vittoria had taken the offensive on every point, and although she hadn't had her way about returning to Rome she'd come off with considerable moral advantage. She'd managed to assume the rôle of an innocent young martyr unjustly persecuted by a cruel husband. The alleged persecution came in handy as a retrospective excuse for the liberties she'd taken over her marital duties, and permitted her to stifle any stirrings of remorse she might have had on the subject.

As for her uncle the Cardinal, recently so dear to her, she now saw him as a mere tyrant, punishing her for no reason. It was certainly true that Montalto was very imperious and liked to control other people's lives. As soon as I myself was twenty-five he tried to make me choose between two prisons: marriage or a nunnery. But as far as Vittoria was concerned it was His Eminence's great love for her that had made him fear the worst, and with good reason. And if Vittoria had still had an ounce of good faith she couldn't have believed he'd acted without cause.

But that was women for you, the wretched sex to which I belong – all flesh and passion! A minute's encounter with a handsome warrior, a letter read and burned, and everything is changed. The kind, affectionate, decent Francesco becomes a cruel husband. The Cardinal is a terrible tyrant. And I, her lifelong friend, am cast aside as useless just because she suspects I mightn't be giving her my wholehearted approval.

I looked at her. How beautiful she was in those loose and simple morning gowns of hers, followed everywhere she went by her long hair! I say "followed" because when Francesco had gone she paced up and down the room, and every time she turned, her golden mane moved with her and swirled around her shoulders like a cape. What a magnificent human animal! What harmony in her form, proportions and features! What energy in her movements!

I sat in a corner with my hands clasped in my lap, saying nothing. I had mixed feelings about her. Although in a way I found her beauty oppressive – what woman wouldn't feel inferior to her? – at the same time, like everyone else, I admired her with all my heart. But I was also frightened of this new Vittoria who'd made a clean sweep of all her former affections, and who was so resolute and ruthless in their destruction.

She stopped in front of me, looked me up and down, and said almost aggressively: "Well, you don't say anything! What do you think of all this! Why don't you speak out?"

I looked at her. My turn now, I thought. She'd said nothing to me about the letter. She hadn't been frank with me, and now she wanted me to be frank with her. And the tone in which she demanded it! But she'd forgotten one thing: I wasn't a man. I was moved by her beauty, but not blinded by it. And I'm not a coward. I could use my claws as well as she could. "If I don't say anything, Vittoria," I said mildly, "it's because no one has said anything to me. I don't know what to think."

"But you can see how I'm treated!"

"Yes indeed. You're guarded as if you were in great danger. But what that danger is I don't know."

"It doesn't exist!" she cried.

"That's not what the Cardinal seems to think, nor your husband."

"Has Francesco spoken to you about it?"

"No, he hasn't!" I cried. "He's like you: his lips are sealed on the subject. But . . ."

"But what?"

"But I noticed he jibbed just now when you said you were guiltless."

"But I *am* guiltless!" she cried in a fury.

"You should know," I answered coolly.

"But you know too," she said, her eyes blazing. "You seem to know my thoughts better than I do myself!"

"Oh, Vittoria," I said, "I make no such claim. If I did, and it were true, there'd be no point in this conversation."

She shrugged, put her hands suddenly to her temples, and said in exasperation: "This hair is too heavy! It gives me terrible headaches! I've made up my mind – I'm going to cut it off."

"This is hardly the moment to sacrifice your crowning glory."

"What do you mean?"

"Just what I say. No more, no less."

She threw me a hostile glance and started to pace back and forth again. Then after a while she stopped in front of me and said: "This conversation has tired me. Leave me, please, Giulietta. I want to be alone."

I withdrew, and in the afternoon she sent Caterina to me with a curt note:

124

"Dearest Giulietta,

I should be glad if you would refrain from visiting me in my room while I am at Santa Maria. I should also be obliged if you would keep Francesco company at meals. I don't intend to join you. Affectionately,

Vittoria"

I liked the "dearest Giulietta"! And I took the final "affectionately" for what it was worth. There was a lump in my throat as I read the note in which she so regally announced my fall from favour. But I didn't cry. I'd already guessed what she'd do. And now I'd joined her uncle and her husband on the scrap heap.

Caterina Acquaviva

I could tell by the foul temper she was in on the journey that the Signora was sad and angry at being snatched away from Rome. But she wasn't the only one! I myself was losing Marcello, because it was decided from the start that he should be left behind. Anyway, wasn't he Prince Orsini's secretary and La Sorghini's guest? He wasn't even informed of the date of our departure, at least not by Signor Peretti. It was I who told him the day and the hour and the destination, as soon as the Signora told me. If you ask me, she had an ulterior motive: she knew the terms I was on with Marcello. And if you want to know what I think, I reckon Signor Peretti would have been well advised not to let his wife know in advance where we were going. But the poor Signore's always too good and naïve; he doesn't know the tricks even the best of us women are capable of. It's true men are sometimes very wicked too. Who'd have thought, after I'd been so nice to them, that Raimondo and Silla would ever threaten to "make lace of my innards"?

But for the moment anyway I'm reduced, like the Signora, to dreaming. Except that I'm even worse off than she is, for I doubt if she's ever really known what love is.

My only consolation is the fact that *il mancino* is here too. Peretti brought him along to fence with, for my elder brother, who excels at everything except honesty, is very good with his blade, and the master, who's put on a little weight, is trying to lose it again by exercise.

Here at Santa Maria, though, *il mancino* — even I, his own sister, often call him that — doesn't talk to me much. And when he does it's only in whispered monosyllables, away from everyone else, and usually just to give me orders. And the way he looks at me I don't feel at all like disobeying.

On the morning of May 3rd he came and found me in the woodshed. It's been re-stocked at last, and I go there to fetch supplies for the Signora.

"Caterina, have you noticed the watch-tower on the cliff above the creek?"

"Yes, Domenico."

"I went and had a look at it the day after we got here. It was empty. But I have a feeling they've put a look-out there since then. We must check."

I made a face.

"You know what'll happen if I go up the tower and there's a soldier there."

"Does that frighten you?"

You see what people are like? Just because I like men my own brother hints that I'm a whore! He should talk! He lives off women!

"Yes," said I, "if he stinks of wine and garlic."

"Caterina," he said severely, "your scented gentlemen have gone to your head. You're forgetting your duty towards your elder brother."

"And is it my duty towards my elder brother to get myself laid by just anybody?"

"No need for that. If you take him some wine he might rather have the bottle than you."

"I wouldn't have to go right to the top of the tower. I could easily hear if there was someone overhead."

"No, you must talk to him. I want to know if there's a look-out there at night as well as in the daytime."

"And it's important for you to find out?"

"It's important for the people you love."

126

"Don't you love them too?"

"I'm doing it for the money," he replied, trying to look superior.

"Your whores aren't enough for you, then!" I said sourly.

His eyes flashed. He looked round, went to the door of the woodshed, looked around again, then came back and gave a couple of slaps, one on each cheek, but not very hard. It wasn't that he didn't want to hurt me – he just didn't want to make a noise or leave a mark.

"That'll teach you to respect your brother, you cow!" he said. "I don't eat with a fork, and I can't read, and I don't fornicate with noble ladies. But I am your brother, and don't you forget it."

"I'm sorry, Domenico," I said, blushing with shame. Not because I'd been slapped but because I'd been rude to one of my elders and betters.

His glance softened at once. "So you'll do as I say?"

"Yes."

"Right, you're a good girl, Caterina. But you must watch your tongue. It works faster than your brain." And he put both his arms round my shoulders and drew me close to him. He's not more than an inch or two taller than I am, and very lean – there's much more of me than there is of him. But he's so strong I seem to melt away in his arms. He kissed me – as usual, not on the cheek but behind my ear and on my neck. *Il mancino* is the only one of all my four brothers and two sisters who's ever shown me any affection. It was a sad day for me when my mother took me out of his bed and made me go and sleep with my sisters. When he hadn't got anything better to do he used to carve dolls for me out of scraps of wood. And later on, after he'd become a bandit (I admired him a lot for that), he used to come and lie low sometimes at Grottammare. And whenever he went away again he'd slip a coin into my hand and say, "Here you are, *bambola mia*, buy yourself some sweets." And yet in those days he was usually broke.

Being a bandit isn't all it's cracked up to be. Father Racasi says it's very wrong to live off women, and as he's very learned I suppose he must be right. But it brings in much more money than being a bandit, and it's not so risky.

Father Racasi had to stay in Rome to take care of his parish, and the Cardinal has given us a Franciscan as a confessor instead. His name is Barichelli. He's dark, and young still. But he's got so much hair you can hardly see his forehead, and so many whiskers his beard comes nearly up to his eyes. I've already confessed to him once. I guessed why he was here. Before he gave me absolution he told me to remember my body was "only a piece of mud, and that one day I'd return to dust." No doubt that's true, but to judge by the way men look at me my little piece of mud must be very attractive. And when I'm with Father Barichelli and he lowers his eyes I can't help wondering whether it's so that he can meditate or so that he can take a peek at my nipples. If it's the first, as I'd like to believe, will you please tell me why his nostrils start to quiver?

As for the Signora, she refuses to see Father Barichelli, on the grounds that she wasn't consulted over the change of confessor. But clearly that's only an excuse: back in Rome she wouldn't see Father Racasi after the Rusticucci palace was segregated, because she suspected he'd been involved.

During the afternoon of the day that *il mancino* gave me my orders, I went to the watch-tower twice. Once by stealth to make sure there was somebody there, and then a second time, more boldly, to take the look-out some wine. He was a young soldier belonging to the papal army, and he wasn't either ugly or dirty, only very shy. He was so impressed by my airs and graces and my elegant Italian that he didn't dare set about anything but my bottle of wine. I was partly flattered and partly rather disappointed. I let him have a drink out of the flask, but didn't leave it with him, and made him promise not to say anything about my visit. By questioning him skilfully I found out that the watch started at dawn and went on until nightfall. I also learned that the look-out was supposed to give the alarm if he saw a ship approach the coast and launch a boat.

When I told *il mancino* about this conversation he listened impassively and made no comment. Two days later, on May 5th, he came and said goodbye: he was riding to Rome with a letter to the Cardinal from Signor Peretti. But on the 8th he was back again. And the next day, when I went to fetch the Signora some wood — the weather was still very cold — he crept up behind me in the woodshed, put his hand over my mouth, and kissed me on the neck. It was by the kiss that I knew who it was.

"Caterina," he said, "I've got two things to ask you. The first is this: on the edge of the castle grounds, just by the steps down the cliff on to the beach, there's a little house. The doors and windows are secure, the roof is sound, and it has two fireplaces, one at each end. The bishop used it to undress in before he went bathing in the creek, and also to get dry and dress again afterwards – that's why it's so well heated. I want you to go and see it, and then get Vittoria to go and stay there. Don't ask me why," he said curtly, "because I shan't tell you."

"I'll try to persuade her," said I, "but it may be difficult. She's not easily influenced, to put it mildly."

"Insist," he said in a curious tone. "And you can even be a bit mysterious."

These words, and the voice in which he uttered them, sent a little shiver down my spine.

"If you succeed," he said, "you'll have to sleep there too, of course. There are two rooms, or rather one room divided into two by a curtain. And there are two windows looking out on the sea. On the night of the 12th to the 13th May, whatever the weather, you're to put as many lighted candles in the windows as you can muster. Leaving the shutters open, of course."

"And what am I to say to the Signora to explain all this?"

Il mancino drew himself up to his full height and looked at me coldly. "Tell her what you like," he said. "From now on this is your affair, not mine. I haven't said anything. Do you hear, Caterina? I haven't said a word to you about all this. I leave again for Rome tomorrow."

"So soon?" I said, throwing myself into his arms. He hugged me to him, planted his usual little kiss on my neck, and slipped away without another word. As soon as he'd gone and I'd thought over what he'd said, I trembled with joy, hope and fear. My visit to Santa Maria was taking a decidedly new turn.

Luckily I still had a little time left in which to induce the Signora to go and live in the little house on the cliff. I began by asking the majordomo if I could go and see it, and after I'd given him a few little smiles he agreed. I liked the place, and at my request the majordomo had a fire lit in each of the two fireplaces. They drew very well, and as soon as the flames had taken hold he sent the servant he'd brought with him away and started fondling me. I let him: from the look of him I didn't think he'd be able to get very far. And sure enough, after a few moments and much gasping for breath, he stopped of his own accord. But he seemed very pleased with himself, and thanked me for my kindness. And when I asked him he lent me the key to the house.

But I didn't dare speak to the Signora about it straight away. She was still in a very bad temper. She wouldn't speak a word, and refused to see Signor Peretti, Father Barichelli or even Giulietta.

I was outside the door and overheard her quarrel with Giulietta. Poor Giulietta! Why did she have to go and defend the Cardinal and Signor Peretti? She *will* always judge people! As I think I've said before, she criticises me for showing off my bosom. Opportunity would be a fine thing, for her! But she's a typical old maid. It's not that she's ugly, though she is a bit scraggy. It's that Vittoria is too beautiful. Giulietta grew up in the shade of a lovely plant that drank up all the sun and left her all pale and weak in comparison. When she and her cousin are in the same room, who wants to look at her? And if you ask me, a woman needs men to look at her from the very first minute she's born. She needs warmth to be able to grow properly.

Sometimes I'm seized with terror at the thought that one day I'll be old and shan't have that warmth any more. Father Barichelli thinks he's very clever when he threatens me with the torments of Hell. But one day I'll be in my own hell while I'm still alive. I'm in it already when I just say the words, "One day I'll be old."

The watch-tower, the little house on the edge of the cliff, the candles in the windows, the steps down to the beach – I wasn't a fool, I had a good idea of who was going to turn up on the night of the 12th. All I hoped was that he wouldn't be alone.

But I hesitated to tell the Signora what my brother had told me. As she hadn't received any more letters (I'd have known if she had), and as she'd declared she was "guiltless", I didn't know how she'd take my revelation. My mother was right when she said noblewomen were very proud and felt they owed it to themselves to have airs and graces and virtue. In the end I decided not to tell her anything unless she positively refused to go and live in the little house. *Dio mio*, the way things turn out! To think of me, who have so much respect for Signor Peretti, helping his wife to be unfaithful to him! I'd never have done such a thing if it hadn't been for my brother and Marcello. Those two can make me do anything they like.

The Signora put all the blame for the shutting up of the Rusticucci palace and the move to Santa Maria on Father Racasi: she hadn't the slightest suspicion about my reports to the Cardinal. I was even the only person she wasn't surly with. Ever since she'd refused to have her meals with Signor Peretti and Giulietta she'd made me eat with her in her room. And she made me presents of clothes and jewellery every day. I was really quite ashamed sometimes, she was so kind and generous. Well . . . kind? Yes and no. She was always kind to me. But the way she treats Signor Peretti!

On May 10th, very early in the morning, I asked the majordomo to have the house on the cliff thoroughly cleaned and to have a good fire lit. And while I was combing out the Signora's hair I told her of my "discovery". As she hadn't left her room for a week and was dying of boredom in spite of her Petrarch, she was very interested. But she made some objections. She didn't want to go through the grounds: the soldiers were camped there, and she didn't want to set eyes on her gaolers.

"But, Signora," I said, "they're not in that part of the grounds at all. And there's a path that goes round by the wall – that's the way I went, and I didn't see any soldiers."

I didn't mention that they'd certainly seen me. There was a covered way all round the parapet, with here and there little turrets that were bound to contain sentries.

But either my arguments or the desire to stretch her legs – the sun was shining for the first time that rainy spring – finally won her over, and I took her to see the little house. She fell in love with it at once, and even started talking again! It didn't smell nearly so musty as the palace – it must be much less damp! And it was so pretty, the cheerful way the fireplaces faced each other! And you were so near the sea you felt you were almost on it. And what did she need with a palace, she said, when it was only a prison to her? A little cottage was ample! She'd never been afraid of solitude, nor, thank God, of poverty.

I agreed with everything she said, but only thought the more. Fancy talking of poverty, with the sort of meals we were served! And calling it a "cottage" – you could tell she'd never set foot in the house I was born in in Grottammare! To me the cottage on the cliff was a veritable palace!

The main thing was, I didn't even have to suggest she should go and live there. She decided on that herself, straight away. She didn't even consult Signor Peretti – she knew he wouldn't dare utter a word against it. She just sent for the majordomo and gave her orders there and then. He was to bring everything that was needed: carpets, hangings, her dressing-table, her trunks and two beds. And now, at once! The Signora reminds me of her mother when she orders people about like that.

She was happy and busy all that day, supervising the removal herself. The dressing-table must be put there! No, there! And the bed would be much better in this corner! Send someone to check if the cistern's full. It was. Stock the woodshed! We soon had enough wood for a whole winter. Clear the overgrown patch of land in front of the cottage. It was done. But don't touch the trees at the back – they hid the view of the hated Santa Maria. I felt like saying the view wouldn't bother her anyway because there weren't any windows on that side of the house. And I wasn't going to tell her, either, that though it seemed a perfectly good place to dress and undress in, like the bishop, and for drying oneself and having a light meal after a bathe, it struck me as draughty, inelegant and, despite the bright sunshine, rather sinister. It was only about ten feet away from the edge of the cliff, which at that point fell in a sheer drop down to the sea. I wouldn't have done what the Signora did for anything: she went and stood on a rocky spur projecting right over the empty air and the waves breaking on the reefs far below. The tiny promontory was covered with long rough grass that I was sure must be slippery when it rained. Just to the right was the top of the steps leading down to the beach.

The next day the sky was clear for once and the sun bright and hot. The Signora, who'd recovered all her usual energy after her first night in the little house, decided to bathe. Naturally I was supposed to go with her and follow her down those horrible steps. I was nearly dead with fright! And what would we find at the bottom? Just a tiny beach about five feet by ten, with a little cave giving on to it.

"That shows the cliff is full of holes and could collapse at any moment," I said.

"*Come sei stupida!*"* said the Signora. "In two or three centuries, perhaps, at the very soonest."

* How stupid you are!

But I soon got my own back. No sooner had she dipped one foot in the water than she took it out again: it was freezing! And as the little beach was in the shade in the morning, she was cold in nothing but her thin bathing shift. So we came back up again, and although going up was not so bad as going down I suffered just as much. As soon as we were back on the little promontory I fell down with my face in the rough grass and wept.

"No one would think you were the daughter of a master fisherman," said the Signora.

She was in a bad temper again, cross about the unsuccessful trip to the beach. And the next day, May 12th, was even worse. When I opened the shutters – they opened from inside, thank God – I couldn't see one bit of blue sky. Everything was grey, with low, threatening clouds and a leaden sea covered with white-caps. It was very chilly, with gusts of rain dashing every so often against the windows. As soon as I'd folded back the shutters I drew aside the red silk curtain that divided the room in two, stoked up both fires and made both beds. The Signora meanwhile stood at the window, looking out at the sea. When I'd finished she walked to and fro for a while about the room, repressed a sigh, sat down on a little chair by the fire and plunged into her Petrarch.

I could see how it was. The enthusiasm for the little house, and for the cheerful way the fireplaces faced each other, was over. Now the walls pressed in on her, and the nearness of the sea, so delightful a couple of days ago, got on her nerves. She wished she were back in the Rusticucci palace. Who knows if she didn't wish she were back in the palace at Santa Maria? But she'd never admit it. She was too proud. She relapsed into silence and Petrarch and didn't say another word. And that meant I couldn't say anything either. This was very disagreeable, partly because I'm talkative by nature and partly because I was anxious. It was that same evening at nightfall that I was supposed to put the candles in the windows. "Whatever the weather," Domenico had said.

It was the weather that was worrying me. I felt very down in the dumps as I stood behind the Signora brushing her hair. It took a good hour and a light hand: the Signora's scalp was very sensitive because of the weight of her hair when she was standing up. But so as not to be left with nothing to do afterwards, which I dreaded, I made the brushing last

133

as long as possible. Unfortunately the Signora was obviously on edge too; she grew impatient and told me to stop. I put the brush away, and while I was about it, tidied the dressing-table. Then I'd finished and had nothing left to do. It wasn't I who did the washing and ironing – that was the duty of another maid, in the palace. For the first time I wished I did do the washing and ironing – it would have stopped me fretting myself over silly ideas. I've got such a vivid imagination! I'd just had a vision of my poor Marcello, all white in the face, his eyes shut, being washed up by a wave . . .

"Signora," I said, "with your permission . . ."

"Oh Caterina," she cried, "you are a nuisance! Must you keep talking? You can see I'm trying to read!"

Read or dream? I hadn't noticed her turning the pages very often. I'm not stupid. And I've got eyes.

"Forgive me, Signora, but with your permission I'd like to clean your jewellery."

"But I cleaned it myself not long ago!"

"Gold can never shine too brightly, Signora."

"All right, clean it then, clean it, if it'll keep you occupied!" she said, shrugging. "But for goodness sake don't make a noise! And stop tearing round the room!"

"Yes, Signora."

I put a small saucer of soapy water and another saucer with a sponge on it on one of the broad wooden window sills, took the jewels out of their casket and spread them out on a red cloth. I'd have enjoyed myself if I hadn't been so worried. The window sill came about up to my waist, just a comfortable height for what I was doing. And I was looking straight out over the sea, which would have been very pleasant if it had been a bit calmer. But it looked to me as if it was getting rougher.

When I'd finished cleaning one of the rings I glanced at the Signora – she wasn't turning the pages any more often than before – and slipped it on to my little finger. That was the only one it would fit, because the Signora's hands are much slenderer than mine. Still, the ring looked just as good on me as it did on her! So do the necklaces! But I only try them on when I'm alone in her room – I need to be able to look at myself in the dressing-table mirror. The effect they make on my pretty bosom! –

enough to make anyone's mouth water! Especially the pearls: they show to great advantage on my smooth dark skin. What I really mean is, my skin and the pearls show one another off, especially as I've got such a pretty neck, round and soft and without a wrinkle. I don't know how any man worthy of the name could see my neck with a beautiful necklace round it and not want to cover it with kisses.

I was a bit ashamed of forgetting my anxiety and only thinking of myself, though, when there in front of me the sky was getting darker and darker and the sea ever more rough. I could hear the waves crashing like drums at the foot of the cliff, and the wrench of the shingle as they receded. I felt as if the cliff were trembling beneath me, but it must have been an illusion. The truth was I'd never set foot on a boat, and never bathed in salt water. At home in Grottammare it's regarded as unhealthy.

When the majordomo and three or four of his staff brought our midday meal the Signora was obliged to open her lips, if only to eat and to thank the majordomo for his extra trouble. When he'd gone she glanced out of the window and said idly: "I hope the weather improves."

"Oh yes," I answered fervently, "I hope so too, with all my heart!"

She looked at me, surprised by my tone. But I was afraid I'd said too much, and fell silent, looking down at my plate.

The afternoon was awful. The weather didn't improve. It got worse. The rain fell in torrents and wind raged, throwing such violent gusts against the window that although they did shut properly the water seeped in underneath. The sill on which I'd cleaned the jewellery was flooded. I mopped the water up with rags, which I then stuffed as best I could between the wood and the stone. It didn't keep the rain out altogether, but it helped.

But things got much worse when the storm really broke. What with the noise of the waves and the peals of thunder, the din was deafening, I was sitting idle on a little low chair by the fire, starting at each flash of lightning. How I wished the Signora were frightened too, so that we could cling together for comfort. In the Rusticucci palace, in the winter, the Signora sometimes used to ask me to get into bed with her because she was always cold and I was always warm. I loved that!

I glanced at her now and then. And do you think she jumped when the lightning lit up the windows and the thunder growled as if it would never stop? Not a bit of it! There she sat as calm as a Madonna, with her feet on a little stool and her golden hair hanging down behind her chair and carefully arranged by me on the carpet. I was the one who'd have to comb it out if it got tangled! And that was the very devil of a job, I can tell you!

She was wearing a pale blue house gown which must have been very comfortable, for it didn't have hoops or petticoats underneath. She was beautiful, flawless. Even I, who've practically never been away from her for years, have never got used to her loveliness. Sometimes when I look at her I can't believe my eyes. I say to myself, it's impossible a woman should be so beautiful!

She was quite undisturbed by the roaring sea, the howling wind or the fall of the thunderbolts. She was either reading or dreaming. Sometimes she'd let her book fall into her lap and sit staring into space, her lips moving. She might have been praying. But she wasn't. I knew what she was doing: she was learning one of those Petrarch sonnets by heart. In the Rusticucci palace she sometimes used to recite one aloud when everyone was bustling around her washing her hair in a tub. It was very pretty indeed, the way she spoke it. But I can't understand that kind of Italian.

Late in the afternoon I heard a noise outside, and, looking through the window, I saw Signor Peretti, the rain streaming down over his bare head and shoulders. There was a knock at the door, but when at a sign from Vittoria I went to open it, it was the majordomo and not Signor Peretti who entered. I tried to shut the door behind him as fast as I could, but had to pit all my strength against the wind blowing off the sea and into the room.

"Signora," said the majordomo, bowing low, "Signor Peretti earnestly requests you to spend tonight in the palace because of the storm."

"Thank him, majordomo," said the Signora loftily, "but this house is quite sound, and I feel as safe here as I do in the palace."

"Signora," answered the majordomo awkwardly, "Signor Peretti told me to insist."

"Insisting will make no difference," said Vittoria with a scornful smile. "I've made up my mind. I shall stay here."

The majordomo bowed and withdrew. I opened the door just a crack to let him out, and when I'd shut it after him I could see him through the window, shouting into Signor Peretti's ear because of the hellish uproar of the wind and waves. Signor Peretti seemed to be wondering whether he should come in and speak to the Signora himself. He took a couple of steps towards the door. But at the last moment he changed his mind, turned round and went away. I thought that was a mistake.

I was sure of it a few minutes later, when the Signora looked up from her book and said: "What a poor specimen of a husband I've got! Afraid of the rain and a few flashes of lightning. Instead of coming himself he sends his majordomo."

"But, Signora," said I, "Signor Peretti wasn't afraid! He was there, outside the door – I saw him through the window. He was soaking wet. He just didn't like to come in because you've said you won't see him."

She looked at me, and suddenly her great blue eyes filled with tears. "What?" she said, her voice faint and plaintive. "You too, Caterina? So you're against me as well?"

I was shattered by her tone, by her tears, by the way she looked at me. I threw myself at her feet, seized her hands and covered them with kisses. "Oh, no, Signora!" I cried. "I'll always be on your side, whatever happens!" And I started weeping too. She took her hands away and stroked my hair. I felt so happy kneeling there with my face in the folds of her gown.

Then after a while she said gently: "There, there, it's all over. We've made it up. You're a good girl, Caterina."

I rose and went back to my seat by the fire. Yes, I was a good girl. Everyone said so. And perhaps they took advantage a bit. But it was true, too. I *had* seen Signor Peretti with my own eyes, standing in the rain and looking miserable outside his wife's door, not daring to come in. And I didn't see how it was betraying the Signora and being "against" her to tell her so.

At about six o'clock the wretched majordomo, accompanied by four servants, came through the pelting rain to bring us our evening meal. I gave the old boy a smile on the sly, which pleased him no end. We'd been great friends since I'd let him take a few little liberties, as I've already mentioned. I noticed that the Signora too, realising how much trouble she was giving him, was very gracious to him once more, and he went away drenched to the skin but enchanted. As he left I gave him another smile to finish him off. Amazing that I could still enjoy playing such tricks in the midst of all that nervousness and anxiety.

For night was falling and it was time for me to follow Domenico's instructions and put as many candles as I could in the windows – without closing the shutters, of course. I did so with some apprehension, for it was a very strange thing to do, especially with the gale rattling the window panes.

"Have you gone crazy, Caterina?" said the Signora, looking up from her book. "What are the illuminations for? You'd do better to close the shutters!"

"Signora," I said gravely. (I'd prepared my answer.) "I'm thinking of the people at sea."

"But you're not at Grottammare now."

"We didn't have candles at Grottammare, Signora. In the winter we only had the light from the fire. If we needed more light we just put a few more twigs on."

"My dear Caterina, put out those candles! They might as well not be there, with the lightning flashing all the time."

"Excuse me, Signora, but you've been reading and haven't noticed. The storm moved away some time ago and there isn't any more lightning."

"What does it matter?" she said. "Why must you keep arguing? Just do as I tell you!"

I looked at her. "Forgive me, Signora – I want to ask you a question. I've been in your service for six years. Have I been a devoted and affectionate maid to you?"

"Of course. But that's no reason why I should indulge all your whims and fancies."

"Oh Signora!" I cried earnestly, "it's not a whim! It's a matter of life and death!"

My seriousness surprised her. She looked at me and hesitated. But the habit of command got the better of her and she said curtly: "Now then, Caterina, no nonsense, please! Do as you're told! Put out the candles and close the shutters!"

I really was in a corner. I stared at her in terror, not knowing what to say or do. Our eyes met, and she sensed and was intrigued by the strength of my resistance.

"I can't make you out, Caterina," she said more mildly. "You're not usually so obstinate."

"Oh, Signora, forgive me!" I cried. "But supposing your brother Marcello were at sea in such weather – wouldn't you like him to see lights in the distance to guide him to you?"

She was astonished – so astonished that if I'd been her I'd have asked a few questions. I thought for a minute she was going to. But no, that's just what she didn't do! She changed her mind, shrugged, and said nonchalantly – or rather with an assumption of nonchalance: "Oh well, do as you like! I'm tired of arguing. But remember, Caterina, I shan't overlook your waywardness another time."

I heaved a deep sigh. "No, Signora. Thank you, Signora. Forgive me, Signora."

I was all repentance, gratitude and humility. I could afford to let her bear off the honours now she'd given in. She was soon deep in her book again, but I'm sure she didn't read a line of it. She was asking herself all the questions she'd have liked to ask me.

At least she had her book to keep her in countenance. I just sat on my little low chair with nothing to do, clasping and unclasping my hands in my lap and longing to get up and move around. I knew what I'd have done if I'd been the mistress instead of the maid. When the Signora's nerves got the better of her she paced up and down, and no one said her nay. But if I did that I was "tearing about" and a nuisance.

Minutes went by, perhaps hours – who knows? Only the Signora had a watch, and I certainly wasn't going to ask her the time. Anyhow, it was late; very late. I watched the candles in the windows, their tall flames quivering in the draughts. They'd already burned down by about a third of their length, and the wicks were beginning to smoke. I'd found something to do: I got up and trimmed them. Then I blew up both the fires with the bellows and threw some more logs on. That gave me away. At bedtime, even in winter, people don't put more logs on the fire – they just cover up the ones that are there with ashes. But the Signora, though she'd been watching me, didn't ask any questions.

I sat down again, and to tell the truth I grew more terrified every minute. True, I'd never been on a boat, but I was a fisherman's daughter and had heard plenty of tales about storms and shipwrecks.

The Signora turned towards me. "Why haven't you gone to bed yet, Caterina?"

I could have said the same: I'd never known her sit up so late.

"I'm not tired, Signora."

Our eyes met. She looked away. She didn't say anything and neither did I. In this world only men are allowed to tell the truth. Women are taught hypocrisy in their cradles. So there we sat together, silent, though each of us knew full well why the other was trembling. For I could tell she was frightened too. She had more self-command than I had, but her face was drawn, her eyes were anxious, and her book lay idle on her lap. She'd stopped even pretending to read.

Suddenly someone started banging at the door, and a voice shouted: "Open up! Open up! It's me – Marcello!"

I ran and opened, and Marcello appeared in the doorway. He was scarcely able to stand, and soaking wet. His doublet was in shreds, and there was blood running down his cheek.

"Come and help me with the Prince," he gasped. "He fell just before we got to the top of the cliff."

"Is he dead?" cried Vittoria.

"No, no!" said Marcello.

Without stopping to throw on a cloak Vittoria flew out of the room like a madwoman, right into a terrible wall of wind and rain. Marcello followed her, and I followed him. But even with all three of us it was no easy matter to carry a man of the Prince's height and weight back into the house. Finally, however, we laid him down in front of the fire, and with unspeakable relief I closed the door behind us. Vittoria was already kneeling on the hearth-rug, raising Orsini's head and cradling it on her bosom.

"He's only fainted," said Marcello. "He was coming up the steps in front of me, and tripped. He must have fallen on his bad leg, and the pain made him pass out."

We were all like drowned rats. I gazed in horror at the Signora's blonde locks, all flattened and tangled by the rain.

"We must get his clothes off," said Marcello, "or he'll catch cold."

"But you're hurt too, Signore," I said to Marcello. "Your cheek is bleeding."

"It's nothing. A wave banged my head against a rock."

"A wave?" I said. "Didn't you come by boat?"

He managed to laugh despite all the blood on his cheek: "It broke up when we hit the creek!"

"Stop chattering, Caterina, and help me!" said the Signora impatiently.

I helped her undress the Prince. It wasn't easy, because he was so heavy. When we'd managed it I rubbed him down with a towel, and so did the Signora. He was a fine figure of a man, as well set up and muscular as a statue. The wound in his thigh was bleeding, but the colour soon came back into his face, and he blinked.

"Caterina," said the Signora, "warm some wine and give him a drink."

She rose to her feet, drew the red silk curtain across the room, and went behind it. I poured some wine into a pewter tankard, added a lump of candied sugar and put it in the embers between some stones.

"Blow the candles out, Caterina," said Marcello. "The Prince told the captain of the galley we'd put them out if we got ashore safe and sound."

"I thought it had broken up."

He laughed.

"Not the galley, *stupida*. The little boat we were supposed to come ashore in."

"Let me wipe the blood off your cheek, Signore."

"It'll dry on its own. Better go and help Vittoria undress, and rub her down. I'll give the Prince some wine."

I went through to the other side of the curtain, but the Signora was already as naked as the day she was born and drying herself with a towel. I twisted her hair up and wrapped it in another towel, holding it away from her back so that she could dry herself there too.

"How is he?"

"Better, Signora. He's opened his eyes. As soon as he's had a drink he'll be himself again."

"God be praised," she murmured.

If I'd been her I wouldn't have praised God for that, even in a whisper.

141

"Signora," I said, "you ought to sit by the fire and let your hair dry properly."

"Sit and wait," she said, "when he's braved death to reach me?"

She hastily threw on a simple gown that she got out of the trunk herself as I held her hair out behind her. Then I put another towel over her shoulders and let her hair fall free. The damp would soon get through both the towel and the gown, but what could I do?

The Signora was unrecognisable. Who had ever said her eyes were cold? In that room, lit only by the glow from the fire, they looked as if they were shooting forth flames. As she went round to the other side of the curtain – where her sin awaited her – she seemed to be dancing on air.

I shivered, and remembered that I too had got drenched to the skin. Before I undressed I put log after log on the fire, stoking up the flames till they reminded me of the Hell that threatened all four of us if I was to believe Father Racasi. But I only half believed him. It was bad enough to have to die one day – *Madonna santa*, if we had to look forward to eternal torments as well, what price divine mercy?

Hell or no Hell, as I was taking off my bodice and skirt I suddenly started to feel gloomy, despite the fact that Marcello was there on the other side of the curtain. But it was man, not God that frightened me. The very second the Signora committed adultery it would become Signor Peretti's duty to kill her. And me too, as her accomplice. Worse still, if I didn't betray her guilt when I confessed to Father Racasi, it would be a bad confession and I'd be damned. And this business would mean death for Marcello too: he wasn't a nobleman, and he had suborned his sister. Only the Prince would escape, because he was a prince. *Dio mio*, was that justice?

My mood changed completely as soon as I was naked. I turned round and round in front of the fire, and as the warmth spread through me so did an intense joy. Why couldn't I just live happily without asking myself questions? Like a pretty little dog lying in front of the fire with her muzzle between her paws?

A hand raised a corner of the red silk curtain, and Marcello came round to my side of it. But I restrained my impulse to rush towards him. I could see at a glance that this wasn't the moment. For a man who'd just emerged from a brush with death, he didn't look upset or even tired. His face was expressionless. But I knew him. If I went near him now he'd push me away. I knew what I had to do. I went and curled up by the fire, taking up as little room as possible and not saying a word. I didn't even look at him.

Marcello undressed absentmindedly and in silence, hanging his doublet and hose over a couple of stools to dry. Then he warmed himself back and front by the fire, but apparently without experiencing the pleasure I'd felt. I glanced at him now and then, but only briefly. For he's as sensitive as a woman and guesses everything. I could tell he was in a foul temper, and began to be afraid he was going to let me crouch in front of the fire all night without touching me. And yet this was all his doing! Right from the start! If it hadn't been for him, none of tonight's events would ever have happened! And there he was, silent, tense and solemn as a judge. How complicated these people were! He and the Signora were just the same! But the Signora was a woman, so I could more or less make her out! But him!

Suddenly he came over to me. Without a word he grabbed me by the hair with one hand and put the other over my mouth (just like the first time). Then he pulled me to my feet, shoved me over to the bed, lay down on top of me, and roughly possessed me. He lay there with all his weight on me, looking at me with blazing eyes and whispering in my ear: "If you cry out at the end as you usually do, I'll strangle you – do you hear?" And he clutched both my arms so hard I'd have groaned with the pain if I'd dared. At the same time, although his distorted face hung directly over me, he refused to kiss me. He just gasped, as he came and went inside me, "You're just a little whore, and I hate you!" And then, suddenly, he could have done and said anything he liked as far as I was concerned – beaten me black and blue, crushed me to death, insulted me. Everything changed into bliss.

When he'd finished, he withdrew and rolled to one side, overcome by fatigue from one moment to the next. He just shut his eyes and slept like a babe. I propped myself up on my elbow to look at him. The fire cast a red glow on his naked body. He was superb. And when he was asleep he was mine, the fool! He'd had his little male triumph, but my pleasures still went on – I could feel their traces inside me. I wouldn't change places with you, Marcello, and it's your little whore that tells you so.

I laughed silently. That's what I was like now: I made love without crying out and I laughed without making a noise. That's how men like us to be. Even the Signora fell into line, to judge by the silence reigning on the other side of the curtain. That must have been my last thought before I fell asleep, for when I woke up in the morning I was thinking the same thing.

6

Aziza

Paolo refused at first when I asked him to let me go with him on the galley taking him to the launching point off Santa Maria. Then he remembered I was a good sailor after being his servant so long at sea, and he gave in. He agreed soon afterwards to let Lodovico go too, but reluctantly, and, it seemed to me, less out of friendship than because of his superstitious respect for family bonds. I was proved right when, before transferring to the little boat in which he was supposed to go ashore, he handed over the command of the galley not to Lodovico but to his mate. And he gave the mate his instructions privately, and in a whisper.

The voyage from Naples to Santa Maria took three days. The nearer we got to our destination the rougher the sea became, and the more anxious I was at the danger of Paolo's venture. But knowing how set he was on it I didn't say anything. I didn't even let him see how terrified I was, but stayed with him up to the last minute as cheerful, lively and obedient as I'd always been, and as he liked me to be. He availed himself of me twice during the voyage, which astonished as well as delighted me. But it also made me feel humiliated, in a way. For obviously there wasn't the slightest connection, for him, between what he was doing with me and his great love for Vittoria.

As we were approaching Santa Maria, Lodovico sent Folletto to ask Paolo if he could speak to him. Before agreeing, Paolo told me to lie on his bunk with the curtains drawn and listen carefully without being seen or heard. I did so, but the curtains didn't quite close, and through the gap I could keep an eye on Lodovico. Paolo asked him to sit down opposite him at the little table fixed to the floor at which he took his meals. All I could see of Paolo was the back of his right shoulder, but I could guess what his expression was from the tone of his voice, that I knew so well. All the time they were talking I lay clutching the edge of the bunk with both hands, for the galley was pitching and tossing, and every so often I could hear huge waves crashing against the hull, and the beams creaking and groaning.

"Well, Paolo," said Lodovico, "you see what the weather's like! Don't tell me you still mean to launch a boat in the dark and go ashore with that intriguer! It would be madness!"

"If Marcello was only an intriguer, would he be sharing in my folly?" said Paolo. "Intriguers aren't usually keen on risking their own skins – you ought to know that."

"Never mind about Marcello," said Lodovico. "You must see for yourself – there's a raging sea and you're bound to perish."

"We all have to die some day," said Paolo jokingly. "Come to think of it, what have I got to live for?"

"You have a duty to Virginio."

"He's amply provided for in my will. And with me always away at sea, he was brought up by his uncles, and is more of a Medici now than an Orsini."

"But he's still your son."

"And you're my first cousin," said Paolo ironically. "And Medici's my brother-in-law. We're a very united family."

"Please, Paolo, be serious! I had a terrible dream the other night about this mad escapade of yours. The boat was sinking on its way back to the galley, and Marcello, Vittoria and you were all drowning."

"That would be very sad for us," said Paolo, still speaking lightly. "And for you too, Lodovico."

"Can you doubt it, Paolo?" said Lodovico, with what sounded to me a very hollow ring.

"No, not in the least. I know I've been a good kinsman to you, *carissimo* – open and generous. Though I fear Virginio wouldn't be the same, much as you've been taking his interests to heart lately."

"Why do you say that, Paolo?" asked Lodovico, visibly uneasy.

"Because Virginio's a Medici now. And the Medicis, being bankers, keep a tight hold on their purse-strings."

146

"You're being unfair to me and to them, Paolo. You don't like the Medicis."

"On the contrary – I like them very much. But I have a grudge against them for badgering me to kill their sister after she was unfaithful to me."

"But you did it in the end," said Lodovico. "And for other reasons that are perhaps less honourable."

"A great deal could be said, *carissimo*, about the honour of the elder branch of the Orsinis. And about that of the younger branch too."

I couldn't see the Prince, but I sensed a cutting edge to his voice that meant there was a certain kind of smile on his face. Lodovico reacted to his tone too, and his face tensed for a moment. But he managed to control himself.

"But you can't deny, Paolo," he went on coldly, "that you only decided to kill Isabella after you'd met Vittoria Peretti."

"The decision did follow the meeting, but contrary to what you and Raimondo may have supposed, it wasn't a consequence of it. As a matter of fact I'd made up my mind before I wrote to Vittoria, and before she gave me her ring to plight her troth. I'd already received reports from the majordomo at Bracciano that Isabella was giving herself to muleteers and scullions. The scandal had to stop."

This was a great surprise to me. Up till then I'd thought the same as Lodovico. But knowing how truthful the Prince was, I couldn't doubt what he'd just said. Lodovico didn't believe him, though – that was obvious from the look on his face. It was a strange face, too. At first glance it was very attractive, but in the long run its vulgarity made it seem ugly.

"I believe what you say, since it's you who say it," said Lodovico in a tone that hovered somewhere between insolence and suavity. "But let's leave Isabella out of it. Paolo, I appeal to your commonsense! Look at the sea! You don't stand a chance in a hundred of getting ashore! How can you commit such folly!"

"Because I love Vittoria," said Paolo, still in the ironical tone he'd been using with his cousin throughout.

"How can you love her when you've only seen her for a couple of minutes?"

"There," replied Paolo as before, "we're talking about one of the mysteries of the human heart."

147

He laughed and stood up. Then, putting his arm round Lodovico's shoulders with every appearance of the warmest affection, he led him to the door, and as soon as he was outside, locked it behind him.

Then to my great surprise and delight he came over, drew the curtain and lay down beside me, slipping his arm round my neck and putting my little head on his strong shoulder.

"Well, Aziza, my wasp," he said with a smile, "what do you think of my fine cousins?"

"A couple of leeches, Good-for-nothings. But they're not both the same. *Il bruto*, in spite of his nickname, isn't altogether heartless, and he does feel some affection for you. Lodovico, on the other hand, is just a snake. He's never been grateful for all you've done for him, and now you've cut off supplies he hates you."

"So why do you think he wanted so much to come with me?"

"To report to the Medicis and Virginio."

"Very shrewd, my wasp. Your black eye isn't the only thing that's sharp about you."

"Sharp she may be, but the wasp doesn't understand everything. For instance, why did you let him come with you, knowing what you do?"

"It's in my own interests to handle him carefully. If it came to open war with the Pope, he and his brother and the rest of his family would represent a considerable amount of support. What's more, Lodovico has the ear of the people, and without their support no rebellion is possible."

I listened. He spoke calmly, even cheerfully. And yet at nightfall he was going to trust his life to a nutshell on a raging sea. "A chance in a hundred," Lodovico had said. What would become of me if he died? Would Virginio sell me to another master? By Almighty God, I wouldn't bear it! I'd still got the little dagger which Abensur gave me and from which I got my nickname. And there and then, with my head on my adored prince's chest, I vowed to myself that I wouldn't survive him.

"Any other questions, my wasp?" said Paolo.

"Yes."

Oh, how I've come to regret that "yes"! What torture I'd have been spared if I'd never uttered it. And what madness was it that seized me, to want to fathom Paolo's feelings? If only I'd answered "no" I know very well what would have happened. The roughness of the sea kept throwing us together on the narrow bunk. And the desire I could feel stirring within me, as well as the terrible risks he was about to run, would have excited him too.

Instead I was as stupid as a real wasp banging itself against a windowpane. I asked the same absurd question that Lodovico had already asked and Paolo had evaded with a jest: How could he love Vittoria when he'd only seen her for a couple of minutes?

This time, unfortunately, Paolo didn't evade the question. He answered with a sincere and circumstantial account, uttered with fervour and enthusiasm and without an inkling of how much he was hurting me. For he really was a good master — fair, patient and considerate.

"You know," he said, wedging his right leg, the one with the wound, against the side of the bunk, "when I met Vittoria at Montalto's house, that wasn't the first time I'd seen her. I first set eyes on her six years before, when she was still living in Gubbio. I was riding through the little town at the head of quite a large troop of soldiers, and as I had some time to spare I asked a well-dressed passer-by what was the finest sight to be seen in the place. He was a very old man, but his black eyes sparkled when he answered:

"'Some will tell you it's the ducal palace, but I say it's Vittoria Accoramboni. And as it happens —" he added, "I'm on my way to see her now. It's Tuesday today, and every Tuesday and Saturday afternoon Vittoria washes her wonderful hair. When it's sunny, like today, she dries it on a balcony overlooking the street. It's a sight not to be missed, and let me tell you, as long as my poor old legs will carry me I shan't miss it! So if you want to see it too, Signore, just come along with me.'

"I was very taken by this ancient. So close to his end and still going out of his way, quite disinterestedly, to contemplate feminine beauty. Delighted and amused, I dismounted and threw my reins to my squire, then walked along with the old man at his own slow and tottering pace. On the way he told me his name was Pietro Muratore: he was a frame-maker, and said wryly that his frames were often more beautiful than the pictures they were intended for. Because of my buffalo-hide doublet he took me for an ordinary captain and spoke to me quite familiarly. I didn't tell him who I really was for fear of embarrassing him.

"Vittoria Accoramboni was sitting on a low-backed stool, her incredibly long fair hair spread out behind her on a kind of frame. A little Moorish slave girl kept the sun off her lovely face with a big white umbrella which she shifted from one hand to another as she got tired. Her mistress wore a loose pale-blue gown with folds that fell freely about her statuesque figure like an Ionian tunic. Her bare feet pointed up the resemblance to a Greek goddess: they were perfectly shaped, and plain for all to see on a little footrest outside the shade of the umbrella. No doubt Vittoria liked to feel the warmth of the sun on them, and didn't mind if they did get brown.

"According to what Muratore had told me beforehand – for now he was speechless in contemplation – Vittoria had just turned fifteen. But she was already a picture of womanly beauty. The little Moorish slave girl didn't look more than ten. She too was very pretty, small and well formed, with a clear pale complexion, hair like a raven's wing, big black eyes, a small nose and a large mouth."

"Like me!" I cried, but with very mixed feelings.

"Yes, Aziza. And as you'll see, the resemblance plays a part in the story. The little Moor struck me as an important element in the picture spread out before me. It was as if a great artist had put her there not only to prevent Vittoria's complexion being spoiled, but also to act as a foil to the pink of her skin, the blue of her eyes and the splendid golden tresses spread out in the sun. As a matter of fact I only guessed that Vittoria had blue eyes. I couldn't see them at first because they were lowered. She was reading."

"But how could you see even as much as that, Paolo? She was on the balcony and you were down in the street."

"There was a little church opposite the house with a raised porch level with the balcony. And Vittoria's admirers – men and women of all ages – used to take it in turns to go and stand on the porch for a few minutes, lost in silent admiration. Even some of the parishioners coming out of the church, their thoughts still caught up in their prayers, lingered on the porch to join in the almost pagan worship of Vittoria's beauty.

"'But we can't see her eyes!' I said to Muratore. I'd spoken in a reverential whisper, but even so the reproachful glances directed at me told me I'd disturbed the worshippers around me.

"'Wait,' whispered Muratore, twitching my sleeve to remind me of the respect due to an idol.

"And sure enough, after a while Vittoria put her book down in her lap. With her left hand keeping the volume open at her place, she turned her head, looked at our little group with her great blue eyes, and gave us a slight nod. It was neither haughty nor familiar, but done with truly regal dignity and grace. A thrill ran through us all: the women bowed and the men doffed their hats. I followed Muratore's example and did the same. Then he took me by the sleeve and indicated that it was time to go. When we'd gone a little way he pointed out that the porch was small and it was only right to make way for others.

"'Man lives as much by beauty as by bread,' said he."

There was a pause.

"He was a wise old man, Paolo," I said. "What's become of him since?"

"I inquired about him when I got back to Venice," answered the Prince. "He died soon after I met him in Gubbio. All that's left of him for me is his name and the memory of the bright little black eyes in his wizened face. Isn't it strange he should have played such an important role in my life? But how can I talk of Providence without casting aspersions on the Almighty and thus offending the Pope? Of course," he added mischievously, "there may be another God called chance."

"Oh Paolo!" I said with a smile (though the Madonna knows how little I felt like smiling!), "you're not a good *roumi*! You're not even a good Muslim! There's only one God!"

"But chance took a hand again during my first fight with the pirates," said Paolo, "when I captured Abensur's felucca and bought a little Moorish girl who looked just like Vittoria's."

I swallowed.

"Was that why you bought me?" I asked in a strangled voice.

I remembered how he'd stared at me as soon as he saw me.

"No, Aziza," he said, not noticing the emotion in my voice. "I'd have bought you anyhow. And since then," he added carelessly, "I've congratulated myself a hundred times over on my bargain. But it's true that in all the years we've sailed the seas together, I've never been able to look at you without seeing you holding a white umbrella over Vittoria's face."

"But that wasn't me!" I cried.

"I know! I knew the very first day, after I'd asked you about yourself."

"In short, then, I've acted as a reminder of the delightful picture you saw that afternoon in Gubbio."

"Yes. Exactly. Thanks to you I could always conjure her up in my mind as alive and fresh and charming as when I actually saw her."

I said nothing. What was there to say? I'd had the answer to my question, but it was horribly painful. Of course I'd known from the beginning what my place was in his heart and in his life. But it was even smaller than I'd thought. A brown hand holding a white umbrella over Vittoria's bright face. That was me.

Paolo Giordano Orsini

I used the three days of the voyage to get the carpenter to lay an extra deck fore and aft on the little boat I meant to use to go ashore. Underneath I ordered him to put all the cork he could find, to make the craft as buoyant as possible and easily rightable if it capsized. For the same reason I had the false bottom reinforced, so that if we keeled over Marcello and I could brace ourselves against it and use our weight to get ourselves afloat again. This manoeuvre is easy in theory but difficult in practice: the boat must be light and the two men must cooperate well. But I'd often done the trick successfully in my youth, even in rough seas. As a further precaution I had the oars lashed to the rowlocks with hempen cords so that they shouldn't float away if we were swamped by a wave. I chose ropes rather than chains because they stood the strain better.

I also made sure we were dressed as lightly as possible, without boots or swords and armed only with fighting daggers. The mate insisted on our wearing cork belts. I agreed, but without any illusions about how much use they'd be in those seas.

The great problem was to launch the boat when the time came, get ourselves down into it, and pull away before the waves dashed us against the side of the galley. So the whole operation was carried out in the lee of the ship, and I also had oil poured on to the water. This surprised the landlubbers, but it's very efficient at calming the waves over a small area. In this case it prevented the boat from overturning when it reached the water. We installed ourselves as quickly as we could, for the galley was taking the wind on the beam in order to shelter us, and this exposed her to danger. As soon as we were clear she went about and we, no longer in her lee, were driven towards the shore. The wind was so strong our oars served chiefly to keep us headed towards the land – and towards the lights. When I turned my head I could see them shining in the windows of the little house that *il mancino* had described.

Although night had almost fallen there was still a greenish twilight over the sea, so whenever we sped along the crest of a wave I could dimly make out the shape of the little cottage where I knew Vittoria Peretti was waiting for me. The thought made me wild with happiness. But my joy was tinged with incredulity, for my idol had seemed completely inaccessible until this moment, when I was risking my life to be with her. If I'd had ten lives I'd have staked them all for her.

However, I kept a cool head. I shouted brief orders to Marcello as he sat on the thwart in front of mine, telling him when and when not to use his oars so as to keep us in line with the flow of waves. But I knew the worst danger in stormy waters was not the sea itself but the shore, where you risked being smashed to pieces. When the lights on the cliff disappeared from view I realised we were now too close to see them. Our lives were going to depend on the next few seconds and whether we managed to find the entrance to the creek.

There was still just enough light for me to see the great fringe of foam where the waves broke against the foot of the cliffs with a savage roar. We were approaching so rapidly the rocks seemed to be hurtling towards us. With the wind so strong and visibility so poor, all I could do was act swiftly and trust to luck. I shouted an order and steered to the left. The wall of rock that had been facing me passed miraculously by on the right. And I realised to my immense relief that I'd somehow found the entrance.

I rose up from the thwart with joy, but my jubilation was short-lived. The sea was rushing into the creek with such force we could no longer control the course of the boat. I just had time to deduce from the spray surrounding it that we were heading for a reef less than a stone's throw away, when a wave came and hurled us over it. I hoped for one wild moment that we might get past it unscathed, but the bottom of the boat scraped on the rock, another wave washed us off the thwarts, and we found ourselves half swimming, half choking in the water. Then suddenly our feet touched the sandy bottom of the inlet.

Strangely enough, just as we thought we were safe we had another bad moment: the backwash was so strong that as soon as we reached the shore we were sucked back again into the sea. I yelled in Marcello's ear. What we must do was dive into the next incoming wave and when it landed us on the beach clutch on to the sand with both hands. But the undertow dragged us back three or four times, and we'd probably have had the worst of the unequal struggle if it hadn't been for a sudden lull that allowed us to struggle as far as the cave at the head of the inlet.

Luckily the cave was at an angle to the face of the cliff, and we were now protected from the pull of the receding waves. We could yield to our exhaustion and collapse on the sand, though we were still not out of the water. However, where we lay motionless it was only a few inches deep, and its gentle to-ing and fro-ing, faintly echoing the undertow, felt soothing and friendly after what we'd just been through. But the wavelets themselves, sometimes washing up to my neck, struck much colder than the waves that had tossed us about out in the creek. The chill could do nothing, though, to detract from the sense of comfort and content I felt as I sprawled there with the water coming sometimes up to my chest and sometimes higher.

Wet and cold as I was, I must have fallen asleep for a couple of minutes, for all of a sudden Marcello was shaking me and shouting into my ear that we ought to take advantage of another lull in the waves to climb up the steps in the cliff. I remember that by then the thought of the house where Vittoria was waiting for me had become quite unreal. I felt a strong pang of regret at the idea of having to leave the womb-like cave where I'd found refuge from the hostility of the world.

Emerging from our shelter was like plunging back into a nightmare. We were immediately buffeted again by the sea, which, even after we'd found the steps, seemed to be trying with malevolent persistence to pluck us off them. I realised dimly that we could only move when the waves were receding, and that when they broke the only thing to do was cling on like a starfish to any holds there were in the cliff. So our ascent was very slow, and I can remember, while it lasted, feeling absurdly indignant with whoever had carved out the steps for not thinking to fix an iron handrail beside them. It didn't occur to me they'd only been put there for people to bathe in summer.

Halfway up we were beyond the reach of the waves, but the wind was gusting so fiercely we were still in as much danger as before of being dashed off the face of the cliff. In fact it was even worse: drenched as we were, the wind chilled us through and through and made our movements and our hold on the rocks less sure. I had several attacks of vertigo when I was tempted just to let go. My mind was so numbed, disoriented and divorced from all logic that I saw the resulting fall not as a crash to my death but as a respite that would enable me to survive. But I went on climbing automatically, blindly imitating Marcello. He was ahead of me, and I was vaguely surprised to see him outstripping me, his elder and his leader. It was only then I'd noticed he was in front of me. Up till then I'd thought he was behind.

What happened next was total confusion. I felt as if instead of standing on rock I was on something soft and slippery, like grass. But when I lifted my foot to climb to the next step I seemed to walk into a void, and pitched face forward on to the ground. I felt an acute pain in my thigh and then I fainted, either from the pain or perhaps from exhaustion.

But although I couldn't move, see or speak I didn't quite lose consciousness. Without understanding what was said I could hear voices murmuring around me, and was aware of being borne along on friendly arms and put down on a rug in front of a big fire. But I was only conscious intermittently. Sometimes I saw things and sometimes I didn't: there was a continual alternation in my mind of darkness and light.

Then suddenly I felt my head being raised and my clothes being taken off, and in the surrounding hum of talk I made out two female voices, one high-pitched and the other low. I felt immensely relieved, though I wasn't thinking of Vittoria. I seemed to be back in my childhood, when my mother and her maids used to lift me out of the bath and dry me in warm towels. I seemed to be living that delightful experience all over again. Women I couldn't see, with sweet, musical voices, were rubbing me briskly down and bringing back life and warmth to my body. Then one of them dressed the wound in my thigh so carefully the pain was quite bearable. But it did serve to bring me round a little, and, still quite dimly, I began to make out two faces leaning over me, one fair and one dark. I couldn't make out the colour of their eyes, but I could see the expression, which was gentle, anxious and friendly. I made an effort to smile, but found to my regret that I couldn't. It was as if my face muscles were frozen.

One of the women dried my hair and put a cushion under my head. Then they both disappeared. I had a horrible sense of being abandoned, but it didn't last long. Almost at once someone raised my head again and a man's voice said, "Drink, my lord, it will do you good." My eyelids flickered, and this time I recognised Marcello quite clearly, though I still didn't realise where I was or what I was doing there. I took several deep draughts, but then to my great surprise the receptacle was taken away. I was very annoyed with Marcello and was beginning to frown, but when the rim of the tankard was put to my lips again and more of the warm, sweet, rough liquid poured down my throat, I kept my eyes shut until I'd drunk the last drop. Then I opened my eyes wide and emerged at last from darkness into a dazzling light. I recognised Vittoria.

It couldn't have produced a greater effect on me if I'd been a hermit praying in his cave and the Virgin Mary had suddenly appeared to me wearing a halo. Vittoria's face seemed to radiate all the beauty in the world. As I looked at her with love changing into adoration, she leaned over me with a mild and motherly air and spoke. I could tell from the intonation that she was asking a question, though I couldn't actually understand a word. But the music of her voice was so soothing and consoling I felt myself melting with happiness just to listen to it.

With a patience I found touching she repeated her question, and this time I understood the first couple of words: "My lord." I shook my head, and tried, by saying, "Paolo," to make her understand that I wanted her to call me by my Christian name. The one word cost me a great effort. She must have realised this, and, not wanting to cross me in my weakened state, smiled and replied: "Paolo."

She then repeated her question, and this time I understood. She was asking me if I wanted something to eat and drink. I nodded. But this didn't satisfy her.

"Say yes, Paolo."

I made an effort: "Yes."

She bent over me: "Yes, Vittoria."

I made another effort, looking up at her great blue eyes as they looked down at me, patient, indulgent and sweet: "Yes, Vittoria."

She seemed satisfied with that, gave me a ravishing smile, and went and busied herself by the fire. I then saw her body, which until then had been concealed from me, so to speak, by the nearness of her face. It was clad in a loose house gown, very like the one she wore long ago on the balcony in Gubbio. I followed her every step, her every movement. I felt that for me she took the place of all existence, and that I existed only through her.

She came back after a moment with a tumbler. She held it out to me but I didn't take it. I think I could have done, but I wanted to re-live the moment when she raised my head on her arm and held the tumbler to my lips. This she did. And my strength and awareness revived at the feel of her warm arm against my neck and at the nearness of her face and bosom, so that I enjoyed the experience much more intensely than before. This must somehow have communicated itself to her, for her breath began to come faster.

I didn't take the loaf she held out to me, either, though the mere sight of it made my mouth water: I hadn't eaten for some hours, which may have been one of the causes of my weakness. So she crumbled some bread into the sweetened warm wine in the beaker, and fed it to me with a little spoon – rather anxiously at first, then more certainly as she saw how greedily I swallowed it.

She fed me two or three little flat loaves, and watched me with delight as I ate. When I'd finished she went and put the beaker down by the fire, then came and knelt by me and wiped my mouth with a napkin. I seized her hand and kissed it adoringly.

"Oh Paolo!" she exclaimed joyfully, "you're moving at last! Your eyes are brighter! The colour's coming back into your cheeks!"

And bending over me she put her lips lightly on mine. I kissed her back, trembling lest she find my kiss too ardent and be shocked. But my arms settled the matter of their own accord. They quite involuntarily closed around her body, and with indescribable relief I felt it melt into mine.

157

When I woke up the next morning at dawn I wondered what I was doing stretched out on the rug in front of the fire. Then it all came back to me. As soon as I'd seen Marcello fall asleep the previous night I'd left him alone in the bed. He wouldn't have been comfortable with me there. It's too narrow for two.

I got up, my back hurting a bit from sleeping on the floor, and went and had a look at Marcello. A cannon ball wouldn't have woken him: I could cry out as much as I liked without making him hate me. But of course I had no reason to cry out now.

There were still some live embers under the ashes, and I rekindled the fire. Not that it was really cold, but the temperature might fall when it got light and I wanted the room to be nice and cosy when he woke up. The doublet and hose that he'd draped over the stools the night before were dry, but because of the sea-water they were stiff and covered with white streaks. They ought to be washed, or at least rinsed in fresh water and dried again. But I didn't dare do it unless he said so. He might need them in a hurry, to run away or hide.

I was glad to have him there, the brute, even with his sulks and foul temper. But at the same time I was frightened to death, and that's the truth! Those two had thrown themselves right into the lion's jaws. Just two of them, with a couple of daggers against forty arquebusiers! It would all end badly, I could feel it. What would my poor parents do when the priest in Grottammare announced from the pulpit that their daughter had been hanged for aiding and abetting adulterers? Would anyone in the village ever speak to them again?

The light began to creep through the shutters of my window, so as they were inside the glass I opened them a crack to see what the weather was like. The sky had cleared and there were patches of blue between the clouds. The sun would soon be above the horizon in the east.

Very gingerly, so as not to wake Marcello, I opened the window for a breath of morning air. Then, hearing a sort of rustling in the grass, I leaned out, and to my amazement I saw the Signora, a little cape thrown over her indoor gown, pacing up and down on the stretch of turf in front of the house. She threw her head back (which she ought not to have done, for it made the ends of her hair trail in the wet grass) and breathed deeply. How beautiful she was! A live statue of a goddess!

Perhaps she'd scold me, but I didn't care – I went out and joined her. But before I did so I parted the red silk curtain and had a peep into the other part of the room. The Prince was asleep, naked, on Vittoria's bed. I lingered a moment. What shoulders he had! What a "*boccone da re*",★ as my mother would have said. Not surprising, as he really was a prince. I slipped out quietly. Vittoria saw me, but far from scolding she seemed happy to see me. She was happy anyway. Everything delighted her that morning.

"Caterina," she cried, her eyes sparkling, "see how lovely the world is! And how lovely it smells! Of damp grass, and earth, and woodsmoke!"

As she spoke she came up to me, threw her arm round my shoulders and drew me close to her. It was the first time she'd ever done such a thing. I was quite overcome. But I knew which of us loved the other more. Still, then I was used to it. I'd always given more than I'd received.

"It smells of the sea, too," I remarked, just for something to say.

"The sea that brought him to me!" she whispered fervently to herself.

To hear her you'd have thought the sea had been created for that one purpose! I glanced at her out of the corner of my eye. My instinct told me she wasn't the same woman she'd been the day before. She looked like someone who'd gone to sleep in hell and woken up in heaven. I couldn't help feeling sad: what she'd experienced the previous night she'd have experienced long ago if she'd married someone other than Peretti. Poor Signor Peretti! Even in his own bed he'd had to obey the Cardinal! And now he'd lost his Signora, and for ever.

She was silent. Even though he wasn't present the Prince's arms were still about her and she was still clinging round his neck. And there we both were walking up and down the turf without a word while our men still slept. We were breathing in the air and the earth and I don't know what. The Signora was radiant. But she was absolutely unaware of the real situation. And if I'd told her all four of us might be killed within the hour she wouldn't have believed me.

She linked her arm through mine, and as she was half a head taller than

★ Morsel fit for a king

me I had to stand on my toes to be level with her. But when I saw her making for the rocky spur overhanging the cliff, I snatched my arm away and said: "I'm sorry, Signora – very sorry! But you wouldn't get me over there, not for a king's ransom! That huge drop underneath! You'd only have to slip on the wet grass and you'd smash your head in, ten fathoms below."

"*Come sei stupida, Caterina,*" she laughed. "Why should I slip? And where's the grass? It's all rock. Come on!"

"No, no, Signora, I can't! I'm sorry, Signora, but that spur looks so insecure! Sticking out like that! What if it gave under your weight?"

She laughed again.

"It could hold a hundred like me. Come along, Caterina!"

"No, Signora, I'm sorry. It gives me a stomach-ache just to watch you. Look, I'm trembling!"

"You really are trembling, silly little thing! Really, there isn't any danger!"

"Not for you perhaps," said I, retreating step by step towards the cottage. "But I've no head for heights – they draw me to them!"

"Come on!" she cried gaily. "It's just your imagination playing you tricks, Caterina! There's no danger! Look!"

As she spoke she advanced to the tip of the spur, which was no wider than the back of a stool. But the further she advanced the further I retreated! And finally I found myself with my back to the door of the cottage, trembling like a poplar leaf. She was absolutely certainly going to fall! I threw my skirt over my head – I didn't want to see her go, didn't want to hear the terrible scream when she felt the ground give way beneath her.

But even through my skirt I could hear her keep saying, "Come on, come on, Caterina!", and her teasing laughter. And then, suddenly, nothing! I uncovered my head.

The Signora was standing upright on the very tip of the spur. Her long fair hair, gilded by the rising sun, floated out behind her in a little breeze that flattened her gown against her body. But she wasn't laughing any more. She was pale and frowning, and her blue eyes were blazing, fixed haughtily on someone to the left of me. I turned and saw Signor Peretti, bareheaded and beside himself with anger, advancing with drawn sword at the head of a dozen arquebusiers. He halted, and the soldiers halted fifteen paces behind him.

"Madam," he said in a low, toneless voice, "the look-outs on the tower saw the wreckage of a boat in the creek this morning. One of them went down to collect the débris, and on a piece of the prow he saw the name of the galley it belonged to. The galley belongs to a nobleman I shall not name. I've come to make sure he's not hiding in your house."

Whereupon he made for the door of the cottage. When he found me standing there he looked at me in bewilderment, as if he'd never seen me before.

"My lord," said Vittoria, without raising her voice but pronouncing each word with emphasis, "I will not tolerate your entering my quarters without my permission, and, worse still, accompanied by soldiers. So listen carefully. If you touch that door I shall jump off the cliff."

"Jump off the cliff?" murmured Peretti, turning pale.

"You heard what I said."

What struck me about this exchange was that neither of them shouted or stormed. They just spoke to one another quietly. It was almost as if they were trying not to wake the Prince. But the truth was, as I realised later, that they didn't want to be overheard by the soldiers, standing fifteen paces away with their ears flapping.

A long silence ensued. The hand Signor Peretti had reached out towards the door fell back to his side. To say he was pale is to put it mildly: his face was drained of blood. He looked at the Signora. I could tell what was going through his head. He knew his wife. He knew that if he opened the door she'd do what she'd threatened to do. And of course he had no doubt by now about whom he'd find inside, at his mercy.

Madonna santa! He was frowning, his hand was moving forward again. He was going to open the door.

But no! He didn't open it. He fell back a pace and sheathed his sword, though his hand shook so much he had difficulty finding the scabbard. Then he swept Vittoria a low bow and said with dignity, in a low but firm voice: "Don't worry, Vittoria. I've never been cruel to you yet, and I'm not going to start now, however much circumstances may seem to force me into it."

Then he turned on his heel and left, followed by his men. Vittoria

161

looked after him with an expression I'd never seen on her face before. She, who'd just been so bold, was trembling in every limb. Without a word she stretched out her arms to me as if she needed my help to get back on firm ground. And I went and got her! I, who've got such a bad head for heights!

Somehow, heaven knows how, with the one dragging the other, we were both safe and sound at last outside the door again. Then the Signora took me in her arms, hugged me with her cheek against mine, and whispered in a strangled voice: "Oh Caterina! How noble he was!"

Marcello Accoramboni

It was Peretti's noble gesture that spoiled everything. It's true that if he hadn't made it the Prince and I wouldn't be here to deplore his magnanimity. We'd both be dead with a sword through our hearts – dead, as Father Racasi would say, "in the filth of our sins". Vittoria would be lying broken to pieces at the foot of the cliff. And Caterina, though surviving for the time being, would have been handed over to the secular arm and hanged soon afterwards – the longest suffering for the one who least deserved it.

Peretti and his henchmen had made little sound, and the interview between Peretti and Vittoria made even less. What woke me up was the sound of my twin sister sobbing. Even when I was a child I couldn't hear her crying without tears coming into my own eyes, whether or not I knew the cause of her grief.

In this case her sobs were muffled twice, once by her own efforts to stifle them and once by the fact that they had to reach me through the door opening on to the cliff. But they were loud enough to rouse me and to wring my heart. I dressed in haste, and had scarcely finished when Vittoria came into the cottage, followed by Caterina. Vittoria drew aside the red silk curtain and came through to my side of the room. She glanced at me, then without a word took off her informal gown and began to dress properly.

Whatever Tarquinia may say, there's never been any false modesty between us, from when we were young until now. Anyhow, *la superba* has

162

never understood our relationship. She's always thought it equally scandalous that I won't touch or kiss Vittoria and that she is quite prepared to undress in front of me. Tarquinia doesn't realise there's no need for any posturings between us.

When she was dressed Vittoria went round to the other side of the curtain and, waving aside Caterina's help, sat down at her dressing-table. I knew what she was going to do. She was going to cover up the traces of her tears, and not only out of vanity but also because she was ashamed of having wept. Vittoria loves heroes, and sees herself as a heroic character. I noticed that all the time she was attending to her face she never once looked at the sleeping Prince. I find this all the more astonishing now I know what had just happened between her and Peretti out on the cliff.

When she'd finished she beckoned Caterina to come and brush her hair, which she did without uttering a word. There were two reasons for this unusual silence: the Prince being still asleep, and the look on Vittoria's face, which she could see in the mirror. As for me, I poked up the fire, and when the flames had revived went and sat in front of it on a little low chair. From there I could see Vittoria in *profil perdu*, as Raphael liked to draw his models: just the brow, the outline of the cheek and the upper part of the jaw, with the nose guessed at rather than seen. Her face looked like marble. I wondered what this stern expression signified.

Caterina's brush made hardly a sound, and I don't think it was so much that which woke Orsini as the tension between the three of us in the little room. I could see the Prince quite clearly. When he woke he immediately gave a start of joy at seeing Vittoria just a few feet away from him. He propped himself on one elbow, his eyes brightened, his whole face lit up with a smile. He suddenly looked much younger, and he said in a clear, cheerful voice: "I wish you good morning, Vittoria."

I glanced sharply at Vittoria. Apparently the Prince's greeting struck a very wrong note, for after a moment she said in a low, distant, toneless voice, without looking at him: "It isn't a very good morning, my lord. It very nearly started with a massacre."

Caterina stopped brushing. Orsini sat up, pulling the sheet over his nakedness. Vittoria swung round on her stool to look at him.

"What?" he said. "What do you mean, Vittoria? Were we nearly discovered?"

"Nearly!" she exclaimed. And in a voice seemingly devoid of any emotion she told him what had just happened out on the cliff between Peretti and herself. I listened in astonishment, and I could see Orsini heard it with growing uneasiness. For it was plain to him that the hero of this story was not himself, who'd risked his life to be with his lady, but Peretti, who had spared the guilty lovers when he had them at his mercy. I reflected that Peretti wouldn't have acted differently if he'd been the wiliest man on earth, for his clemency had completely reversed the situation in his favour. But the strange thing was, and all three of us were conscious of it, that he hadn't acted out of calculation or guile, but simply on an impulse of the heart.

When Vittoria had finished her account — which she gave with downcast eyes, in a flat voice and without adding any comment — she swung round again to her mirror and signed to Caterina to proceed with her task. She said no more. We didn't speak either, and all that was to be heard in the silence was the insistent swish of the brush on Vittoria's hair. All three of us were crushed by Peretti's magnanimity. Law, custom and honour bade him kill us. He had flouted them all to spare his wife, and incidentally us too.

I glanced at the Prince. His eyes were lowered and his powerful chest was heaving as if he found it difficult to breathe. As long as he was confronting the sea, storms, dangerous reefs or an unequal battle alone against forty other men, he was a hero. As soon as someone else refrained from meting him out his just deserts, he became a mere thief, robbing a husband of his wife's affections. He felt as if he were diminished in Vittoria's eyes. And so he was. He had only to look at her sitting at her dressing-table with that icy expression, and hear her addressing him ceremoniously as "my lord". Where were the "Paolo's", the "carissimo mio's" and the sighs of the previous night?

Poor Orsini, who'd lost everything just as he thought he'd won it, realised he was clasping only a memory and was beside himself with rage and despair. But fury is a poor counsellor, and although he wasn't really lacking in subtlety he set his teeth and said: "I don't accept Peretti's mercy. My mind is made up. I shall go and challenge him in his palace. Right away."

Vittoria's reply was devastating. "If I understand you correctly, my lord," she said with crushing scorn, not even deigning to look at him, "you propose to go and ask Peretti, who just spared you, to lend you a sword to kill him with. What courage! What a glorious feat, for you, the finest swordsman in Italy, to kill a mere amateur in fair fight" — she put a savage emphasis on the word "fair". "And how delicate of you, by doing that, to proclaim *urbi et orbi* that I yielded to your advances!"

She turned round, looked at him fixedly, and added deliberately: "Since we're talking of my honour, my lord, don't you think yours requires you to do nothing henceforward that might directly or indirectly threaten Signor Peretti's life?"

The Prince, thank God, now recovered himself. To the question that sounded the knell of all his secret hopes he made answer in a voice that was firm enough: "I do think so, indeed."

"Do you promise?"

"I promise, since you require it."

He had spoken coldly. He wasn't used to being treated as Vittoria had just treated him, and both his attitude and his tone indicated that he wasn't disposed to endure any more of it. Picking up his doublet and hose from where they'd been hung to dry, he parted the curtain and came round into the part of the room that I'd slept in myself.

After a moment I got up, went over and took the brush from Caterina, and began to officiate in her stead. It was a task that required close attention and the use of both hands: one to take a big swathe of Vittoria's tresses, the other to handle the brush so as not to add to the weight and pull of the long mane of hair. I'd been doing it since I was a child, and I loved the job. It was the only real contact I'd ever had with Vittoria. And it seemed to exert some kind of magic: I felt as if through those threads of gold I found my way more easily amid the labyrinth of her thoughts.

I looked at her in the glass. She was pale, her eyes were lowered, her face still. But her hands kept clasping and unclasping themselves in her lap.

"Haven't you been rather harsh?" I said quietly.

She glanced rapidly up and then down again, darting me a brief but very plain look in the mirror meanwhile. No, she wasn't harsh. She was only trying to teach herself to be so. Her mind was made up, and already she was suffering almost more than she could bear.

The Prince put aside the curtain, strode resolutely out of the other half of the room, and came and stood to the right of Vittoria. He was completely dressed, with his doublet buttoned up to the neck. His face was pale but firm.

"Madam," he said, "the finest gift is spoiled when the giver stops loving us. Allow me to return the jewel you gave me."

And he put the ring decorated with a V down on the dressing-table. Vittoria raised her eyebrows and gave me a black look in the glass.

"I didn't give you anything, my lord," she said.

"That's what it pleases you to say now, madam. To my infinite regret."

He'd spoken in a subdued voice and I saw Vittoria start. But I knew she wouldn't tell him how the ring had come into his possession. She did what she'd always done: she covered up for me.

"How is it," she asked in a gentler tone, "that I haven't noticed this ring on your finger since you've been here?"

"I've always worn it with the V turned inwards. I thought it more discreet."

This exchange had taken place in quite friendly, even tones, but they knew it was only a lull and that the storm would soon break over them again.

"My lord," Vittoria went on with an effort, "there can be no sequel to last night. I cannot be your wife, because I'm married already. And I won't be your whore."

"Madam," replied Orsini indignantly, "I've never thought of you in such terms."

"Your mistress, if you prefer."

"And you don't wish to be that any more?"

"No."

"Isn't it rather late to think of that?" he exclaimed in an outburst of fury. But he regretted it at once, for clasping his hands behind his back so hard I saw his knuckles whiten, he went and stood by the fire, shoulders hunched and head bowed.

"It's never too late to mend," said Vittoria haughtily.

"That's a question of morality which we won't discuss," Orsini answered in a low voice shaking with anger. "When I left my galley

166

yesterday evening, madam," he went on, "I told my mate that if I didn't return by dawn it would be because my boat had been damaged. In that case he was to wait until nightfall, and if he saw lights in your window again, send another boat to fetch us. Until then, may it please you to grant me your hospitality. I shall try to incommode you as little as possible."

She didn't answer. He bowed stiffly, drew back the curtain and went round to the other side again. I gave the brush back to Caterina and joined him. As he was occupying the only chair, I sat on the couch. He was leaning back with his powerful shoulders against the back of the chair, his long legs stretched out before him, staring into the flames.

I looked at the flames too. If I'd had the heart I'd have admired them. They came from a clump of heather root, which produces smaller, steadier flames than other kinds of wood. The root was round and solid like a skull, and out of the glow around its edges leapt little bluish, almost transparent will o' the wisps not more than a couple of inches high. Oh, it wasn't the grand passion, that crackles and flares. It was the low flame that can kill you by inches. But for us, though we had nothing else to look at, there was no question of dying. We were all too abjectly alive, and judging by the Prince's face, pretty humiliated to be so.

An hour later there was a knock at the door. Orsini didn't move and neither did I. If Peretti had changed his mind and the affair was going to be finished off ingloriously here and now, *Dio mio!*, so be it! I was weary of the frantic business called life. What did it all lead to, anyway?

But the knock heralded only a majordomo and some servants with a meal. The majordomo couldn't see us because of the curtain. And apparently he didn't suspect our presence, for he hung about chattering like a magpie.

When he'd gone Caterina brought us our share of the food. As I took the tray from her she stroked my hands. Did our ration come out of hers and her mistress's? Or had Peretti had extra amounts sent? I could see the Prince was dying to refuse the offer. After what had passed, wouldn't it be the last straw to take food and drink from Peretti? But on second thoughts he must have decided it would be childish and unrealistic to refuse, and silently, with downcast eyes, he began to eat, and with a good appetite too. It was a long time since the bread and wine

Vittoria had fed him last night.

Caterina, who hadn't shrunk from peeping through the curtain during the night, had told me of that poetic scene. Yes, Vittoria had fed the Prince with a spoon, like a baby! And now she'd cast him from her bosom as if he'd bitten her. I couldn't get over it. What changes of fortune the unfortunate Prince had gone through in a few hours! One after the other he'd been a tenderly nursed casualty, a babe, a cherished lover, and this morning a rejected one. What a farce human affection was! All love began and ended in our own heads. And our heads were as wild and empty as goat bells.

I thought that day would never end, and by the look of him the Prince felt the same. But where could he go? In front of the cottage was the sea, and behind it the castle grounds full of soldiers. And why should he risk his death now Vittoria had dismissed him? True, if *I* lost my sister's love I'd just as soon lose my life too. But Orsini didn't love Vittoria in the same way as I did. Witness the fact that he'd hated her just now when she treated him so cruelly. And now, in front of her fire, he loved and hated her by turns. For a day at least he was imprisoned in the worst of all jails — one shared with a woman who's stopped loving you. He thought she'd stopped loving him, anyway.

In the middle of the afternoon he turned to me and broke his silence.

"Marcello," he said, "I noticed there were some books on the other side. Will you ask if I can borrow one?"

I liked his impersonal way of putting it! I got up, raised a corner of the curtain and went round to "the other side". There, for some reason I don't understand, I delivered my message in a whisper. There weren't "some" books — there were three. Vitoria was holding one of them: the Petrarch. The others were on the mantelpiece. Vittoria looked up and stared at me as if I'd appeared from nowhere, and took an age to reply to my question. Caterina devoured me with her eyes meanwhile. She at least was a simple, straightforward creature: love certainly didn't begin and end in *her* head.

"Give him a book, Caterina," said Vittoria flatly.

"Which one, Signora?" asked Caterina, no doubt to remind me that she could read.

"Whichever you like."

This wasn't very gracious to the Prince, and didn't even give Caterina the chance to show off her learning. She fetched one of the other two volumes at random and handed it to me. It was Ariosto's *Orlando Furioso*.

I didn't know what Orsini was going to think of this choice, which wasn't really a choice at all, but I thought it rather unfortunate. Vittoria had made me read the poem long ago, when she was trying to educate me. It tells how Orlando, a proud paladin in the service of Charlemagne, underwent incredible dangers to win the love of the beautiful Angelica, only to be steadily rejected by her and lose his reason. Not very cheering in present circumstances. Still, Orsini was a cultivated man and a lover of the arts. Perhaps he'd enjoy it for the style.

The hours crawled by. The Prince was buried in his book. On the other side of the curtain Vittoria was reading too. The irony of the situation amused me. If Peretti had come in then he'd have been edified by the innocence of our pastimes.

I heaved a sigh of relief when it got dark and Caterina put a lot of lighted candles in the windows. An hour later I suggested to the Prince that I go down to the beach and wait for the boat, then come and tell him when it arrived. He agreed. I made my farewells to Vittoria, who received them coldly. She might have been angry with me about the ring. And I don't blame her. But if I exceeded her intentions I only translated her desires. Last night had proved it.

I'd scarcely got as far as the turf outside when the door opened behind me and Caterina ran out with a handkerchief that I'd left behind. I wouldn't be surprised if she'd stolen it herself as an excuse to see me alone. She threw herself into my arms and squirmed about trying to kiss me on the lips. I reckon she wouldn't have minded being laid there and then, on the grass. She always knows exactly what she wants, and with her attractions she'll never have any trouble getting it. I disengaged myself from the little octopus's tentacles, but not roughly. Strangely enough I was quite touched.

It was getting darker by the minute, but I climbed down safely to the beach and stood in front of the cave that had served us as a refuge. Despite its ferocity against us the night before, the sea, as fickle as all females, scarcely washed up as far as my feet.

I could see little in the dusk, but by straining my ears I could hear a

169

regular clicking noise which I soon recognised as the sound of oars: the boat sent from the galley to pick us up. It had managed to avoid the reef we'd struck ourselves. Of course, the sea had been too rough last night for us to steer properly.

In the darkness the boat was upon me before I could make out its shape. A shadow jumped into the water to prevent the boat scraping on the sand. As I approached the shadow drew back.

"It's me – Marcello."

I thought I knew the voice that replied.

"Geronimo?" I asked.

"Yes, Signore."

But it was only when our faces were almost touching that I really recognised him. He looked very scared to be there.

"I'll go and fetch the Prince."

"*Per l'amor di Dio*, be quick, Signore!"

"Don't worry, there's no danger!"

I groped my way back up the cliff. It was very strange, but although that was only the second time, I felt as if I'd been doomed to do it for ever. And while it was much easier now than it had been before, it still seemed mortally difficult. Perhaps because it was linked in my mind to failure.

As soon as I got to the top I dropped to my knees. There was a light in the window of the watch-tower overlooking the creek, and I could see the look-out's head silhouetted against the glow. Perhaps I'd spoken too lightly when I told Geronimo there was no danger. I didn't know if the rough grass by the cottage hid me from view – the candles in the windows lit up the turf quite brightly.

So I crawled as far as the door, glad I was dressed in black. As I tapped on the oaken panel I called: "Caterina, put out the candles and close the shutters, and then open the door."

She did as I said. The turf was plunged in darkness again, and I stood up and went in. Thank goodness the fires on the hearths had burned right down.

"My lord," I said. "The boat's here. But the look-out is on the alert. It's time to go."

Vittoria was standing by the fire. Orsini stood facing her. Despite all his experience of the world and his princely self-assurance, I had the impression he didn't know what to say or do. He made to kiss her hand, but it didn't come out to meet him.

"Madam," he said.

But he didn't go on. No words seemed suitable.

Finally he just bowed and straightened up again haughtily, then turned abruptly on his heel. When he reached the door Vittoria, till then as still and impassive as marble, stepped forward, halted, then said in a subdued voice: "Goodbye, Paolo."

The goodbye sounded final enough, but she had called him by his Christian name, and she hadn't done that since the scene with Peretti. Orsini turned his head, looked at her, and hesitated. Then he put an end to his own hesitation by marching resolutely out of the cottage. To put it plainly, he didn't dare go and take her in his arms. If you ask me, he was wrong there, clever as he is. It's no use being a great captain if you can't fathom female ambiguity better than that.

7

Caterina Acquaviva

After Marcello and the Prince had gone, the Signora insisted on going to the door to see they got away safely. The night was inky black and very cool for the time of year. We listened hard but couldn't hear anything, and all we could see were some little lights bobbing about out at sea: the Signora said they must have been lit on the Prince's galley to guide him back. We didn't go farther than the doorstep: there was still a light in the watch-tower and though it was faint we were afraid of showing up in it.

Back inside the cottage I helped the Signora undress and she went straight to bed. But when I'd nearly finished taking my own clothes off on the other side of the curtain she said she was cold, and asked me to come and get in beside her. Sure enough, I found her hands and feet were like ice. Mine were boiling hot. This always surprises the Signora, though it's really quite natural, seeing I'm running about all day and she doesn't do anything, not even put on or take off her own skirt by herself. It's very odd when you think about it – noblemen and noblewomen need a nursemaid to look after them from the cradle to the grave. They'd be lost without us.

As soon as I got into bed with her the Signora put her feet on mine and I got hold of her frozen hands and put them between my breasts. I didn't say anything though. I didn't want to annoy her with my chitchat – she was quite capable of turning me out again as soon as she was warm. And I preferred to stay. She was so beautiful and she smelled so nice. What a pity she wasn't just an ordinary girl like me. Then we could have spent most of the night talking about our menfolk.

But I was mistaken. She did talk about them, though not in the way I'd have expected.

"Tell me, Caterina," she said. "Last night – did you sin with Marcello?"

I wondered whether or not I should lie. I was sure she hadn't heard anything, but on the other hand I didn't think it wise not to tell her the truth. That's never really worked with her.

"Well," I said sanctimoniously," you know what Signor Marcello's like, Signora. When he wants something it's impossible to resist him."

"And of course," she said ironically, "you did put up a lot of resistance!"

"No, Signora, not much – resistance makes such a noise! And I didn't want to disturb you while you were asleep." I said that very innocently.

"Be quiet, you little witch," she said.

But she didn't sound really annoyed. And I was glad to have got back at her and shown I wasn't as stupid as she always made out. In bed we weren't a great lady and a chambermaid, only two women, even if I did use a certain amount of ceremony.

"Tell me, Caterina," she went on, "are you going to confess to Father Barichelli about having sinned last night?"

"Of course, Signora. I'm a good Catholic."

"But he'll want to know who you sinned with. Then what will you tell him?"

"The truth, of course, Signora."

"Will you really, Caterina?" she said, sounding very frightened. "Don't you realise the truth brings dishonour on me?"

"How is that, Signora?"

"Come now, Caterina – who's going to believe the Prince mounted all that expedition and launched a boat in the middle of a storm just so that Marcello could come and see you on the sly?"

I said nothing. So the Signora was under no illusion about the links between Father Barichelli and the Cardinal, nor about the priest's discretion. This conversation was like walking in a swamp – I was going to have to step carefully if I didn't want to get sucked under.

"I didn't think of that, Signora."

"And now I've made you think of it, what are you going to do?"

"I don't know, Signora."

173

"Come now, Caterina," she said crossly, "you must see you can't tell Barichelli who it was you sinned with."

"Who shall I say it was with, then?"

"Well, you could say it was a soldier! There are about forty of them in the grounds."

"What if he asks me his name?"

"The soldier didn't tell you."

I thought about it, and decided to be a bit awkward.

"Oh Signora!" I said. "What shall I look like, not knowing the name of the man I've granted my favours to?"

"Oh Caterina, don't start giving yourself airs! Can you swear to me it's never happened before?"

"No, Signora," I said firmly. "No. It never has happened to me before."

That was a lie. I lied first of all because I didn't like her accusing me of putting on airs, and secondly because even if she didn't believe me she'd never be able to check.

But I knew she was anxious, and I didn't want her to go on worrying too long: she was already disappointed enough at the way things had turned out. But I resisted a little bit longer so as not to give in too easily.

"I'm sorry, Signora," I said, "but I don't like the idea of lying to my confessor."

"Oh, it's not serious! You won't be lying to him about the fact – only about the person."

She was right. And anyway I'd never told the whole truth to my confessors, especially when they started going into details the way old Father Racasi did. Father Barichelli was more discreet, perhaps because he was younger. You might almost think he was afraid of me. He was the one who blushed when I told him about the naughty things I'd done.

"Very well, Signora," I sighed. "I'll do as you say."

"Thank you, Caterina – you're a good girl. Go to your own bed now. I'm sleepy."

I was disappointed that she hadn't said anything about the Prince. But it had been naïve of me to think she would. She asked me for my secrets, but she didn't tell me hers. Her hands were warm now, and even her feet were beginning to thaw out against mine. I'd served my purpose. Thank you, Caterina. Go to bed now, Caterina. I was furious and felt like crying. But if I cried now, all I'd get was "Don't be a nuisance, Caterina!"

"Goodnight, Signora," I said in a strangled voice.

"Goodnight," said she.

But as I sat up to get out of bed she caught me by the arm, drew me to her, and kissed me on the cheek.

And I quite melted! That's me all over! One little kiss on the cheek and I melt!

Next morning, after dressing with the utmost care, the Signora asked me to deliver a note to Signor Peretti. Unfortunately I couldn't read it on the way because it was sealed. But I soon saw its effects, for at ten o'clock Signor Peretti turned up at the cottage, alone and unarmed.

"Caterina," said the Signora, "go for a little walk in the grounds. I want to be on my own."

"In the grounds! With all those soldiers!"

"You needn't go far. Go on, Caterina, do as you're told!"

"Yes, Signora."

And on the pretext of going to fetch my cape I went round to the other side of the curtain and quietly unlocked the little door at the back of the cottage that opens into the woodshed. Then I went out of the front door, shut it behind me, and went round the house and into the woodshed. There I quietly lifted the latch of the little door, opened it an inch or two, and put my ear to the crack. I'd taken the Signora at her word: I hadn't gone far.

At first I couldn't hear a word, and supposed they must be very embarrassed at finding themselves face to face after what I'd seen happen the day before. I waited a minute or so. Finally one of them decided to speak first, and you won't be surprised to hear it was the Signora.

"Monsieur," she said, "I have been guilty of a few small offences against you, and I want to tell you exactly what they amount to. In Rome I received a letter from a great nobleman whom I'd met briefly at your uncle Montalto's house. I read the letter. It's true that far from answering it I burned it immediately. But it was wrong of me to read it, and I ask you to forgive me."

"Vittoria," said Peretti quietly, "it's a pity you didn't admit this wrong to me the day after you committed it."

175

"I did admit it the day after – to my confessor," said Vittoria with suppressed anger. "And the real pity is that you should have heard about it through his indiscretions. And that, having heard, you didn't say anything about it to me."

"But I didn't hear about it from Racasi!" cried Peretti – very tactlessly, if you ask me.

"From your uncle, then! What's the difference! What I say before God is repeated by the priest to the Cardinal and by the Cardinal to you! How despicable! And can you tell who it was that decided I should be cooped up first in the Rusticucci palace and then in this wilderness here, if it wasn't your uncle?"

"He's your uncle too, madam," answered Peretti sorrowfully.

"No!" cried Vittoria. "A thousand times no! He's no longer my uncle after the tyranny he's imposed on me through you!"

"But after all, madam," said Peretti more firmly, "events have shown our precautions had some justification. There's every reason to believe that the nobleman of whom we're speaking made a desperate bid to join you here."

"Bid!" cried Vittoria violently. "Was that the reason you tried to rush on me sword in hand with a score of your henchmen? If so, let me tell you that if there was a bid I swear to God it was neither instigated nor agreed to by me!"

When I heard that, I did admire the Signora! She'd managed to lie and tell the truth at one and the same time. Who'd have thought, to hear her, that Orsini had ever set foot in our cottage?

"And yet I repeat, madam," Orsini went on, "the wreck of a boat belonging to one of Orsini's galleys was found in our little creek."

"What does that prove?" said Victoria vehemently. "Nothing! Neither that the Prince was on the galley, nor that he was in the boat, nor that the boat succeeded in putting ashore. The fact that it was smashed proves rather the opposite."

"And yet," said Peretti, "you gave weight to my suspicions when you threatened to throw yourself off the cliff if I forced your door."

"Fie, sir," cried Vittoria scornfully. "How can you refer in my presence to the grotesque scene that so cruelly insulted me? The sudden incursion, the naked sword with which you threatened me, the

176

henchmen! It was enough to drive me mad! I didn't know what I was saying or doing. Of all the outrages I've suffered at your hands in the last month, that was by far the worst! How can you blame me for the senseless things I said in such horrible circumstances? And all for a letter burned as soon as read! And read without thought of harm, out of childishness, out of feminine curiosity! . . . For you can't seriously suppose, Francesco," she went on in a gentler voice, addressing him for the first time by his Christian name, "that I'm in the least interested in that cripple. A man I saw only for about a minute at your uncle Montalto's!"

Another silence. I admired the Signora but I didn't envy her. She must have had difficulty getting that "cripple" out.

As for Peretti, could he tell her she was lying when he had no proof of it? The proof he needed today was inside the cottage yesterday. And now it was gone and he'd never get it. All he had left was doubt.

How I'd have loved to be invisible in a corner of the room, to see them staring silently at each other like stuck pigs! I knew how the Signora would look: regal and dignified. But poor Signor Peretti — I couldn't imagine him!

"Madam," he said at last in a subdued voice, "you asked to see me urgently. Was it just to argue about this, or have you anything else to say?"

"Yes, Francesco," she answered calmly. "I want to ask you something. As I've just admitted, I made a mistake, and that mistake has made you suspect me. Francesco, if we return to Rome and I'm set free again, I swear to you as I hope to be saved that you'll never again have cause to doubt me."

Silence again. My neck ached from stretching out to hear what came next.

"Vittoria," he said uncertainly, "I'll think about it."

He didn't say any more. He just went. I heard the front door shut behind him. Then I scuttled as fast as I could out of the woodshed and round the house, only this time on the side by the cliff so as not to meet Signor Peretti. I sat and waited two or three minutes on the top step of the stairway down to the beach before going back inside to the Signora.

She was sitting in the chair with her hands clasped in her lap and her eyes fixed on the hearth, though the fire wasn't lit. It wasn't nearly so cool this morning.

I didn't know what to do. I pretended to tidy up the dressing-table, and then I just tore about, as the Signora puts it. Finally, so as not to get on her nerves, I sat down on the little low chair.

After a moment she looked at me and said: "We're going back to Rome, Caterina."

"Is that what Signor Peretti's decided?"

"Not yet. But he will."

"Are you glad, Signora?"

"Yes," she said. "I am."

And she went over to the window and leaned on the sill looking out at the sea with her back to me.

"Leave me, Caterina," she said.

I went round to the other side of the curtain and took the opportunity to lock the little door to the woodshed again. Then I lay down on my bed. It was sure to be some time before she called me. I knew what she was doing there with her elbows on the window sill and her head in her hands. She was weeping.

Marcello Accoramboni

In the boat going back to the galley I asked the Prince to grant me an interview alone before he said anything to Lodovico. He agreed, and as soon as we were on board he told his cousin he had to change his clothes and would see him later. Then he took me aft to the quarter-deck and asked me to wait. Five minutes later he came back and took me to his cabin, where I noticed at once that the curtains of his bunk were drawn. I deduced that his little Moorish slave girl was hiding behind them – the Prince had let me glimpse her once or twice, being rather Moorish in these matters himself – but as I knew through Folletto that she was fanatically devoted to him, her presence didn't stop me telling him what was on my mind.

"My lord," I said, "I suppose you intend to tell Lodovico your venture failed."

"What do you mean?" he asked, raising his eyebrows.

"That you found the lady less than pliable and she turned you down."

"Honour requires me to say that," replied Orsini at once, "if only to protect her reputation."

"But there's something else I'd like you to do too, my lord."

"Something else?"

"Yes, my lord. I'd like you to terminate my duties as your secretary."

At that he started and looked at me with a mixture of sorrow and anger. "What, you want to leave me, Marcello?"

"Only out of necessity, and with reluctance," I declared. "But it's absolutely necessary that I go. There are so many witnesses to your expedition here on the ship that before long the secret's bound to leak out. There'll be all sorts of conjectures. If you dismiss me when we get back to Rome it'll strengthen your version of the affair – the one that says you failed. And that version's the one that will do the least harm to Vittoria's reputation."

"But it would mean I wouldn't see you again," said the Prince sadly, looking away.

I knew what he valued in me most was my resemblance to Vittoria. Just the same I was touched, and replied warmly: "I'll always be entirely at your service, and you'll only have to ask for me and I'll come. You know you can always reach me through *il mancino*."

He looked at me, then came over and took me in his arms. And so we parted.

Next day as I was on the poop deck having some target practice with a pistol and a playing card, Lodovico came up and said loftily: "They say you're quite a good marksman, Accoramboni."

"Yes, Signor Conte. I'm not bad with swords either."

"I regret all the more that your low birth prevents me from crossing them with you."

"I don't know what you mean by low birth, Signor Conte. Birth is the same whether it be low or high. So is death."

"Still," he said mockingly, "I don't see the point of being such an expert fencer if one's not a nobleman."

"Unfortunately I have to be an expert: certain people dislike me."

"I take pride in being one of them," said Lodovico provocatively.

179

"Would you like to know why?"

"Signor Conte, if you want to be unpleasant, go ahead. Haven't you just said your birth exempts you from having to bother about me?"

"Exactly. I'd be demeaning my sword if I crossed it with yours."

"You're quite safe, then. I'm listening."

Upon which I concentrated my attention on loading my pistol. Then I walked over, fixed another card in the target, and came back and waited.

"*Primo,*" he said, "I think you're an intriguer who's wormed his way into the Prince's good graces out of self-interest."

"So far I've never accepted one piastre from him. Can you say the same, Signor Conte?"

"*Secundo*, I think you're a pimp who lives at the expense of a rich widow."

"You've said that before, and I've given you my answer."

"*Tertio*, I consider you a vile seducer."

"Your *tertio* is the most interesting charge, Signor Conte. Can you be more precise?"

"You tried to corrupt your own sister in order to deliver her over to the Prince."

"You're not subtle enough, Signor Conte. I helped the Prince gain access to Signora Peretti only so that he might see that her virtue is unassailable, and that there'd be no point in his having her abducted. After which I resigned from my post as his secretary."

"I already knew that."

"Is that why you're trying to provoke me?"

"It's one reason, but not the main one."

"You haven't yet told me what that is."

"No."

"You whet my curiosity."

"The main reason is that I can't stand such incredible arrogance in one who was born, like you, in the mud, of the people."

"And what are you going to do about it?"

"Chastise you."

"I don't see how, if you won't accept my challenge."

"The streets of Rome are dangerous, and accidents will happen."

"What sort of accidents, Signor Conte?"

"I don't know — a tile falling off a roof, a stabbing by a crazy passer-by. In short, Accoramboni, you might die from some quite fortuitous cause."

I turned the barrel of my pistol in the direction of his stomach and said with a gracious smile: "So might you."

He went extremely pale and fell back a pace, his hands in front of his belly with the palms towards me, as if to protect himself.

Then a voice said: "Marcello!"

I turned and saw the Prince's head appearing just above the level of the deck.

"Lower your weapon, Marcello."

"Certainly, my lord. But the Count of Oppedo took fright for nothing. The cur wasn't armed."

The Prince climbed slowly up the ladder to the deck, looked coldly at Lodovico and said: "You're behaving very recklessly, cousin. You refuse to fight Marcello, then insult him and threaten him with an accident. Do you want to suffer the same fate as Recanati?"

"My lord," said I with a little bow, "I have no intention of killing the Count of Oppedo. Having been born, as he puts it, in the mud and of the people, I'm too low for his insults to reach me."

"You see, Paolo!" cried Lodovico, "the rascal still defies me! And in front of you, too!"

"He's not defying you. He's making clever replies to your stupid insults. You should thank both of us — if you weren't my cousin he'd have put a bullet in your stomach by now. Marcello, go down to my room, please. I want to talk to you."

"With your permission, my lord, I'd like to empty my gun first. Accidents will happen."

"Very well."

I cocked the pistol, noticing out of the corner of my eye that Lodovico had edged a little way behind the Prince. My target was a playing card — a knave of spades, if I remember rightly — fixed in a cleft stick that I'd wedged in the lid of a chest.

I aimed carefully and fired. I hit the knave of spades right in the middle.

"You're a remarkably good shot, Marcello," said the Prince. "Yet strangely enough your hand is shaking."

181

"Yes, but my eye is accurate. It makes up for my hand."

I bowed to him, nodded to Lodovico who didn't respond, and went down the ladder. But at the bottom, instead of going straight to the Prince's room I stayed where I was and listened.

"Lodovico," said the Prince, "I don't understand you. All this is ridiculous. What are you up to? You've got this insane hatred for Marcello — as soon as you set eyes on him you started insulting him. What do you expect? Do you think he's going to go on all fours to you and lick your boots? You're a fool, cousin. You know the sort of man you're dealing with: Marcello's a *disperato* — he sets no value on his own life, he's afraid of nothing, he's ready for anything. I tell you again: if you weren't my cousin he'd already have put a bullet through you. Just like this playing card. Here, take it, keep it — it'll serve as a reminder. And if you're thinking of engineering an accident, drop it. I'd never forgive you."

I don't know how Lodovico answered this reprimand, for hearing footsteps overhead I hurried along to the Prince's cabin. I knocked before I went in, not wanting to disturb the little Moorish girl, and it was a good minute before Folletto came and let me in. As soon as I was admitted to the holy of holies I noticed the curtains of the bunk were drawn. Since I was hungry, I also observed that the table was laid for two. I looked at Folletto, raising my eyebrows and pointing to my stomach. He nodded: Yes, the Prince had invited me to eat with him. I was amused to think how this would make Lodovico hate me more than ever.

The Prince came in and signed to Folletto to withdraw. Then, as always, he came straight to the point.

"Marcello," he said, "I heard the beginning of your conversation with my cousin, and I was very struck by something you said. You said, 'I helped the Prince gain access to Signora Peretti only so he might see that her virtue's unassailable.' Tell me, please — was that really your reason?"

"No. What I said then was the truth as adapted for Lodovico."

"And what is the truth as adapted for Marcello?"

I looked him in the eye, thought for a moment and said: "As far as I can make out, the truth is that I serve Vittoria's desires but wouldn't act against her will."

"And what would you do if her desires got the better of her will?"

"If that was clear beyond all possible doubt, I'd serve her desires."

The Prince put his hands behind his back and paced back and forth as well as he could in the confined space. Then he looked at me and said nothing. From what had just been said I concluded he hadn't given Vittoria up. I can't say I was particularly surprised.

Then: "Sit yourself down!" he said, suddenly cheerful, nodding me to a chair at the table and clapping his hands to summon Folletto.

"Marcello," he went on, "one more question. If I hadn't interrupted when your pistol was aimed at Lodovico, would you have shot him?"

"No, but I wanted to. And at one point I nearly did."

"When?"

"When he started saying I'd corrupted my sister. If he'd said one more word against her I'd have fired. But he's shrewd enough to know that — that's why he didn't go on. As a matter of fact he's careful to keep all his taunts from going too far. He's really just a coward."

"That's what makes him dangerous," said the Prince. "Watch out for yourself in Rome, Marcello."

Caterina Acquaviva

To say I was glad to be in Rome again is putting it mildly! I couldn't see myself spending months at Santa Maria, especially as we didn't have any good weather all the time we were there. It was as if blue skies and a hot sun had been waiting for us back in the courtyard at the Rusticucci palace. What's more, in Santa Maria I'd spent only one night with Marcello in a whole fortnight, and in Rome I was almost certain to see him more often.

But if the Signora was pleased to be back in Rome and free again, she didn't show much sign of it. She was neither cheerful nor sad. She didn't talk much. Most of the time she seemed to be dreaming. She took her meals with the rest of the family and no longer shut the door of her room against Signor Peretti. But nor did she quite open it when he asked to go in. She kept me with her, and though she spoke to him nicely she didn't encourage him to stay. I felt quite sorry for him, sitting wretchedly there in a corner, talking of this and that and not daring to claim his rights as a husband. If you want my opinion, I think he was a bit too considerate. No man in Grottammare would behave like that with his wife! He'd better not try!

Sometimes the Signora herself seemed rather embarrassed at the way she was treating her husband, but not to the point of opening her arms to him. She must have been put off him in the Prince's embrace, and was making him pay for forcing her to choose him instead of her hero. That's what we women are like when the devil gets us by the innards – too kind to the one and too cruel to the other.

We hadn't been in Rome a fortnight when one day I was in the Signora's room brushing her hair and in came Marcello without even knocking. *Madonna mia*! My heart started to pound just at the sight of him! But do you think the wretch so much as brushed my hand or gave me a single glance? It was the same with his sister – hardly a look at her in the mirror as he stood behind her fumbling in his doublet for a letter. He put it down on the Signora's jewel box without a word.

"Who is it from?" said she without batting an eyelid.

"Can't you guess?" he answered coldly. "Do I have to explain?"

She didn't hesitate for an instant. She seized the letter, held it briefly in the flame of one of the candles, then set it down in a saucer and watched it burn. Her guardian angel must have been pleased. Still, I'd have been a bit worried in his shoes. She'd burned the letter, but she hadn't forbidden her brother to go on acting as an intermediary between herself and the Prince. She'd have been afraid he might obey.

Marcello took leave of her at once, if you can call it that: he just nodded and went. He didn't look at me, either. I went on brushing with a heavy heart, not knowing if I'd dare go to his room when I was free. I didn't have much time to wonder, for after a few moments the Signora said in a subdued voice: "That will do, Caterina. Go to bed."

"But Signora, I've only half finished!"

She looked daggers at me. "Don't argue! Do as I tell you!"

In spite of that I did stay long enough to tidy the dressing-table, though not long enough to make her angry. She sat looking at the ashes in the saucer as if by some magic this might turn them back into the letter she hadn't read. But only the devil could do that, and after what had happened at Santa Maria who could blame him for staying in the background for a bit?

"Goodnight, Signora."

That was just formality — I'd be surprised if she did have a good night. She didn't answer; she hadn't heard me. And just as I was going out of the door it struck me she'd sent me away not because she wanted to be alone, but rather because she hoped I'd go and see Marcello and get him to tell me what she hadn't dared ask. As I've got such a kind heart I was only too glad to do this errand, not to mention to have such an excellent excuse for going to see Marcello.

He'd nearly finished undressing when I went in, without knocking. He's so handsome my throat went dry and my legs started to tremble with longing. But I got an icy welcome.

"What are you doing here?" he said with a scowl.

"With your permission, Signore, I've come to see you."

"My permission? Did I ask you to come?"

"No, Signore."

"And is this a public place, that you just march in without knocking?"

"I didn't like to knock, Signore."

"'Didn't like to'? Why not?"

"If I had you would have asked who it was."

"Naturally. So?"

"I was afraid if I said who I was you'd tell me to go away!"

"Well, I'm telling you to go away now. What's the difference?"

"The difference is that I've seen you," said I humbly. But at the same time my eyes were boldly looking him up and down.

He laughed. It looked as if I'd won. But I knew that with him everything could suddenly be lost at the last minute, so I persevered in my humility. There's not a slave girl in Rome more slavish than I can be! Pride? — you know what you can do with that!

"Take your clothes off," he said.

I had so many buttons to undo that my hands shook with impatience.

"Do you know what you are, Caterina?"

"No, Signore."

"The most clinging octopus in creation."

"Yes, Signore."

"Do you know what an octopus is?"

"Yes, Signore. I caught a little one once at Grottammare. They cling to you with their tentacles. But if you twist their heads round they let go."

"Unfortunately I can't twist your head round."

Fat lot I cared what he said. What mattered was he'd said it in a low, sibilant voice and looked at me with those eyes of his, like a tiger's. I waited with delight for him to leap on me, drag me into his lair by the scruff of the neck, and devour me.

Which he did. When it was over, instead of saying, "Go away now, Caterina, I'm tired," he seemed inclined to jest for a bit. He propped himself on his elbow and delivered himself of a string of insults – but his voice was soft and his eyes were kind. It was now or never.

"Signore, may I ask you some questions?"

"Fire away."

"Are you still with the Prince?"

"No. I've left him. I'm not his secretary any more."

"So have you gone back to live with your old woman?"

His eyes darkened and he gave me a box round the ear. A good one. Richly deserved. "That'll teach you to be disrespectful to Signora Sorghini. And to me."

"Sorry, Signore."

"Anyhow, I never left her. The only difference now is that I don't go to Montegiordano any more."

"So how did the Prince get the letter to you?"

He shrugged. "Can't you guess who was the go-between?"

"Yes."

"So why ask stupid questions? Do I ask you questions?"

"Signore," I said, rather vexed, "you might well ask me how I confessed the sin I committed at Santa Maria."

"But I don't. I presume you didn't mention my name."

"You see, Signore – I'm not as stupid as all that!"

He laughed, rolled me over on my back and lay on top of me, gripping my wrists and holding my arms outspread. Then he knocked his forehead against mine, rubbed noses with me, and said through clenched teeth: "Yes, Caterina, you *are* stupid! And ugly too! Very ugly! The ugliest girl in all Italy! And your breasts are as shapeless as a sack of wheat on a donkey's back."

He looked at me with his tiger's eyes, and all I could think of was "Rape me!" It's delightful to be raped by a man you love! But then of course it's not really a rape. Nothing's perfect.

The following evening on the stroke of ten, as I was brushing the Signora's hair, Marcello came again. You must be wondering why I brush her hair at night and not in the morning. But I do both. At night I brush it before I plait it into a couple of braids — loose enough not to pull on her scalp but tight enough to prevent her hair getting tangled in her sleep. In the morning I brush it again to undo the plaits and make them "melt into a single rippling mantle." That's how Signora Tarquinia describes it.

Well, my Marcello appeared again without knocking — despite his reproaches to me — and without a word or a glance for anyone put a sealed letter down on the jewel box. Immediately, as if she'd been waiting all day for this moment, Vittoria picked it up, set light to it in the flame of one of the candles, put it down in a saucer and watched it burn. We all watched it burn.

Not a word from anyone. The Signora didn't tell Marcello not to bring any more letters, and Marcello didn't say it was hardly worth his trouble to do so. He just nodded and left. And later, when I went and tried to talk to him, he told me roughly to be quiet.

The same silent scene was repeated the next night, and the next, and so on for a week. I wondered what the Prince found to say all the time. He must often have repeated himself.

On the eighth day — a Friday if my memory serves — there was an important change. Marcello spoke. When the daily letter had duly been reduced to a heap of ashes, he glanced at the Signora in the mirror and said dryly: "What a farce! Don't expect me to keep it up indefinitely!"

And the next day, Saturday, it was in vain that the Signora let the brushing go on and on instead of telling me to stop and braid her hair. Finally, at eleven o'clock, when my arms were nearly dropping off, I started to do the plaits of my own accord. Her face in the mirror was impassive, and I couldn't see the expression in her eyes because she kept them lowered, but I could tell the Signora was as unhappy as I was that Marcello hadn't shown up, though not for the same reasons. She must have been wondering whether it was because he'd had enough of watching her just burn the letters, or if it was the Prince himself who'd got tired.

On the days that followed we still waited for Marcello in vain. It was a horrible time for both of us. Sometimes the Signora was so agitated she got angry with me for nothing; sometimes she just lay face down on the bed with her head buried in the pillow, refusing to go down to meals and closing her door again on Signor Peretti.

Finally at eleven o'clock on the Thursday evening — we'd got into the habit of sitting up — Marcello came in, nodded to the Signora at her dressing-table, and — a thing he'd never done before — sat down on the bed with his legs apart and his hands clasped between them. And he stayed like that for a good quarter of an hour, with his head bowed and not saying a word, while the Signora fidgeted about on her stool, biting her lips.

But bite them as she might she could finally hold out no longer, and said in a quavering voice: "Haven't you brought anything?"

"What do you mean, 'anything'?" said he, looking up.

"Don't pretend you're surprised!" she cried angrily. "You know very well what I mean!"

"I know. But I'm still surprised. I brought you a letter from the Prince every night for a week and each time you burned it. Tonight I don't bring anything and you ask me for a letter. What for? To burn it? No wonder I'm surprised!"

"I don't care a rap if you're surprised or not! Tell me straight out: did the Prince give you a letter for me?"

"Yes."

"Well, what are you waiting for? Give it to me!"

"So that you can burn it?"

"It's none of your business what I do with it! You're just supposed to give it to me, that's all!"

"Unfortunately I can't," he said casually.

"What do you mean, you can't?"

"I burned it myself!"

"You burned a letter addressed to me!" she cried, beside herself. "But that's disgraceful!"

"Why? Isn't that what you'd have done with it yourself?"

"That doesn't matter — you had no right! It was my letter!"

"Not at all," said Marcello calmly. "As you weren't going to read it it wasn't anyone's letter. A letter's written to be read. If you burn it instead of reading it, it isn't a letter any more — it's just paper."

"But it was for me to decide whether I read it or not!"

"What do you mean — 'decide'? Your decision's already made — no question about it! For a whole week, without hesitation, you've burned every letter I've brought you. And you know very well you'd have done the same today."

"But it's I who'd have done it!" cried the Signora.

"Come, Vittoria," he said patiently, "this is childish. I was just as capable as you of reducing today's letter to ashes. And that's what I've done with them all."

"What do you mean — 'all'?"

"The Prince has written to you every day since Friday. Six letters altogether. I thought I was obeying your wishes. I burned all six of them."

She stood up, pushed me aside and faced him, her eyes blazing: "You're a scoundrel!" she cried. "You'd no right to do such a thing! You've betrayed the Prince's confidence!"

"Write and tell him so!" he mocked. "I'll deliver the note!"

"Get out!" she cried.

And she snatched the brush out of my hand and threw it at him. But he ducked and she missed. He picked up the brush, put it back carefully on the dressing-table, then left without a backward glance.

He'd scarcely closed the door than she threw herself down all anyhow on the bed, not bothering about her hair. I could see at a glance that all my brushing was wasted!

But I was flabbergasted as well as annoyed. Close as Vittoria and Marcello were to one another, they often quarrelled. But never before had I seen them have such a violent row. The poor Signora was sobbing on the bed, her lovely face buried in the pillow. I didn't know what to do. Should I leave her and go and see Marcello in his room? Or stay and try to comfort her? I didn't really have much choice. It was up to her to dismiss me or not. And because we'd been waiting up for Marcello she hadn't sent me to bed till eleven o'clock for six days! That was a long day's work! It was true I didn't really have all that much to do, and it was certainly better to be a lady's maid in the Rusticucci palace than the wife of a master fisherman in Grottammare. I knew how they treated their women. More clips round the ears than kisses . . .

There was a knock at the door. The Signora took her head out of the pillow and said: "Don't open. Ask who it is."

I did so.

"It's Signora Accoramboni," said an authoritative voice.

"I'm sorry, mother – I can't see you," said the Signora firmly. "I've got a bad headache."

"I don't really like talking to you through the door, but I want to ask you a favour. My maid's ill. I'd like you to lend me yours to undress me."

"I'm afraid that's impossible. I don't lend my maid."

"That's not very gracious of you, Vittoria."

"I am as you've made me. Get Giulietta to help you undress."

"She's asleep."

"Undress yourself then. You've got all your arms and legs."

"Vittoria! You treat your mother like the fifth wheel of a coach. You're a monster of rudeness."

"So you've often told me. Goodnight, mother."

"Your night can only be a bad one after the way you've treated me."

"Don't worry – it will be. Goodnight, mother."

I could hear *la superba* crossing the ante-room where I slept when the Signora really was unwell. She slammed the door angrily and flounced out on to the gallery. I was glad the Signora had put her in her place.

"Caterina," said the Signora behind me, "do you think Marcello really did burn those letters?"

I turned round. "Perhaps not," I said. I hadn't any idea. I said "not" to please her, and "perhaps" to be on the safe side.

"You know what a tease he is . . ."

"Yes, Signora."

"Caterina, go to his room, please, and if he's there bring him back to see me."

"Yes, Signora."

I went towards the door, but just as I was going to turn the handle it opened of itself and Marcello burst through like a jack-in-the-box. After what had happened you might have expected the Signora to give him a cool reception. But not a bit of it. She gazed at him anxiously. He looked round and took in everything: the Signora lying on the bed, her lovely hair in tangles, her eyes red, a tear-drenched handkerchief in her hand. And he said to her wryly: "The 'fifth wheel' says you're a monster of rudeness. I regard Flaminio as a monster of devoutness and Giulietta as a monster of chastity. And you regard me as a monster pure and simple. But don't think you're an exception, Vittoria. You're the most interesting specimen in the whole family: you're a monster of wilful blindness. As soon as a fact is inconvenient you tuck your head under your wing and pretend it doesn't exist."

"What does all that mean?" asked the Signora, but with much less resentment than I'd have expected.

She was obviously handling him with care, afraid of what he might say.

"Nothing unkind. I'm never cruel to you except to be kind – for instance, to stop you lying to yourself, which in the long run could endanger your soul. I didn't burn your letters, Vittoria. I even numbered them so that you could read them in chronological order. Here they are."

And he took them out of the pocket in the armhole of his doublet and threw all six of them on to the bed. The Signora was overcome. You'd have thought those letters were a holy sacrament. She didn't dare touch them at first. But when she finally made up her mind to she didn't even try to conceal her eagerness. She just seized the letter marked with a 1, broke the seal with trembling fingers, and devoured it.

"Well, you've plenty to keep you occupied," said Marcello. "So I'll leave you. I have to see someone. I'll be back in an hour."

She didn't answer. She hadn't heard. She didn't even notice him go out.

"Caterina," she said without looking up, "bring a candlestick closer."

It didn't even occur to her she'd be better off sitting reading them at the dressing-table than lying on the bed. I could tell this was going to take a long time, a very long time because no doubt she'd read every letter more than once, so I moved a low table close to the bed and brought one of the candlesticks over from the dressing-table.

Then I sat down on a stool in a corner, leaned against the wall and watched her. I envied her. When a man takes the trouble to write to you every day it means he really adores you. I can't think of anyone who'd do that for little me. Of course, I'm much more get-at-able. Can you see a Pope and a Cardinal mustering forty soldiers to guard my virtue?

The Prince would have gone wild if he could have seen her then, lying there in her nightgown with her arms and a good part of her bosom bare. I noticed her breasts were as firm as mine, only not so big. I don't say that to criticise — just to do myself justice. The Signora's a hundred times better-looking than I am; quite simply she's a pearl of a woman. Especially like that: reading the letters over and over, wrapped in her long hair (two hours' brushing for me tomorrow), her lovely face flushed with emotion, her cheeks shaded by her long lashes, her bosom rising and falling.

Time passed. Fascinating as I found the situation, I couldn't help feeling sleepy. But I wasn't going to interrupt the Signora to ask if I could go: she looked too absorbed. Or was I staying on out of self-interest? Marcello had said he had to see someone, so he wasn't in his room.

There's something diabolical about Marcello. You've only got to mention or even think of him and he appears. He pops up in the Signora's room without even knocking at the door. It's true they're twins and don't mind if the other one sees them without any clothes on. The contrast with family modesty at Grottammare! There everyone's shocked if you show an inch of bare skin! And the acrobatics to get out of your nightgown and into your day clothes without letting anyone see anything! I remember as if it was yesterday the slap and the scolding I got from *il mancino* one morning because I got out of the bed I shared with him and crossed the room naked. I was only ten years old, and thought he'd like to see the little body he caressed every day. Yes, but the caressing took place at night, and under the bedclothes, and while both of us pretended to be asleep.

So in came my Marcello, and as the Signora looked up inquiringly he said point-blank: "There's more than one way into Margherita Sorghini's house. In the days when she didn't want anyone else to know about our liaison, I used to go in through a back way, off a little cul-de-sac only just wide enough for one person. On the left there's a small porch opening straight into a corridor, and the corridor leads to a little chapel that Signora Sorghini has turned over to some mendicant friars. She's very pious, and acts as their patron. The chapel's open to the public, but hardly anyone goes there. And further down the corridor there's another door. It's painted dark green, and here's the key to it."

He threw it adroitly into the Signora's lap.

"If you open that door you'll find a staircase, and if you have the patience to go up three flights of stairs you'll come out on a flat roof where Signora Sorghini has had a tent put up, with curtains to keep out the sun and the wind and prying eyes. It's a charming spot, surrounded by lots of red and white geraniums, and if you go there tomorrow during Vespers you can rest without being disturbed. Signora Sorghini won't be there — she and I leave tomorrow at dawn for her house at Amalfi, to enjoy a month's sea breezes."

After that he left, without so much as a glance at me. The Signora seized the key, and not just between finger and thumb. She clasped it to her bosom with her whole left hand, and her right hand round that to make doubly sure it was safe. Oh, that little key wasn't going to run away! It was so cosy there between her breasts!

"Signora, may I go now?"

"Goodnight, Caterina," she said absently, staring into space with a faint smile on her lips.

I went to Marcello's room. It was empty — the wretch hadn't even waited to say goodbye to me. I looked round incredulously. The place couldn't have been emptier. Worse still it was going to be empty for a month, since he was leaving at dawn with his old woman. I said it again: his old woman! I'd say it a hundred times if I liked!

If I'd been the Signora I'd have thrown myself on Marcello's bed and buried my face in the pillow. But that's not my way. I blew out the candle he'd left burning, went out on the balcony and leaned with my stomach against the balustrade. There was a fine moon and down in the patio I could see our little white cat lying full length with her claws out. She was scratching at the ground and growling, with her eye on a male tabby hiding under a bush. Where had he sprung from? Where had she found him? She was growling, our little Moujoute, ready either to scratch the tom or accept him. But anyhow, when he'd taken her he wouldn't get away without a good clout. And serve him right! The tears were streaming down my cheeks. I wiped them away. But that's how it was

193

with my mistress and me: when one laughed the other wept.

Lodovico Orsini, *Count of Oppedo*

I nearly fell for it. But only nearly. I'd had my suspicions from the start, knowing Paolo and being pretty sure that if necessary the vile Marcello could give his master points in Machiavellian cunning. And when I went and reported to Francesco de' Medici in Florence, he was sceptical too.

"Women being what they are," he said, "that is, virtuous only when they're forced to be, it's hard to believe Paolo found Vittoria intractable and only slept beside her like a brother. Especially as up till now he's never had a heart or body refused him in the whole of Italy! And he's a fine-looking fellow, not to mention being the sort of hero the weaker sex dote on! What's more, would Paolo have boasted about it if he really had failed?"

I too thought the whole thing looked like a put-up job, and that Marcello's dismissal was very likely just a trick. Paolo showed such affection for the scoundrel, inviting him to his own cabin on the ship and leaving me, his own cousin, to eat with the mate!

Medici gave me ten thousand ducats for my trouble and to cover the expenses I'd incurred in coming to see him. He asked me to keep a close eye on what happened, so that Virginio's inheritance wasn't ever threatened by his father's remarrying. I saw Virginio several times while I was in Florence, and with an eye to the future tried to get into his good books. In spite of his youth I found him thoughtful, cool and cautious, seeing much and saying little. In short, a Medici already, with none of the legendary Orsini rashness. He didn't give me one piastre. But perhaps he knew his uncle had already paid me. Not that I considered the Medicis rewarded me adequately for my services. But as Paolo had made up his mind not to give me another penny, I had no choice. I wished I was still with him, though. I don't really like the Medicis. They smell too much of banks and trade.

Back in Rome I put a spy on Paolo's tail, selecting him with care from among the outlaws I gave bed and board to in my palace. This was in contravention of papal law, since as a member of the younger branch of the Orsini I don't have the right of asylum, as I think I've said before. An injustice if ever there was one!

The man I chose was a monk who'd had to renounce the cloth to escape being sent to ecclesiastical prison. But I got him to wear his habit again to trail the Prince, for Rome is full of monks and nothing escapes notice so easily. Also, while a mask attracts attention, no one looks twice at a cowl modestly pulled down over the eyes to ward off worldly temptation.

As Paolo often went out on horseback I provided the monk with a mule. It couldn't have kept up with the Prince's horses on the highways outside Rome, but inside the city, with its congested traffic, it managed very well. As Vittoria Peretti had given up riding, or at least so I'd heard, I had reason to suppose that if the two of them met it must be in some discreet spot in Rome itself.

Over a week went by without the monk's pursuit bringing any result whatever. But on the ninth evening he asked to see me and presented himself with his hands shaking, his eyes staring, and his knees practically knocking together.

"Signor Conte," he said, "I've found out what's going on. But I'd be obliged if you'd relieve me of my task. If I don't desist I'm a dead man."

"And what is going on, Giacomo, and where?"

"It's in the widow Sorghini's house."

"Good heavens! What a coincidence!"

"There's a cul-de-sac behind the house with a porch in it. The porch gives on to a corridor, which leads first to a little chapel that's kept unlocked and then to a dark green door that's kept locked. The Signora has a key to the green door, and so has the Prince."

"And where's the danger to you?"

"It's a mortal danger, Signor Conte. I shan't escape it twice. When I saw the Prince go into the corridor I waited a few minutes and then followed. As he wasn't in the chapel I knew he must have gone through the green door. So as I'm very religious by nature, I knelt down at the front of the chapel and started to pray . . ."

"Spare us your piety, Giacomo!"

"It didn't prevent me from watching the door of the chapel, Signor Conte."

"How could you see it, kneeling in the front?"

"I'd made a hole in the back of my cowl so that I could see if I turned my head."

"And what did you see?"

"A signora coming in, followed by her maid. Both were masked and hooded, and wearing long cloaks down to their ankles in spite of the heat. But when the signora knelt down and crossed herself, some of her hair showed under her cape, long as that was, and I knew who it was."

"They were praying, I suppose."

"Fervently but briefly. And when they got up and left the chapel I followed. But before I got through the door someone burst out of a confessional, shot out a huge arm and grabbed me by my cassock. He pinned me against the wall with his other hand and stuck the point of a dagger under my chin. 'What are you doing here and where are you going?' he hissed. 'As you can see, Signore,' I said humbly, 'I'm a monk and I often come here to pray. Signora Sorghini has put her chapel at our disposal.' 'Monk?' says he. 'We'll see about that!' And he tore off my cowl and felt my tonsure. Thank God I'd thought to go to the barber's, so it was as smooth as an egg. But that wasn't enough for him — he went on to search my pockets. He only found a rosary and a few religious medals I'd put there on purpose, but he was still suspicious. He made me recite the *pater*, the *ave*, the *credo* and the *confiteor* in Latin. But I didn't make a single mistake. And believe me, Signor Conte, it's a long time since I prayed so hard."

"Well, your prayers were answered: you're still here."

"This time he let me go — yes. But it would be folly to tempt fate again."

"Who do you think it was?"

"One of the Prince's men, there to protect the Signora."

"How can you be so sure?"

"Signor Conte," said Giacomo proudly, "I may be afraid, but I'm not a coward. I stayed and waited for the wretch, and trailed him later in the afternoon. When the Signora came out of the Sorghini house again, the man first followed her back to the Rusticucci palace, then went on to Montegiordano. I deduce from that he was one of the Prince's soldiers. He's tall, wears a coat of mail and a sword, and keeps a dagger and a pistol in his belt. He had a good look at me in the chapel with his nasty black eyes, and I don't want him to see me again."

"Don't worry, Giacomo, your part in the play is over, and you won't have to appear again. For your own good, padlock your tongue for ever and pocket these piastres."

I spent that night thinking what to do. I considered two alternative courses of action and weighed up the consequences of each in turn. The first was to inform Signor Peretti anonymously of where and when the guilty lovers met. Unfortunately, everything I knew about him led me to suppose he wouldn't kill his wife, but at the worst only shut her up again in some fortress like Santa Maria. From which I didn't doubt that the Prince would sooner or later manage to free her, and, if Peretti should happen to meet with a fatal accident, marry her. The very opposite of what I wanted.

The other solution, more radical and more attractive from every point of view, was to have Vittoria killed by a hired assassin. But this would be difficult, and dangerous for me. Vittoria only went out in the daytime, and she was protected by the wily and resolute armed giant whom Giacomo had come up against: you'd have to be wily to think of hiding in a confessional! Moreover, a hired assassin might be caught and speak under torture, and through him the Corte might find its way back to me. If that happened I wouldn't give much for my chances: even if I escaped death from the papal courts, Paolo would finish me off.

I could have written and told the Medicis all about it and let them decide what was to be done. But I knew they were too circumspect to give me advice or to make any move until I'd got the chestnuts out of the fire myself. I'd be lucky if they let me have a few for myself when thanks to my efforts Virginio came into his full inheritance.

While I was still undecided which course to take I was very surprised to get an invitation from Monseigneur Cherubi, then visiting Rome. He was staying in a palace rented by the Patriarch of Venice, whose right arm he was. You may remember he'd been dismissed by Cardinal Montalto for repeating something he'd said to the Pope.

Monseigneur Cherubi was an amiable fellow: frivolous and imprudent but not at all a fool, inquisitive as a squirrel and talkative as a magpie. He was unique in the Vatican, where there are so many clever men, because, contrary to all logic and expectation, he'd made a nice career for himself in the Church through an endless series of gaffes. The reason was that his clumsiness was rather soothing to the Machiavellian schemers with whom he was surrounded. It amused everyone and harmed no one.

I was even more astonished when I saw that only Cherubi and I were to be present at the meal he'd invited me to. I concluded the tête-à-tête had been organised — perhaps at the instigation of Gregory XIII, whose protégé Cherubi was — to worm information out of me about Paolo. I sat down at table highly tickled by the situation.

Most of the meal passed in the usual chat. Monseigneur Cherubi was a big fat man with a face the colour of a Parma ham. He was a great trencherman and a heavy drinker, so the fare was excellent. But when we got to the sweets his appetite seemed to slacken, as did his table talk, and I sensed we were approaching serious matters. But they came sooner and more abruptly than I expected.

"Conte," said he in his jovial, tipsy voice, "I'd like to ask you a question that was put to me by His Holiness but that I couldn't answer. In your opinion, has the inevitable happened between your cousin and Signora Peretti?"

I laughed, first because the word "inevitable" struck me as piquant coming from a prelate, and second because laughing gave me time to think before I answered.

"Monseigneur," I said gaily, "your question has a virtue I greatly admire: it is frank. And I ask nothing better than to answer it, at least if you'll promise in return to satisfy my curiosity about the Holy Father's feelings on the subject."

"I'll tell you what I know," said Cherubi, apparently throwing Vatican diplomacy to the winds. "You know me," he added with a chuckle, putting his hands on his belly: "Round in speech and square in business."

I laughed too, beginning to wonder if Cherubi hadn't done better out of his gaffes than others out of their wisdom. A gaffe isn't only a diplomatic blunder: in naval parlance it's a long pole with a hook on the end to pull another boat towards you or push it away from you. As Cherubi's gaffe was clearly designed to bring my little barque alongside his great galley, I decided not to offer any resistance.

"Yes, Monseigneur," I said, "the inevitable has happened. I can't prove it, but I am certain of it."

"Oh, how unfortunate!" said Cherubi gravely. "The Holy Father will be very sorry to hear it, and as he has the gift of tears no doubt he'll shed a few."

He said this without a trace of irony, as if he shared the Pope's sorrow in advance.

"But what can he do?" I asked.

"That's just it — nothing. That's what's so awful about it. Telling the husband wouldn't do any good. He'd only lock the flighty creature up again, and sooner or later our hero would manage to set her free!"

He was right, but there was something here that intrigued me. Adultery wasn't all that rare a sin even in the papal state, and I was eager to know why the Pope found this example of it so distressing.

"I understand the Holy Father's apprehensions," said I. "No doubt he's afraid Peretti might meet with a fatal accident."

"The Holy Father," answered Cherubi, "has never expressed such a fear. But men being what they are, such an eventuality can't be excluded. What do you think?"

I said very guardedly: "Your Eminence, Paolo Orsini is my first cousin. Apart from his son, I'm his nearest relative. And I'm very fond of him."

"Exactly. Who knows him better than you do?"

"It's certainly true Paolo is very passionate," I went on. "And like all passionate people he's unpredictable. And his fame as a soldier has rather gone to his head. In my opinion he wouldn't be restrained by the laws of the State. He thinks he's above them." As I was suavely delivering myself of all this, while being richly entertained by a senior dignitary of the Church, I suddenly remembered with amusement that at that very moment my two rascals were holding travellers to ransom in the Nora mountains and perhaps, being rather bloodthirsty by nature, even slaying them.

"So you don't rule out the idea," said Cherubi, "that Peretti might meet with an accident?"

"Unfortunately no. And now, Your Eminence, may I ask you a question?"

"By all means."

"If our hypothesis were to prove correct, would the Vatican dare arrest Paolo?"

"It would be better to deprive him of the fruits of his crime."

"You mean you'd imprison Vittoria?"

"When you want to break a chain," said Cherubi sententiously, "you attack the weakest link."

At these words I felt a wave of satisfaction surge through me. But it didn't last long. I soon saw the flaw in this plan.

"But our hero would take up arms to free her."

"Probably," said Cherubi impassively. "But we think we could get the better of him if . . ."

"If . . . Your Eminence?"

"If you don't join forces with him."

Now we're getting to it, I thought. Here at last is the reason for this invitation, this openness, these frank answers. Not only would my men be a useful back-up for Paolo, but as I had the ear of the lower orders, the revolt would become a popular uprising if I joined it. And that development would be highly dangerous for the Holy Father.

I was silent for a moment, not because I didn't know what I was going to say but to lend more weight to it.

"Monseigneur," I said at last, "you must know I have no sympathy for this caprice of my cousin's. And despite my great affection for him I'm too mindful of my duties to His Holiness to rule out *a priori* my remaining aloof from any conflict that may arise out of Paolo's follies. But I must point out that my neutrality will have to be negotiated when the time comes."

"And so it will be," said Monseigneur Cherubi.

"Through you?"

"With my mediation."

He smiled as if he was glad to have used a phrase that was different from mine. I smiled too. I was nicely replete after an excellent meal, and the prospect of "negotiating" my neutrality when the time came was very pleasing. The Vatican was rich and my purse was empty – the Medicis' ten thousand piastres had only bailed me out temporarily.

"However," Cherubi continued, "that's only a hypothesis. It's highly unlikely a man of honour like our hero would go so far as to defy the law."

"Highly unlikely," I echoed, an octave lower.

The meal was over. I stood up, made an excuse, and cut the leave-takings short. The future was beckoning to me in the most seductive of manners, and I was anxious to be on my own to examine it more closely.

8

Gian Battista della Pace,
Bargello della Corte

At nine o'clock on the morning of July 6th I went to the Rusticucci palace, together with my assistant, my clerk and a surgeon, to record the death by murder of Signor Francesco Peretti, adopted son of His Eminence Cardinal Montalto and third chamberlain to His Holiness Pope Gregory XIII.

The mother of the deceased, Signora Camilla Peretti, was watching over the body in the audience chamber, together with his mother-in-law, Tarquinia Accoramboni, and two of the latter's children, Giulietta and Flaminio. According to Signora Tarquinia, Signora Vittoria Peretti was shut up in her room, "out of her mind with grief" and unable to talk to anyone.

I requested the family to withdraw and ordered the surgeon to examine the body. He observed a wound from an arquebus bullet in the right leg. The shot, which had been fired from behind, had broken the victim's femur and caused him to fall, but death itself was due to a stab wound in the heart delivered by a dagger, probably when the victim was already lying defenceless on the ground. According to my assistant, Signor Peretti's sword was found unsheathed several yards away from the body. This detail intrigued me until it was explained by the testimony of Filippo, a footman, the only witness to the murder.

Filippo★

Bargello: Filippo, I'm told you were the last person to see Signor Peretti alive.

★ This interrogation took place in a room in the Rusticucci palace (Note by Bargello's clerk).

Filippo: I didn't have anything to do with it, Signor Bargello! Don't blame me for the murder – please! *Affè di Dio*, I'm innocent!

Bargello: Come now, Filippo, don't be silly! And stop shaking like a leaf! Sit down on this stool. No one suspects you. Just answer my questions.

Filippo: Yes, Signor Bargello.

Bargello: Do you know why Signor Peretti ventured out alone in the streets of Rome at half past eleven at night?

Filippo: Well, first of all, Signor Bargello, he wasn't alone. I was with him. I went in front with a torch to light him along.

Bargello: But you weren't armed.

Filippo: No, Signor Bargello. Anyhow I couldn't have used a weapon because I was carrying the torch.

Bargello: How was Signor Peretti armed?

Filippo: He only had a sword.

Bargello: Why do you say "only"?

Filippo: I was surprised he didn't take his pistols too – he was usually so careful.

Bargello: Where did he keep his pistols?

Filippo: On his bedside table. They were always kept loaded and primed, and no one was allowed to touch them, not even to dust them. As I said, he was very prudent.

Bargello: It wasn't very prudent of him to walk about the streets of Rome at night so lightly armed and escorted.

Filippo: That's what I thought, Signor Bargello, when he told me to go in front with a torch. To tell you the truth my heart was in my boots.

Bargello: Do you know the reason for this nocturnal errand?

Filippo: No, Signor Bargello. But I know where we were going. Signor Peretti told me.

Bargello: Where?

Filippo: To the Montecavallo palace.

Bargello: But it's been shut up for a week.

Filippo: I know. I was surprised.

Bargello: There were quite a lot of things that surprised you about all this.

Filippo: Oh yes, Signor Bargello! There were indeed! Lots of things!

Bargello: For example?

Filippo: For example, that Signor Peretti didn't take more people with him. There are half a dozen able-bodied men in the Rusticucci palace, not counting the door-keeper, who's an old soldier.

Bargello: What time was it when Signor Peretti decided to go out?

Filippo: I was just going to bed. It was almost eleven o'clock. *Il mancino* had just brought him a note.

Bargello: Do you know what was in it?

Filippo: No, Signor Bargello.

Bargello: Signor Peretti received the note at eleven o'clock, but he didn't go out till half-past. What happened in that half-hour?

Filippo: All the family were there in the patio begging him not to go out.

Bargello: What do you mean by "all the family"?

Filippo: Signora Camilla, Signora Tarquinia, Signorina Giulietta, Signor Flaminio. They clung on to Signor Peretti begging him not to risk his life. Oh, Signor Bargello, you ought to have heard them! The cries and lamentations!

Bargello: What about Signora Vittoria?

Filippo: The Signora's not one to cling on to people. But she did speak to Signor Peretti after.

Bargello: After what?

Filippo: After he'd shaken off all the others.

Bargello: Did you hear what she said to him?

Filippo: No, there was too much noise. Everyone was shouting and crying. But I could tell from the way she looked that she was trying to stop him going out too.

Bargello: How did she look?

Filippo: Very frightened, very anxious. She was wringing her hands.

Bargello: How long did their talk last?

Filippo: I don't know. A good ten minutes, I should think, but in two parts.

Bargello: How do you mean?

Filippo: At one point the Signora left Signor Peretti and went over and spoke to *il mancino*. Then she came back to Signor Peretti again and went on begging him.

Bargello: How do you know she was begging him if you couldn't hear what she was saying?

Filippo: I could tell by what she looked like.

Bargello: You must have heard her – you were lighting the scene up with your torch.

Filippo: Signor Bargello, I'm not a liar! I'm telling you the truth! There was a terrible din going on all round me. And there were three torch-bearers in the patio, and I wasn't the one nearest the Signora.

Bargello: And then what happened?

Filippo: Signor Peretti sent Piero to fetch his sword.

Bargello: You heard that time.

Filippo: No, I didn't, Signor Bargello! But I realised what he'd said when I saw Piero come back with the sword. Please, Signor Bargello, don't keep calling me a liar!

Bargello: I'm not calling you a liar. What happened next?

Filippo: Piero came back with the sword in its scabbard and the belt to hang it on.

Bargello: And then?

Filippo: The master unsheathed the sword and threw the belt and the scabbard angrily on the ground.

Bargello: Angrily?

Filippo: Yes, he looked beside himself with fury. Then he barked at me to lead the way with my torch, and rushed out like a madman. I'd never seen him in such a state. Out in the street he told me we were going to the palace at Montecavallo, and shouted at me to go "Faster! Faster!" He was hurrying along hell for leather.

Bargello: And then what happened?

Filippo: You know very well what happened – they went and killed him!

Bargello: Come, Filippo, don't cry. Men don't cry.

Filippo: Why not, if they're unhappy? And I'm unhappy twice over — first because Signor Peretti was a good master, and also because I don't know what will become of me now he's dead.

Bargello: Tell me how it happened.

Filippo: Signor Bargello, would I had never been born, to see such a thing! What a misfortune!

Bargello: Now, now, Filippo — get on with it, please!

Filippo: I'm sorry, Signor Bargello, I really don't know what I'm doing . . . *Bene*, you know the street leading up to the Montecavallo palace? It's very steep and the master had to slow down. He was tired by then too. Half-way up the street I heard a shot behind me. I turned round, and there was Signor Peretti lying on his back on the ground. His right thigh was bleeding. But he hadn't let go of his sword.

Bargello: So what did you do?

Filippo: I threw down my torch and ran away.

Bargello: Instead of helping your master?

Filippo: Helping him? How? And with what? I hadn't even got a knife! And the others had got an arquebus! And now everyone at the Rusticucci palace has got it in for me! You ought to hear them! "Filippo hasn't got the balls of a baby rabbit!" It's not fair! I'd like to have seen them! How would they have fought the bandits? With their teeth?

Bargello: Calm down, Filippo! Calm down!

Filippo: I didn't just run away, Signor Bargello. When I saw the murderers weren't coming after me, and that they couldn't even see me because the torch had rolled away down the hill, I crept back. I didn't make any noise because I was wearing felt shoes. So I hid in a doorway and listened. I heard everything. I was in the dark and the bandits were lit by the torch lying a few yards below Signor Peretti's body. So I could see them as plain as I see you. They'd walked calmly up the hill to where he was lying. There were two of them.

Bargello: What were they like?

Filippo: Very polite.

Bargello: What do you mean by that?

206

Filippo: Signor Bargello, once again — I'm telling the truth! They spoke to Signor Peretti very politely.

Bargello: They spoke to him?

Filippo: Oh yes! Quite a conversation! I couldn't believe my ears!

Bargello: What did they say?

Filippo: First the master — he was still holding his sword — threw them his purse with his left hand and said, "If that's what you want, take it!" And the taller one answered: "With respect, Signor Peretti, we'll get your purse anyway when you're dead. Our job is to murder you." "And who gave you the job?" "A monk. He pointed you out to us and told us who you were last Sunday when you went to Mass at Santa Maria de la Corte with your lady wife." "Do you know why the monk wanted me to die?" "If you ask me, Signor Peretti, he was only an intermediary." "What made you think that?" "A joke he made." "What did he say?" "I'm sorry, Signor Peretti, it was a very indelicate joke." "Tell me anyway". "He said Signor Peretti had too beautiful a wife to keep her to himself." Then the other bandit said to the tall one, "Barca, you shouldn't have repeated that. It's very coarse."

Bargello: Barca? Did you say Barca?

Filippo: Yes, Signor Bargello.

Bargello: Make sure you've got that name, clerk. Barca. What was he like?

Filippo: Tall, broad-shouldered, with a beard right up to the eyes.

Bargello: And the other one?

Filippo: Short, beardless, slim, with a soft voice. If you ask me he was the other one's faggot.

Bargello: Faggot?

Filippo: From what I've been told there are men who act as women to other men.

Bargello: Go on.

Filippo: After that . . .

Bargello: After what?

Filippo: After Barca had repeated the joke, Signor Peretti said very crossly: "Well, what are you waiting for? Why don't you finish the job?" "Signore," said Barca, "you've got a sword but we haven't.

We've got to wait till the arquebus is reloaded." "Here you are," said the little one, "it's ready." And he handed it to Barca. He aimed it at Signor Peretti, but it didn't go off. "Use your daggers, then," the master ordered.

Bargello: Ordered?

Filippo: It's the truth. And that's still not the most amazing thing. When Signor Peretti told the two bandits to use their daggers, Barca said reproachfully: "Signor Peretti – a dagger against a sword?" Then the master did something quite incredible. He drew back his arm and hurled his sword down the hill with all his might! It rattled down over the cobblestones. Oh Signore, I can still hear it! (He wept.)

Bargello: Come, Filippo, pull yourself together!

Fillippo: Madonna mia! Why did he do it? Disarm himself with armed bandits all round him!

Bargello: Perhaps he thought it was hopeless to struggle. There were two of them.

Filippo: But if he'd held them off I'd have had time to go for help. I did go, but it was too late.

Bargello: What happened after Signor Peretti had thrown his sword away?

Filippo: The two murderers took their time. They leaned over and undid his doublet. When the master got impatient, Barca explained he wanted the doublet for himself and didn't want to spoil the fine buffalo-hide by making a hole in it with his dagger. I ran away then, and rushed like mad to the Rusticucci palace to raise the alarm. When I got back with all the able-bodied men in the house, the master's body was still warm.

Domenico Acquaviva (*Il mancino*)

Bargello: Acquaviva, I've got some questions to ask you.[*]

Il mancino: Here, Signor Bargello? In this cellar? Surrounded by instruments of torture? Have you forgotten I'm no longer a

[*] This interrogation took place in a room in the Rusticucci palace (Note by Bargello's clerk).

bandit?

Bargello: Your present career is just as immoral.

Il mancino: But it's no threat to law and order. And among the pleasures it's brought me, Signor Bargello, is that of having done you some small favours.

Bargello: It's a treat to talk to you, Acquaviva. You express yourself so well.

Il mancino: It's a pleasure I can do without – except, as I said, when I can be of use to you.

Bargello: That's twice you've reminded me. But there's no need – I remember. However, my gratitude isn't endless. It'll depend on how you answer my questions.

Il mancino: I'll tell you the whole truth whatever you ask.

Bargello: Who? Where? When?

Il mancino: I don't follow.

Bargello: I'll concentrate on the "who" – the rest will follow. Who gave you the note you delivered yesterday, Thursday, at eleven o'clock, to Signor Peretti?

Il mancino: A monk. At the Mount of Olives tavern. At ten o'clock in the evening.

*Bargello:*Did you know him?

Il mancino: Didn't know him from Adam.

Bargello: What did he look like?

Il mancino: Difficult to say – he kept his hood down over his eyes. You know how modest monks are in the company of ladies. And some of the ladies where we met were showing off their charms.

Bargello: What sort of height and figure?

Il mancino: Short, slim, long thin hands almost like a skeleton's. But he could guzzle enough for half a dozen. Scar on his left thumb.

Bargello: Good! Pity you're on the wrong side of the law. You'd have been useful to me on the right side. What did the monk say?

Il mancino: He asked me to deliver the note straight away to Signor Peretti – said it was urgent. He gave me twenty piastres to do it.

Bargello: Didn't you think it a rather suspicious errand at that time of night?

Il mancino: From just anyone it would have been. But not from a monk. I'm a good Catholic.

Bargello: Was the note sealed or only folded?

Il mancino: Folded.

Bargello: So what could be easier than to unfold it and read it before delivering it to Signor Peretti?

Il mancino: Yes, for someone who could read.

Bargello: And you can't?

Il mancino: Alas, no, Signor Bargello. I can neither read nor write.

Bargello: You speak Italian remarkably well for an illiterate.

Il mancino: So everyone says. Perhaps I was meant for better things.

Bargello: So you don't know what was in the note?

Il mancino: As a matter of fact I do. Signor Peretti read it aloud when I gave it to him.

Bargello: And what did it say?

Il mancino: You know that as well as I do, Signor Bargello.

Bargello: Never mind. Tell me.

Il mancino: The note purported to be from Marcello Accoramboni, and asked Signor Peretti to come to his aid. He was lying wounded on the steps of the Montecavallo palace.

Bargello: Why do you say "purported"?

Il mancino: Because Marcello Accoramboni couldn't have sent the message. He's been in Amalfi with Signora Sorghini for the last ten days.

Bargello: He could have come back to Rome yesterday.

Il mancino: You'd have known if he had. Everyone has to go through the police and the customs to enter Rome.

Bargello: They never used to give *you* much trouble.

Il mancino: That's different. I was a bandit. I knew the ropes.

Bargello: You could have told him.

Il mancino: I don't give away information.

Bargello: So I've noticed. One day we must come back to these ropes of yours, Acquaviva.

Il mancino: As you like. But there isn't much point. When one door closes another opens.

Bargello: Let's get back to the note. You don't think it was genuine, then?

Il mancino: With all respect, Signor Bargello, neither do you. Why would Marcello Accoramboni put his name to a note that would send him straight to the gallows as soon as his brother-in-law's murder was discovered?

Bargello: He might have been counting on protection in high places.

Il mancino: In Amalfi?

Bargello: Not in Amalfi, no. But perhaps in Montegiordano.

Il mancino: From what I've heard, Marcello Accoramboni hasn't got any connection with Montegiordano now.

Bargello: Is that all you've heard, Acquaviva?

Il mancino: Yes, Signor Bargello.

Bargello: And yet your sister is Signora Peretti's maid.

Il mancino: True, Signor Bargello.

Bargello: Perhaps she'll be more willing than you are to consult her memory?

Il mancino: My memory has nothing to reproach me with except my past. As for Caterina, she confessed regularly to Father Barichelli at Santa Maria. And in Rome she confesses to Father Racasi. She'll confess to you too, if you like. You'll find her as open as the day.

Bargello: We shall see.

Il mancino: Signor Bargello, don't be too hard on my little sister.

Bargello: No harder than on you. I'm trying to find the truth.

Il mancino: It may not be where you think.

Bargello: What do you mean?

Il mancino: Whoever ordered this murder is trying to incriminate Marcello Accoramboni.

Bargello: Thank you for your valuable help with my inquiry.

Il mancino: You're making fun of me, Signor Bargello.

Bargello: A little, perhaps. Let's go back to when you gave Signor Peretti the note. Did he ask you what you thought?

Il mancino: Yes, Signor Bargello. And I strongly advised him not to venture out into the streets of Rome at night.

Bargello: But you'd done that yourself to bring him the note!

Il mancino: That's different. I'm known. Dog doesn't eat dog.

Bargello: And did Signor Peretti listen to you?

Il mancino: No. He seemed determined to go to his brother-in-law's aid. So I went and saw Signora Tarquinia Accoramboni. She asked to see the note, and declared loud and clear that Marcello hadn't written it.

Bargello: And that's when all the family came running, and all the screaming and crying started?

Il mancino: That's right. There must soon have been about twenty people out in the patio, counting the servants. Even those who'd gone to bed got up and came out. And they were all running hither and thither in the torch-light, weeping and wailing and waving their arms about. Just like a play.

Bargello: It seems Signora Peretti asked to see you at one point. What did she say?

Il mancino: Seeing Signor Peretti was so set on going to the rendez-vous, she asked me if I'd go with him.

Bargello: And what did you say to that?

Il mancino: I absolutely refused. Even if he took an escort of ten! I said that in my opinion the rendez-vous was a trap, and the only thing to do with a trap was stay well away from it.

Bargello: What did she do then?

Il mancino: She went and told Signor Peretti what I'd said, and begged him not to go. She was very emphatic about it.

Bargello: I imagine she threw herself in her husband's arms.

Il mancino: No. She's not like that. She's rather regal.

Bargello: How do you explain that?

Il mancino: Everyone's worshipped her for her beauty ever since she was a child.

Bargello: Did you hear what she said to her husband?

Il mancino: No. Not really. There was too much noise.

Bargello: Where was Caterina just then?

Il mancino: With the Signora. She follows her about like a shadow.

Bargello: So she can tell me what the husband and wife said to one another.

Il mancino: Signor Bargello, please, don't be too hard on my little sister. She's very sensitive. One little slap and she sheds tears.

Bargello: One would think you loved women, to hear you talk. And yet you live off them.

Il mancino: Signor Bargello! I've never asked my sister Caterina for money!

Bargello: Don't get excited. I wasn't talking about her – I meant the girls at the Mount of Olives.

Il mancino: That's different. I may live off them, but they owe their lives to me. If I wasn't there they'd all get themselves murdered by their customers.

Caterina Acquaviva

When Filippo brought us the terrible news that Thursday-to-Friday night I thought the Signora would go out of her mind. She wept and wailed and scratched her cheeks and literally tore out her hair. And it was worse when the servants brought Signor Peretti's body back covered with blood. She threw herself on it, sobbing louder than ever and getting her nightgown and even her hair all stained with her husband's gore. She was shaken by violent spasms, sometimes letting out heart-rending shrieks and sometimes groaning like a brute beast. But, thank God, she couldn't utter a word. I say thank God because she'd lost all self-control and I was half dead with fear she might say more than she should in front of the family and the rest of the servants.

Fortunately in the end it was all too much for her and she fainted. And with the help of Giulietta and two of the servants I was able to get her to her room.

As soon as she was on the bed I sent the servants away. Unluckily I couldn't do the same with Giulietta, who looked like settling in for good. She hadn't been allowed in the Signora's room since their quarrel at Santa Maria. So now she was putting on airs of importance and pretending to be indispensable, and I could tell from her prying eyes that she was preparing to stick her long, old maid's nose into everything. Who knows, I thought – she might even send me away on some errand so that she can search the room and try to worm the Signora's secrets out of her when she comes to.

So I got in first. I pretended to search among the pots and phials on the dressing-table, and said: "Signorina, I can't find the Signora's smelling salts. Would you be kind enough to fetch yours?"

I could see she was dying to send me for them. But I knew she wouldn't. She's got an obsession about tidiness and can't bear anyone else to touch her things. She hates anyone even to set foot in her room, and stays there all the time her maid does the dusting. So she said grudgingly, with a decidedly poisonous look: "I'll go and get them."

The venom was because the silly fool is madly in love with Marcello, and by dint of spying she'd found out my relations with him. She immediately complained to Signor Peretti, Signora Camilla and Signora Tarquinia. Several times, but without result. A fat lot they cared: the son of a good family having an affair with a little lady's maid like me! They cared much less about that, anyway, than about his publicly living in sin with an old woman! And who'd dare confront Signora Vittoria and ask her to dismiss me?

As soon as Giulietta had gone I locked the door of the ante-chamber and tried to revive the Signora with little slaps on the cheek. Already her eyelids were flickering and she was getting some colour back. I pitied her: sorrow was going to return with consciousness. But I kept my head, and as soon as I saw she was able to understand I said: "Signora, I've locked the door. I thought you wouldn't want to see anyone."

"No," she said feebly. "No one."

When Giulietta came back and couldn't get in, she called out to me from the gallery. I had some trouble finding the right tone of voice to say: "I'm sorry, Signorina. The Signora told me to lock the door. She doesn't want to see anyone."

"Who says so?" said Giulietta crossly.

"The Signora, of course, Signorina."

"I don't believe you."

"Signora," said I, turning to my mistress, "Signorina Giulietta doesn't believe me."

"Come, Giulietta," said the Signora, faintly but distinctly enough, "leave me, please. I want to be on my own."

214

"Very well! As you wish!" said Giulietta furiously. "I was only trying to help."

It was a pity I couldn't be both inside the door to head her off, and outside to see her nose grow longer. I sighed. *Madonna mia*! It had been a narrow squeak. And I'd been right to be afraid, for no sooner had I shut the second door – the one that led from my little room to the mistress's bedroom – than the Signora burst into a torrent of jumbled words which would have been all too clear to Giulietta if she'd heard them.

"The wretch!" she said. "He's killed him! He's broken his promise! His oath! Francesco spared him, and this is his reward! A despicable ambush! A cowardly murder! Hired assassins! He didn't even have the courage to kill him with his own hand! Oh, how hateful! How hateful! I'll never forgive him! He, a hero? A fine hero! A Turk wouldn't have acted worse! But I'll avenge Francesco! I'll dishonour the coward publicly! I'll confess everything! Everyone shall know how he suborned me, lulled me with fine words, sullied me with his filthy love. Everyone shall know how nobly Francesco had mercy on him, and with what baseness he in return . . . Oh, I hate him, I hate him!"

I listened, amazed and terrified. I couldn't get a word in. She rose and paced about the room. The silence of the initial shock was succeeded by a flood of broken words, uttered (fortunately) in a low voice as she strode back and forth biting her knuckles – tearless now but with flashing eyes and lips twisted with rage.

When at last she paused for breath I said quietly but firmly: "Confess everything, Signora? You're not serious! They'd put you on public trial for adultery. And because you married into the nobility, they'd do you the great favour of strangling you with a red silk cord."

"Very well!" she cried, looking up, her eyes starting out of their sockets in her passion. "I'll die! I have so much to expiate! Wasn't it because of me that Francesco died?"

"You're right, Signora," I answered coldly. "Being strangled with a red silk cord is nothing. It only takes a minute. A minute's soon over, even if the seconds seem long. When you don't belong to the nobility they hang you with a rope, and *il mancino* says that takes twenty minutes."

"Why are you telling me that, Caterina?" she asked, taken aback.

215

"Because *I* don't belong to the nobility, Signora. And if you confess, I'll be hanged as an accomplice."

"I hadn't thought of that," she said.

If she hadn't been my mistress I'd have told her that didn't surprise me, and that she didn't usually think much about other people. It's not that she's not generous. It's just that she's been worshipped too much. Ever since she was a child! Those sessions on the balcony in Gubbio!

"Not to mention Marcello," I added. "He'll be hanged too."

"But he had nothing to do with that horrible murder," she cried. "He's in Amalfi, and the note wasn't in his handwriting!"

"They'll say he came back to Rome secretly and disguised his handwriting. And as for you, Signora, if you reveal your liaison with Paolo, who's going to believe you didn't have a hand in your husband's murder?"

"Oh!" she cried, "but that's shameful! I couldn't bear such a suspicion! I'd kill myself!"

"And then you'll be damned! But the fact that you're dead won't stop the judges hanging Marcello and me. The sole survivor of this business will be the Prince. He'll get off scot free. Can you see the Pope daring to attack him in his fortress at Montegiordano? That'll be the only outcome of your revenge! Work it out! The Prince safe and sound up in his fine palace, and, far below, four dead bodies: you, me, Marcello and Signora Sorghini."

"Signora Sorghini?"

"Of course. She's an accomplice too. Didn't she lend you her house?"

"That's true," she said, and dropped on to a chair, overwhelmed.

Reality was beginning to break through. She'd have to give up the heroic rôle of the adulteress making public confession and dying in the odour of sanctity.

"And of course," I added, "once you're dead all the women in Rome will be wilder about the Prince than ever and throw themselves at his head."

"Caterina," said she, "don't speak to me of that abject creature!"

I'd probably been hurting her terribly, but there it was — it was about time she suffered! Other people existed too. Ever since this conversation had begun I'd been trembling all over, with cold shivers at the top of my spine. I could almost feel the noose tightening round my neck.

"Signora," I said, after a moment, "where did you hide the key to the Sorghini house?"

"In my jewel box. What do you want it for?"

"I'm going to put it in Marcello's room."

"Why?"

"If they search his room it'll be quite natural for them to find the key there. Whereas if they find it in your room . . ."

"So you think they'll search my room?" she said faintly.

"I'm sure of it."

"How can you be so sure?"

"Signora, I'm *il mancino*'s little sister. I've been hearing about what the police get up to all my life."

"Do as you like, then," she said wearily.

I had no trouble finding the key to the garden of delights (poor Signora, they'd been so brief). It looked quite dull there in the jewel box amid the pearls and the precious stones and the gold.

"Signora," I said, "be so good as to lock the door after me so that no one can intrude on you while I'm gone, and then let me in again when I come back."

"Go, then," she said.

I didn't meet a soul either going or coming. Everyone was round the dead man in the audience chamber, lamenting his departure to a better world or, in the case of the servants, lamenting their own futures and wondering who was going to pay them now the third chamberlain to the Pope was no more.

When I came back I found the room all lit up. The Signora had lit the candles on the dressing-table and was now burning the six letters Marcello had brought her in a saucer, one by one. I didn't say anything. I was glad she'd started taking precautions at last. And while she looked icily on as the letters she'd read with such love scarcely two weeks ago were reduced to ashes, I was already thinking what we ought to say to the Bargello so as not to contradict each other.

The next day, when I saw the Bargello shut himself up with Filippo, I thought it would soon be my turn, and hoped I'd be interrogated before the Signora. I'd advised her to say she'd be ready to answer questions at the end of the morning. I wanted to go first so that I could tip her the wink.

I went into my little room to set myself to rights and change into a bodice with a low square neck, the kind that suits me best. On reflection I decided to leave nothing to chance, and undid the two top buttons, not so much to show more as just to catch the eye. I also rehearsed my part. Though I was pretty sure of myself deep down, I couldn't help feeling rather nervous: I'd never seen this man before in my life, and didn't know the sort of person I had to deal with. My heart turned right over when Pietro came and told me the Bargello was waiting for me in Marcello's room. I didn't know if it was right, but I said a little prayer and asked God to let him be the sort of man who likes women, and not one of the others.

He opened the door to me himself, and when he locked it and turned round and looked at me, that one look was enough. I knew my prayer had been answered.

And so much the better, thought I, as on closer inspection he proved to be a good-looking fellow: quite tall, broad-shouldered, slim-waisted, with curly brown hair. His aquiline nose and piercing black eyes made him look rather severe, but you only had to look at his mouth to see he was no cold fish. Nor did it escape me that he hadn't brought his clerk with him, as he had for Filippo.

"Caterina," he said gravely (but with his eye resting briefly on my neckline), "I have some questions to ask you about what took place at Santa Maria between the unfortunate Signor Peretti and the Signora."

"Well, Signor Bargello, it's very simple – they quarrelled. The Signora was angry with the Signore for shutting her up at the back of beyond just for reading a letter that she burned immediately afterwards and never answered."

"Who delivered the letter?"

"Signor Marcello. At the time he was secretary to . . ."

"No names, please!"

I looked at him. The Prince was lucky! Not only would *he* not be questioned in *his* palace, but his name wasn't even going to be mentioned in the inquiry.

"Was that all they quarrelled about?" said the Bargello, who'd understood my reaction perfectly and didn't look very comfortable himself. That made me feel rather well disposed towards him. He struck me as the sort of policeman who wouldn't hesitate to go and question the Prince in his palace if only anyone ever had the courage to order him to.

"No, Signor Bargello. There was another bone of contention. The Signora didn't like living in the palace at Santa Maria – she preferred a little house on the cliff, and she went and stayed there. One night there was a terrible storm, and next morning they found the wreckage of a boat on a little beach at the foot of the cliff. At which Signor Peretti arrived in a fury, sword in hand, while the Signora and I were walking about quietly in front of the cottage enjoying the morning sun. Signor Peretti rushed up to us brandishing his sword and yelling that the boat must have belonged to the nobleman who'd written to the Signora. I intervened, and Signor Peretti, without meaning to, wounded me slightly in the shoulder. Would you like to see the scar, Signor Bargello? The Signora was furious and overwhelmed him with reproaches, and he went away. But he came back two days later and apologised, and they were reconciled."

"How?"

I gave him the glad eye and said: "How do you think a husband and wife are reconciled, Signor Bargello?"

"I don't know," said he. "I'm a bachelor."

And he smiled. What a smile! And the little black moustache that went with it!

"*Bene*," said he, growing serious again. "Now let's turn to the night of Thursday to Friday. How are we to explain the fact that Signor Peretti disregarded the pleas of his whole family and committed the unbelievable folly of going out in the streets of Rome, alone and at night, armed only with a sword? No one's been able to tell me why he did it!"

The Bargello now seemed to be dangling a bait of some importance in front of me, and I wondered if it was to the Signora's advantage, or to mine, that I should bite. I decided it was. He'd surely have been told I was with the Signora all the time that night, and must have heard all she and Signor Peretti said to one another. As a matter of fact I'd discussed this point with her while she was burning the letters, and we'd agreed on our version of what had happened. It wasn't too far from the truth, but nor was it close enough to compromise the Signora. As I thought about all this, much faster than it takes to tell, I was using various wiles to distract

219

the Bargello's penetrating glance from my face. I didn't quite know if I'd succeeded. Those black eyes of his might let themselves dally and stray a little, but they soon came back to fix themselves on mine.

"I don't know," said I, pretending to hesitate, "if the Signora would really like me to tell you this . . ."

"Come along, my beauty," said he. "Don't stand on ceremony, Speak! I'll be grateful if you do."

"Well, that Thursday there was a little dispute between Signora and Signor Peretti. The Signora had had a very bad headache all day, and in the evening, when Signor Peretti came and asked to spend the night in her room, she was rather reluctant . . ."

"Rather curt, perhaps?"

"Well, let's say she wasn't very amenable. Signor Peretti got cross, and there you are! You know what it's like when that happens!"

"No, I don't. I'm not married."

"They both dug up old resentments. In particular, what had happened at Santa Maria."

"His turning up in front of the cottage, brandishing a naked sword?"

"Among other things."

"There were other things?"

"Yes. But if you ask me they were very trivial."

"Tell me about them."

"The day after the quarrel outside the cottage there was a terrible storm. Signor Peretti sent the majordomo to tell the Signora he feared for her safety and ask her to return to the palace."

"And she blamed him for that? He was only trying to look after her."

"She blamed him for sending the majordomo instead of coming himself. She said he was afraid of the thunder and lightning."

"Just like a woman! And how did Signor Peretti take that?"

"Very badly. He said: 'You dare to tell me you think I'm a coward?' He was white as a sheet and grinding his teeth — he could scarcely speak. But when he did, I heard him for the first time say disagreeable things to his wife."

"For example?"

"'You're a madwoman! Quite mad! You read too much, and your head's full of heroes out of books!' And he went out and slammed the door."

"And this all came up on the night of the murder . . . At what time?"

"Just before eleven. At least, I think so. My brother arrived just afterwards with the famous note. Unfortunately he can't read. Otherwise he'd never have delivered it."

"Not even for twenty piastres?"

"Signor Bargello, my brother owes a great deal to Signor Peretti. It was thanks to him his banishment from Rome was lifted."

"And thanks to me . . . I've been told the whole family gathered round Peretti, shouting and weeping and begging him not to go."

"Yes."

"But the Signora didn't join in?"

"She's not one for clinging round people's necks or throwing herself at their feet. But when Signor Peretti had got rid of the others she spoke to him."

"What did she say?"

"That the note from Marcello was a forgery, and the rendez-vous was a trap and he mustn't fall into it. But he wouldn't listen. He was still angry after their quarrel, and whatever the Signora said he just answered, 'I'll show you if I'm a coward!' He kept on saying that."

"And what did the Signora say?"

"That she hadn't meant he was a coward — it was a misunderstanding, and she asked him to forgive her. But he wouldn't listen. He just kept repeating what he'd said before."

"I see," said the Bargello.

He put his hands behind his back and looked at me silently out of his piercing grey eyes. For the first time since he'd started questioning me I felt rather afraid.

"That's all very fine, my beauty," he said.

He must have liked the sound of that, because he said it again. "That's all very fine, my beauty. I'm sure you're telling me the truth. Well, more or less . . ."

A pause, another piercing look, and he went on: "And you're a good girl, Caterina. You've got a kind heart. You're very fond of your mistress. You're very fond of *il mancino*. And there's certainly someone else you're very fond of, perhaps even in this room. But that's of no consequence. I'm not your confessor. Only . . ."

He looked at me, pulled a face, and was silent, as if he expected me to ask a question. But I didn't say anything. Perhaps that was a mistake. But I simply couldn't open my mouth. A little shiver ran down my spine.

"Only," he said, "there's one thing that surprises me. It seems to me that if the Signora had *really* wanted to prevent Signor Peretti from going, she had a way of stopping him."

Again he waited for me to ask a question, and again I said nothing. This time I was sure it was a mistake. But although I was furious with myself I still didn't speak. There was nothing I could do about it.

"You don't ask me what that way was?"

"Yes," I said feebly. "What was it?"

"Come now, Caterina," said he, "you know very well what it was. So why do you ask?"

"Signor Bargello!" I said angrily. "First you tell me to ask you a question, and then when I do you reproach me!"

He laughed, but wryly.

"What a sly little minx it is!" he said. "Come, Caterina, don't try to slide out of it. Tell me frankly, if you'd been in the Signora's shoes, what would you have done to keep your husband at home? Especially when he'd just asked you to let him spend the night with you."

"Oh, Signor Bargello," I cried, "why ask me when you know the answer? But I'm not the Signora. She's a queen! And once she's said no it's not easy for her to go back on it."

"You mean it didn't even occur to her?"

"Yes!" I answered at once, "but too late! He'd already gone! And she bitterly regretted not having thought of it sooner!"

Although I sounded genuine enough, what I said was at the same time true and untrue. It was true she regretted it now. But it wasn't true she regretted it then. I'm sure that at the time the idea never entered her head.

As for the Bargello, I couldn't tell whether he believed me or not. His grey eyes, fixed on mine, were impenetrable. All he did was shrug his shoulders after a moment, as if, after all, such speculation was beside the point. Then suddenly his expression changed and he said with an air of detachment but with a playful little curl of the lip: "Now let's see that scar on your right shoulder that Signor Peretti's supposed to have given you."

"Do you doubt it, Signor Bargello?"

"I shall until I've seen it."

"As you please, Signor Bargello."

And I started unbuttoning my bodice, slowly and enticingly, but without overdoing it. The Bargello's mouth now seemed more expressive than his eyes, for the simple reason that I couldn't see his eyes any more. He'd lowered them to follow my performance.

When he finally passed his hand over my scar I was surprised to find his fingers so soft and his touch so delicate.

"To be frank," he said with a little laugh, "I couldn't say whether this scar is a year old or only a month, or if it was made by a sword or a thorn. Perhaps someone did hit you, but only with a rose. You're such a good girl. And not only have you got a good heart, Caterina, but what covers it isn't bad either."

So saying he held my left breast in a swift, light caress that made me quiver from head to foot.

Dio mio! I'd been so frightened, and now it was all right! I let him undress me and do as he liked with me. *Madonna mia*! the questions he'd asked! A lot of little traps with teeth ready to snap on me like twenty tigers if I fell in, and a rope at the end of it!

It was such a relief not to have to puzzle my brains any more about what I ought or ought not to say — and then say it fast enough to make it look natural. Now all I had to do was let myself go. It gave me a special thrill, deep down, to be made love to by a man who'd frightened me so. Now he was no longer asking me questions, with his eyes boring into mine! Now his eyes were down by my neck, and his mouth was there too, biting! No more words, thank God! Instead, panting and sighs. I was in my element now! And so was he, with his masculine pride!

But which of the two of us was being had — that's something I'd very much like to know.

While I was out my clerk received two letters, one forwarded by His Excellency the Governor of Rome, the other handed to one of my men by a beggar who ran away. The first was signed; the second was anonymous. Both were very curious.

The letter forwarded by the Governor was signed by Cesare Pallantieri. I knew him very well, having had him banished from Rome for his crimes. In the letter he said that with the help of Marcello Accoramboni he'd had Peretti murdered, because of a quarrel they'd had recently. He didn't say what the quarrel was about, nor where and when it took place. I assumed someone had paid him to write me this billet-doux, which seemed to have two purposes: to exculpate whoever really instigated the murder, and to incriminate Marcello Accoramboni.

Despite the fact that it was anonymous, I took the second letter more seriously. It said that while Signora Sorghini was out of Rome, Vittoria Accoramboni had secretly met with "a certain nobleman" in her house. She got in through a little door at the back to which she had a key.

I went to the place immediately, and found it just as described in the letter. There was a narrow cul-de-sac behind the house with an open porch leading into a passage. The passage led to a door, also left unlocked, which opened into a little chapel Signora Sorghini was said to have lent to some mendicant friars on condition that they prayed for her soul. But further down the same passage there was another door. This door was locked, but must have led into the Sorghini palace, or at least to the roof.

Thanks to some obliging neighbours I was able to look out on this roof from the window of a house nearby. There were masses of geraniums round the parapet, and in the middle stood a large tent closed in with white curtains. And white indeed must be the souls of those who dallied inside them!

One can easily imagine a closely masked signora going into the innocent ground-floor corridor as if to say a brief prayer, kneeling down for a moment in the chapel, then going up to the roof through the little door. The gate may have been strait but it certainly didn't lead to salvation.

After referring to Governor Portici for his approval, I decided to have the Rusticucci palace searched. My men didn't find anything in the Signora's room, but in Marcello Accoramboni's they discovered a key that fitted the back door to the Sorghini house. But that didn't prove anything against his sister: Marcello was known *urbi et orbi* to be La Sorghini's lover.

I questioned the neighbours who'd let me inspect the Sorghini roof. The husband's answers were evasive, but the wife was more forthcoming. Before La Sorghini went away she'd sometimes noticed the tent curtains not quite closed, and caught a glimpse of a big white couch and a bath.

"On the roof! *La Sorghini, che svergognata!*★ And would you believe it, Signor Bargello, one day I even saw that good-for-nothing Marcello outside the tent, basking naked in the sun in broad daylight!"

"Naked, Signora? In broad daylight?"

"Well, I would have seen him naked," said she, blushing, "if it hadn't been for all the geraniums."

"And what did you see, Signora, *after* La Sorghini went away to Amalfi?"

"Nothing," she said regretfully. "The curtains were always closed."

And so what might have been crucial evidence went up in smoke. Of course, imagination can always complement reality. Just as the lady next door could see Marcello naked even if the geraniums were in the way, so I could imagine Vittoria on the white couch, disporting her lovely body and long hair in the arms of "a certain nobleman". But what would that prove?

Governor Portici and I got a good hundred or more other letters after the first two, all anonymous and all accusing and insulting Vittoria Peretti, her brother, her mother, her maid and indirectly "a certain nobleman", though without naming him (courage wasn't these correspondents' strong point, even though they did write anonymously). Five or six of the letters addressed to the Governor criticised my inquiry and accused me of incompetence for not yet having brought it to a successful conclusion. We read and re-read these missives in search of the

★ What a shameless hussy!

slightest serious clue, but didn't find one. So we burned them.

A week later Alfaro, my assistant, told me that on the Saturday following Peretti's murder a former soldier had been arrested for stabbing a drinking companion in a tavern. The murder had been committed in front of witnesses, so there was no question about the man's guilt and it took the judge only about ten minutes to sentence him to hang. The sentence was to be carried out in three days' time, and the prisoner was asking to see me. He had some confessions to make.

"Confessions?" said I. "He's already been found guilty!"

"He says he committed another crime and wants to relieve his conscience before he dies."

"His conscience! Let him relieve it by confessing to the chaplain. I can't hang him twice!"

This conversation took place outside the entrance to the Corte. My squire was holding my horse ready for me to mount and ride home. I was hungry and eager to get outside my dinner. But when I was in the saddle I turned and said to Alfaro, out of pure routine, I suppose: "What's this conscientious convict called?"

"Barca."

"Barca! Did you say 'Barca'? God in Heaven! That changes everything! Bring him to me!"

"Now, Signor Bargello?"

"This minute!"

I dismounted, threw the reins to my squire and rushed back into the Corte. "Hurry, Alfaro, hurry!"

He was such a slowcoach!

When at last Barca appeared before me, his hands and feet in chains, I was no longer in any doubt. He was just as Filippo had described: tall, dark, broad-shouldered, with a beard up to the eyes, and very polite. He looked like a brute and sounded like a lamb.

"You wanted to speak to me?"

"Yes, please, Signor Bargello."

"What for?"

"To confess to another murder and ask you a favour."

"A favour? Would you prefer the galley to the gibbet?"

"Oh no, Signor Bargello, I'm a soldier. If I have to go I prefer to go quickly."

"Let's hear about this other murder."

Barca drew himself up, took a deep breath, and said solemnly: "It was I who killed Signor Peretti, Signor Bargello."

"On your own?"

"No, Signor Bargello, my dear friend Alberto Machione was with me. But I was the one who shot Signor Peretti. And I was the one who finished him off with my dagger."

"You're going to a lot of trouble to clear your dear friend Alberto Machione, Where is he?"

"I killed him."

I looked at him.

"You killed him?"

"Yes, Signor Bargello. He was the one in the tavern."

"So he wasn't as dear to you as all that."

"Oh yes, he was!" said he, his eyes suddenly brimming with tears, "his death was a sort of accident."

"Tell me about it."

"Well, we went for a drink in the tavern after we'd done the job. And we quarrelled about the loot. He wanted the dead man's doublet as well as half the piastres! And all he'd done was be there and re-load the arquebus! Well, we'd drunk a lot of wine, and things got hot, and I stabbed him."

"For a doublet?"

"It was a very fine doublet, Signor Bargello. Real buffalo hide! With pockets in the armholes!"

"Where is it?"

"The turn-key of the prison took it!" said Barca in despair, tears streaming down his cheeks in torrents now. "He'd no right to do that, Signor Bargello! No, he'd no right! I know the rules. My things belong to me until I'm executed. And when I'm dead they're supposed to go to the hangman, not the turn-key! It's a disgrace, Signor Bargello! The turn-key's not only robbed me — he's robbed the hangman as well!"

"We'll talk about that later," I said impassively. "Now let's get back to the facts. Tell me about the murder of Peretti."

In his soft voice Barca gave me an account that exactly coincided with

227

Filippo's. As soon as he'd finished I spoke. "And did you kill Signor Peretti to rob him?"

"Oh no, Signor Bargello," said Barca, shocked. "I'm not a thief. I'm a soldier, even if I'm not in service at the moment. I only kill to order."

"And who ordered this murder?"

"A monk in a tavern."

"Did you know him?"

"No, Signor Bargello."

"Tell me what he looked like."

"It's difficult. I never saw him without his hood. He was small and thin. I don't know his name."

"Why did you do what he told you?"

"He paid me."

"How much?"

"A hundred piastres."

"And you killed a man for a hundred piastres?"

"Signor Bargello, when I was a soldier I killed men for much less than that. And, as I said, I was not in service, and I was broke. Everyone has to eat."

"Whom did you serve under when you were a soldier?"

"Prince Orsini. He sacked me a couple of months ago – and Machione."

"Why?"

"He suspected us of immorality."

"What sort of immorality?"

"You know, Signor Bargello."

"And was he right?"

"No."

"You don't sound very sure."

"Signor Bargello!" he said angrily. "What do you want? Isn't hanging enough? What would satisfy you? Would you like me to be burned as a sodomite?"

"No, no, of course not! Calm down, Barca. All this is between ourselves. In your opinion, might your former master have ordered this murder, using the monk as an intermediary?"

"I did wonder about it, seeing how beautiful the widow is, and given the monk's rude remark. But on reflection I don't think so."

"Why not?"

"The Prince wouldn't have chosen soldiers to do a murder. He'd have used bandits. And there's no shortage of them at Montegiordano. The courtyard's full of them."

"Why bandits?"

"They do that sort of thing better than we do. It's their profession."

"You don't think you made a very good job of it?"

"Terrible. The arquebus wasn't a good idea, Signor Bargello. If Signor Peretti had had a pair of pistols Machione and I would have been dead ducks before we got near him."

He was right. The arquebus was a typical soldier's idea and not at all appropriate. It's noisy and unreliable, especially at night, in poor visibility. Bandits would have hidden in a doorway and stabbed Peretti from behind, not forgetting to dispatch the torch-bearer, too, as the only witness. Moreover there are so many of them in Rome that if they'd been caught it would have been impossible to work back from them to the person behind them. Using a soldier or an ex-soldier was tantamount to putting your signature to the murder. Could I believe the Prince had been so stupid? Wasn't it more likely that the real instigator of the crime had chosen two of Orsini's former soldiers purposely in order to incriminate him? In my view there were too many fingers in this affair pointing at him and Marcello. It was as if someone were trying to influence my judgement.

"Well, Barca," I said, "is that all?"

"No, Signor Bargello. As I said, I want to ask you a favour."

"Tell me what it is."

"I'd like the turn-key to give me back my doublet."

"Forgive me for reminding you, Barca, but you'll only be able to wear it for three days."

"Never mind. I'd like to be decently dressed on the scaffold."

"Right. You shall have it back."

"Thank you very much indeed, Signor Bargello!" he cried.

He made to kiss my hands, but the guards wouldn't let him, and at a sign from Alfaro they led him away.

"Alfaro, go to the prison and make sure Barca gets his doublet back.

229

And see he's well treated and well fed until the end."

"Now, Signor Bargello?"

"Now. Why will you always procrastinate? And tell the hangman to strangle him on the quiet before he puts the rope round his neck."

"The hangman usually asks the condemned man ten piastres for that."

"Ten piastres isn't much for a buffalo doublet he wouldn't have got if Barca hadn't complained about it. And if that consideration isn't enough, tell him it's an order."

I went home and ate and drank heartily as usual, then spent the afternoon writing my report. I went into the most circumstantial detail with all the different testimonies, and concluded that as things stood it was impossible: *primo*, to find out who had organised the murder; *secundo*, to say definitely that there'd been guilty relations between Vittoria Peretti and "a certain nobleman"; and *tertio*, still less to show that Vittoria Peretti (or anyone belonging to her entourage) had been an accomplice to the murder. I was forced to the reluctant conclusion that she'd had nothing to do with it.

I handed in my report to Governor Portici the same evening. The Pope had expressed a wish to see it, and Portici wanted to read it first. The next morning he sent me a note saying my report was "most excellent" and he was taking it to the Vatican that day.

A week went by, and Portici sent for me. I noticed his eyes as soon as I went in: they were evading mine. He looked simultaneously worried and embarrassed. After a long irrelevant preamble he finally told me His Holiness had decided to incarcerate Vittoria Peretti and her maid in the Castel Sant'Angelo.

I was struck dumb. When at last I could speak I said: "As the case stands, there's not enough evidence to bring Vittoria Peretti to trial."

"The Vatican is aware of that. Therefore it doesn't intend to try her. Only to imprison her."

My surprise was succeeded by stupefaction.

"For how long?"

"Long enough for the Prince to stop thinking of marrying her."

"So the Vatican," said I with an effort, "believes there was a guilty relationship between her and the Prince?"

"Yes."

I gazed at Portici open-mouthed. "Your Excellency, were you able to find out what that belief is based on?"

"No. I came up against a brick wall."

After a moment I went on. "If they did commit adultery it seems very unlikely the Signora would have admitted it to her confessor. Or the Prince to his."

"Very unlikely."

"I don't know if Cardinal Montalto is going to like seeing his niece imprisoned without trial."

"His Holiness has never sought to please Cardinal Montalto."

That was true, but it wasn't for the pleasure of upsetting Montalto that the Pope was incarcerating his niece. I was silent, and to tell you the truth I was overcome with resentment. If the Vatican had another police apart from the Corte and followed its recommendations rather than mine, what purpose did I serve?

"Excellency," I said . . . Then I stopped and counted ten. The Pope is not only the head of Christendom, he's also my sovereign, and I owe him loyalty and obedience.

"Speak freely, della Pace," said Portici kindly. "Your words won't go beyond this office."

"Excellency, don't you think this imprisonment will be felt by all concerned as a crying injustice?"

"I'm afraid so. But among the Holy Father's entourage there are some who think . . ."

He sighed, and went on with an effort:

". . . who think injustice is better than disorder."

"But injustice often engenders disorder," said I angrily.

"What are you thinking of, della Pace?"

"Of a rebellion by the great nobles. Or one of them."

"That possibility didn't escape me either," said Portici. "I mentioned it in the Vatican but I was told there was no danger — every precaution had been taken to prevent it."

9

Monsignor Rossellino (il bello muto)

Although His Eminence Cardinal Montalto goes to bed late and sometimes reads late into the night, he invariably rises at half-past five in the morning. He says for a monk to get up later than that only encourages sloth and lust. That's why (though it's only one of the reasons) the Franciscans in Venice, whose lax ways he tried to reform when he was still only a bishop, conceived a great hatred for him and intrigued to get the Senate to turn him out of the Republic.

However, His Eminence allows me to get up a quarter of an hour later than he does, since because of his infirmities it takes him longer to dress, and even then his valet has to help him. But it's understood that on the stroke of six I meet him in the palace dining room. This would be a very pleasant little place if only the Cardinal would allow a fire there in the winter. But in that as in everything he's inflexible: "We'd be tempted to linger over our meals if we weren't so cold," he says. But in the study we share we do have a fire, though a small one, so that his rheumatic hand can hold a pen. All this is due to austerity, not avarice. His Eminence owns some fine woodlands, and we have enough logs in store to keep us amply supplied through ten winters.

As for what we eat early in the morning, it's very frugal. When I think of the breakfasts I used to have at the Contessa's I'm ashamed in retrospect at my greed, and happy I can no longer succumb to a sin bound to lead a man on to others even more serious.

As we enter the dining room one after the other on the stroke of six, Sister Maria Teresa, who's very old and fabulously wrinkled, brings us each a bowl of hot milk and a few slices of rye bread. That's all. On

Sundays she adds a couple of little goat cheeses, except during Lent, when we observe a very rigorous fast.

His Eminence doesn't open his lips during breakfast except to eat his bread, which he dips in the milk first as his teeth aren't very good. They laugh in the Vatican at this Spartan fare. "Montalto doesn't eat," they say. "He fills himself up like an ox for a day's ploughing."

Although this is said in a far from charitable spirit, it has some truth in it. One day when I asked His Eminence why he dined so lightly in the evening, he said: "I don't need much. I don't work at night."

The Cardinal says a short prayer before he rises, and another, not very long, in his oratory after breakfast. I've heard him say to a young priest who was always stringing together Paters and Aves: "Don't think you have to say the same thing a hundred times over. God isn't slow-witted."

He prays standing up: he can't kneel because of his crutches. Then he goes into his study, where with my help and that of his valet he drops on to rather than sits down on the chair behind his desk. He then becomes entirely transformed, and sets about his day's work briskly and cheerfully.

I greatly admire this alacrity, and have only once seen it fail him. That was on the day Filippo brought the news that Francesco Peretti had been murdered.

In an instant the Cardinal's firm countenance was ravaged by the most pitiful despair. For what seemed an interminable while he sat slumped in his chair, so overcome with grief and virtually stupefied that I turned my head away with a mixture of consternation and embarrassment. I was ashamed to witness this moment of weakness in a man whose fortitude I revered. I described this interval as "interminable" because it was so painful to me, but, thinking about it later, I don't suppose it lasted more than five minutes. Then the Cardinal turned to Filippo and said faintly, "Tell your mistress I'll come and see her in the morning." And to me: "Order my coach to be got ready and come and fetch me in an hour's time." Then he waved me imperiously away, and hid his terrible countenance in his great hands.

When I returned an hour later to tell him the coach was ready, I found him as I'd always known him till then: his eye commanding, his voice loud and his face impassive. This stoical calm didn't fail him even in the

Rusticucci palace, when he saw the blood-stained body of his adopted son and prayed at his bedside, leaning on his crutches. But the prayer was brief, and leaving the hall where the corpse lay without a backward glance, he summoned the family and the majordomo into another room. He spoke first to the majordomo, telling him to go at once and calm down the servants, who were in an uproar of tears and lamentation. "Tell everyone to go about their ordinary duties," he said, "and to do so in silence."

Then, alone with the family, he called for an account of the money available in the palace. It soon appeared that the only person who could answer this question was Giulietta Accoramboni, whom Francesco Peretti had greatly respected and who had acted as his steward. She went and got the papers in which she entered receipts and expenses, and read them out. Despite their grief the family were plunged into consternation by what emerged: without the emoluments the Vatican paid to the third chamberlain, the palace could only carry on for about three more months.

Tarquinia then announced that she would now take over the household finances. At which Vittoria said angrily and scornfully, "You!" The one word spoke volumes. Tarquinia opened her mouth to reply, but the Cardinal crushed her with a look and said in a voice that brooked no argument: "Giulietta was an excellent choice on Francesco's part. I shall stand by it."

Then he sent away everyone except Giulietta and discussed with her how to reduce expenses. The first thing, clearly, was to dismiss half the servants. The majordomo was called in to help draw up a list of those who were to go. Giulietta, pen in hand, tried to include Caterina's name among these, but the Cardinal said severely, "Do you want to drive Vittoria to despair?" and the Signorina drew in her horns.

Later on Giulietta expressed the hope that the Pope, of his indulgence, might bestow a small pension on his third chamberlain's widow.

"Don't count on it," said the Cardinal. "The Pope will shed plenty of tears on Francesco's death, but that's about all."

He spent a good hour with Giulietta examining Francesco's assets and deciding how they might be realised to support the family. He advised selling a couple of farms that brought in practically nothing and investing the proceeds with the Medicis in Florence. When Giulietta objected that the Medicis were known to practise usury, the Cardinal shrugged his powerful shoulders and said: "Do you want to be more Catholic than the Pope?" He was alluding to the fact although usury was forbidden by the Church, Gregory XIII had entrusted the Medicis with large sums of money which were intended to yield a profit.

Finally, when Giulietta said she didn't even know how she was going to pay for Francesco's funeral, this man whom some people called a miser replied: "There's no question of your paying anything – I'll see to it." And he drew his purse out of his cassock and gave it to her, saying: "Do what you think best, but no ostentation."

After that he didn't speak for some time. Giulietta, completely subdued by his authority, didn't dare breathe a word either.

"Giulietta," he said at last, "you're the only member of the family with an ounce of commonsense. What frame of mind would you say Vittoria is in now?"

"She's overwhelmed with grief."

"And remorse?" asked the Cardinal, with a piercing look.

"No," said Giulietta. "In my opinion she hasn't any reason to feel remorse."

For a moment that must have seemed endless, the Cardinal gazed at her as if to plumb her very soul. But she didn't flinch.

Two days later, referring to this exchange, the Cardinal told me: "There are three possibilities. Either Vittoria is not guilty of adultery and Giulietta is telling the truth. Or Vittoria is guilty and Giulietta doesn't know. Or Vittoria is guilty and Giulietta knows but is lying to protect her."

I looked at him inquiringly. He went on, with a sigh: "How is one to tell? Women are a complete enigma. They're taught to dissimulate from the cradle."

I asked him by means of signs whether he thought Vittoria had been an accomplice to the murder.

"No!" he answered emphatically. "A thousand times no! I'll never believe it!"

To return to the night of the murder, when we arrived back at the palace after His Eminence's conversation with Giulietta, I asked him if he intended to go to the meeting of the consistory that was to be held that day.

"Of course," he said. "I must. It will be an ordeal, and it would be cowardly to avoid it."

Before the meeting of the consistory began it was customary for the seventy cardinals to kneel at the Pope's feet and do him homage. This ceremony took some time, as the Pope addressed a few words to each of the cardinals. As what he said was amiable enough but unimportant, like the cardinals' replies, the other prelates were in the habit of conducting private conversations at the same time. They did so in respectfully low voices, but so many people were bound to produce quite a loud buzz, which only stopped when the first chamberlain announced that the meeting was about to begin.

On the day in question, however, the hum of voices, like that of bees round a hive, was interrupted long before the chamberlain's announcement, and much more abruptly than usual. A profound silence fell as soon as everyone saw His Eminence Cardinal Montalto going forward in his turn to salute the Holy Father.

The room in which the consistory was held was oblong, with the Pope's throne on one of the shorter sides and the prelates' stalls facing each other along the longer ones. As soon as His Eminence appeared in the central aisle, dragging himself along on his crutches, all heads on both sides of the room turned to watch his slow progress. All eyes were riveted on him, all ears strained to hear what he and the Pope would say to one another.

By that time none of the cardinals, and I dare say no one in Rome, was unaware of the murder, and no one could doubt the gravity of its implications for both men. It was a blow to the Cardinal's affections, and a blow to the Pope's authority. For though the crime had probably been committed for private reasons, the assassination of the Pope's third chamberlain could only be an insult and a challenge to the Pope himself.

His Eminence was exempted from kneeling to the Pope because of his infirmities, and a stool had been placed for him. But the first and second chamberlain both had to help him lower himself on to it, and this seemed to add to the drama of the conversation that was to follow.

There was certainly no handsomer old man than the Pope either in Rome or in the whole of Italy, nor one more healthy and alert. His snow-white hair framed a face with regular, aristocratic features. His pink cheeks and blue eyes gave him a youthful look even at seventy, and his expression was full of sweetness and nobility. If I hadn't known the faults and weaknesses that lay behind that magnificent appearance, I'd have been the first to be won over by his lofty demeanour, melodious voice and affable manners. What a poor figure my poor master cut in comparison, slumped on his stool with his hunched shoulders, dishevelled hair and beard, crooked nose, prognathous jaw and bushy eyebrows! He might well have been compared with Socrates, whose roughness and ugliness shocked people at first, though it was only from the undiscerning that they concealed his virtue, wisdom and fortitude.

The Pope, a consummate actor, was silent a moment, thus lending weight to what he was about to say. When he finally spoke, in a voice both loud and musical, it was clear he was addressing the cardinals in general rather than the individual before him.

"My very dear son," he began (how could he say otherwise in the circumstances, little though he really loved Montalto?), "we were deeply afflicted to learn of the cowardly murder of which our beloved son and chamberlain Francesco Peretti was the victim, and we wish to convey to you the indignation and sadness that overwhelmed us when we heard the dreadful news . . ."

At this point the Pope's eyes filled with tears, which continued to run down his cheeks for the rest of his speech, though without at all impairing the harmony or clarity of his diction. He went on: "We cannot but see the work of the devil in a base assault that bereaves us of the most worthy of our children. But how can we forget that a human hand collaborated with the Evil One in a crime that cries out to heaven for vengeance? May heaven hear our prayers and supplications and aid us in the search for the assassins and whoever armed them, that they may receive the wages of their iniquities here on earth before they are summoned to answer to the divine judge . . ."

He went on in this vein, angry and vengeful, for a good ten minutes. Although his tears continued to flow he expressed himself with such energy and forcefulness that even I would have been impressed if I hadn't known how little of those qualities he'd shown in the exercise of his power.

The Holy Father's tears dried up at the same time as his eloquence, and he gave a courteous and condescending wave of the hand to invite the Cardinal to speak. The general attention redoubled and the silence grew more profound as all the cardinals strained their ears to hear what my master would say. The Holy Father himself, while retaining his usual haughty reserve towards him, wore a look of eager curiosity that to me seemed tinged with malevolence. God forgive me if I was mistaken!

His Eminence spoke in a faint, toneless voice interrupted by coughing but devoid of any emotion. By contrast with the winged eloquence of the Pope his answer was brief.

"Most Holy Father," he said, "I thank you for your kind interest in my family. As for me, I already have one foot in the grave and I regard this bereavement as just one more test sent by my divine master before He calls me home. That is why, far from asking that the murderers be sought out and punished, I forgive them with all my heart for the evil they have done me."

Upon which the Holy Father gave another wave of the hand and the two chamberlains helped His Eminence back on to his crutches. Then, without another word, the Pope blessed him and he made his way back to his stall. I could tell the consistory was more astonished than edified by what he'd said. For although Christians consider the forgiveness of injuries the highest of virtues, it's one that is seldom practised even in the Vatican.

I learned what the Pope himself thought before the end of the consistory, when I unwittingly overheard a conversation between two prelates. The cardinals never hesitate to talk about my master in my presence: because I'm dumb they think I'm deaf as well. But how can I tell them they're mistaken? They wouldn't be able to understand the signs.

As soon as my master had – alas, so painfully – turned his back on the Pope and regained his seat, the Holy Father bent over to one of his familiars and said: "*Veramenta costui è un gran frate!*"*

This was repeated from one to another and didn't take more than half an hour to reach me. Perhaps I should here recall that my master was once a Franciscan, and that Pope Gregory XIII shared the popular Roman

* He really is a typical monk!

238

prejudice that members of the religious orders are hypocrites. In other words, the "forgiveness of injuries" was just a sham: Cardinal Montalto's only concern was to become the next Pope, and he was letting Prince Orsini off lightly so that he wouldn't be his enemy when it came to the vote.

When we got back to the palace I, as in duty bound, told His Eminence what the Holy Father had said. He shrugged his great shoulders, set his teeth and replied: "And I might have been stupid enough to ask that fellow for justice! You'll see, Rossellino! Apart from weeping and talking he won't do a thing!"

A week later "that fellow" (as His Eminence hadn't shrunk from calling the Pope – the only strong language he ever used in that connection) sent him the Bargello's report. His Eminence read and re-read it. His face showed no reaction and he made no comment. But when, a week later again, he heard that Vittoria had been arrested, all impassiveness was at an end. "What an injustice!" he cried in a fury. "And what a mistake!"

A little while later, sensing he was still preoccupied by this affair, I ventured to ask him by signs why he considered Vittoria's arrest a mistake.

"It's doubly so!" said he. "*Primo*, because there's nothing in the Bargello's report that points to her guilt. *Secundo*, and more important still, it's a political error. If the Pope thought the Prince guilty he should either have had the courage to confront him, or else done nothing at all. Arresting Vittoria was just ridiculous. Pretending to act when you're not really acting at all only exposes the weakness you're trying to hide."

Lodovico Orsini, Count of Oppedo

I didn't feel very comfortable when Paolo sent a messenger asking me to go and see him at Montegiordano. Even before the messenger arrived I'd had various reasons to be worried. The two scoundrels operating for us in the Nora mountains, harassed up hill and down dale by the Corte, had had the bright idea of coming to Rome and taking refuge in my palace. This was all the more stupid and dangerous because, for all my own and

Raimondo's efforts, the younger branch of the family has never been granted the right of asylum that Paolo enjoys at Montegiordano.

Raimondo, impulsive as ever, wanted to do away with the two idiots there and then.

"If the Corte arrests them," he said, "they'll talk under torture and that'll be the end of us."

"Now then, *Bruto*," said I. (He scowled at the sound of the nickname, so I put my arm round his neck and kissed him on the cheek.) "How can you kill them without all the men who camp in our courtyard knowing? And how much would they trust us after that? If we don't respect our own right of asylum, which of them is going to respect us?"

"And what do we do if the Bargello and his henchmen turn up at our door?"

"Keep them talking long enough to hide the bandits in the cellar and then let them in."

"Let them in?"

"Yes, if there are not too many of them."

Raimondo pulled a face, and was about to speak when Paolo's messenger arrived and gave me the note. I took my arm from round Raimondo's neck and said: "I'll be at Montegiordano in an hour."

And I threw the messenger a piastre.

I regretted it immediately; funds were low. Why, just because you're a nobleman, should you always do what the peasants expect of you? In a way, they're our masters! The trouble I've gone to to please the mob! Including setting up a barrel of wine for them outside my house in Rome at holiday time! So that they can guzzle for nothing!

"I don't like the sound of this," I said gloomily.

"Why not?" said Raimondo. "Paolo's our cousin and head of the family. He may have stopped funding us, but he's still fond of us."

"To be frank I think it'll be dangerous for me to go to Montegiordano today."

"Dangerous?" said he in amazement.

"Yes."

"Why?"

"It would take too long to explain."

"I know, I know! I'm a fool!"

240

"Come, *carissimo*, don't be cross. I have my reasons for not telling you. And it's safer for you to know nothing. Still, I'd feel safer if you'd come with me."

"Is it as bad as that?" said Raimondo.

You couldn't call Raimondo handsome, but his big mug isn't entirely without expression, and I could see from the way he was looking at me that he was simultaneously annoyed by my secretiveness and anxious for my safety.

"*Carissimo*," said I, putting a hand on his shoulder, "forgive me for leaving you in the dark. Let's put it in a nutshell and say I've been a bit of a Machiavelli. I'll explain later."

"Who's Machiavelli?"

"I'll explain that later too. Meanwhile, will you arrange for me to have a large escort?"

"Large?"

"About thirty men."

"Thirty?"

"Please, Raimondo, stop echoing everything I say! I'll need some noblemen too. Who've we got here today?"

"Silla Savelli," — he started with him because he was his bosom friend — "Pietro Gaetano, Emilio Capizucchi, Ascanio di Ruggieri and Ottavio di Rustici."

"*Tutta la crema*!★ Why are there so many of them?"

"We had a party last night with some girls, and they got drunk and stayed the night."

"That's where all the money goes!"

"You're not so economical, either!"

"True! Anyway, Raimondo, will you please tell them to get ready? I'll need them all."

"You mean you need five of the noblest sons of Rome as well as me to help you face Paolo?"

"Yes."

"What have you done to him to make you so frightened of him?"

"Nothing but good. But he thinks it's harm."

★ All the nobs!

241

"More mysteries," said Raimondo.

I left my escort in the courtyard at Montegiordano and, with my heart thumping and Raimondo following me like a shadow, I went up to meet Paolo in his favourite little room on the second floor. He was standing by the window, looking down into the courtyard.

"I see," he said drily as he turned round, "that as well as a large escort you've brought a lot of high society with you. Silla Savelli! Pietro Gaetano! Emilio Capizucchi! Ascanio di Ruggieri! Ottavio di Rustici! But what are you thinking of, Raimondo? We can't leave all those noble young men to fret in their saddles till we've finished talking. Raimondo, please go and tell my majordomo to get them some wine and a meal, then go and do the honours of my dining hall."

Graciously as it was framed, this was an order, and Raimondo, curious though he was to hear what we were going to say to one another, obeyed. So I was left alone with Paolo, willy nilly.

"So here you are!" said he, his lips smiling but his eyes scathing. "You came! Thank you. I'm in a quandary, Lodovico. The Pope has insulted me."

I raised one eyebrow.

"He's arrested Vittoria," he said.

"The main thing is," said I, "that he hasn't arrested you."

"He hasn't arrested me because he knows very well that I didn't have Peretti murdered. But by arresting Vittoria he gives everyone to understand that I'm the murderer. That's how the Pope has insulted me."

"How can you expect people not to think you're the murderer?" I asked. "Your expedition to Santa Maria has probably leaked out."

"Rumour isn't proof. I've managed to get hold of a copy of della Pace's report. He concludes that the murder was perpetrated in such a way as to make everyone think Marcello and I did it; but he doesn't believe we did."

"Della Pace's a clever man," said I smiling on one side of my face. "So you're cleared."

"Except that the Pope, by arresting Vittoria, designates me *urbi et orbi* as the guilty party!"

"Well, what are you going to do?"

242

"Take up arms and overthrow him."

"Paolo! You can't mean it! Attack the head of Christendom! He'll excommunicate you!"

"And if I succeed in turning him off his throne his successor will absolve me. Anyhow, it's not the Pope I'll be attacking, it's the ruler."

"And I suppose you invited me here to ask my advice."

"Not at all. My mind is made up. It's your help I'm asking for. You have a good army and the ear of the people."

"My help in attacking the Pope!" said I, pretending to be taken aback. "But Paolo, I'm a good Catholic!"

"So am I."

"But the risks are enormous! You're asking me to stake my property, my palace and my life in a completely unpredictable contest!"

"Isn't it the duty of all the Orsinis to take up arms when one of them is insulted?"

"But Paolo," said I with a faint smile, "don't you think it would be better if we spoke frankly? You want to attack the Pope not because you've been insulted, but to set Vittoria free. And that's why I refuse to help you. Vittoria's a widow. I have Virginio's interests very much at heart. So I don't want you to marry her."

"In short," replied he with a piercing look, "it suits you that she should be shut up in the Castel Sant'Angelo?"

His tone and look made my blood run cold. I didn't know what to say.

"Would you like a drink, Lodovico?" he asked.

"No – no, thanks. I'm not thirsty."

"You must be! You've been swallowing all the time we've been talking. Besides, it's very hot. Come on, pour yourself a drink. Pour one for me too. And take whichever glass you like. Then you won't think I'm trying to poison you."

He laughed, and I, rather mirthlessly, joined in. When I'd filled the glasses, Paolo took the one I handed him, and seeing I didn't touch mine, emptied his in one gulp. So I decided to drink too, but though the wine was excellent I had difficulty in swallowing it.

"Lodovico," he said conversationally, throwing himself on to a chair, "I've just heard something very strange. The Pope has sent a big sack of piastres from the Vatican to Cardinal de' Medici's palace in Rome, and *he's* sent it to the Patriarch of Venice's palace, also in Rome, where Cardinal Cherubi's staying. According to my information that sack contains fifty thousand piastres."

"That's a lot of money."

"Indeed. And isn't it strange such a large sum should be travelling about from one palace in Rome to another? And who knows who Cherubi will pass it on to? Do you know Cherubi, Lodovico?"

"Yes. I met him once. I dined at his house."

"Really!" said he with a little smile. "And what did you talk about?"

"This and that."

"Did you talk about me?"

"Among other things."

"What did he want to know?"

"Whether you were Vittoria's lover."

"And what did you say?"

"I said I didn't know anything about it."

"Well," said Paolo icily, "that was a good answer. And you're a good kinsman, Lodovico. And I wish you a good day."

At that he stood up and looked at me with a terrifying expression. My knees turned to water and I backed out of the room, afraid he might plant his dagger between my shoulder-blades if I turned round.

Down in the courtyard I called for Alfredo – he acts as squire to both Raimondo and me as we can't afford one each – and told him to go and fetch Raimondo and his noble friends. It took him a good ten minutes to drag them away from their entertainment. I could see Raimondo had had too much to drink again. He was red in the face and shouting, and as he walked along he was slapping his sword and obviously looking for trouble.

"Well, what's the matter with you, *carissimo*?" he bawled. "You're as white as a sheet! If anyone's insulted my elder brother – *affè di Dio*! I'll spit his liver on my sword!"

"No one's insulted me! And you're as red as a turkey-cock. Come, to horse! Help him, Alfredo!"

"I don't need Alfredo!" cried Raimondo, not even noticing that Alfredo was putting his foot in the stirrup and giving him a good boost from behind into the saddle.

Once he had mounted, however, he sat straight as a ramrod. His horse started to buck, but he brought it under control at once and gave it a little tap with his riding crop.

"What, beating your horse, Raimondo?" cried Silla Savelli.

"A woman, a mare and a walnut tree . . ." began Raimondo, who'd never struck a woman in his life, being as soft and easy-going with the opposite sex as he was rough with his own.

"Shame on you, Raimondo!" said Pietro Gaetano, laughing. "My mare has nothing but caresses from me! I couldn't bear to hurt her!"

"A crop never hurt a horse," said Ascanio di Ruggieri. "Their hide's too thick. It just annoys them, that's all."

This was debatable, and the discussion went on with much shouting and laughter as we rode through the courtyard. The outlaws and bandits who filled it made way for us grudgingly, looking askance at the handsome young men in their glistening doublets who didn't even deign to glance at them and jabbered at the tops of their voices as if Montegiordano belonged to them. Turning round in the saddle, I saw Paolo standing at the second-floor window, motionless as a statue, looking down at us. The sensation of having his eyes on me, the huge courtyard, all those men totally devoted to him – it all weighed one down. I spurred my horse and was the first through the gateway. Out in the street again I felt better. Paolo had understood or guessed everything and I'd got off lightly. It was almost too good to be true! His whore shut up in Sant'Angelo! Paolo paralysed by my neutrality! And later this evening, fifty thousand ducats falling into my money-bags like rain! Alas, how little a man knows of his own future! A word, a gesture, and in a few seconds it all collapses!

We were about a hundred yards from our own palace and I was already imagining the festivities with which I'd celebrate my success, when our troop was brought to a halt. A score or more horsemen were riding towards us with arquebuses by their sides and della Pace at their head. He greeted us politely, and as the street was too narrow for us to pass, suggested his party should go back a little way to let us through. I agreed, and he turned his men round, but in the subsequent confusion I saw – and my eyes nearly started out of my head at the sight – that our two bandits from Nora were tied on to one of the police horses, the reins of which were

245

held by a particularly gigantic officer.

"Bargello," I yelled, "what's this? Have you broken into my house in my absence and abducted two of my men?"

Della Pace took off his hat and rode back towards me, closely followed by his men.

"Signor Conte," he said politely, "I'm extremely sorry to have had to do it, but I was ordered to arrest these two bandits by His Excellency Governor Portici. And I didn't break in. I rang and was let in. My men did the rest."

"But you've violated the Orsinis' right of asylum!" shrieked Raimondo, red as a beetroot.

"Forgive me, Signor Orsini," said della Pace, "but the right of asylum belongs to the elder and not to the younger branch of the family."

"Elder or younger, what do I care?" shouted Raimondo. "Just you untie our men and give them back to us, you scoundrel!"

"Signore," said the Bargello, putting his hat on again and speaking more stiffly, "you forget you are speaking to the Bargello."

"Don't you get mixed up in this, Raimondo," I said. "Let me talk to the Bargello!"

"I'll get mixed up in it if I like!" screeched Raimondo – the wine had given him the courage to disobey me. "You heard me, Bargello, you scum! Untie those men and hand them over!"

"Signore," said the Bargello, "you insult me, and that's unworthy of both of us. Have you forgotten I'm a nobleman too?"

"A lousy flea-ridden minor nobleman!" roared Raimondo.

"Be quiet, Raimondo, and let me speak!" said I.

"Minor nobility, perhaps," said the Bargello grimly, "but none of my servants has ever gone robbing and murdering travellers in the Nora mountains!"

"Wretch!" shouted Raimondo. "You dare to cast aspersions on the Orsinis' honour! I'll make you eat your words!"

"Come, come, Raimondo, you go too far," said Silla Savelli, who was gentle and conciliatory by nature.

"Let me speak!" Raimondo was foaming at the mouth by now. "I'll flay this rascal and his stinking policemen alive! And in the meanwhile," raising his riding crop, "I'll give him a good hiding!"

"Signore," said the Bargello, "I advise you not to use violence. The fuses of our guns are lit, and my men don't like being defied or insulted."

"We'll see!" roared Raimondo, raising his crop still higher.

At this point Silla Savelli, who was on Raimondo's right, urged his horse closer and grabbed him by the wrist. But Raimondo shook himself free and brought his crop down as hard as he could on the Bargello's face.

There was a moment of stupefaction. I watched incredulously as the blood welled up and started to run down the Bargello's cheek. Then he turned in his saddle. Contrary to what I said later, for the good of the cause, he didn't give the order to fire. He just showed his men his bloodstained face. They fired immediately. The noise was deafening, and by the time the smoke had cleared from the narrow street the police and their leader had turned and ridden away. I dismounted. Five of our people were lying on the cobblestones: Raimondo, Silla, Pietro Gaetano and two of the escort.

I sent at once for a barber-surgeon, who gave me little hope for Raimondo and Silla. And an hour later they both died, before they could be given extreme unction. They'd been so close in life that they'd shared everything, even their mistresses. And now they'd breathed their last almost together.

The news of the police's fatal volley spread swiftly all over Rome, and by one o'clock in the afternoon all the nobility of the city had gathered in my courtyard to file past the dead and injured in grief and anger. They all shook their fists and swore vengeance on the Bargello and his men. And already the ordinary people, who loved the nobles as much as they hated the Pope, were besieging my door and demanding weapons, as well as torches "to go and smoke the old fox out of his lair in the Vatican".

Paolo arrived an hour later. There was a stir among the nobles when he appeared, for everyone knew of his military talents and already regarded him as the leader of the rebellion.

He knelt and prayed for a long while by the two bodies, and when he stood up Alfredo, who was beside him, told him in detail what had happened. Paolo walked past me and pretended not to see me, then changed his mind and came back. He put his arms round me, kissed me on the cheek, and whispered: "Now you *have* to be with me!"

In my opinion, nothing is worse for a country than secret diplomacy. If some of a ruler's officials agree with him on a policy the others know nothing about, the latter may in all good faith take contradictory measures that completely undermine the secret plan. A government may thus find itself in the dangerous and ridiculous position of a snake that instead of biting the enemy bites its own tail.

And that's exactly what happened over Lodovico Orsini. I, the governor of Rome, was kept in ignorance from beginning to end of the Vatican's negotiations about him. These were designed through Cardinal Cherubi, to ensure Lodovico's neutrality if Prince Orsini declared open war on the Papacy.

The consequences of this secrecy have been extremely grave. I list them below for the edification of those who may wish to conduct their politics on sounder principles.

First: if I'd known the Vatican intended to negotiate with Lodovico Orsini I'd have advised them against having anything whatever to do with that vice-ridden, debt-riddled gentleman.

Second: I'd have told the Vatican of the Corte's suspicions concerning the two bandits who were robbing and murdering wayfarers in the Nora mountains, and how those suspicions had become certainties when the bandits in question took refuge in Lodovico Orsini's palace.

Third: should the Vatican have disregarded my advice and treated with Lodovico Orsino just the same, I would certainly not have ordered the Bargello to go and force an entry into his palace and arrest the two bandits there. Knowing how proud Lodovico is, and how violent his younger brother Raimondo (known as *il bruto*), I'd have been afraid such an intrusion would end in bloodshed. As, alas, it did.

In the subsequent skirmish two gentlemen fell who belonged to a couple of the most important families in Rome, and this sounded the knell of all the Vatican's plans. For it soon became evident that after Raimondo's death Lodovico could not remain neutral. Nor could the Roman nobility be indifferent to the death of Silla Savelli. And Prince Orsini wouldn't miss the opportunity to assume the leadership of a rebellion that might enable him to free Vittoria.

Though they didn't choose it knowingly, the conspirators couldn't have taken up arms at a more propitious moment. Popular discontent was at its height, for reasons I shall now explain.

As both leader of Christendom and head of a sovereign state, the Pope exercised two powers, the spiritual and the temporal, which together gave him unlimited sway. But Gregory XIII used his powers unwisely. Above all he too often confused the papal tiara and the princely crown.

The year before the rebellion, being short of money, he'd taken back from certain gentlemen the fiefs his predecessor had granted them. And when some of these gentlemen complained a little too boldly of how they'd been despoiled and ruined, Gregory XIII promptly and without more ado excommunicated them, thus adding injustice to expropriation.

There were many excommunications for non-religious reasons during Gregory XIII's papacy, and these, as well as dealing cruel blows to innocent people, also scandalised many of the faithful. And that wasn't the only example of how the spiritual power was made to serve the interests of the temporal. More than once the Pope issued a *precetto* against a political opponent – an irrevocable decree annulling his marriage. If the unfortunate victim refused to quit the marital home he found himself living in concubinage, and thus in a state of mortal sin, with the woman he loved, and who only the day before had been his lawful wife. This was an abuse that angered the Pope's least sophisticated subjects as well as his theologians. The latter murmured under their breath that marriage was a sacrament in which the husband and wife were the ministers, and therefore no external authority had the power to set it aside.

But Gregory XIII used his temporal power arbitrarily too. Nepotism had always been the main weakness of the Papacy, but Gregory XIII's indolence and thoughtlessness allowed the nephews to whom he entrusted the main instruments of power to wield it without let or hindrance, according to their mood, their purse, or their mere likes and dislikes. They didn't hesitate to throw people into Papal prisons without charge or trial, and for an unlimited period – honest people whose only crime was to have displeased or opposed them.

I feel some qualms about mentioning one class of Gregory XIII's enemies. They weren't very numerous, but their animosity was all the fiercer for having to remain secret. I refer to those Lutherans whom the Inquisition and fear of the stake had reconverted to the old religion. These people still had a strong hidden affection for their former opinions, and couldn't forgive Gregory XIII for celebrating a Mass of thanksgiving on hearing of the massacre of the Protestants in Paris on St Bartholomew's Day. Some Catholics, even in Rome, were shocked by this, and by the public bonfires the Pope caused to be lit on the same occasion.

Worse still, Gregory XIII's government managed to be weak as well as tyrannical. Not daring to attack Prince Orsini after Peretti was murdered, he imprisoned a woman who appears not to have been involved in the crime. And then, having provoked Prince Orsini by incarcerating the woman, he tried to paralyse him by purchasing the neutrality of a dubious character who might otherwise have been his ally. As Gregory XIII didn't dream for a moment that this *combinazione* could fail, he had no alternative plan ready and took no special precautions, such as reinforcing his Swiss Guard while there was yet time.

The uprising took him completely by surprise, and was all the more threatening because the people soon joined the nobles. They did so partly because they hated the Pope's nephews and the Papal police, and partly because they were attached to Lodovico, and to all the great households, for the largesse they bestowed. This bounty cost the aristocracy little enough, for they were as harsh and extortionate towards their peasants as they were generous towards the lower orders in the towns. The reason for this was that the peasants were scattered about the countryside and the nobles weren't afraid of them, whereas they had to handle the townspeople carefully: their number and concentration made them dangerous, and they could be turned without undue expense into a useful following.

I sent spies to all the nerve centres of the city as soon as della Pace, his face all bloody, told me about the confrontation that had cost Raimondo Orsini and Silla Savelli their lives. (The Bargello hadn't given the order to fire, contrary to what Lodovico said later — one more lie made no difference to the wretched fellow.) The spies brought back very alarming news. The nobles were swiftly organising themselves under Prince Orsini, and handing out knives to their various followers while prudently keeping the arquebuses for themselves. The mob was already swarming through the streets, chasing the Papal police and murdering more than one of them. This state of affairs brought all the cut-purses and cut-throats out of their holes, ready for robbery, looting, murder and other villainies.

I informed the Pope's nephews that they should take refuge as quickly as possible in the Vatican (their servants were being molested already), and went there myself with della Pace. I immediately put the whole place into a state of siege, barricading all exits except one and training the cannon on the besiegers. The Vatican had already sent for immediate help from the Spanish troops stationed in the Two Sicilies under the command of an Austrian general. But anyone who knew how long it took Philip II of Spain to make a decision, and how long it took the Austrians to carry one out, knew nothing would come from that quarter for at least three weeks. And the way things were going it would be too late in three days. People were running round outside the Vatican with torches, shouting that they were were going to "smoke the old fox out."

At night, by a little secret door that I'd left open though strongly guarded, I sent out several emissaries. One had orders to try to get into Montegiordano, where the rebellion had set up its headquarters. There was so much bustle and activity that he succeeded, and found the nobles both excited and embarrassed at finding victory so near. They scarcely knew what to do with it. They were also worried lest the mob get out of hand: although they alone had guns, they were afraid they'd no longer be safe in their own palaces.

The emissary to Montegiordano was a monk, a man of courage and resource. Seeing how anxious the nobles were, he was bold enough to speak to Prince Orsini in private, explaining who he really was and asking him on what conditions the rebels would make peace with the Pope.

The Prince took him into a little room, locked the door and said: "There are two conditions. First: a coach with my coat of arms on it and surrounded by a platoon of my soldiers will be waiting at midnight outside the little door at the back of the Castel Sant'Angelo. Two women prisoners unjustly detained there by the Pope will come out and get into the coach. If they haven't appeared by one in the morning, my men will attack one of the gates of the Vatican with a battering ram."

"And the second condition, my lord?"

"It's one that everyone else insists on, though I myself find it very repugnant. All the nobles are clamouring for della Pace's head."

"That's horrible, my lord!"

"Yes. But it's the price the Pope has to pay for peace."

"But, my lord, even if the Pope agreed to sacrifice his Bargello, it's doubtful if the people would be satisfied with that. They're crying out for him to abdicate."

"Don't worry. We're the ones with the troops and the guns. We'll cut the mob to pieces."

"What, my lord? Your allies?"

"What else can we do? Do you want this hateful anarchy to go on? In the end we ourselves will be the victims."

"My lord, I shall report your conditions faithfully."

"Remember the two go together. If the first isn't fulfilled there'll be no point in fulfilling the second."

"My lord, forgive me for speaking frankly – but what would happen if only the second condition were fulfilled, and the nobles were satisfied with that?"

"I'd continue the siege myself, and the people with me. Would you like to wager on whether I can capture the Vatican by tomorrow at noon?"

"You'll be excommunicated."

"Are you here to negotiate or to threaten?"

"My lord, pardon me for my straight speaking. May I go on, or shall I say no more?"

"Go on, please. I find your conversation very instructive."

"What will happen if the Vatican fires its cannon on the besiegers?"

"I have cannon too. And instead of just tickling your main gate with a battering ram I'll blow it to smithereens. You know what will happen then. The mob will pour through the breach, and loot and kill all in its path!"

"And you'd allow such carnage?"

"How could I stop it?"

"Oh, my lord! All this because of a woman!"

"I'm sorry, father, but that subject's outside your competence. Go

252

back whence you came and report my conditions word for word."

When the monk, safely back within our walls, told me all this, I could scarcely believe my ears. The second condition – that della Pace's head be thrown to the mob – seemed so utterly insulting to the person it was addressed to. Rather than repeat it to the Pope myself I decided to take the monk with me and let him tell his tale.

I found the Holy Father with the captain of the Swiss Guard and a dozen or so senior Vatican dignitaries, all in a state of the greatest alarm and discussing whether or not to let our cannon take a hand. The captain of the Swiss Guard was very much against it, saying to fire them would be ineffective in the city, where there were plenty of walls for the assailants to shelter behind. "It will only enrage them more!" he declared in his heavy German accent.

But the Holy Father had noticed me, and guessing that I brought news beckoned me forward. After kneeling and kissing his slipper (a ceremony he didn't curtail, even in those circumstances), I told him about the monk and requested him to hear what he had to say.

While the monk was speaking I watched the faces of the Pope and his advisers and was amazed to see them show immense relief. But when the monk had finished the Holy Father, instead of indulging in his usual eloquence, merely asked his counsellors for their opinion. There was a long and embarrassed silence: none of them wanted to be the first to speak. The subject was an extremely thorny one, and they didn't know, and couldn't guess, what the Pope's wishes were in the matter.

The silence must have irritated the Pope, for he turned to one of the cardinals present and asked imperiously: "Cherubi?"

The choice was no accident: Cherubi was well-known for his frankness and his gaffes.

"Most Holy Father," he trumpeted, "I think that if the proposed negotiations were successful we'd get off very lightly."

"Very lightly?" murmured another cardinal.

"I mean," went on Cherubi, not in the least put out by the interruption, "things might be much worse. For instance, if the nobles decided to unleash the mob. That's why we ought to treat with the nobles while there's still time."

"But the conditions are very harsh," said another of the cardinals, "especially the second."

I noticed he spoke very softly and hesitantly, not at all like Cherubi.

"No doubt the conditions are harsh," went on the latter, "especially the one concerning della Pace. All of us here are fond of della Pace. We respect him. We've got nothing against him. But it's through him the trouble started, so he'll have to put up with being the means of stopping it. The Most Holy Father must be as courageous in sacrificing him as Abraham was in sacrificing Isaac."

As the Pope heard this speech with some signs of approbation, no one else dared protest. But to compare the demands of a band of bloodthirsty nobles to a command from the Almighty . . . !

"My most dear sons," said the Pope, suddenly desperate to have the discussion over and done with, "which of you shares Cardinal Cherubi's opinion?"

It escaped no one that this way of putting the question dictated its own answer. Every hand was raised except two.

I then did something extremely audacious. I threw myself at the Pope's feet and panted: "Most Holy Father, if anyone has to be sacrificed, let it be me! I was the one who ordered della Pace to arrest the two bandits. So I was really responsible for the fatal incident!"

Gregory XIII seemed taken aback. He gazed down at me out of his big blue eyes as if he didn't know what to say.

"My dear Portici," said Cherubi loudly, "unfortunately it's not your head the rebels are after. And even if we gave it to them it wouldn't satisfy them. So there's no point in going back on our vote. What I suggest," said he, looking at the captain of the Swiss Guard, "is that the thing should be done discreetly and without warning, so that the person concerned hardly even notices he's being killed. The head can be separated from the body afterwards."

I looked at the Holy Father. He was nodding gently, but it was impossible to say whether this was a sign of approval or of senility. It suddenly struck me he was exploiting his great age to appear weaker and less alert than he really was. As recently as the previous day I'd seen him laughing, lively and incisive and holding his slim frame perfectly upright.

"Most Holy Father . . ." I made a last effort.

But he immediately interrupted me. "My very dear son," he said,

254

"believe me, I'm terribly grieved that the tyranny of circumstance has forced us into this painful decision. I am the first to deplore it – and I should like to be left alone to offer my suffering and affliction up to the Lord." His pink cheeks streamed with tears.

"My very dear son," he said, blessing me, "go in peace."

But despite his tears and his blessing, the Holy Father never forgave me for the embarrassment I'd caused him. He took his revenge at leisure, a few months after peace was restored. While I was enjoying a summer holiday at my villa in Ostia he wrote and told me I needn't come back: it was time for me to rest from the exertions of my office. The style of the letter was suave and flowery, but the fact remained: not only was I relieved of my duties as Governor, but I was also banished from Rome.

Alfredo, squire to Raimondo and Lodovico Orsini

I've not got much to say, and as I haven't the gift of the gab I'll say it simply. Forgive me if I use the Venetian dialect – I can understand Italian but I don't speak it very well.

To start with I was Lord Raimondo Orsini's squire, then I was squire to his brother Count Lodovico as well. I knew both of them well.

They used to call Raimondo *il bruto*, mostly because of his mug. Mine's not much better. In fact, I'd say it's worse. If I was judged on that alone I'd go straight to the gallows.

But I'm not really a bloodthirsty type. It's true I've stabbed about half a dozen people in my time, but always on orders from my masters – never on my own account. And to tell you the truth I wouldn't have liked to be a bandit in the Nora mountains, like some I might name.

To get back to Raimondo, he was only a brute when he'd had too much to drink – and with him, "too much" was a lot – and then you had to watch out. But he was kind-hearted. The trouble he went to, killing the Duchess Isabella at Bracciano! And afterwards he cried his eyes out. And never stopped praying. As bad as a priest! She *was* very beautiful. I've never seen such a fine figure of a woman. But even so. After all, she had betrayed Prince Paolo with just about everybody.

I've got happy memories of that time in Bracciano. After the thing was done and Raimondo had finally finished saying his prayers, we really enjoyed ourselves. Guzzling, boozing, wenching – a whole week of it. None of the maids in the castle escaped, whether they liked it or not. You can imagine! With the duchess dead, we were the masters!

But the brutal side of Lord Raimondo was his undoing. If he'd let Lord Lodovico do the talking that day it wouldn't have happened! But he would go and work himself up! Of course, he *had* been drinking. Still, insults were one thing, but hitting the Bargello on the cheek with his crop was going too far! Mind you, the Bargello didn't give the order to fire. He turned in his saddle so that his men should see the outrage he'd suffered. Unfortunately the fuses of their arquebuses were already lit. I found out afterwards why, and I'll tell you.

When they came into our courtyard to capture the bandits our men showed their teeth, and as there were a good many of us the policemen took fright and withdrew into the gate tower. There the Bargello ordered them to light their fuses before renewing the attack, and this time our lot were less obstreperous.

So – that's the explanation. It was simply because the Bargello's men had their fuses already alight that they fired. And also because they were very fond of him. If they hadn't been they'd just have laughed at him getting hit in the face. Not in front of him, of course! But the fact is, good masters are mourned, and bad ones you wouldn't mind giving a shove to help them into the next world.

The policemen didn't wait to aim – they just fired at random into the crowd! It's a miracle there were only two dead. I was just behind poor old Raimondo, and the bullet that went through his chest grazed my arm. But I'll tell you what was the most unfair, and that was the death of poor Lord Silla Savelli. You couldn't find a nicer, gentler young man, and very polite with ordinary people too. He even tried to hold Raimondo's hand back when he lifted his riding crop. And all he got for his kindness was a ball in the head.

I'm not ashamed to say it – I wept for Raimondo. The more so as I only had one master now: Lodovico. I won't say anything about him one way or the other. It's not for me to judge. They say he has a special devotion to the Madonna and prays to her every day, morning and evening. But if you ask me he's not the sort of person the Madonna would like very much

— not if she knew him as well as I do.

Perhaps I didn't explain very clearly about the arquebuses and the lighted fuses. I'd better have another try.

What I mean is: if the fuses hadn't already been lit, the policemen wouldn't have fired. Why not? Because they wouldn't have lit them without being ordered to by the Bargello. You may say they *fired* without being ordered to. But it's not the same thing. It only takes a second to fire. But it takes some time to light a fuse. You've got to get the flint out of your pocket, strike it, light the touch, blow on it to keep it burning till it's close to the fuse, and blow again: a whole rigmarole. And in that case the Bargello would have had time to say: "What do you think you're doing? I haven't given you any orders!" And on our side, even if he hadn't said anything, we'd have seen what they were up to. And we'd have had time to drive them away with a few good thumps from the flat of our swords, without even having to kill them. Don't forget there were thirty of us and only twenty of them.

You see what a small thing it revolved around: just those lighted fuses. And the enormousness of the result! By the next day the city was being put to fire and sword. All the nobility were mobilised, and all the people out on the streets. *All* the people, good and bad — and as it turned out there wasn't much to choose between the two: respectable artisans took to murdering and looting along with the riffraff. All the policemen they could lay their hands on were slaughtered down to the last man! The same with the servants of the Pope's nephews. The nephews themselves would have met the same fate if they hadn't taken refuge in the Vatican. Anyway, their palaces were looted, and they weren't poor!

The Vatican itself was surrounded and besieged, with people rushing around in all directions shouting "Abdicate! Abdicate! Death to della Pace!", and even "Death to the Pope!". Yes, you heard me: "Death to the Pope!" — and all of them devout Catholics, God forgive them!

The nobles held slightly aloof, on horseback. Their soldiers and other followers on foot were all armed with arquebuses. Some of the latter were the kind with wheels (though in my opinion this newfangled version isn't reliable) and some were the usual sort, with fuses — and you can be sure they were lit!

Some distance back from the crowd, and in front of the main body of

257

the nobles, was Prince Paolo on his white mare. Close on his right was Marquis Giulio Savelli (poor Silla's father), and on his left Count Lodovico. Here there was silence. And apprehension. For seeing the populace on the rampage like that they began to fear for their own palaces. What struck me most of all was that they weren't doing anything. Nothing at all! And when I ventured to ask Count Lodovico what they were waiting for he only snapped, "For the moon to fall into our pockets!"

True, there was a moon, and it was almost as light as day. You could have read a book (if you knew how to read). Prince Paolo was able to consult his watch every so often; he said the time aloud. He was also able to read a note that his squire trotted up with. Afterwards he looked radiant. We didn't know what was in it until later.

Suddenly: "Let's get it over with," said Prince Paolo.

And he ordered a salvo of muskets to be fired at the windows of the Vatican. As no one had been foolish enough to stand by them not much harm was done except to the glass. Just a little tickle, really. But it pleased the populace, who applauded as if it were a show.

Prince Paolo looked at his watch again and advanced three cannon. They weren't very big and there were only three of them. And the gunners on the other side were arranging sandbags and screens to shelter themselves from our arquebuses. Meanwhile the horsemen tried to clear a way through the mob so the cannon could fire at the gate of the Vatican. But the horsemen weren't enough, and it took two ranks of foot soldiers to hold back the idiots prepared to be made into mincemeat just to get a better view.

I could see the gunners inside were taking their time arranging their shelter, and so could the mob. They shouted to our side to "Hurry up! Get a move on!" and Prince Paolo sent a dozen or so soldiers forward with a battering ram. They began to attack the gate. But their efforts were rather half-hearted, and they produced no result. When the mob saw this they yelled "Harder! Harder!" and the hotheads among them shouted "Let us handle the battering ram – then you'll see!" The double row of soldiers had all they could do to hold them back.

Then in a second-floor window, over the gate that had been battered to so little effect, a white flag appeared. Uproar! And after a moment a box was let down on a rope!

"Go and see what it is, Alfredo!" said Count Lodovico, his eyes blazing.

I spurred my horse forward and told one of the soldiers to leave the battering ram and go and open the box. He did so: it contained della Pace's head, the neck still dripping with blood. I seized it by the hair and galloped off so that the mob couldn't snatch it away.

Prince Paolo was our general, so I offered the head to him. He declined it with disgust. The same with Marquis Giulio Savelli. But don't imagine Count Lodovico was so sensitive! He grabbed the head by the hair and pranced about in front of the mob brandishing it at arm's length and shouting "Della Pace! Della Pace! Victory! Victory!" And when they all rushed towards him, he threw it to them.

I shan't say what happened next, and what those scum of the earth did with it. It makes me feel ill just to think of it.

The nobles were silent. If you ask me they weren't feeling too happy. After all, della Pace was a nobleman too – of second rank, but honourable. And a good man, respected by everybody. And they were revolted by the fact that Gregory XIII had been such a poltroon as to sacrifice a loyal servant to save his own throne. I was ashamed of him myself. And of the good Christians who kicked that poor bloodstained head about as if it were a football.

And don't go thinking that was enough to calm them down! They were beside themselves, the beauties! The cries of "Abdicate! Abdicate!" "Down with the tyrant!" and "Death to the Pope" started up again. They piled kindling up against one of the smaller gates of the Vatican. They jostled the soldiers and got the battering ram away from them. Then ten, twenty of the mob began battering at the main gate, and this time it was serious.

Prince Paolo turned in his saddle and asked the nobles: "Shall we let them go on?"

What a question? They certainly weren't going to do anything of the kind! After the Pope it would be their turn! The answer was unanimous. They were all quite determined! In the twinkling of an eye they'd changed sides!

Prince Paolo ordered his cannon to be swung round, and without warning he fired on the people. The crowd was so dense that the cannon balls wrought havoc. And scarcely had the mob recovered from their first stupefaction than a volley of musket shots rang out. Men fell by the dozen, dead or wounded. The rebels began to fall back. Another volley! There was no need to aim, there were so many of them. They fell like flies all over the place. It was a real massacre. As the rebels' retreat intensified, Paolo turned to the nobles and ordered a charge. The hiss in the air as they all unsheathed their swords! Their war swords, double-edged! No messing about with the flat of them! Cut and thrust for anyone who didn't run fast enough!

As Count Lodovico, bloodthirsty as ever, was about to join in the onslaught, Prince Paolo held him back, saying: "*Carissimo*, go home now. And please stop trying to be a Machiavelli! If it hadn't been for you none of this would have happened. And, believe me, all this bloodshed is pointless: the prisoner of Sant'Angelo is in my house at this moment, and God willing I shall marry her tomorrow."

And he turned and rode off, leaving Count Lodovico white as a sheet. He ground his teeth like a madman: I almost expected the upper ones to get stuck in the lower. Work it out: he was one of the two cuckolds in this business – he'd lost his brother Raimondo and fifty thousand piastres, and the Prince was going to marry Vittoria!

The other cuckold was the people. They'd helped the nobles, and the nobles, as soon as the demands of their vendetta were met, had hacked them to pieces. The day after the massacre a Franciscan went through the streets of Rome saying he'd heard the devil laugh when the nobles turned their cannon on the populace. For a piastre he'd describe or even imitate the laugh, and by the end of the day he'd collected a small fortune. The following day he vanished, and a good thing for him that he did, for his victims, ridiculed by their neighbours for their credulity, were looking for him everywhere to beat him up.

I've heard many accounts of the dispute between Raimondo and the Bargello from people who were there, and even from people who weren't. But I've never heard anyone repeat one threat that Raimondo made: "If you don't hand our men over here and now, the biggest bits left of you will be your ears."

I don't know where he picked that up, because he wasn't very bright.

260

At least, no brighter than I am. But he was a good master. It's true I got more kicks than piastres, but when we went on the razzle together he pooled everything, wine and women alike.

All except Caterina Acquaviva. The only person he shared her with was Silla Savelli. He was so fond of him (Silla was as handsome as the day) that some people in Rome said Savelli was his minion. I don't believe it. But anyway, when you're drunk what's the difference?

I often think of them. They were so young! So brave! So full of life! And now they're dead. And they both died unexpectedly, in a state of mortal sin. That's the worst of it. I don't often pray, but when I do it's to ask the Lord to let them into His heaven. I know it's for Him to judge, and He alone holds the balance in which souls are weighed. But a little ounce of prayer on the right side can't do any harm.

10

Caterina Acquaviva

We weren't badly treated in the Castel Sant'Angelo, and the living conditions were passable. We had a couple of quite spacious rooms with a door between, on the second floor. The only thing wrong with them was that the windows were on the small side, and barred. Our meals were brought to us either by an elderly nun or by a young novice who might have been about twenty. The old one lowered her eyes as soon as she came in, and only looked up to find her way out. She didn't answer when we said good morning or goodnight.

At first we thought she was deaf. But when I dropped my hair brush on the floor one day she started visibly, so I knew it must be put on. No doubt she thought our sins might enter into her through her eyes or ears. We were lucky she didn't think of holding her nose.

The young one, who was quite pretty, didn't talk much but had a ready smile and was easily amused. It amazed me a girl could still be cheerful after vowing never to let a man come near her. As she seemed to like me, I got into the habit of showing her out, and I took the opportunity to ask her a few little questions, which she quite innocently answered. That's how I found out our food would have been less good and less plentiful if His Eminence Cardinal Montalto hadn't paid the gaoler. When I told the Signora this she cried, "Oh, so he *is* still fond of me!" And she wept. But they were the sort of tears that did her good.

It was the young nun who brought us our meal the evening the riot broke out. Hearing the shouting and running about, I asked her as we went to the door what it was all about. She either didn't know or didn't want to say, but she looked frightened and was even trembling, and

262

advised me not to look out of the window. As soon as she'd gone I did look: there was a big moon, but all I could see was lots of horsemen galloping about on the other side of the Tiber. The noise seemed to be coming from the direction of the Vatican, but our windows looked out on the river.

There was so much din it would have been impossible to sleep, and the Signora wouldn't get undressed. She was right about that, as it turned out. The thing that had irked her most about her imprisonment was that as soon as she set foot inside the Castel Sant'Angelo the old nun had taken away her books, which della Pace had let her bring with her when he came to arrest us. She wrote a petition to the Pope in Latin asking to be allowed to have them back, but she didn't receive any answer. When I expressed surprise about that she smiled faintly and said: "Who knows? Perhaps the Holy Father can't read Latin!"

But she didn't speak much, and not once did she ever utter the Prince's name or even mention his existence. Several times she did remember Signor Peretti, and each time she spoke of him with affection. She seemed much fonder of him now he was dead than she'd been when he was alive.

She clamoured so much to have her books back that the nuns finally lent her a New Testament. She read it assiduously, and after a few days she almost knew it by heart and could recite whole passages. But sometimes she said things that surprised me about the Gospels. For instance, one day she looked up from her reading and said:

"I don't understand why St Matthew goes to all that trouble listing Joseph's genealogy. What's the point, since he wasn't Christ's father? He'd have done better to give Mary's family tree."

"Signora," I said, "if he didn't it's because Mary was only a woman."

"You're probably right," she answered, looking at me as if she'd been struck by what I said.

Then she suddenly started to laugh. "You talk like a heretic, you know, Caterina! How can you say Mary is only a woman when she's the Mother of God?"

I looked at her. I didn't know what to think. First she praised me and then she blamed me. Who was she making fun of – me or St Matthew? She was the one who was a heretic! Or perhaps she was taking it out on St Matthew because she was angry with the nuns for taking her books.

Anyhow, she never really complained. I admired her courage. I wasn't as strong as she was. I restrained myself during the day so as not to annoy her, but at night in bed I cried my eyes out. I thought of my family in Grottammare, and what the parish priest would be saying about me from the pulpit. I thought about my sweethearts too, and went over them in my head. To begin with it did me good, but afterwards it only made me feel more lonely and miserable on my straw mattress. Yes, what a disgrace — all I had to sleep on was a straw mattress. The Signora had a proper bed.

As he was taking us to prison, della Pace, nice man, managed to bring his moustache close to my ear and whisper: "You can both sleep easy. They won't put you on trial. They haven't got anything against you." I told the Signora, but she refused to be reassured.

"We'll be here for years, then," she said, shrugging her shoulders. "Until the Pope dies, at least! And he's as fit as a fiddle."

That night on my pallet I prayed with all my heart that the Lord would take the Holy Father to Himself as soon as possible. I had a few qualms about it afterwards: I wasn't sure it was right for a Catholic to pray for the Pope to die.

I thought of della Pace too, and how I felt when his moustache tickled my ear. If only he could come to the Castel Sant'Angelo and interrogate me alone in a little room there. But even that faint hope disappeared when the young nun told me he wasn't in charge at Sant'Angelo, which had its own Governor.

As for Marcello, I refused to think about the scoundrel. I hoped he was enjoying himself with his old woman at Amalfi. At first I worried a bit about his safety, but the Signora said the Viceroy of Naples hated the Pope and would never hand Marcello over to him.

To get back to the night when we heard all that noise going on round the Vatican, we didn't realise it was an insurrection until we heard the first volley of musket fire. And then there was a great to-do inside the Castel Sant'Angelo, with people running up and down the stairs and muffled rumblings overhead.

To our surprise the Governor appeared in our quarters. Until then he'd never deigned to visit us. He was a fat, pompous man with bulging eyes, who looked about as trustworthy as a lawyer.

264

"Signora," said he with a courtly bow, "I have come to reassure you. The Castel Sant'Angelo is as solid as a rock. You are in absolutely no danger."

"Many thanks, *Signor Governatore*," said the Signora, smiling politely, "but I wasn't at all alarmed."

The Governor seemed rather taken aback at this, and by the Signora's failure to ask any questions about the din inside and out.

"Signora," he said before withdrawing, "it's going to be a long night. If you wish, I'll send you some refreshments."

I could see she was going to say no, so I signed to her behind the Governor's back to accept.

"Many thanks again, *Signor Governatore*," she said. "I'd like some herb tea."

The Governor bowed again, straightened up, and made for the door. He walked as if he expected the floor under his feet to be impressed by his importance.

As I'd expected, it was the little nun who brought the herb tea. She was pale, and her hands were shaking. As I saw her out I asked her what the rumblings upstairs were.

"They're moving the cannon."

"Who's attacking us, then?"

"I don't know. Some sort of wicked people, anyhow."

"Forgive me, sister, but you're trembling. Are you afraid for your life?"

"No," she said. "I'm afraid of the soldiers, if they capture Sant'Angelo."

I nearly said, "Come, come, it's not as bad as all that," but I restrained myself. She was a nice girl and I didn't want to shock her. What a funny world it is! I thought. What some people long for, others dread.

Half an hour later she came back.

"Signora," she said, "on the Governor's orders I've come to help you pack. You're going to be moved. You'll be safer where you're going to."

The Signora didn't ask any questions, and neither did I, though I was dying to. I don't suppose the poor girl knew where we were going anyway.

In a quarter of an hour we'd done our packing and started off downstairs – the Signora, me, and a man with our portable goods. No sign of the Governor.

We went out through a little door guarded on the inside by several men. The noise outside was deafening, but I didn't have time to see anything because a coach was waiting a couple of yards away. It looked golden and shiny in the moonlight. I couldn't see the coat of arms on the door because an officer, hat in hand, was holding it open. To right and left of us men on horseback blocked the view.

Our man gave the luggage to one of the soldiers and left, or rather scuttled away for dear life, slamming the door behind him. The men in the escort started to laugh, but the officer silenced them with a gesture.

The inside of the coach was padded with red velvet trimmed with gold braid; I thought it looked fit for a cardinal, and that they were going to take us to safety in another fortress belonging, like Santa Maria, to some prelate. But I didn't dare ask questions: the Signora sat regally silent, and the officer opposite didn't speak either. He was wearing a black mask. The coach went very fast, but I couldn't see anything of the streets we were passing through: the red velvet curtains over the windows were drawn, and I was too overawed by the officer in his black mask to try to peek out.

To my great surprise the coach slowed down after a little while, then turned a corner and stopped. When the officer jumped out and opened the door for us to alight, I glimpsed a big courtyard full of people. I couldn't see much because a thick black cloud was just passing over the moon. The officer led us up to the second floor and into a small room sumptuously furnished with hangings and rugs. Then he took off his mask. I'd never seen his face before, and observing out of the corner of my eye that Vittoria didn't recognise it either, I wondered why he'd gone to so much trouble to hide it. Anyhow, for a gaoler he was incredibly polite, for he bowed almost down to the ground and said to the Signora with the greatest respect: "Signora, the small drawing room and the two adjoining bedrooms are at your disposal. I hope you will be comfortable here. I have been ordered to do everything I can to that end."

I could tell the Signora was surprised by all this deference, as well as by the gilded prison and the luxurious coach that had brought us here. As the officer was backing out of the room, his hat sweeping the floor, she

266

said eagerly: "Signore, I've never been here before. Can you tell us where we are?"

"In Montegiordano, of course, Signora," he answered, raising an eyebrow in astonishment.

And as the Signora said nothing, he made another low bow and was gone.

"My God!" cried the Signora, putting her hands to her throat.

She went so pale I was afraid she was going to faint, and I rushed over to support her. But she thrust me roughly aside and started to pace to and fro in a furious rage, her fists pressed to her cheeks. I got out of her way and sat down in a corner and said nothing. I knew her too well to think I could calm her down with words. You might as well try to still a tempest by catching hold of the lightning.

Then the Signora turned from white to red, and every so often moved her hands from her cheeks to her throat, as if choking with indignation. She went on marching up and down for about ten minutes, and all she managed to say was: "How shameful! How degrading!" But even with knitted brows and her face tense, she still managed to look beautiful.

At last she sat down – exhausted, I suppose, with emotion – but she held herself rigid, lips clamped together and jaw set, her arms folded over her chest. I still sat quietly in my corner, understanding all too well what was going on in her head, and very uneasy at the way she was taking the situation.

Then came a knock at the door. And, as the Signora remained silent and motionless, another. She signed to me to open.

It was Prince Orsini. I stood back to let him in, and he strode into the room, his presence making it seem smaller than ever. He really was a fine-looking man. Tall, broad-shouldered, with a head like that of a Roman statue. But what I liked most was the determined, triumphant, joyful expression on his face. Unfortunately it vanished at once when he saw how the Signora was looking at him. He stopped and gazed at her incredulously, apparently incapable of speech.

"My lord," she said cuttingly, "can you explain to me how and why I come to be in your house?"

The Prince turned pale, as if she'd struck him. When at last he spoke it was in a strangled voice, though it became clearer as he went on. "I didn't expect this sort of welcome, madam," he said. "I don't think I have deserved it. I've moved mountains to get you out of the Castel Sant'Angelo! I've risen up against my sovereign, I've fomented a riot, I've staked my dukedom, my possessions and my life for you! And the lives of others too, unfortunately. Many others! Blood has flowed in torrents for you tonight! And you ask me for an explanation?"

"Yes, my lord," she said icily.

"Well," said the Prince, his amazement giving way to anger, "since you want an explanation, here it is: your liberty is the price the Pope has had to pay to save his throne."

"And who gave you authority," said the Signora, "to barter me for a throne? Did I agree to this bargain? Did you consult me?"

"Consult you? About trying to set you free?"

"Free? Do you call my being here freedom? Montegiordano is the worst possible prison to me – the very worst! – because it dishonours me."

"What?" cried the Prince, transported with anger. "Do you call it a dishonour to become my wife?"

"Oh!" she cried, rising and looking at him with flashing eyes, "now we have it! You barter me like merchandise, and the merchandise is supposed to say yes to becoming your property for life! If that's what all those intrigues and all that bloodshed were for, let me tell you I'll never be the wife of a gentleman who has broken his word as cravenly as you have done."

"Vittoria!" exclaimed the Prince, white with anger and astonishment, "what are you saying? Why are you insulting me? You accuse me of breaking my word, of acting like a coward? You shall account to me for those words here and now!"

"Account to you?" said the Signora scornfully. "In a duel, perhaps! Take the quickest way and kill me! And if you haven't the courage to do that, follow your natural bent and hire an assassin. Or if, with a last spark of humanity, you spare my life, grant me one last favour and take me back to the Castel Sant'Angelo!"

"Take you back?" said the Prince, aghast.

"You've freed me, haven't you? Well, if I'm free, here is my free decision: I don't wish to stay in your house a moment longer."

"Vittoria, what you're saying is madness!"

"On the contrary, it's very sane. I repeat: every minute I spend here dishonours me, and proclaims to the world that I am your mistress and your accomplice in my husband's murder."

"What are you saying?" cried the Prince angrily. "I had nothing to do with the murder of Francesco Peretti. How could you think for a moment I'd broken the vow I made to you at Santa Maria, not to make any attempt on his life?"

"And how am I to believe you?" asked the Signora.

But I could see she was shaken by his vehemence. She went on more quietly. "Who else but you benefited from his death?"

"Vittoria," he said firmly, "I won't allow you to doubt my word! I repeat that I had nothing to do with the unfortunate man's death. I swear it, as I hope to be saved!"

The Signora, impressed by the gravity of his oath, was silent. Though only for a little while. But when she spoke again it was more in sorrow than in anger.

"Unfortunately, my lord, it makes no difference whether you are guilty or not. No one who learns I am here will believe in your innocence, or in mine. My presence here condemns both of us — you as Francesco's murderer, me as an adulteress and your accomplice. So my decision is irrevocable: I insist that you take me back at once to the Castel Sant'Angelo."

"I say it again — you're out of your mind!" cried the Prince. "Can't you see that if you go back to prison voluntarily it's tantamount to admitting you're guilty and want to be punished? Listen," he went on, restraining his anger. "I can see I haven't convinced you and you mean to stand by your insane decision. Just grant me a delay of one night! And think about it, I beg! Think before you throw yourself into the gaol of your worst enemy for the rest of your life. One night is all I ask! One night's reflection!"

And thereupon he turned on his heel and left. He was so blind with wrath that although he hit his left shoulder on the doorpost as he went out I'm sure he didn't feel a thing.

The Signora sat down on the chair she'd occupied before. Her body was rigid, her arms folded, and her eyes quite dry.

269

I was completely taken aback. I'd expected her to relax and burst into tears. Something like that. But no – there she sat without a tear, her jaw set, and stiff as a ramrod. And suddenly that struck me as a bad sign for the future.

"Signora," I said, "with all due respect – do you really want to go back to prison?"

"Yes."

"For the rest of your life?"

"Yes."

"Even now you know the Prince didn't kill Signor Peretti?"

"I don't know if I can believe him."

"Oh yes, you do! You do believe him, Signora!"

"Why do you ask, if you know what I think better than I do?"

"Because, Signora, if the Prince didn't kill Signor Peretti, there's no reason why you shouldn't marry him!"

"What?"

"If you ask me, it would be more sensible than going back to prison!"

"I don't ask you."

"Forgive me, Signora, but perhaps I have some right to an opinion, seeing that if you go back to prison I go too."

"You don't have to go with me."

"I'll go with you because I love you. But also because I have no choice."

"What do you mean?"

"Can you see me living in the Rusticucci palace under Giulietta's thumb? Or worse still in Grottammare, after all the priest will have said about me from the pulpit?"

"If I listened to you I'd marry the Prince just to please you."

"And because you love him."

She sprang up and came at me, eyes blazing. But for once I stood my ground. I stayed just where I was and didn't budge. I meant to have my say, and without mincing words.

"No, I don't love him, you foolish creature!" said she. "At least, not any more!"

"You might make him believe that, Signora," I answered, "because he's a man. But I'm a woman, and you won't convince me. I know that all

270

the time you were insulting him your one desire was to rush into his arms."

"Wretched girl, how dare you be so stupid?"

"It's no stupider than wanting to go back to prison after you've been let out."

"You go too far! You dare to say your mistress is stupid?"

"I never said that. But I do say my mistress takes too much account of what people think."

"Really!"

"Signora, forgive me, but it's the honest truth. You say you don't want to be dishonoured, and you want to go back to prison so that people won't think you're an adulteress and accomplice to a murder. But what is this honour you're talking about? It's not what you've done – it's what people think about you. But let me tell you, you're too beautiful for them not to say nasty things about you! They'll make out you're guilty whether you marry the Prince or jump back into the clutches of the Pope. The difference is that in Sant'Angelo you'll be subject to snubs and insults all the time. But if you become Princess Orsini people won't dare to gossip. And that's the truth!"

"*Affè di Dio*! You sound just like the Prince! You repeat everything he says, and even everything he doesn't say but just thinks! It's quite simple – you can't see a pair of trunk-hose without falling in love with the man inside them! You adore the Prince! You're on his side about everything! And against me!"

"Not against you, Signora. I agree with him because he's right."

"Well, my little moralist," she said, drawing herself up to her full height and glaring at me, "go and tell the Prince I've had enough of your insolence and chatter, and that I dismiss you from my service! Let him take you into his if he wants to! And let him make you his whore if he feels like it!"

And so saying she gave me two stinging slaps. She hit me so hard I lost my balance. The tears sprang to my eyes. But I didn't lower them. I kept on looking her straight in the face.

"Oh, Signora!" I said. "How dreadful! Fancy hitting me after all the years I've served and loved you! Me, the only friend you have left! Me, who would follow you to hell if necessary!"

271

I was exaggerating a bit there. And the Signora might well have retorted that if I wasn't even keen to go back with her to Sant'Angelo . . . *Madonna mia*! the silly things you say when you're quarrelling with someone! But I really was beside myself. Utterly grieved and humiliated! It was the first time the Signora had hit me so hard! You might ask me what about the clouts I got from *il mancino*? It's not the same thing. *Il mancino* is my elder brother.

As the Signora looked at me, probably not very proud of what she'd done but too haughty to apologise, I turned round, went and picked up my little bundle from the heap of baggage in the corner of the room, and headed for the door.

"And where do you think you're going, you little idiot?"

"I'm going to tell the Prince you're fed up with me and my insolence and my chatter, that you've dismissed me, and that he's to take me into his service if he wants to and make me his whore if he feels like it."

"Caterina!"

"Wasn't that what you told me to say, Signora, with two slaps to help me make up my mind?"

"Oh, you little witch," cried she, "how can you be so irritating?"

But I could see she wasn't sure whether to rage or to laugh.

I didn't have time to see which she'd choose, for suddenly she threw herself on me, hugged me so tight I could hardly breathe, and started planting little kisses on my forehead. As for me, I flung both arms round her waist and buried my face in her neck. As I embraced her I was all melting with love, and weeping.

Weeping for joy, fool that I am.

Marcello Accoramboni

As soon as the news reached me in Amalfi that the uprising against the Pope had set Vittoria free, I borrowed Margherita Sorghini's swiftest horses and made for Rome. I took two footmen with me, all three of us were armed to the teeth, and we rode as fast as consideration for our mounts would allow.

Although della Pace's report had cleared me of my brother-in-law's murder, I took the precaution of sending one of my men ahead to spy out the land before entering the city. He came back grinning from ear to ear. Rome was still plunged in such anarchy "it was a treat to behold, Signore – the customs posts are deserted." And the only policemen he'd seen were corpses rotting in the streets. There was no one to bury them – it was disgusting. But still, it was a pleasant sight for anyone who'd had anything to do with them . . .

The only trouble I had was getting into Montegiordano. Finally, after much shouting, the guard sent for the majordomo, who recognised my face despite the dust it had gathered on the road. I was overjoyed to hear that Vittoria was in the palace, but as it was late I decided to wait till the morning to go and see her.

The advantage of being the master is that at the end of a day's journey the servants have to see to the horses before they rest themselves. Whereas I, as soon as I was in the room the majordomo had shown me to, could sit on the bed and start to take my boots off. But before I had time to remove the second one I'd keeled over and was sleeping like a log.

The first thing I noticed when I woke up was that I was still wearing one boot. The next, which disturbed me considerably, was a monk sitting at my bedside with his cowl down over his eyes. Beside him was a candle, almost burned out. "Am I dead?" I thought.

"Signore," said the monk, "forgive this intrusion. I made the majordomo let me in. I must speak to you urgently."

He threw back his cowl and revealed his face. I blinked and began to see more clearly. It was *il mancino*.

"Domenico," I said, laughing. "What's the habit for? Are you going to exchange the tavern for the monastery?"

"I'm too young yet to repent," said *il mancino*, "and with your permission, Signore, I'll take this thing off – it's a hot night and I'm stifling."

He emerged in trunk-hose and shirt and as I'd always known him: small, lean, muscular, straight as a ramrod, bright-eyed and quick-tongued.

"I didn't want to be seen entering the Prince's house," he said.

"Why not?" I asked. "The Prince is at the height of his power! What are you afraid of?"

"The backlash. There's always a backlash. The Prince's success is precarious. What he's done can't be done twice. He's made himself too many enemies, not to mention the Pope. He exploited the nobles' vendetta to free your sister, and cut the people to pieces after making use of them. If he's insulted by the Holy Father again, he won't be able to count on either the aristocracy or the mob."

"Domenico, you're wasted organising your troop of whores. You ought to be governing the State."

"Governing the State is much the easier of the two," said *il mancino* seriously. "All you need is a few clear rules. The first is, never do things by halves. If I'd been the Prince, once I'd taken up arms against my sovereign I'd have dethroned him and killed him while I was at it . . . But forgive me, Signore, I'm wasting your time and mine," he said with his usual meticulous politeness. "I really came just to put you in the picture."

Then, in the elegant and distinguished Italian that always astonishes me in one who can neither read nor write (though he must be a very good listener), he gave me a vivid account of everything that had happened between the murder of Peretti and the riot.

"In a nutshell," he said, "whoever organised the murder was trying to incriminate the Prince, your sister and you. And that's what della Pace thought, though he couldn't prove it. But, thank God, I've got my own ways of finding things out! I'd noticed that the monk who gave me the note for Signor Peretti was a heavy drinker and had an eye for the women, so I knew where to look for him. His cowl had concealed his face, but I'd seen he was very thin and had a long scar on his left thumb. So I set what you kindly call my troop of whores to work, and one of them finally spotted him, and, with what bait you can easily guess, lured him to the tavern. I shut him up in my cellar, put a dagger to his throat, and made him talk. Peretti was killed on the orders of Lodovico. The Prince knew nothing about it . . . Excuse me, Signore – you don't look very surprised."

"I suspected as much. But it's marvellous to have proof of Lodovico's tortuous manoeuvres."

"Too tortuous, Signore! Much too tortuous! One should never overdo things. That's my second rule of government. Most machinations rebound on their perpetrators. That's what I call the law of the backlash."

"What did you do with your monk?"

"Locked him into my cellar and started looking for della Pace, to hand this useful witness over to him. Unfortunately the riot caused by the death of Raimondo and Silla broke out, della Pace just had time to take refuge in the Vatican, and the next I saw of him was a bloody head being kicked about by the mob. I don't mind telling you I wept."

"You! Wept for a police lieutenant!"

"Yes, Signore. He was an open, straightforward man, loyal to his sovereign and abnormally honest. That was his undoing. Believe me, Signore, a virtuous Bargello can't last very long in a State that's corrupt."

"You could always hand your monk over to della Pace's successor."

"Oh, Signore! Forgive me, but you haven't got much head for politics. It's not in the Pope's interests, especially now, to proclaim the Prince's innocence. My witness wouldn't have time to open his mouth. He'd end up in a sack, and the sack would end up in the Tiber. As for me, I'd be banished. You know I'm barely tolerated in Rome as it is. No, the only person I can negotiate with now about my witness is the Prince himself. On condition, of course, that he uses him carefully."

"How do you mean?"

"Just to convince Cardinal Montalto that he had nothing to do with his nephew's murder."

"Why Montalto?"

"Because he's the Signora's uncle, and probably *papabile* when the present Pope dies."

"You amaze me! What makes you think he might succeed?"

"A very weighty reason: when Gregory XIII dies, the cardinals will want to elect a Pope who's virtuous. The backlash, Signore! The backlash! Would you like to bet?"

"God forbid! You're too deep for me! What do you want in exchange for your witness?"

"The Prince owns a big piece of land east of Rome. There's a little road that goes through it that he owns too. There's nothing on the land except a tavern built there illegally. I'd like the Prince to let me buy the land for a modest sum."

"So that you can own the tavern?"

"Oh no, Signore! Our laws are more complicated than that. I could own the land without owning the tavern, even though it has no right to be there. But if I do own the land I can block the road that leads to the tavern, ruin the tenant's custom and force him to sell."

"For a modest sum."

"That goes without saying."

"I suppose your third rule, Domenico, is to use a nice, simple, legal *combinazione* rather than a complicated intrigue. What do you want me to do?"

"Introduce me to the Prince."

"All right, I will."

As soon as *il mancino* had gone I went straight to Vittoria's room and knocked on the door. I heard Caterina's slippers clattering hastily over the tiled floor at the sound of my voice. She opened the door, breathless, a candlestick in her hand, and clung to me without any shame, even in front of her mistress. I shoved her roughly aside, so that she dropped the candlestick and the candle went out. And do you know what the little octopus did? – she flung her arms round my neck and embraced me in the dark! I was very annoyed by this second assault, but I'm so susceptible to female curves that it took me a few seconds to pull myself together. Then I pushed Caterina away, struck my flint and re-lit the candle.

Vittoria was propped up on her elbow, her hair done in long plaits for the night. She fixed her blue eyes inquiringly on mine. It was almost a year since I'd last seen her. And strange as it may seem, her face, familiar as it was, seemed to be wearing a new expression, at once more mature and sadder. No doubt this was a reflection of her long captivity in Sant'Angelo, the unjust suspicions that had hung over her, and her own doubts as to the Prince's complicity in Peretti's murder.

I sat on the edge of the bed and told her all about the evidence supplied by *il mancino's* prisoner. She listened wide-eyed, and as soon as I'd finished she leaped out of bed, half-naked as she was, and rushed madly to the door.

"Where are you going?" I cried.

"To see the Prince!"

"But you don't even know where his room is!"

"Show me!"

"In the middle of the night?"

But she wasn't listening. She was already out in the gallery. I just had time to snatch up the candlestick, then stride along fast enough to light her way. Caterina was at our heels.

I shall never forget the look in the Prince's eyes when he saw Vittoria burst into his room, her long plaits hanging down her back. A child seeing his beloved mother arrive after he'd given up expecting her wouldn't have looked more intensely and naïvely happy. He made to rise, but she didn't give him time. She ran and knelt at the side of the bed, took his face in her hands and kissed it wildly.

"Oh, Paolo!" she said in a low, breathless voice, "forgive me! forgive me! I was so unfair to you! I'll be your wife whenever you wish."

His Eminence Cardinal Ferdinando de' Medici

When I heard the grievous news that Paolo Orsini had married Vittoria Peretti at Bracciano (in the very castle where my sister Isabella had perished, in circumstances all too well known), I immediately asked Gregory XIII for an audience for myself and my brother Francesco, Grand Duke of Tuscany.

I made my request by word of mouth, for as his Secretary of State I have the privilege of seeing him every day. The biggest problem was not obtaining the audience, but getting Francesco to come with me.

What bound Francesco to Florence was not so much affairs of state, which he bothered about as little as possible, as his chemical experiments and Bianca. For the throne of the Grand Duchy of Florence was occupied, alas, not by a prince alive to his duties, but by a chemist and a lover.

I am well aware that when, several years later, Francesco and Bianca died rather suddenly after dinner one day in their villa at Poggio, odious rumours were put about by my enemies accusing me of being a second Cain and having murdered them. This Spanish or rather Jesuitical slander (for it's well known that there's an affinity between the two terms) rested on the fact that Francesco died without an heir, so that I was obliged to abandon the purple and succeed him as Grand Duke. I treated the vile accusation with nothing but silence and contempt.

Having recalled these slanders only to deal with them as they deserve, I now return to the time of my aforementioned journey to Rome, and the trouble I had persuading Francesco to come too. I knew how weak my elder brother was, and how every night Bianca would undo any resolution I'd managed to instil in him during the day.

As a matter of fact, Bianca hated me, and although as a churchman I myself may not entertain such an unevangelical sentiment, it's true I didn't care much for her either. I'd raised my eyebrows when Francesco installed her at the court as reigning mistress after our father's death (thus mortally offending his wife, the Grand Duchess Giovanna of Austria), instead of being satisfied with a few discreet affairs with girls whose lack of birth or brains would have made them harmless. My anxiety increased when the Grand Duchess died, and I hastened to suggest several good matches that would have brought Francesco substantial property, useful alliances and princely connections. But he found excuses to reject them all, and secretly married Bianca, though he dreaded my wrath so much he didn't dare make it public for several months. I can't describe the grief and indignation I felt at seeing my brother fall into this carnal trap and betraying his princely duties so unworthily.

Bianca opposed Francesco's going to Rome because she had a good idea of the object of our journey, and didn't want Francesco to do anything against Vittoria Accoramboni and her marriage to Prince Orsini.

She'd only met the Prince once, and had never seen Vittoria, but how could she fail to be struck by the likeness between their two extraordinary careers? True, neither Vittoria nor Bianca was of really low birth, but their family connections, though respectable, placed them far below the ducal and grand-ducal unions to which they'd had the audacity to aspire. Neither was without learning, wit or love for the arts, but who would believe it was these qualities alone that had made illustrious princes wed them? The truth was that both had fleshly charms, and the princes concerned, forgetting the lessons of *Genesis*, yielded to the magic of appearance.

Alas, they share this weakness with the whole of Italy, perhaps with all the world. As for me, I don't mind telling you it fills me with rage when I see sensible, educated men in Rome or Florence making idols of women

278

like Bianca and Vittoria, and, just because they are beautiful, paying them the homage due only to God. Such pagan worship is corrupting, and does incalculable harm.

To return to the journey to Rome, I finally prevailed and Francesco came away with me, leaving Bianca in Florence, tearful, anxious and full of resentment. She could only just bring herself to kneel and kiss my ring before we left. I raised her up kindly, but you should have seen the look she darted at me with her blazing eyes! She'd have killed me if she could! I suppose it's as a joke that our good Italians call women "the gentle sex".

Naturally I made the most of the opportunities afforded by the journey to lecture my brother on the subject of Vittoria and Paolo. But I only half convinced that weak spirit: all I could get out of him was a promise to support, if only by his presence and his silence, what I myself was going to say to the Holy Father.

He scarcely kept us waiting at all. And as soon as we'd kissed his slipper and received his blessing, he looked at us with an expression that reflected both the loftiness of his position and some inner satisfaction.

"Well, my beloved sons," said he without beating about the bush, "what do you want of me? I'm listening."

I began by congratulating him on looking so well, on his flourishing health and eternal youth – an exceptional favour from heaven and blessing from the Almighty. He listened benignly and lapped it all up like a kitten with a bowl of milk. Then he reminded me modestly that he was mortal like the rest of us. But it was obvious from the way he said it that he didn't really believe it.

This preamble took a good quarter of an hour, and I didn't hurry it, knowing how much store Gregory XIII set by such assurances of long, not to say eternal, life. It's true he astonished everyone in this respect. At over eighty years old he had a face as smooth as a baby's, with pink, delicately rounded cheeks, unwrinkled eyelids, and eyes of periwinkle blue that lent him a disingenuous look about which it paid to be sceptical. In fact he was jovial, selfish, unwilling to put himself out; a lover of luxury and ease, of jewellery and the arts, but disinclined to improve his capital city; authoritarian, but neglectful of the State and even of Christendom; affable and lively to everyone who approached him, but inwardly an unforgiving bearer of grudges. With his subjects he was tyrannical in the extreme, not by nature but because of his situation and out of fear and caprice.

When I'd delivered my little compliment I waited with an air of extreme respect, and only when His Holiness asked for the second time what I wanted of him did I come to the point.

"Most Holy Father," said I, "the Grand Duke of Tuscany and I heard with profound affliction of the marriage of our beloved brother-in-law and cousin Paolo Giordano Orsini to the widow Peretti. It seemed to us that the circumstances surrounding the death of the unfortunate Peretti made this union an object of scandal in the State, in the Church, and in Christendom as a whole."

"Alas, that is true, my beloved sons," said His Holiness with a sigh, "but what can I do? The inquiry carried out by the unfortunate della Pace" – and here two tears rolled down his pink cheeks, but only two, making me once again admire his unfailing self-command – "did not find any evidence that Vittoria had committed adultery, nor that she had been involved in that heinous crime. At the most there were strong presumptions, in the sense of the Latin adage, *Fecit cui prodest*.★ But presumption isn't proof."

"Nevertheless, Most Holy Father," I answered humbly (for I knew how Gregory XIII disliked being contradicted unless it indirectly served his purpose), "in people's minds the Prince's subsequent marriage to the object of his desire has considerably strengthened the presumption."

"Indeed," said His Holiness, "the presumption is strong, very strong . . ."

"Especially, Most Holy Father, as before his marriage the Prince went so far as to use force against the head of Christendom! And isn't it obvious that if he was so carried away by passion as to commit that abominable crime against the Pope, he might easily have prefaced it by hatching a plot against His Holiness's third chamberlain? Whoever can do the greater can do the less . . ."

"Well reasoned, my son," said the Pope. "The presumption is indeed extremely strong . . . Many, including perhaps myself, might call it conclusive . . ."

★ The one who did it is the one who profits by it.

"Your moderation does you credit, Most Holy Father, and if Your Holiness will allow me to say so, I admire the exemplary magnanimity and evangelical leniency with which, when safely re-established on your throne, you forgave the deadly insult of the insurrection. You didn't even, as you might have done, punish its leader with excommunication."

At this, Francesco started and gave me a reproachful look which I pretended not to notice. He'd always been very friendly towards Paolo Giordano.

"By forgiving him," said the Pope, lowering his eyes, "I only did my duty as a Christian. Moreover," he added, glancing up and giving me a meaning look, "it wasn't as easy as all that. If I'd excommunicated the person you allude to I'd have had to excommunicate the Count of Oppedo, the Marquis Savelli and all the other Roman nobles. They were all involved in the uprising. And although the person you refer to was the leader of the revolt, he didn't aim at my abdication and death. He treated with me. And when he'd got what he wanted he crushed the mob."

"And what *did* he want, Most Holy Father?" said I indignantly. "A woman! The woman you'd imprisoned precisely to prevent him from marrying her! So he marries her in deliberate violation of your wishes! A misalliance frowned upon by the whole of the Roman nobility!"

"Presumably, at least," said Francesco suddenly. "We've only been here since yesterday evening, so we haven't had time to ask them."

My brother's interruption, which didn't at all please me, brought an almost imperceptible smile to the Pope's lips. He could easily guess how reluctantly Francesco was backing me up, especially on the subject of unsuitable marriages. I decided not to insist further on this point, for fear of widening the rift that had just appeared between Francesco and me.

"But, Most Holy Father," said I, "there are other even weightier reasons against this insane marriage. As you know, my sister Isabella had a son, Prince Virginio, from her marriage to Prince Orsini. Until now it went without saying that Virginio would inherit all his father's possessions. But in view of Paolo Giordano's blind passion for this intriguer, it's to be feared he'll make a new will that will seriously damage our nephew's interests."

The Pope was silent a moment, looking from Francesco to me, and from me to Francesco again.

"Does the Grand Duke agree," he asked gravely, "with what the Cardinal has just said?"

"I fully agree with *that* aspect of things," said Francesco, implying that he didn't agree on the question of misalliance.

But this nuance escaped the Pope, who smiled once again. The longer the audience lasted the more charming a mood he seemed to be in. Bright-eyed, rosy-cheeked, his lips parted eagerly, he seemed to be enjoying every minute of it.

"My beloved sons," he said finally, "what cure do you suggest for the ills you have so well described?"

"In order that crime should not profit the person who committed it," I declared, "and that an innocent son may not be harmed by the consequences of this scandalous union, I respectfully suggest that Your Holiness issue a *precetto* annulling it."

"Does the Grand Duke agree!" said the Pope.

"Yes, Most Holy Father," said Francesco, more firmly than I would have expected.

It's true he was very fond of Virginio, and, being childless himself, treated him like a son.

"So," said the Pope, straightening up on his throne, his eyes shining, "your joint request is this: you ask me for a *precetto* annulling the marriage of Prince Paolo Giordano Orsini to the widow Peretti. Is that it?"

"Yes, Most Holy Father."

"And are Cardinal de' Medici and the Grand Duke of Tuscany ready to send me that request in writing?"

"Yes, Most Holy Father," said I.

"Yes, Most Holy Father," said Francesco, after a pause.

There was a gleam of triumph in the Pope's eye. But only for a moment. He swiftly bowed his head.

"In your request, my beloved sons," he said, "it would be best if you omitted your fears on the subject of Prince Virginio's material interests, for they are hypothetical and judgment in such a case may not take account of hypotheses. Nor should you stress the question of misalliance, if misalliance there be" – here he glanced briefly at Francesco. "For that is too worldly a consideration, and therefore open to challenge. The only element that should be taken into account is the scandalous aspects of

282

this marriage, at least as you see it."

"Most Holy Father," I said, "in drawing up our request I shall take care to follow your valuable advice with accuracy and respect."

"Even so, my dear sons," said the Pope firmly, "do not be sure of success. There are many thorns on this path and few roses. As you know, I have been much criticised in the past for issuing *precetti* to annul marriages. There has been plenty of grousing, especially on the part of the theologians, a dire and disputatious lot who think they know the divine will better than I do. I should not wish to expose myself afresh to such detractors, especially in the case of the leader of an insurrection, against whom ill-wishers might think I bear a personal grudge."

He lowered his eyes as he said this, then swiftly looked up to deliver himself of some of the sprightly ecclesiastical pleasantries that were his stock-in-trade.

"I'll see, I'll see. Patience is the thing. Rome wasn't built in a day. And in Rome nothing is done in a day, especially in the Vatican . . . Go in peace, my most dear sons."

He gave us his blessing and we backed out of the room, as etiquette requires. Neither of us opened our mouths so long as we were still inside the immense palace, where it's said that even the walls have ears.

I ushered the Grand Duke of Tuscany into my coach, sat down beside him, and ordered the officer in charge of my escort to take me back to my palace. He knew which one.

I've got two palaces in Rome, but for reasons of economy I live in the smaller one and let the larger one out at a handsome rent. That makes my peers, the cardinals, laugh up their sleeves: "What's bred in the bone will come out in the flesh," they say. "Medici is the son and grandson of bankers." It's true. But then *I* don't have to keep body and soul together by selling my vote in the conclave to Philip II of Spain.

As soon as I'd drawn the curtains of the coach, Francesco turned to me.

"Well, what do you think? Will the Pope issue the *precetto*? He seems very undecided."

"Ah Francesco!" I smiled. "You were right to study the chemistry of matter − the chemistry of the soul is beyond you. If the Holy Father hesitated it was before our visit. Now he is as pleased as can be. We've served Paolo Giordano's head up to him on a silver salver, if you'll forgive

283

the metaphor, and he doesn't have to soil his own hands cutting it off. He can tell the Sacred Congregation we asked him to issue the *precetto*. And what's more he can prove it by showing our written request."

There was a moment's silence.

"I said what I did for Virginio's sake," said Francesco. "But it grieves me, just the same. Poor Orsini! He raised a whole revolution to set that woman free and make her his wife. And when the *precetto's* issued she'll only be his whore."

11

Paolo Giordano Orsini, Duke of Bracciano

It was on July 28th 1584 that I received by special messenger, in Bracciano, the *precetto* annulling my marriage. It was handed to me by a courier at seven o'clock, as Vittoria and I were about to have dinner. As I broke the seal and read this monument of iniquity and hypocrisy, I could scarcely believe my eyes.

Nowhere did it actually say that I, with Vittoria's complicity, had had Peretti killed for the sole purpose of marrying her, but everywhere it suggested as much with hints much worse than assertions, all wrapped up in a style of ecclesiastical suavity.

The decree, it said, had been issued by the Holy Father and his counsellors after much reflection and "a most painful moral debate", and at the express request of Cardinal de' Medici and the Grand Duke of Tuscany.

Trembling with rage from head to foot, I handed the *precetto* to Vittoria without a word. During all the time I'd been trying to take it in, she had been looking at me with growing anxiety.

When she had read the decree, Vittoria paled and set her teeth, but did not weep. She read it twice, the second time more slowly, then folded up the parchment and handed it back to me in silence.

"Well, what do you think, Vittoria?"

She came and put her head on my shoulder.

"This decree hurts us," she said, "but not as much as it would like. We're alive, and we love one another."

"Nevertheless," said I, holding her close, "it's infamous. I should have let the mob invade the Vatican and tear the old fox to pieces."

"No, no, Paolo," she said eagerly, "you were right to do as you did. If a Pope had been slain on his throne it would have been a terrible scandal throughout Christendom."

"But that same Pope," said I, "now takes a petty revenge on me for saving his life."

Unexpectedly she started to laugh.

"But you did begin by threatening his life, Paolo! You made him tremble inside his golden palace! That's what he can't forgive! On the other hand," she said pensively, "I don't see where Cardinal de' Medici and the Grand Duke of Tuscany come into it."

"They're defending, or think they're defending, or pretend they're defending, Virginio's interests. The Medicis are bankers. They see everything through a prism, and the prism is money."

Vittoria looked at me with raised eyebrows. I went on: "They're afraid I might change my will in your favour. While I was away at the wars, they brought Virginio up at court in Florence and made a Medici out of him. They already consider that when I die everything I own should come to them by way of Virginio."

"My God!" she said. "A cardinal, thinking like that?"

"This one was a Medici before he was a cardinal. But he's got another motive too: he hates women. The more beautiful a woman is the more he hates her. There isn't any kind of snub he hasn't inflicted on poor Bianca!"

"But he's never so much as seen me!"

"He doesn't have to see you to hate you. Your reputation for beauty is enough. Worse still, your wit and love of the arts, far from finding grace in his eyes, only make matters worse."

"Oh Paolo!" she exclaimed, putting her lovely bare arms round my waist, "how small and lonely I'd feel in this cruel world if I didn't have you!"

I was silent for a moment, full of love and compassion, but also deeply concerned about the uncertainties that lay in the future, and about my unhealed wound. Of late it had gnawed at the roots of my new-found, unending, insatiable happiness at being able to see Vittoria all day long, and to feel her warm soft body, wrapped in her long hair, beside me at night.

When one's in love there's a charm even in sadness. The night that followed the arrival of the *precetto* was, despite that terrible blow, or perhaps because of it, delicious as well as melancholy. We spent it in one another's arms, as if we wanted to prove that the decree had no power to separate us. Asleep or awake it was the same: our embraces were never-ending. We used very few words; those we did speak were added caresses.

It was only as the first rays of the sun appeared, and the birds began twittering wildly in the trees, that we spoke again of the Pope's ordinance.

"I notice," said Vittoria, "that not content with annulling our present marriage, he forbids us ever to marry again in the future. Isn't that rather strange? Why the extra precaution?"

"The Pope is old, and he's afraid his successor might annul his decree. He's trying to tie his hands in advance."

"What a Machiavelli! And what relentlessness! Is there any chance he might be brought to reverse his decision before he dies?"

"Only one," said I, "and it's a very small one. This is the first time a *precetto* has been aimed at one of the leading families. I shall appeal to the solidarity of the nobles. Tomorrow I shall leave for Rome."

"Without me?"

"Oh, Vittoria! How can I expose you to the gibes of the mob? I'll feel happier knowing you are inside the walls of Bracciano, guarded by your brother."

So I left for Rome next day, taking care to be accompanied by a strong escort. It was a good thing I did. For the same crowds that before had so often acclaimed me when I appeared in the streets now greeted me with scowls: they bore me a deadly grudge because of the way I'd suppressed the insurrection after having incited it. Wherever I went I met with nothing but averted looks, clenched fists, muttered insults, people spitting in front of my horse's hooves. At one point someone threw a stone that hit my squire on the ear and made it bleed. It was only with the greatest difficulty that I restrained my men from retaliating. But I wasn't going to give Gregory XIII the chance to say my presence in Rome always caused disorder. I decided I would only go out in a coach without my coat of arms on it, and with my escort not wearing livery.

As soon as I'd dismounted – and I did so painfully, for my wound hurt every time I made a sudden movement – I summoned my secretary and dictated a letter respectfully requesting an audience with the Pope. I sent it off at once, and received a polite but curt reply the next morning: the Pope apologised for not being able to see me, but he was unwell and had to keep to his room.

The Pope's reputation for good health was such that I didn't know if this excuse was to be taken seriously. My brother-in-law Cardinal de' Medici could have enlightened me on this point, but since he had inspired the *precetto* I could no longer look on him as a friend. For the same reason I didn't feel I could go and see the Florentine ambassador: although, personally, he had been very close to me, I couldn't disregard the attitude the Grand Duke of Tuscany had adopted over my marriage. As for Lodovico, I'd tacitly excluded him from my affections since the revelations of the monk *il mancino* had brought to see me.

I felt very depressed. The feeling had a number of sources: Vittoria's absence, my wound, the Pope's refusal to see me, my unfriendly reception by the Roman people, the hostility of my in-laws, and Lodovico's betrayal. The world I'd always inhabited seemed to be collapsing about me and leaving me to stand alone.

After a moment or so, I made an effort to pull myself together. I had many friends among the Roman nobility, the oldest and trustiest being no doubt Marquis Giulio Savelli, whose son Silla had been killed at the same time as Raimondo Orsini in the scuffle that had provoked the insurrection. I sent him a note asking him to see me, and a few hours later, in the evening, received the following reply:

"Carissimo Paolo,

I am in bed and unable to see you. I only just have the strength to write you this note. I can guess the reasons for your visit. As far as I am concerned, I was infuriated by the *precetto* that undid your marriage, and I did not conceal my opinion from those about me. But I'm sorry to have to tell you that I was about the only member of the Roman nobility to take this position. Almost all the rest blame you for what they call your 'misalliance', and for that reason the *precetto* was not objected to. No doubt this is partly due to the aristocratic prejudice so rife among us; but another cause is probably jealousy pure and simple, because your wife is so beautiful and so accomplished.

As you are a great general, I don't suppose I need warn you to be extremely careful in circumstances where the balance of power has turned so much against you. For if at the moment you were to attempt anything against the Holy Father, you would do so without the support of Lodovico, who is banished and hunted, or of the people, who hate you now as much as they loved you before, or of the nobles.

Bide your time, *carissimo*: the Pope is eighty-four years old and despite his healthy appearance he can't live for ever. The last time I saw him I thought I detected a change: he was less glib and more tearful.

As for me, I'm bound to die before he does. Silla was my favourite son, and his loss has been a terrible blow. My health fails more each day. I don't much care: I have lived long enough. And in vain, it seems to me now. I regret many of the things I've done; especially having brought about della Pace's death. It was unjust and cruel, and it didn't give me back my son.

Please give the Signora your wife my greetings and respects. Perhaps the present Pope's successor will be more favourably inclined to you both.

As for me, I shall remain, even in the jaws of death, your old and faithful friend:

Marquis Giulio Savelli"

Comforting as the affection in this letter was, it didn't escape me that it sounded the death knell of any hopes I might have invested in the solidarity of the nobility. The Pope had been extremely clever. If he'd excommunicated me immediately after the insurrection he would have incurred the opposition of all the nobles who'd taken part in the revolt and might fear a similar fate. By merely annulling a marriage of which they in any case disapproved, he set me apart from them and, at no danger to himself, turned me into a scapegoat.

As to the decree itself, I had certain doubts as to its validity, and decided to consult a theologian. I sent a note to Father Luigi Palestrino, asking him to come and see me. He sent me his answer by word of mouth: I was to send a coach without my coat of arms on it to fetch him at nightfall, and I wasn't to repeat anything he said when he saw me. If I disobeyed he would publicly deny everything. This caution seemed only natural under the current tyranny, so I accepted these conditions.

Father Luigi Palestrino's body was so thin and attenuated that you wondered how it managed to carry his enormous head. His head itself was also out of proportion, for while the brow was wide and monumental and full of bumps, the lower part of the face was insignificant, with a ridiculously small nose, hollow cheeks, a mere slit of a mouth and a weak chin. His complexion was paler than his habit, or rather so wan that you wondered if it was really blood that he had in his veins. But when, at my invitation, he'd sat down – his frail person occupied only about a quarter of the chair – and briefly waved away the wine I offered, he asked me what I wanted of him in a voice that surprised me both by its strength and by its diction.

Without a word I handed him the *precetto*, which he seized with the eagerness of a squirrel pouncing on a nut. Then he started to dissect the contents so swiftly with his inquisitive jet-black eyes that I was quite taken aback: he had hardly started reading it than he seemed to have finished.

Then he shut his eyes and remained silent so long I grew impatient. But at the very moment I was opening my mouth to ask what he thought of the *precetto*, he opened his eyes – I don't think he could have seen me start to speak *before* he opened them – and with the same rapid, peremptory gesture as he'd used to refuse the wine, said in his strong, precisely articulated voice: "My lord, pray do not ask me any questions. There is no need. I shall answer without being asked not only all the questions you can think of but also those you can't."

"In that case, father, speak. I'm listening."

"The first thing you have to understand, my lord, is that marriage is a sacrament in which the ministers are the husband and wife, and that it is regarded by the Church as indissoluble, especially since the Council of Trent. However, one of the two spouses may ask the Pope for an annulment if he or she can argue that his or her consent to the marriage was obtained by deceit or violence, or that the union has not been consummated physically, or that it has been barren. This last point is very debatable, as Henry VIII found out when he asked Clement VII to release him from his marriage to Catherine of Aragon on the grounds that she hadn't given him a son. But she had given him six daughters. So she wasn't barren. Henry, seeing the weakness of this argument, put forward another. Catherine was a near relative, and this consideration, although weak enough since their kinship didn't come within the prohibited degrees, might at a stretch have received Clement VII's approval if Catherine's nephew, the Emperor Charles V, hadn't opposed it with all the power at his command. In this he was wrong, for without his opposition the divorce would have been granted, and the schism that separated England from the Vatican and the rest of Christendom would never have happened. Small causes, great effects . . ."

"Father," said I, "this is all very interesting, but it hasn't got anything to do with my *precetto*."

"Oh yes it has, my lord – indirectly. The object of my preamble was to establish the general rule: the annulment of a marriage is requested by one of the spouses. So it is very surprising that an annulment should be pronounced by the Pope without either of the spouses having asked for it, as in your case and in that of many previous *precetti* issued by Gregory XIII in the course of his pontificate."

"So do you think, father, that these *precetti* constitute a misuse of power?"

"I didn't say that. I said that they are very surprising. And may I remind you, my lord, that it was agreed you wouldn't ask me any questions?"

"Forgive me, father. I'm not used to obeying. But perhaps I could get used to it if I tried."

The irony was lost on Luigi Palestrino. Or at least so I thought. He went on without batting an eyelid.

"As the two spouses are, as I said, the ministers of the sacrament of marriage, it's hard to see how any authority external to the marriage, even the head of Christendom, could lawfully abolish that sacrament. Unless the said marriage is surrounded by circumstances that make it scandalous. And that, my lord, is what the *precetto* suggests in your case. The weakness of its argument resides in the fact that it suggests this in

291

veiled and allusive terms: it doesn't state it clearly, and it doesn't establish, or even try to establish, your guilt."

"Because there isn't any proof of my guilt," said I. "And perhaps because there's no belief in it either. Father – is there any way out?"

"None. You can't appeal to the Pope against the Pope."

"Even if I prove my innocence?"

"Not even then."

"So there's no solution?"

"When Gregory XIII dies you can appeal to his successor. He might find it excessive that Gregory XIII, not content with having annulled your marriage, forbade you to marry again. It's as if he were trying to tie his successor's hands, and his successor may be annoyed and free you from having to obey that clause. You might also take advantage of the *interregnum* between the death of Gregory XIII and the election of his successor."

"How could I do that?"

"My lord, I will tell you, but only when the time comes. For the present I must take my leave."

He rose, and to my great surprise a smile appeared on his thin lips. It vanished almost at once, but it had undoubtedly been there.

"My lord, you have asked many questions. Despite all your good intentions you have been an unruly client. But that's hardly surprising if one remembers you used to fight against the pirates in the Adriatic, and in so doing became to a certain extent one of them. Now, however, it's not a matter of rushing on the enemy but of learning a virtue you lack: patience. But don't worry, my lord – your case is far from desperate."

And, having made me a low bow, he headed for the door.

"Father," said I, taking a purse from my doublet, "you're forgetting this."

Luigi Palestrino skipped back, snatched the purse with his squirrel-like swiftness, tucked it away somewhere, bowed again and vanished somehow through the door. He was so famous as a theologian that people came to consult him from all over Christendom. And each time he must receive some kind of largesse – which, as I'd just found, he didn't ask for but didn't refuse either. I wondered what he used the money for. He certainly didn't spend it on food.

That night, for the first time since I'd been in Rome, I saw a gleam of hope. Palestrino was right: up till then I'd been too inclined to attack, even if the enemy galley was the Vatican. Now my grappling irons were no longer available, and I had to get used to the waiting, the procrastination, the stratagems and intrigues of peace.

Il mancino

I was in my room at the Mount of Olives, doing my accounts – there weren't many customers at that late hour, and such as there were belonged to the docile kind that let themselves be fleeced without a murmur – when *la sorda* came up to tell me four armed horsemen had just come in and a fifth was minding their horses in the stable.

"How are they armed?"

"Swords, daggers and pistols in their belts."

"Hell! Are they robbers?"

"Not by the look of their horses."

"So you thought to take a look in the stables? There's something inside your pretty head then, *cocca mia*."★

"There's something inside my pretty ass, too," she said, laughing.

Normally I don't like my girls to use bad language, but this time I let it pass.

"And what did you do in the stable?"

"I stroked their fine horses. Their coats were quite dry. So they hadn't ridden far."

"So they're from Rome. What about the man looking after them?"

"From Calabria, but very well turned out for a servant. A leather jerkin."

"So you made up to him to loosen his tongue."

"I couldn't loosen anything – neither his tongue nor his fly. The cold fish wouldn't have anything to do with me. Told me in that jargon of his that he was a married man and faithful to his wife."

"Let's get back to the four in the tavern."

"That's what I did. They didn't want any girls either. Only wine – the

★ My pet

293

most expensive. The tallest of the four — he had his hat pulled down over his eyes — asked to see you."

"How is he dressed?"

"Buffalo doublet, the sort soldiers — captains — wear."

"And his hat? Out of shape? Weatherbeaten? Faded? The feathers all bedraggled?"

"Not at all. The felt quite new and the feathers fresh as paint."

"Not a captain, then. Right — bring him up. But first post three of my men behind the curtains in the mezzanine window with their arquebuses. What does this so-called captain look like?"

"Tall, very broad-shouldered. A fine masculine mouth, wide and firm. That's all I could see because of the hat. He speaks quietly, but like someone used to being obeyed."

"Wait a little while before you show him up. And when he's here, sit on the stairs and warn my men if the other three try to come up. And send all the girls straight to bed, except the ones who are occupied."

When I was alone again I felt quite tense. I don't like the unexpected. Nor am I keen on having four men armed to the teeth bursting in on me at one o'clock in the morning, even if their mounts do reek of the aristocracy. There are some barons who are brigands, and even some counts who are not much better, like the Count of Oppedo. And talking of him, he wouldn't be very pleased if he knew what I'd done with his monk. I slipped a knife into my left boot, then loaded a little lady's pistol and put it in the left armhole pocket of my doublet.

There was a knock at the door. I went and opened it, but stood right behind it with my hand in my armhole pocket.

"Hey, *mancino*!" cried a voice I thought I recognised. "Is this any way to greet people?"

I just peered round the door, without really showing myself. But the visitor saw me, smiled and nonchalantly took off his hat.

"My lord!" I cried, bowing to the ground. "You here! You only had to say the word and I'd have rushed to Montegiordano."

"It would have taken too long for a messenger to come and go," said the Prince, "and I leave for Bracciano tomorrow at dawn. The pavements of Rome burn my feet. But I wanted to see you."

"I'm at your service, my lord. Pray be seated."

"Thank you."

He made a little grimace as he sat down.

"*Mancino*, what happened about the monk? Did Cardinal Montalto agree to hear him?"

"He saw both of us, and in great secrecy."

"And what happened?"

"The Cardinal listened extremely closely. Especially to the monk."

"And what did he say?"

"As far as the monk is concerned, there's what the Cardinal said and there's what the Cardinal thought. What he said wasn't very encouraging."

"I'm listening."

"*Testis unus, testis nullus.*"★

"Do you understand Latin, *mancino*?"

"I learned that kind of Latin from a little misunderstanding that arose once between myself and a law-court."

"What was his reaction to your own evidence?"

"Nothing. He just lectured me about my 'unfortunate way of life'. I agree with him. Who knows, perhaps with a bit of education I might have climbed higher. They say the Cardinal himself used to mind the pigs when he was a boy."

"That's what they say. Let's get back to the monk."

"The Cardinal lectured him on renouncing his vows. He was so severe the monk went down on his knees and wept."

"What makes you think the Cardinal took his evidence more seriously than he cared to admit?"

"His face, terrible as it is, couldn't quite hide how glad he was to hear it."

"And why do you think that was?"

"Because the monk's evidence cleared his niece."

The Prince was silent for a while, eyes downcast, but then he seemed to rouse himself. He looked up and said brightly: "What's the situation about the tavern on that piece of land I sold you?"

"It's mine now. The work I had done on the road leading past it took

★ One witness is no witness.

295

so long the owner lost all his customers and handed it over to me. Unfortunately I haven't got enough money left to do it up."

"There may be a remedy for that. Cardinal Cherubi would like to get hold of the little wood adjoining the land to enlarge the grounds of his house. I'll sell it to you."

"Without my having to pay for it at once?"

"Without your having to pay for it ever. And when it's yours you resell it to Cardinal Cherubi."

"I expect there's a condition attached to that transaction."

"It's verbal and confidential. The Cardinal is to give you a daily account of the Pope's state of health."

"A rather surprising condition, coming from a humble inn-keeper like myself."

"It won't surprise the Cardinal, coming from a neighbour who kindly clears the undergrowth from the wood he's just sold him. Cherubi's a simple man. He talks to everyone he meets when he's out taking his constitutional."

"And perhaps he'll need your Venetian connections when the aged Patriarch of Venice gives up the ghost?"

"Perhaps. You're very well-informed, *mancino*. Where do you get your information?"

"From my girls, my lord. I blush to say it – from my girls. They don't mix only with the lower orders."

"*Mancino*, it's very important I should know as soon as possible when Gregory XIII's end is near. You know that kind of thing is often hushed up in the Vatican. Sometimes they even delay the announcement of the Pope's death."

"My lord, when the time comes I'll gallop to Bracciano with the news myself."

"It's a bargain. Come to Montegiordano tomorrow morning. I'll have gone, but my majordomo knows all about it and he'll sign the deed of sale for me. Don't see me out – I know the way."

Then, with a nod, he left. I noticed he was limping badly and had some difficulty negotiating the stairs. I shut the door behind him, though I was sure *la sorda* would be in after he'd gone to find out what had happened.

I sat on the stool the Prince had just vacated, filled a clay pipe with good tobacco, struck my flint and meditated for a while in a pleasant cloud of smoke. I was making money so fast that one day I'd have to quit my present "unfortunate way of life". But I'd miss it. I was fond of my girls, in a way.

La sorda burst in, hopping about like a flea with excitement. She came and sat on my lap, and I told her about the monk and the land, but not about the condition attached to the re-sale. She looked at me with eyes like saucers, full of admiration that I'd won the trust and protection of a great prince. When I'd finished speaking she started to caress me. What with the time of night and the pipe, she hadn't chosen a very good moment. But seeing it came from the heart I didn't stop her.

His Eminence Cardinal Cherubi

I am well aware I have been greatly blamed, by among others the cardinals who were in the Vatican on the day of the insurrection, for suggesting to His Holiness that he should sacrifice della Pace. Certainly that sacrifice, dictated though it was by the need to save the Pope's life, was in itself a horrible thing. But most of those present, including His Holiness, had already accepted it in their hearts when I was bold enough to express aloud what everyone else was thinking.

Once the danger was over His Holiness might, like others, have looked at me askance. But on the contrary he was kind enough to say he was grateful for my courage and frankness.

I claim no credit for these qualities. My character is such that I say what I think quite spontaneously. Thus I've never made any mystery of the fact that I'd like to succeed the Patriarch of Venice when it pleases the Lord to call him home. I know it's not usual in the Vatican for people to reveal their aspirations so ingenuously; they tend rather to hide them and then let them leak out at the most propitious moment. But I do things differently. Having been born in Venice I think I know the people there, and I consider myself especially suitable to represent the Church in the Most Serene Republic. It's a perfectly legitimate ambition, so why should I hide it? And isn't it best, when one aims at a particular office, to declare oneself as soon as possible, if only to cut the grass from under the feet of candidates less determined or slower at making up their minds?

According to the gossips my frankness has made me the clumsiest prelate in the Vatican, and at the same time the one who's done best out of his gaffes. That strikes me as a contradiction in terms. If my blunders have helped my advancement, were they really as maladroit as all that?

Anyway, there can be no doubt that after the insurrection I became the Pope's most valued adviser. Some considered my influence excessive. It was considerable, it's true, but how could it be excessive when it was always exerted in the cause of moderation?

After the terrible evening when he'd feared for both his throne and his life, the Pope did his best to make himself invulnerable by recruiting more Swiss Guards and buying cannon. But the stronger he grew from the military point of view, the weaker, rasher and more irresolute he was himself. He never had had much resilience, and what spirit he did possess seemed broken by the strain he'd gone through. He just gave himself up to resentment.

As soon as he was re-established on his throne, he at first wanted both to excommunicate Prince Orsini and to annul his marriage by means of a *precetto*. I was against both these measures; they looked too much like revenge. I said as much to the Holy Father, and to begin with he was angry. But when I pointed out that he couldn't excommunicate the Prince without excommunicating the whole of the Roman nobility too – a thing not only impossible but also almost comically absurd – he fell back on the *precetto*. And there was no dissuading him from that.

When the decree was promulgated the Pope was very pleased with himself. And again when, with some reason this time, he banished the Count of Oppedo. And yet again, when, on the pretext of being unwell, he refused to see Prince Orsini in the Vatican. After that he relapsed into apathy, and seemed just to drift as if he had no further real aim in life.

One day, seeing the Venetian ambassador, Armando Veniero, emerge from a Papal audience with rather a worried look on his face, I took him by the arm and asked him what was the matter.

"I'm afraid," said he, "the Pope isn't as fond of Venice as he used to be. I asked to speak to him about a problem that's currently troubling the Republic. He saw me for five minutes and scarcely listened to what I said. You'd have thought he wasn't in the least interested."

"Armando," I said, drawing him into a window recess and whispering in his ear, "don't worry. It's not Venice in particular – the Pope isn't interested in anything these days. He cuts his audiences as short as possible and doesn't pay much attention even while they're going on. He can't even be bothered now with important affairs of State or of Christendom."

"Oh, so that's it!" said Armando. "I noticed he was rather weepy."

"He's always had the gift of tears," I replied. "The difference is that now they come to his eyes unbidden, and whether the context is suitable or not."

"How sad," said Armando. He didn't look very sad to me. "The trouble is I don't know what to say in Venice."

"What's the difficulty?" I asked. "You know how much I love the Republic. And how much I hope one day it will love me . . . "

At this Armando, who was not unaware of my ambitions, managed a smile at the same time friendly yet full of diplomatic reserve.

"Venice would like to conclude an extradition treaty with Rome," he said. "The Republic is full of Romans who've fled from the rigour of your laws. No doubt you have the same difficulty here in reverse."

"Well," said I, "I'll talk to the Holy Father about it, and if I don't manage to engage his attention I'll get a clerk to draw up a memorandum. Then at least there'll be a written and dated record of your suggestion, which can be revived and dealt with more effectively under the next Pope."

A few days later I found the Holy Father deep in one of his melancholy moods, and when I ventured to ask him the reason he said lugubriously: "The Castel Sant'Angelo was struck by lightning last night. It destroyed the standard flying over it. That's a bad sign, my friend, a very bad sign."

He wouldn't say any more, but when he'd withdrawn into his apartments the first chamberlain, seeing how intrigued I was, whispered: "As Your Eminence was born in Venice you're not familiar with the superstitions current among the lower orders in Rome. When lightning strikes down the flag over the Castel Sant'Angelo it's supposed to mean the Pope's going to die before the end of the year."

"And does His Holiness believe it?"

"It looks like it. And it's all the more surprising because the standard has been struck by lightning twice before, and this is the first time the Holy Father has taken any notice."

One day a little while later I happened to pass a certain prelate who shall be nameless on one of the Vatican staircases. He smiled at me and stopped. I smiled back and halted too. I may mention that a landing between two flights of stairs is the best place in the Vatican for exchanging confidences. If you position yourself properly you can see whoever is coming up or down in time not to be overheard.

"My friend," said he, "you see the Holy Father every day – haven't you noticed a change in him?"

This question and the raised eyebrow that went with it really constituted an offer: "You can tell me what you know and I'll tell you what I know." I decided to accept, as the person concerned was usually well informed. I didn't mention what the Pope had said about the standard over the Castel Sant'Angelo, though: I regarded that as confidential. But I did describe the much less significant impressions his brief audience with the Pope had made on Armando Veniero.

The prelate listened avidly and said with a knowing smile: "Yes, that confirms it! Without going so far as to say he's failing, one might apply the famous phrase and say Homer's nodding. Yet he still looks very well. And he eats and sleeps well.★ It's as if the inner man were falling asleep. I consider it very significant that he's stopped insisting so much on the eminence of his position. Did you know that some evenings he has himself carried to his son Giacomo's house in a litter, and takes part in that useless young fellow's goings-on? Oh, nothing really depraved goes on, apart perhaps from some dancing by scantily clad Moorish slave girls. But it would be disastrous if a thing like that got out."

Upon which, having greatly contributed to its getting out, he left me, a little twinkle in his eye belying his sanctimonious sighs.

To tell the truth, His Holiness was coming to rely on me more and more. He would send for me at any hour of the day, or even of the night when he couldn't sleep. As soon as he saw me he'd say, "Cherubi, I'm in the dumps – amuse me."

It wasn't very difficult. When he liked a story you could tell it a

---

★ Not so, at least during the last months of his life (Cherubi).

hundred times over and he still enjoyed it. So long as you repeated it exactly. He'd even ask you to tell it again.

"Cherubi, tell me about having a meal at Montalto's."

"Well, to start with, Your Holiness, the dining room was always freezing. His Eminence wouldn't have a fire lit."

"Why not?" said the Pope, who'd asked the same question a dozen times before.

"Because people would be tempted to linger at table if they weren't cold. And then, the nun who waited on us . . ."

"No, no, Cherubi, you're going too fast. Montalto used to make little jokes in French about eating."

"Quite right, Your Holiness. He'd say" — and here I imitated Montalto's deep voice — "that *chère* leads to *chair*, and after the *panse* comes the *danse* . . ."★

"Excellent! Excellent! Go on!"

"The meal the nun brought us . . ."

"No, no!" cried the Pope, "You're still asleep, Cherubi! You're forgetting half of it! You haven't said what the nun was like."

"Well, Your Holiness, she was old and fabulously wrinkled. And so thin she looked like a skeleton. And so bony she creaked as she walked. All she needed was a scythe."

"Excellent! Excellent! Go on, Cherubi!"

"One day before the midday meal she told us with horror something had held up her supplies and all she had to give us was a couple of eggs. 'That's all right,' said Montalto. 'Give the larger one to Cherubi — he's a big eater — and Rossellino and I will share the little one.'"

"Excellent, Cherubi! Excellent!"

Although his recent memory was unreliable, he could remember perfectly what had happened several years before. Nor had he forgotten his various grudges, which sometimes gave rise to malicious remarks.

"Do you remember what Montalto said the first time he saw Vittoria? 'No one could see her and not love her, or hear her and not adore her.'"

He laughed and added sourly, though under his breath: "Well, our saintly friend must be pretty peeved now to see his beloved niece living

---

★ Good cheer leads to flesh, and after stuffing (paunch) comes dancing (Tr.).

in sin with a pirate."

One day he granted me a rare favour, and one that not many prelates in the Vatican could boast of: he showed me his collection. Unlike his predecessors and his illustrious successor, Gregory XIII didn't go to much expense to beautify the Eternal City. On the other hand he spent money like water adding to his collection of jewels. This was the work of a lifetime, for which he'd arranged a special room with showcases lined with mirrors, so that the gems were reflected to infinity. Tall windows lit them up by day, and Venetian chandeliers with countless candles illuminated them at night. My visit took place during one of His Holiness's bouts of insomnia – he hadn't hesitated to send for me, as was his habit by now – so an unfortunate footman, also routed out of bed, though no worse off than I was, had to spend half an hour lighting the candles in all the chandeliers and then snooze against a doorpost for a couple of hours until the inspection was over.

If I hadn't been drowsy myself – I'm a person who needs plenty of sleep – I'd have been dazzled. The Pope unlocked every showcase himself and took the marvellous specimens out one by one, exhibiting them to me and stroking them with his plump smooth hands, though he was too jealous of them to let me actually hold them. There were quantities of precious and semi-precious stones from all over the world, though most were from the Indies, Brazil, Ceylon and Siberia. Some of them were new to me, though I didn't like to ask their names. They all had sumptuous gold settings engraved by the greatest masters. The Pope told me he'd had an expert in to value his treasures, but thought his estimate too low and had sent for a famous artist from Lombardy to make another one.

All the time he was showing me his jewels a distant smile hovered on his lips, and his somewhat vague glance seemed to lose itself in the glow of his stones and of their reflections in the mirrors. Throughout our visit – and it seemed a very long one to me – he looked bright and fresh, but as soon as it was over he was overcome with weariness. He dropped on to the chair I pushed forward for him, his neck resting on the back and his eyes closed. Even then he wouldn't leave until the footman had put out all the candles. He explained in a faint voice that he wanted to lock the room up himself, with three keys he always carried about with him. When finally the last candle was out he got up, and leaning on my arm but with a firm and unerring hand, he locked the door. It was very heavy, and strongly reinforced with iron.

I escorted him back to his room, where a servant was waiting to undress him. As he passed from my arm to that of his chamberlain he looked up at me and said as if in surprise: "You here, Cherubi? Is it day already, then?"

At the same time, heaven knows why, great tears were coursing down his pink cheeks. Perhaps he was grieving deep down at not being able to take his treasures with him when his time came.

But in spite of all the signs of decay in his demeanour, memory and intelligence, his health remained good. If I may so express it when talking about a Pope, his animal being was still magnificent, especially considering he was just entering his eighty-fifth year.

This thought occurred again to me and many others on April 4th 1585. That day on the stroke of noon the Pope emerged from the Vatican to go to the Medici palace, where the Cardinal had invited him for the midday meal. I can see him now in St Peter's Square, preparing to mount his white palfrey – straight as a ramrod, slim, smiling, with sky-blue eyes and rosy cheeks. He was wearing a red hat, a white cassock, and a red velvet hood that matched the harness of his magnificent mare. Two hundred officers and court dignitaries were there on horseback, waiting to escort him through the streets of Rome. He stood for a moment in the midst of them, chatting to Cardinal de' Medici: he was a head taller than the Cardinal, and presented such a picture of elegance, dignity and nobility that we were all amazed. We were even more astonished when he took the reins from his squire, waved him aside, put his foot in the stirrup and swung into the saddle with a lightness and vigour that left us open-mouthed.

Very unusually for the time of year there'd been a frost that morning, but the sun had melted the rime and dissipated the fog, and was now high overhead, pleasantly warming our shoulders. Care had been taken to station Swiss Guards all along the Pope's route, but the ordinary folk, though they didn't actually applaud, seemed admiring rather than hostile when they saw our splendid procession.

Many stupid things have been said about the Medicis, and they've often been taunted for dabbling in banking and commerce. But I must say

303

Cardinal de' Medici's reception was worthy in every way of a great prince of the Church, and combined splendour with the most exquisite taste. Although Gregory XIII ate moderately and was a gourmet rather than a gourmand, on this occasion he willingly lingered at the table, conversing cheerfully with those about him. When the meal was over, Cardinal de' Medici, who was also the owner of some valuable jewels, offered to show them to the Pope. He accepted gladly, saying to me with a bright smile, "You come too, Cherubi, and tell me whether you think they're better than mine."

As a matter of fact the Medici jewels were not as good as the Pope's either in quantity or quality, save for a monumental salt-cellar, a reproduction of the one Benvenuto Cellini made for King François I of France. It consisted of two naked figures, a man and woman, one representing the Sea and the other the Land, sitting with their legs entwined, an allusion to the way sounds and inlets relate to the continents. The Land, a woman of ravishing grace and beauty, rested her hand on a charmingly carved little temple designed to hold the pepper. The Sea held a boat, intended to hold the salt.

The Pope gazed at this magnificent piece and stroked it with his plump hands as if he couldn't bear to tear himself away. Finally, as I'd expected from the start, he offered to buy it. The Cardinal, who must have been cursing himself for having shown it to him, was a picture of embarrassment. To sell his treasure was something terrible to contemplate. But the Pope was so vindictive it might be dangerous to refuse.

A Medici isn't easily caught out, however, and the Cardinal didn't hesitate for long.

"Sell it to you, Most Holy Father!" he exclaimed, throwing up his hands. "Certainly not! But it would give me great pleasure to make you a present of it, provided you'll leave it with me long enough to have a set of drawings made so that I can keep at least the memory of it."

So saying he put it back in its place, locked the showcase, and escorted the Pope out of his palace with the utmost courtesy. He was using a typical commercial trick: he was gaining time.

Outside we were disagreeably surprised by the temperature. The sun was hidden by big black clouds and the air had grown quite cool. I noticed that after he'd mounted his horse His Holiness shivered, and when he dismounted in the courtyard at St Peter's he shivered again. A severe attack of fever ensued and the Pope took to his bed. When the remedies of the Vatican doctor proved of no avail, Andrea da Milano was sent for. He was a descendant of Giovanni da Milano, famous professor of the equally famous school of medicine in Salerno, which was unrivalled in Europe except at Montpellier. The pre-eminence of both these schools, I'm told, derives from their incorporation of Jewish and Arab medicine, passed on to them by the Jews when they were expelled from Spain.

Andrea da Milano examined his patient, took his pulse and uttered soothing words. But having seen me constantly at the Pope's bedside – His Holiness, who was quite lucid, insisted on my staying with him – he signed to me to join him in the ante-chamber. When we were alone he spoke quite differently. "Both lungs are affected, Your Eminence. But His Holiness has an exceptionally sound constitution. His heart is excellent, and he may recover."

But by the next day there was no change, and Andrea da Milano, on his own with me, was much less hopeful. "Frankly, Your Eminence, illustrious as the patient is, I'm disappointed in him. He has no resilience. He's not putting up a fight. Instead of helping the doctor he's helping the disease."

The following day he was franker still. "It's time to give him the last rites."

I sent for Cardinal San Sisto, one of the Pope's nephews, and he came running, weeping copiously (a talent no doubt inherited from his uncle). As His Holiness was drowsing at the time I took the liberty of leaving him for a while and going home to my palace. There I ordered a light meal, after which I went out for a breath of air and to have a look at a little wood I'd just added to the grounds of the house. There I met the former owner, Domenico Acquaviva, busy clearing the undergrowth. As soon as he saw me he threw himself at my feet and kissed my ring.

"Good work, Acquaviva!" I said. "And many thanks for your kindness!"

There was a silence. Then Acquaviva said: "Your Eminence, everyone's saying His Holiness is very ill. Has all hope been abandoned?"

I nodded. "Alas, yes, my son!"

At that moment a footman ran up to tell me Cardinal de' Medici was waiting to see me in my palace. I went in at once and found Medici in the main hall, striding up and down as far as his meagre stature permitted.

"Cherubi," he said briefly, forgetting for once his courtly manner, "how is the Pope? I haven't seen him for three days."

I threw out my arms, then let them drop again. "At this moment San Sisto is giving him extreme unction."

"How very sad!" said Medici sanctimoniously, bowing his head.

But there was a faint smile on his lips, though it disappeared as soon as he felt me looking at him. Then there was silence between us as we shared a secret joke. Medici had won. Now he wouldn't have to send his precious salt-cellar to the Vatican.

12

Reverend Father Luigi Palestrino, Theologian

It was on April 10th 1585 that Gregory XIII breathed his last. I prefer that expression to "rendered up his soul", which wrongly confuses the soul with a breath, whereas there is nothing material about it and no image or metaphor drawn from the terrestrial world can convey any idea of it.

I distrust the frivolous and reckless way people speak, and am particularly shocked when they talk or even write that a child's soul is created by its parents at the moment of conception. That is pure heresy. The son of Adam possesses no such privilege. God alone has the power to create a soul.

The point is irrevocable and beyond dispute. What is debatable, however, is the point at which the soul is breathed into the infant: whether at the moment of conception or at the moment of birth. Whichever alternative one chooses there are difficulties. If you say the infant receives a soul only at birth, that means it didn't possess a soul during its nine months in the uterus. But if the infant receives a soul at the moment of conception, should it not be baptised while still in its mother's womb? For what would happen to that soul if the mother were delivered prematurely and the child were born dead?

The reason we theologians are always arguing with one another is on the one hand because we are trying to deal with points in our Holy Religion which Revelation has left obscure, and on the other because we cannot back up our various theses with definite proof. I'll cite just one example: ever since St Thomas Aquinas we have been discussing whether angels have any material being. Aquinas, of course, denied it, but despite his eminent authority some of us are very far from accepting that point of view.

But let us return to Gregory XIII (who, permit me to observe in passing and without acrimony, did not look with favour on theologians. He resented their strictures, or "grousing" as he called it, concerning his matrimonial *precetti*). He died before he could receive unction from Cardinal San Sisto, which caused us great and painful anxiety about the fate of his soul, since his conduct had not always been very edifying either in life, or in his leadership of Christendom, or in his government of the State.

I was very surprised, the day after the Pope's death, when Prince Orsini sent an anonymous coach to me with a note asking me to go and see him at Montegiordano at nightfall. I'd thought he was at Bracciano. And indeed he had been there the previous day, but having apparently still maintained sources of intelligence close to the Holy Father, he'd had warning of his imminent death and ridden in to Rome as fast as he could during the night.

This wasn't very good for his injured leg, as I saw at once on entering the room where he was waiting for me. He was half lying in his chair, his left leg stretched out in front of him. He had both hands on his thigh, as if to curb the pain, and his lower lip was slightly twisted. But this significant glimpse lasted only a second, for as soon as he saw me the Prince stood up with military swiftness and hastened forward to greet me, though with a pronounced limp. Then, still holding both my hands, he made me sit down in the chair he had just left. I was touched by such affability, especially in one with so many sources of suffering, both physical and emotional.

"Well, father," said he, coming straight to the point, "the last time we met, you said it might be possible for me to take advantage of the *interregnum* between the death of Gregory XIII and the election of the next Pope. What's the situation now the *interregnum* has begun?"

"My lord," said I, "I'd be obliged if you would refrain from asking questions in general. And from asking this one in particular: it's unnecessary, for I know very well why I'm here."

Far from being vexed at this, he just smiled. And I understood why he was much loved by women: there was something so warm about him. Yet without knowing why, I felt a kind of pity. So great, I might almost say so

308

exemplary a prince: brave, intelligent, well-educated, an enthusiastic friend of the arts, and physically so tall and broad and athletic . . . Such a fine figure of a man — but made of flesh, and flesh so precarious, so ensnared in this fleeting world.

"My lord," I went on, "an *interregnum* is a very temporary state of society, but it allows great scope to those who, like you, have a wrong to set right. For at the moment the Papal State is without a ruler and Christendom without a guide."

"Am I then to conclude," said he, forgetting my prohibition in the heat of the moment, "that I may make use of the *interregnum* to declare my marriage valid?"

"My lord, that would be madness! You can't treat the dead Pope's decree with such contempt without arousing the wrath of his successor. You must go about it more tactfully. For example, call the theologians together and consult them. Then if, and only if, their verdict is favourable, you can remarry."

"Remarry?" he said, staring. "But I'm married already!"

"Forgive me, my lord, but you are not. You are no longer married in the eyes of the Church. And there isn't a theologian in the world who can annul a papal *precetto*. All he can do is tell you that in his opinion you may remarry."

"But," said he, "what's to stop the next Pope, when he's elected, from issuing a *precetto* annulling my remarriage?"

"Nothing, my lord — absolutely nothing! It's a risk you have to take!"

"My God!" he muttered under his breath, clutching his head. "What tyranny!"

To this I made no reply: in the case that concerned us I wasn't far from sharing his opinion. But my feelings didn't change the principle I held to: *dura lex, sed lex.*★ I believe the benefits that Christendom derives from papal omnipotence are greater than the disadvantages arising from its misuse.

"If you mean to follow my advice, my lord," said I, "here is a list of seven of the most highly respected theologians. Call them together here and let them deliberate."

★ It is a harsh law, but it is the law.

"Why seven, father?" he asked, glancing at the list.

"So as to have a majority, even if only of one. For we shall take a vote – a secret ballot."

"Why secret?"

"So as not to draw the new Pope's anger down upon any one individual if he doesn't agree with our decision."

"Can these theologians be brought together by tomorrow?" he asked anxiously.

"I'll do my best. But first I should like a private interview with the Signora your wife. And please don't question me about it: I shan't answer. You may ask the Signora about it afterwards."

I could see from his frank and open countenance he was glad I'd referred to Vittoria Accoramboni as his wife, though he must have guessed I did so purely out of courtesy.

"I'll call her," he said briskly, "and leave you alone together."

I stood up and bowed. He came over to me with his limping stride and, as before, took both my hands in his: they were so large I felt mine almost disappear in them. He looked at me silently for a moment with an expression of friendship and gratitude. My head just about came up to his chest. What a mountain of a man! What huge bones! What enormous muscles! And probably, inside the giant body, what powerful organs! When his hour comes he'll have difficulty leaving behind so much flesh, whereas with me the job's already almost done! There's so little matter about me, St Thomas Aquinas might have taken me for an angel . . . Forgive my little joke. Life is only a long waiting for death, so it's as well to brighten the time occasionally as it passes.

I sat down again and waited some time for the Signora. This didn't surprise me: the ladies have a reputation for never being ready. I don't know if it's justified. I know very little about them. My mother died giving me birth, and the rest of my family was lost soon afterwards in an earthquake. I was brought up by nuns who were dumb, and I might never even have learned to speak had it not been for the convent's old gardener, with whom I lodged and who became my mentor.

It was early in my twentieth year that I went out into the streets of Rome for the first time and saw some real women. I was taken aback, and thought at first they belonged to a different species from my nuns. The latter had a kind of fusty smell about them, whereas the women I saw in the street were enveloped in a peculiar perfume. I wasn't sure whether I liked it or not. Their eyes were bright and shining and never stopped turning to look at everything. And they spoke in high clear voices that rang in my ears like music. But all these discoveries scared rather than pleased me, and it wasn't long before I got an even more terrifying shock: one of the women in the street, probably just by accident, looked at me. My nuns lived with their lids lowered and their eyes had never encountered mine: that was why the eyes of these real women seemed so brilliant and dangerous. It was as if their glance sent out little pincers that got hold of you and turned you round and round for their inspection. So when this woman looked at me as she passed by, her glance, brief and accidental as it might be, made me shake from head to foot. And ever since then I've been frightened of women.

This probably quite absurd feeling explains my uneasiness as I waited for the Signora, though I was sure the interview was necessary to her and the Prince's cause. My lips were dry, my throat felt paralysed. I noticed my hands were shaking, and hid them in my ample sleeves. What I was most afraid of was that she might see the panic she'd thrown me into — me, a man old enough to be her father.

She came at last. I sprang up. With a gracious wave of the hand she said in a low, sweet voice: "Father, I'm told you want to ask me some questions. I'm at your service."

She was a head taller than I, and as she looked at me with her great blue eyes their light was so dazzling I had to lower my own. Not so far, however, that I couldn't still see her. She seemed very elegantly dressed, though I didn't know the names of her various garments. I did notice, though, that instead of flattening and imprisoning her body like the habits of my nuns, her clothes followed her shape and even seemed designed to show it off. Her fair curly hair was so immensely long it came down to her heels and trailed behind her as she moved. Her face seemed excellently proportioned, with the skin taut over the bones. Her complexion was pink and white, her teeth regular and gleaming white.

"Father," she repeated, as if surprised at my silence, "I'm at your service."

Her voice shook a little, which made me think that in spite of her self-

311

possession she dreaded this interview as much as I did. Then something curious happened: her fear largely dispelled mine.

"There's a slight difficulty, Signora," said I, finding my voice again. "I want to speak to you alone, but at the same time I need to have a written record of my questions and your answers."

"If that's the problem," she said with a ready smile, "I think I can solve it quite easily. I'll sit at this desk and be both your witness and your clerk. Then you'll have my evidence not only in writing but in my own hand."

This was both witty and gracious. I signified that I accepted her offer, and she installed herself on a stool in front of an escritoire. This took some time, as before she sat down she gathered up her Absalom-like locks, then as she took her seat brought them round into her lap. This was probably so that their weight wouldn't trouble her as she wrote. As I watched I wondered what feminine beauty might mean to a theologian. Some saw the hand of the devil in it, but that thesis didn't stand up to scrutiny. The devil could intervene only where things were put to bad use. And there was no doubt that beauty, in itself, was a gift of God. But what for, since the function of women is procreation? All women, beautiful or ugly, can bear children, so I couldn't see the need to bring together so many excellences in one of them. If the purpose of theology was to explain religion, I had to admit that outside the bright circle of Revelation all was darkness, even a detail as trivial in itself as the one I'd been pondering. However it might be, I was sure not a leaf ever fell from a tree except by the will of Providence.

"Signora," I said, "the first question I have to ask is this: Was it at your own desire and by your own will, without threat, blackmail or any other external pressure, that you married Prince Orsini?"

"Yes, it was of my own free will."

"Will you please write all that down, Signora?"

"In our exact words?"

"Yes."

She wrote, and I waited until she lifted her quill from the paper.

"Signora, why did you marry Prince Orsini?"

"Because I loved him and wanted to be his wife."

"How many times had you met Prince Orsini before you were shut up in the Castel Sant'Angelo?"

"Once. At the house of my uncle, His Eminence Cardinal Montalto."

"Did you have any communication with him, written or oral, after that meeting?"

"The Prince wrote to me, but I didn't answer. Am I to write all this down, father?"

"Just the answers. You can leave out the questions."

She continued accordingly.

"In your view, Signora, why did the Pope shut you up in the Castel Sant'Angelo?"

"Because he thought Prince Orsini had murdered my husband, and that I was his accomplice."

"And was that true?"

"No, it was not!" she flared. "Not only was it untrue, but it was categorically denied in the Bargello's report. Della Pace told me so when he came to arrest me."

"Please go on writing, Signora."

She did so, making the pen squeak angrily on the paper. It was obvious she hadn't expected me to ask that sort of question, and was offended.

As soon as she'd finished I said: "Signora, need I say I believe what you say? Should I be here if I thought you were guilty?"

"Thank you, father," she said, evidently moved.

"Let us go on. When you met Prince Orsini at the house of your uncle, Cardinal Montalto, did you speak to him?"

"No."

"How long did you see him for?"

"About five minutes."

"And that was enough for you to love him?"

"Yes." And she added, somewhat belligerently: "Does that strike you as improbable?"

"I don't know," I answered curtly. "I have no experience of human passions, even by hearsay. I'm a theologian, not a confessor."

She looked at me repentantly, as if she was sorry to have spoken to me like that.

"Write, please, Signora," I said gently.

After a while I went on. "Supposing Gregory XIII hadn't shut you up in the Castel Sant'Angelo – would you have married Prince Orsini then?"

"I don't think so. I'd have been afraid people would think I was guilty."

"So how was it you did marry him after he'd freed you from the Castel Sant'Angelo?"

"The harm was already done. Because I'd been imprisoned, no one believed I was innocent."

"Write it down, please."

Then: "Signora, you know of course that as a result of Gregory XIII's *precetto* you are now no longer married to Prince Orsini."

"I know, and it's iniquitous!" she cried passionately.

"I must ask you, Signora, out of respect for the Holy See, to withdraw that comment. Otherwise you'll have to record it in black and white, and it will make a very bad impression on the theologians."

"I withdraw it."

"Here is my last question: If in the near future it were possible for you to remarry Prince Orsini, would you do so?"

"Yes, with all my heart!"

"Is that your considered and unalterable intention?"

"Certainly!"

"Write it down, please."

When she'd finished I asked her to date and sign what she'd written. Although, because of my retired life, the interview had been something of an ordeal (though a much less painful one than I'd ever have believed possible), I was pleased with the Signora. She'd answered my questions clearly, firmly, logically, and – I hoped – frankly. The only thing that bothered me a little was that she'd fallen in love with the Prince after having seen him for only five minutes. If women could forge so rapidly a bond that was going to last a lifetime, they were greatly to be pitied.

The Signora rose, handed me the testimony she had recorded, and took a most gracious leave. Setting aside her beauty, the purpose of which seemed to pose an insoluble theological problem, she struck me as a highly estimable human being. I took the opportunity of being alone to send up a brief prayer that she and her chosen companion might be restored to spiritual peace.

When the Prince returned I handed him the Signora's evidence, without comment. He read it right through, apparently with some surprise.

"Father, one more question, perhaps the last. Why do you lay so much stress on the fact that the Signora married me — and would, if the case arose, remarry me — of her own free will?"

"My lord, I've already told you: in the eyes of the Church the basis of the sacrament of marriage is the intention of the two spouses to give themselves to one another. What I was trying to establish was the soundness and authenticity of the bond that the *precetto* untied."

"I understand that, but in that case why don't you ask me the same questions?"

I couldn't help smiling at such naïvety. "My lord, your wish to marry the Signora needs no further proof. It is public knowledge. You fomented an insurrection to free the Signora from prison, and what are you doing now but moving heaven and earth in order to remain her husband?"

Later on, as the unmarked coach was taking me back, I thought about what I'd just said. "Moving heaven and earth" was a singularly inappropriate expression. Men being made of such changeable stuff, it may be possible to move earth; but the decrees of heaven are immutable and eternal.

His Eminence Cardinal Cherubi

Things started to move the minute Gregory XIII died, so great were the interests, personal and national, involved in the choice of his successor.

As I'd never been *papabile* because of my reputation for clumsiness, and as my only ambition was to become Patriarch of Venice some day, I observed the various manoeuvres and intrigues quite disinterestedly, only taking care to give my vote and support to a cardinal who wouldn't oppose my plans if he became Pope.

No one in the Vatican was naïve enough to imagine the princes of this world wouldn't try to influence the election. The most powerful of these was Philip II, whose possessions included Austria, the Low Countries, Spain, Portugal, and, in Italy itself, the duchy of Milan, the Kingdom of Naples, and Sicily. Not to mention his huge empire in the Americas,

315

source of the gold that maintained both his influence and his armies.

So before the doors were locked upon the conclave, Philip's ambassador, Count d'Olivarès, took care to visit all the cardinals in Rome and put pressure on them to elect a Pope favourable to the interests of Spain. He came to see me too, and spent quite a long time with me, supposing my influence on the conclave to be greater than it actually was. He wasn't stupid, but he lacked finesse. And no one ever had more of the arrogance universally attributed to his countrymen. He spoke to church dignitaries as if he were giving them orders, and lost his temper at the least sign of opposition. Though generous with promises he was equally lavish with threats, which he scarcely took the trouble to veil. My opinion after our meeting was that he was trying too hard, and doing his master's cause more harm than good.

Henri III of France had little chance of influencing the conclave: he had his hands full with the rebellious *Ligue*, who were hand in glove with Philip II. But the French king had some sympathisers among those who mistrusted Philip's power, and these included Cardinal d'Este, who had family connections with Henri III. D'Este's people were very powerful in Italy — they owned the duchy of Ferrara, Modena, Reggio and Rovigo — so he himself was quite influential among us.

We went into conclave on April 21, after Mass, and spent the rest of that day taking possession of our cells and paying courtesy calls on one another, each using his long antennae to try to weigh up the leading candidates' chances, and in some cases his own.

It was rather amusing, leaving our splendid palaces behind and being cloistered each in a modest cell. In a way it made us feel young again, and the feeling was all the more pleasurable because we knew our juvenile discomfort wasn't going to last very long. The conclave, of such great moment for Christendom, for the State and for ourselves, was starting off not only in a state of suppressed excitement but also in a monastic atmosphere lightened by innocent high spirits.

One might have been tempted to go along with that mood if it hadn't been necessary to be on one's guard. But the most amiable words and the friendliest glances might hide calculation. Though my inveterate blundering was usually accepted indulgently by my colleagues, even I felt the need to tread carefully, and to be frank in appearance only.

None of the other prelates raised his voice above a murmur, either. When we tapped on a door we did so quietly. As the scarlet robes passed one another in the narrow gallery between the cells, the only sound to be heard was a smooth rustle – the footsteps were silent. Gestures were slow and restrained. Eyes often lowered. Despite the thickness of the walls, conversations in the cells were whispered. And the talk was all understatement. Smiles, shrugs and glances said more than words, and sometimes contradicted them. No one spoke ill of anyone, except by omission or paralipsis. The silence, meditation and piety on display at our services, morning and evening, would have edified the most sceptical observer.

On the second day the conclave really got started, and the hopes of all the cardinals aspiring to the papacy began to seethe. Almost all of them could aspire, even the most unassuming, for it had sometimes happened that some obscure cardinal was elected just to rule out some other so talented as to be thought dangerous.

On the face of it, Cardinal Alessandro Farnese looked the most likely candidate to me. He belonged to the famous princely family who ruled over the duchy of Parma and Piacenza. He was intelligent and able, a humanist and patron of the arts. Perhaps most important of all, his nephew and namesake Alessandro Farnese, who was half Austrian through his mother, had been made governor of the Low Countries by Philip of Spain, and had won renown for restoring peace there. So the virtues of the nephew were added to those of the uncle, and the favour of Philip II towards both lent convincing weight and lustre to Farnese's candidacy. He hadn't yet offered himself as a candidate, but his position made it inevitable that he should do so.

Everyone was therefore surprised when on the second day of the conclave Cardinal Altemps and Cardinal de' Medici put forward Cardinal Sirleto, who as a Neapolitan was one of Philip II's subjects and so a partisan in his cause.

The motives of the two sponsors were very different. Altemps supported Sirleto because he was pro-Spanish and he really wanted him to succeed. Medici supported him because although he, Medici, was not pro-Spanish, he wished to appear so, and above all he wanted to block the candidacy of Farnese, who seemed to him much more of a threat.

317

Moreover he could expect some recompense from Sirleto: Medici had been Secretary of State to both Pius IV and Gregory XIII, so why not to Sirleto too if he became Pope?*

This candidacy at once met with strong, though mixed opposition. Many of the cardinals didn't want Sirleto precisely because Medici might become Secretary of State for the third time under him. Cardinal d'Este and Cardinal Farnese were against Sirleto for other reasons. The first, with the interests of France at heart, feared a Pope who was a subject of the King of Spain. The second wanted the papal tiara for himself. The votes were counted and Sirleto was eliminated.

At this point two things happened which both contained an element of comedy. One, which happened inside the conclave, seemed important at first but in fact had little effect on the election. The second event took place outside the conclave, and what is worse, in the street, and ruined the chances of the most brilliant candidate.

Just before noon that day – it was Easter Monday – someone started hammering on the trebly locked door of the conclave: it was Cardinal Andrea, who'd just arrived in Rome and was demanding admission. For Andrea was not only a cardinal – he was also Archduke of Austria. That was why he was accompanied by the Spanish ambassador. It was the Archduke who was responsible for the imperious battering that had startled the other cardinals, as was clear when someone opened the judas hole in the door. To tell the truth we were all rather alarmed. To admit the Austrian Archduke was tantamount to having Philip II in our midst during the election. But how were we to refuse, given that Gregory XIII had been weak enough to make him a cardinal?

With our whispered approval Medici had recourse to the method that had proved so successful in the matter of his precious salt-cellar: he played for time. "May it please Your Eminence to defer your entry. The members of the conclave are just about to sit down to their morning meal, and if you came in straight away it would take a good two hours to read you the bulls establishing you as an elector. That would be a great pity for those of us who are hungry and need to recruit our strength."

Though this was politely put it was taken badly on the other side of

* Medici later denies nourishing the ambition Cherubi attributes to him here.

the judas.

"There can be no question," said d'Olivarès haughtily, "of His Eminence the Cardinal Archduke kicking his heels outside a locked door while his colleagues stuff themselves – as no doubt they have every right to do. But if they elect a Pope in the course of the meal, that would greatly infringe on the Cardinal Archduke's rights. So I hereby declare that if he is not admitted at once, the King my master will consider null and void any election in which he hasn't taken part."

This outrageous threat left us aghast: Philip II, through his arrogant ambassador, was by anticipation calling in question the sovereignty of the conclave! So taken aback were we all – even the most Hispanicised among us – that at first we were at a loss what to say or do.

Once again Medici came to the rescue. He went over to the judas hole and said:

"May it please Your Eminence to wait a few minutes. We are about to confer among ourselves."

And he firmly closed the judas. Though he handled the Spanish power tactfully, he also feared it, as did his brother the Grand Duke of Tuscany, and the Most Serene Republic of Venice, and Cardinal d'Este's brother, the Duke of Ferrara. These principalities, though famed and prosperous, were small, and were afraid of suffering the same fate as the duchy of Milan and the Kingdom of Naples. For Philip II's greed for new territories was as vast as his Empire was great.

Someone then remembered that the Archduke of Austria was only a deacon and hadn't received holy orders; his cardinal's title was merely a courtesy one. And according to a bull promulgated by Pius IV, he needed to be ordained in order to enter the conclave and take part in the vote. At first our gathering was delighted at this discovery; but then everybody drew back. Who was going to be bold enough to bell the tiger Olivarès, already banging impatiently on the conclave door with an iron hand that had never known a velvet glove?

Medici declined the task, saying he'd already braved Olivarès' claws twice. They thought of me next, even politely insinuating that one more blunder on my part wouldn't matter. But I firmly refused. Finally, after a hasty consultation of everyone round the table had resulted in nothing but negatives, Cardinal d'Este offered to be the martyr. He didn't get much thanks for it: everyone knew he was pro-French, and so had nothing more to lose from the Spanish faction.

Cardinal d'Este didn't fail to note this ingratitude, but nevertheless marched stoutly over to the locked door, opened the judas and said: "Your Eminence, the conclave regrets it cannot admit you. According to the bull *In Eligendis* of 1503, no one can participate in the conclave who is not in holy orders."

Once again Olivarès spoke for the Cardinal Archduke, and very curtly too: "We foresaw that objection and here is a document that does away with it. It's a bull issued by Gregory XIII, exempting the Cardinal Archduke from having to take orders and giving him the right to vote in the conclave just the same. Read it."

He passed the bull through the judas. Cardinal d'Este took it, unrolled it and read it, some of the others crowding round and reading the scandalous document over his shoulder.

"Well, what do you think, Medici?" said d'Este sourly. "Is it really Gregory XIII's signature? You were his Secretary of State — you must have written the thing out?"

"I don't remember anything about it," said Medici.

This insolence brought him some not very amiable looks, but he didn't seem to care. Drawing himself up — he wasn't very tall — he went and unlocked the door with his own hand.

The Cardinal Archduke then entered, and as soon as the door was locked again behind him we enveloped him in a great swirl of robes, vying with one another in civilities. We also looked at him with some curiosity, for he had been to Rome only once before, staying just long enough to receive his red hat at the hands of the Pope. He was a big fat man with pale blue eyes and an expression polite but indifferent. He accepted our Italian compliments graciously, but as if he didn't really understand them. Someone tried him with Latin. He still didn't understand. French and Spanish were equally unsuccessful. Anyhow, he didn't know any of us, and was quite unfamiliar with our cliques and factions, the various interests at stake, large and small, and of course our numerous intrigues. Those who spoke German tried to rope him into their respective parties. He listened to them politely but without taking the least interest in their suggestions. He was clearly bored stiff, even during Mass, and never opened his lips in the whole course of our discussions, except to yawn behind his glove.

But strangely enough, although the Cardinal Archduke's entrance into the conclave had little direct influence on the votes, outside the conclave it gave rise to an incident that had a considerable effect on the election. The row Count d'Olivarès had caused over the locked door soon leaked out, and the people of Rome, by a kind of wishful thinking, assumed that the Spanish faction was going to win, and that Cardinal Farnese would soon be elected, if he hadn't been elected already. There were great rejoicings, and the mob rushed to sack the Farnese palace. This was not done out of spite: the populace adored the Cardinal, and were acting in accordance with a custom – I don't like to call it a tradition – which says that since a cardinal who succeeds to the tiara gains access at the same time to great wealth, he can well afford to make the people a present of his personal possessions.

We were shocked beyond expression that the Romans should have dared to anticipate our decision, and perhaps even more to see that Farnese was so popular with them. That meant that if we elected him he would rely partly on the Spanish influence and partly on the favour of the people, and could afford to snap his fingers at our opposition. We sent some guards to protect his magnificent palace, and took a vote. Farnese had only ten or so supporters, so he saved his possessions but lost the tiara.

Then Cardinal di San Sisto, who was very influential with the Roman cardinals because nearly all of them had got their red hats from his uncle, Gregory XIII, on his own recommendation, put forward one of them, Cardinal Castagna, as a candidate. Most members of the conclave wanted a virtuous Pope to succeed Gregory XIII, and Castagna was virtuous. But he didn't have a very strong character, and people were afraid San Sisto would be behind him pulling the strings. So he too was rejected.

The next to be suggested was the Grand Inquisitor, Cardinal Savello. He was a Roman, and as soon as his name was put forward all the other Roman cardinals opposed it. They were in a good position to know that Savello was a fanatic who saw the devil's hand in everything, was suspicious of his own shadow, and dreamed of nothing but auto-da-fés and burnings at the stake. Even his colleagues didn't feel safe from him.

His candidacy was soon nipped in the bud.

Then Farnese suggested Santa Severina, thinking that as he was so young he would be easy for him to handle. But this same question of age was used against Santa Severina by those who didn't want a Farnese protégé on the papal throne: "What?" they said, "scarcely forty years old? Are we going to elect a *putto-papa*?★ Terror had eliminated the Grand Inquisitor. Ridicule finished off Santa Severina.

But by now we had been shut up for three long days. Everyone was anxious to bring the matter to an end. We were getting tired of all the manoeuvrings, and of our Spartan conditions. Farnese, still smarting from his failure, sensed this waning enthusiasm and decided to stir things up. He put forward the name of the Spanish Cardinal Torrès, due to arrive in Rome the following day.

I was in my cell ruminating on this staggering piece of news when Medici knocked at the door. I let him in. He was pale, and his brow was streaming with perspiration.

"Cherubi," he said straight away, dispensing with his usual diplomatic precautions, "what do you think of the Torrès candidacy?"

"I'm aghast! A Spanish Pope on the throne of St Peter? Why not Olivarès himself while we're about it! It amounts to the same thing anyway! If Torrès is elected, Olivarès and Farnese will rule for him. They'll be our masters! And the leader of Christendom will be a mere chaplain to the King of Spain! What a disgrace!"

I fell silent, astonished at my own sudden outburst of frankness. But there was no time now for concealment. Medici, Machiavellian though he was, knew this too.

"Since that's how you feel, Cherubi," he said hastily, "come and see me in my cell in ten minutes' time. You'll find others there who think as you do."

Very unusually for him, he shook my hand before he left. His hand was quite damp. The poor fellow was terrified, and with reason. How could a Spanish Pope defend the Grand Duchy of Tuscany against the voracity of Philip II?

Ten minutes later, in Medici's cell, I found Alessandrino, Santa

★ A child Pope. A *putto* is one of the little naked cupids or cherubs often depicted in the painting and sculpture of the period.

Severina, Rusticucci and d'Este, all four of them very tense.

"Farnese," said Medici, "is hatching a very skilful plot. He means to exploit the fact that when a cardinal is introduced into the conclave we all crowd round to greet him. By the time Torrès arrives Farnese hopes to have rounded up enough cardinals to elect him by acclamation, taking advantage of the confusion and the impossibility of counting, in the heat of the moment, who is for and who is against."

"Very clever," said d'Este, "but we can use the same trick. Let's be quick and choose a candidate of our own, campaign on his behalf, and elect him by acclamation before Torrès arrives, when we're all together in the chapel."

"We must hurry, then," said Medici. "Let's pick a candidate at once. I eliminate myself straight away."

"And arithmetic eliminates me," said Cardinal d'Este. "If I stood I'd only get the votes of the three French cardinals, and then probably not all of them — Pellevé's an ardent supporter of the Ligue."

"As for me," said Rusticucci, "my ambitions don't fly that high."

He meant he'd rather get from the next Pope what he'd never been able to get from Gregory XIII — an important position in the State.

"My ambitions don't fly at all," said I. "They sail in the direction of Venice."

"Mine neither fly nor sail," said Alessandrino soberly.

"I don't need to eliminate myself," said Santa Severina, who was indeed "young" and still had the cheerfulness of youth. "I'm eliminated already."

Despite the gravity of the situation, everyone smiled at the *putto-papa*'s sally.

"We must act quickly," said Medici. "Torrès could arrive at any moment. I propose Montalto."

There was a brief silence while everyone weighed the name in his own personal scales.

"He'll make a change from Gregory XIII," said Santa Severina. "He's virtuous, capable and a hard worker."

"I respect him," said Cardinal d'Este. "He refused a pension from the King of Spain."

"But he voted for Farnese," said Alessandrino.

"Mere *captatio benevolentiae*,"* said Medici. "He knew Farnese hadn't a ghost of a chance after the riot."

"What do you think, Cherubi?" asked d'Este, raising one eyebrow.

Everyone turned to look at me, remembering the difference Montalto and I had had in the past.

"I'm extremely grateful to Montalto," I said with an air of mock seriousness, "for 'sending me back to my gondolas'. Otherwise I'd never have become a cardinal. I shall vote for Montalto."

They all smiled, and I thought I'd got out of it rather wittily. If, as seemed likely, Montalto's chances prospered, it would be an advantage to have been one of his main supporters. My Venetian ambitions needed the favour of the next Pope.

"One good thing about Montalto, apart from his virtues," said Rusticucci, "is that since the death of Peretti all his nephews are too young to be given official positions. Gregory XIII's nepotism was unbearable – by the time he'd provided for all his kinsmen there were no important jobs left for those who really deserved them."

Everyone agreed, though with some amusement: in our friend's view, the first among "those who really deserved" high office was Rusticucci himself.

"Alessandrino?" said Medici.

"Oh, I agree," said Alessandrino in his usual lofty tone. "I don't see any reason to oppose the poor old man. We'll be the masters, anyhow."

"Do you think so?" said Medici.

Prince Paolo Giordano Orsini, Duke of Bracciano

My theologians started their deliberations on the *precetto* on April 11th, ten days before the conclave began. Twelve days later they still hadn't reached any conclusion.

Thanks to a clever arrangement that I owe to my grandfather and his architect, anyone speaking in the room I'd assigned to the theologians could be heard in the room overhead. I'd intended by this means to follow their discussions, but as they spoke Latin I couldn't understand a word.

---

* A manoeuvre to obtain goodwill.

So I called in Vittoria. She listened for a good hour, her brow furrowed with concentration, and then reported:

"They keep on weighing the pros and cons, with endless quotations from Scripture and the Fathers of the Church. They can always find some text to support whatever point of view is advanced. They can't agree about anything, not even on what Our Lord is supposed to have thought about the dissolving of the marriage bond. Some say He was for and others say He was against it. They argue passionately, and get very impatient with one another."

"My love, you're as learned as you are beautiful! I'm full of admiration that you can understand these pedants. They may also be very crafty. I shouldn't be surprised if they kept us hanging around indefinitely, until one fine morning the conclave gives us a new Pope and they still won't have reached any decision."

"That's what I'm afraid of too, Paolo. One thing struck me as I was listening to them. Apart from Father Palestrino, who keeps trying to make them stick to the point, they hardly ever mention our *precetto*!"

"Ours!" said I. "How strange that sounds. But you're right, Vittoria – it is ours, like a disease eating away at us or a leech clinging to our skin."

It was a mistake to talk about a disease eating away at us. A cloud passed over Vittoria's lovely face, and I could see she was thinking of the wound in my leg. She worried about it a great deal, however much I tried to hide the fact that it was getting worse.

"But Vittoria," I went on, pretending not to understand why her expression had changed, "don't you worry – I'll hurry them up. I'll tell Father Palestrino in particular not to let the conclave steal a march on us."

I did so that very day.

"My lord," said Palestrino in the loud, clearly articulated voice that always surprised me coming from that frail body, "the good fathers aren't deliberately keeping you waiting – they're embarrassed, and afraid."

"Afraid?"

"My lord, like me they belong to the Church and must obey its laws. You treat them so well they'd like to give a decision that pleased you, but for them there's a danger involved. How do they know if the next Pope will be your friend?"

325

"I understand. But what can we do to make them come to a decision?"

"Chivvy them."

"Chivvy them?" said I in surprise. "But how?"

"If you've really made up your mind to do it, I'll tell you how, my lord, in the morning."

Thereupon he asked to be allowed to take leave, and as I knew he'd only shut up like a clam if I asked any questions, I let him go.

I told Vittoria about our conversation, and we spent a couple of hours not exactly depressed (after all, we were together), but in a very disagreeable mixture of impatience and anxiety. Our marriage seemed to depend on everything except ourselves: on the theologians, the conclave, the next Pope, and heaven knew what else.

At the end of the evening we decided to set our sombre mood aside and play dice. The stakes had to do with love, and we whispered them in one another's ear because Caterina was there, gently brushing her mistress's tresses.

Then came a discreet tap at the door. The majordomo came in, apologising because it was so late, to tell me a monk had arrived and insisted on seeing me. From his description I recognised *il mancino*.

"Let him in! Let him in!" I said. "He's at home here."

You'd have thought *il mancino* was waiting outside the door, so swiftly did he appear before us in his doublet, having shed his monkish garments in the ante-chamber. As soon as he entered, Caterina ran and hung round his neck, covering him with kisses. He bore it with patient indulgence, like one who was used to being adored by women.

"Come, come, little sister," he said at last. "Have you forgotten where you are?"

He freed himself from Caterina's embrace and swept Vittoria a low bow expressive of both respect and admiration, then honoured me with one made up entirely of respect. As I'd already noticed, he was capable of fine distinctions.

Then he drew himself up proudly to his full height, reminding me of a little fighting cock, thin and wiry. Nor was he devoid of beak and claws, for he had a dagger in his belt, another, Italian style, at his back, and a knife in his boot. It was late at night, of course, and the streets of Rome were full of danger.

326

"My lord," he said with dignity, "I wouldn't have ventured to disturb you at this hour if I hadn't got very important information to impart."

"I'm listening."

"His Eminence Cardinal Torrès arrived in Genoa yesterday evening and will set out for Rome tomorrow. He's in a great hurry to get here. And ambassador d'Olivarès is very eager to take him to the conclave as soon as he arrives."

He was silent long enough for me to ask why.

"Because of a plot he's hatched with Cardinal Farnese. When Torrès enters the conclave, Farnese is to round up all the pro-Spanish prelates and have him elected Pope by acclamation."

"A Spanish Pope!" cried Vittoria. "How disgraceful!"

"And how dangerous for you and the Prince, Signora!" said *il mancino*, with another of his gallant bows.

"Dangerous, Acquaviva?" said Vittoria.

"I used to be a general in the service of Venice, my angel," said I. "That's enough to make Philip II mistrust me."

"And your military talents, my lord," said *il mancino*. "Philip hates good generals, Signora, unless they're his, like Alessandro Farnese."

"Acquaviva," I said, "once again your political acumen amazes me. Where did you get the news about Torrès from?"

"One of my girls," said *il mancino*, lowering his eyes modestly. "They call her *la sorda*, though she isn't deaf. She's reliable, faithful and devoted, and she's got plenty of brains."

"But a whore's a whore, after all," said Caterina sourly.

Il mancino scowled at her and Vittoria, half scolding and half protecting her, at once intervened.

"Caterina, come and sit by me on this stool. And hold your tongue."

As soon as Caterina had obeyed, Vittoria put a hand on her shoulder and said with a laugh: "And after all a chambermaid's a chambermaid too."

Il mancino looked swiftly at them both. He was furious with Caterina, yet at the same time grateful to Vittoria for protecting her.

"Well," said I, "what did *la sorda* do?"

"She made friends with d'Olivarès' secretary."

"Friends!" said Caterina derisively.

"Be quiet, Caterina," said Vittoria, giving her a little tap on the cheek. Caterina caught hold of her hand and kissed it.

"The secretary's an Italian," said *il mancino*, "but he speaks Spanish very well and acts as d'Olivarès' interpreter."

"And how did he come to confide in *la sorda*?"

"Out of friendship, as I've said, but also because he was angry at the thought that there might be a Spanish Pope."

"A thousand thanks, Acquaviva. Please take this little purse for your pains. Would you like me to send you back by coach?"

"I thank you, my lord, but that won't be necessary," he said, with an excellent imitation of nonchalance. "My servant is waiting for me in the courtyard with our horses. But may it please your lordship, I'd like to have a word alone with my sister before I go."

"Off you go then, Caterina!"

And by the time *il mancino* had bowed to us and opened the door, she had bounded forward. He ushered her out in front of him, treating her to a stern look as he did so. I'd never seen a girl run so gleefully into a good clip round the ear.

"What are we going to do, Paolo?" said Vittoria.

"Chivvy the theologians."

"But how?"

"I'll know tomorrow morning."

I was up betimes next morning, and when Palestrino arrived I took him aside and told him about d'Olivarès schemes.

"A Spanish Pope!" he cried, crossing himself. "God save us from such an affliction! Those people would burn one half of Christendom to save the other half!"

"Be that as it may, father – the conclave is about to conclude. I haven't a minute to lose. What must I do to hurry the theologians up?"

"To hurry us *all* up, my lord. I mustn't be treated as an exception."

And after signing to me to bend down, he spoke at length into my ear.

When I left him I went and gave my majordomo some orders that surprised him. Then, after he told me all the theologians were now in their room, I went and addressed them in no uncertain terms.

"A word, if you please, reverend fathers. As I don't know Latin I shall speak to you in good plain simple Italian. Your discussions have been going on for twelve days now without result. This delay is very damaging to my cause and I cannot allow it to continue. So I've decided to keep you shut up here at Montegiordano until you've reached a conclusion. You won't die of hunger. You'll be provided with as much bread and wine as you want."

"What!" said Father Palestrino, pretending to be indignant. "Are we your prisoners, then, my lord?"

"No doubt about it, reverend fathers."

"But that's tyranny!" cried another of the priests, as if outraged.

There were various murmurs, and one of the theologians said: "You're subjecting us to force!"

"Reverend fathers," said I firmly, "let us not argue, I beg. I'm not dictating your decision — I'm only speeding it up."

Then with a brief nod I left, locking the door behind me.

I went straight to Vittoria and told her about it. She listened wide-eyed. "They must be foaming at the mouth!"

"That's the impression they tried to give. But really they're delighted. It makes things so much easier for them. If their verdict about the *precetto* displeases the next Pope they can say I used force on them and they couldn't do otherwise!"

I not only kept the theologians in as strict seclusion as the cardinals in the conclave: I also sent the majordomo every hour to ask them how they were getting on.

The pressure produced results. On the stroke of six the majordomo brought me a sealed scroll. I broke it open at once, but it was written in Latin and I had to wait for Vittoria, who was resting in her room, to come and translate it for me.

Here is the result of the consultation as far as I can remember, set down without any attempt to reproduce the ecclesiastical rhetoric of the original:

FIRST POINT

We have diligently studied the *precetto* in which the Most Holy and Late Lamented Pope Gregory XIII annulled the matrimonial bond uniting Prince Paolo Giordano Orsini, Duke of Bracciano, and Signora Vittoria Accoramboni, widow of Signor Francesco Peretti. It seems to us, both because of the imperfect Latin in which it is written and because of the unsoundness of its arguments, that the *precetto* was drawn up not by the Holy Father himself but by a clerk.

SECOND POINT

The reasons given for dissolving the bond are moral. It is suggested, though not clearly stated, that the said marriage was scandalous because Francesco Peretti was murdered on the orders of the Prince, with the Signora as his tacit accomplice. However, not only is no proof offered to support this implicit accusation, but Bargello della Pace's report, which is known to us, also fails to indicate the guilt of the two people concerned.

Moreover, when Signora Vittoria Accoramboni was imprisoned in the Castel Sant'Angelo there was no question of bringing her to trial. Any presumptions against her must therefore have been too weak to be put before the judges.

THIRD POINT

The *precetto* was issued at the request of two influential noblemen whose names for honourable reasons we shall not mention. Both gentlemen are relations by marriage of Prince Orsini. The reasons for their request were moral, and identical with those examined above. We have therefore nothing to add to our previous analysis. But it seems possible that the petitioners might have been moved by worldly considerations, since Prince Orsini's remarriage might have seemed to them to threaten the interests of his son by his first marriage.

FIRST CONCLUSION

Despite the weaknesses, omissions and inaccuracies in the arguments of the *precetto*, it cannot be regarded as null because of the sacred character of its author, the Most Holy and Late Lamented Gregory XIII, deciding and judging *ex cathedra* under the inspiration of the Holy Spirit. Nor is it possible to maintain that the death of the Most Holy and Late Lamented Pope Gregory XIII renders the above-mentioned *precetto* null, unless it be expressly declared so by his successor.

SECOND CONCLUSION

On the other hand, the prohibition in the *precetto* forbidding the parties concerned to contract another marriage cannot now be considered binding. Firstly, because the Most Holy and Late Lamented Gregory XIII, having been summoned by his Creator to enjoy eternal bliss, has left this vale of tears and is no longer in a position to punish the offenders. Secondly, because no one can pre-judge the decision a future Pope may make concerning them, as he cannot be bound by the decisions of his predecessor and possesses complete sovereignty over his own.

As soon as Vittoria had translated this document I went to the theologians and said:

"Reverend fathers, the report of your consultation is a masterpiece of wisdom, prudence and moderation. I am completely satisfied with it, and shall always be infinitely grateful to you. Thanks to you the Signora and I will be able to live again as a Christian couple, in dignity and fidelity. Be good enough to wait here a little while longer and my majordomo will summon you one by one to convey to each of you a more concrete token of my gratitude. Reverend fathers, I ask all of you to pray that the bond you have just saved may never again be broken."

The theologians bowed and uttered friendly murmurs. I left the room, and the first person my majordomo would summon was Father Palestrino, but I wanted to see him myself before he left Montegiordano. When I went up to him and clasped him affectionately in my arms, I was taken aback to find I was embracing a skeleton.

"You're crushing me to death, my lord," he said, a faint tinge of pink appearing in his cheeks. (But can I speak of cheeks?: his withered skin was stretched so tightly over the bones there seemed no trace of flesh.)

"I'm sorry, father," said I, "But I owe everything to you."

"As a matter of fact," he answered, "neither I nor any of the others did very much. And I don't know if we had the right to do what little we did. However, it's enough to enable you to remarry. Only remember that your second union will be precarious until the next Pope has accepted it."

I realised it was true. Our waiting, our anxiety were still not over: we'd negotiated only one step.

On the following day, April 24th 1585, in the chapel at Grottapinta, I married Vittoria for the second time.

13

His Eminence Cardinal de' Medici

The original nucleus of Montalto's supporters consisted of myself, d'Este, Alessandrino, Santa Severina, Cherubi and Rusticucci. Plenty of talent there, but it would take at least six times that number to get Montalto elected by acclamation. So as soon as we'd agreed on his name we all six set about trying to increase our little party through a whispering campaign and all the other devices usual on such occasions.

Admittedly the candidate we were trying to help had already done a lot to help himself. Ever since the beginning of the conclave he'd shown great prudence and skill. He visited every cardinal in his cell, presenting himself quite humbly and without mentioning that he wanted to be elected, but promising that if the opportunity arose he would do all he could for them. For years he'd been at pains to study his colleagues and find out all he could about them, so he knew how best to approach each one.

He effected a reconciliation with Cherubi, whom he'd treated harshly in the past, asking forgiveness for having "sent him back to his gondolas" and adding wittily that one day perhaps it would turn out to be prophetic, and Cherubi would realise his ambition of presiding over the Church in Venice . . .

Montalto's discernment was so keen it amounted almost to divination. While most of the cardinals wrongly supposed I wanted to be Secretary of State again under the new Pope, he realised I was tired of the job. So instead of promising it to me when I visited him in his cell, he spoke only of his attachment to the Grand Duchy of Tuscany and his desire that it should retain its independence "against all comers" (no doubt referring to Philip II). He was well aware that my elder brother, the Grand Duke, was childless, that one day I'd be called upon to succeed him, and that that was now my only ambition.

He showed the same skill in steering a safe course between the Charybdis of the Spanish faction and the Scylla of the French. He promised Farnese his vote and did in fact vote for him, though only when he had no chance of being elected. He spoke to d'Este about the Duchy of Ferrara as he'd spoken to me about the Grand Duchy of Tuscany. At the same time he was affable though dignified with the Archduke of Austria: he was able to be useful to him because he spoke German.

Knowing how fond Cardinal Altemps was of his brother the Marquis, Montalto gave him to understand that the Marquis would make a very good governor of the Borgo.* To San Sisto he praised his brother Giacomo, expressing the hope that after the election he would be confirmed in his post as general of the Papal army. He didn't make any promises to Alessandrino, probably because he was so overbearing; he merely flattered his inordinate pride with equally inordinate compliments. With Rusticucci, whom he considered both more modest and more able, he ventured a few subtle hints, having known for a long time that he aspired to become Secretary of State.

His attentions were so skilfully measured out, and his demeanour so modest and natural, that the less perspicacious swallowed the bait without realising it. The sharper ones among us, knowing he was a man of his word, just stored up his promises and admired his adroitness without necessarily being taken in by it. Before the conclave we had regarded Montalto as a very virtuous and able prelate; but the diplomatic talents he showed now made him rise considerably in our estimation. It must be admitted that when you see a man so cut out for success, as long as that success doesn't do you any harm you feel like helping him and making a friend of him rather than an enemy . . .

I realised our little group would never rally enough people round Montalto unless we managed to win Cardinal San Sisto over. Undistinguished as he was in both heart and mind, he still had a lot of influence over the many cardinals created by his uncle Gregory XIII, for

* The quarter of Rome that includes the Vatican.

the simple reason that he'd engineered their nomination.

In person San Sisto was tall, pale and spineless, like a candle. His character was much the same. He was weak, irresolute and fickle. I don't want to push the metaphor too far and say he melted like a candle, but one day when I was talking to him I got hold of him by the arm in the heat of the moment – and could feel neither bones nor muscles. I wondered for a moment what on earth he *was* made of.

To win him over we put our heads together and came up with a little ruse I don't like to describe as pious, though it did aim at the good of the State and of Christendom. Then we primed Cherubi, and sent him to see San Sisto.

Cherubi is talkative, kind and exuberant, and because he's a blunderer people think he must be straightforward and frank. And he spoke to San Sisto bluntly if speciously.

"My lord, I want to give you a friendly warning. The matter is still very secret, but Montalto's candidacy is so popular that by all the calculations he's the one most likely to be elected."

"What! What!" said San Sisto. "But he's been keeping so quiet! I haven't ever seen him bustling about!"

"He doesn't bustle, my lord, but he does make progress, and his election is almost certain now. If he hasn't approached Your Eminence it may be because he thinks you're against him, as was your uncle – the Most Holy and Late Lamented Gregory XIII."

"But not at all!" cried San Sisto in horror. "I'm not in the least against him! I think both his virtues and his talents make him eminently suitable."

"How is it then that he hasn't approached you?"

"But, now I come to think of it, he has! He said very kind things to me about my brother. If I remember rightly, he even said he hoped that under the next Pope he'd be confirmed in his post as general of the Papal army."

"Well, that certainly was an opening, my lord! And if I were to give Your Eminence a word of advice, I'd say don't let that opening close up again and leave you out."

"I'll think about it," said San Sisto, very shaken. "And many thanks, Cherubi, for your kindness, and for speaking to me so frankly."

335

When Cherubi told us the result of this interview we decided San Sisto was so spineless and changeable that we'd better strike while the iron was hot. We sent Cardinals Riario and Gustavillanio to see him: they'd just been won over to our cause and spoke to him in the same strain as Cherubi. As a final touch we sent Alessandrino.

The choice of messenger was mine, and I may say in all modesty it was very apt, and took into account the characters of both men.

Alessandrino was the most imposing of all the cardinals, and that was why for all his talent he never had the slightest chance of being elected Pope. He was tall, strong, still young, and intelligent; but he was also imperious and arrogant. But the considerations that prevented him from ever being *papabile* also made him an influential voice in all the conclaves in which he took part.

He was much briefer and more abrupt with San Sisto than Cherubi had been, and didn't bother addressing him as "my lord" or "Your Eminence". They were of equal rank, and he didn't see why he should use such courtesies to an individual he regarded as his inferior.

"San Sisto," he said, taking him by the arm and drawing him aside in an authoritarian manner no one else in all the conclave ever used, "I want a word with you, please. Do you respect Montalto?"

"Oh, very much, very much," said San Sisto hastily.

"A word of advice, then. Wake yourself up, my friend, and exert yourself in his favour. In any case you'll only be in at the victory. His candidacy is so well sewn up he's bound to be elected. And you don't want the next pope to have a grudge against you, do you? You don't want him to treat you as your uncle treated him?"

"What? What? Is his election as certain as that?"

"Consider it already done, my dear fellow," said Alessandrino, fixing him with his black eye. "It's up to you to decide whether to act. I'm only giving you some friendly advice."

"Decide? Act?" said San Sisto. "But how can I decide to support him without consulting the cardinals my uncle created?"

"Do you mean to say," said Alessandrino, "that you, their leader, are going to follow them? Shouldn't you do the opposite and show them the way?"

"I ought to consult them, anyhow," said San Sisto, who seemed

336

utterly confused. "What's the difference?"

"It lies in how you ask the question. For example, if you say, 'What do you think of Montalto's candidacy?' you leave them free to decide for themselves. But if you say, 'I'm going to vote for Montalto. What do you think about that?', you'll be guiding their choice."

"That's a good way of putting it," said San Sisto. "I must remember that."

When Alessandrino told me about this I remembered that the Cardinal Archduke of Austria, as well as being Philip II's cousin, was also one of the cardinals created by Gregory XIII at his nephew's instigation. So, summoning up the little German I knew, I went to his cell and began very prudently to sound him out.

"My lord, some of us, including Cardinal San Sisto and myself, are considering voting for Montalto, whom we regard as a very saintly and able man. What do you think?"

"Who? Who did you say?" exclaimed the Cardinal Archduke.

"Montalto."

"Who's he?" said the Archduke, yawning behind his glove. And the *homo germanicus* looked down at me out of his big pale-blue eyes, as well he might, since my head only came up to his stomach.

"Your Eminence must know Montalto! He's about sixty-five and uses . . ."

And as I didn't know the German for "crutches" I mimed Montalto using them.

"Oh, him!" said the Cardinal Archduke. "Of course I know him! A charming old man! He's been very useful to me! How could I forget that it's thanks to him I've been allowed to have an armchair in my cell? What did you say his name was?"

"Montalto."

"Oh yes, Montalto! I must fix that in my memory. Montalto! Well, why not Montalto? He's a very amiable old fellow! And supported by San Sisto! And he speaks German, too! A Pope who speaks German – what an honour that would be for Austria!"

And without much rhyme or reason he started to laugh, or rather to chuckle, his big belly shaking. I laughed politely too. The Austrian Archduke clearly didn't take our little Italian affairs very seriously.

"What I'd like to know, Your Eminence," I insisted, "is whether Montalto's candidacy would be agreeable to Spain."

The Cardinal Archduke was serious again, and took a folded piece of paper out of the inside pocket of his robe.

"This," he said, unfolding it, "is a list of the cardinals my cousin" – he was referring to Philip II – "absolutely doesn't want to have as Pope."

I was staggered to hear him speak so undiplomatically, and more astonished still when he adjusted his spectacles and began to read the list of black sheep aloud. Aloud! I found it amusing, but not surprising, that my own name was on the list, as well as those of d'Este, of the French cardinals (with the exception of Pellevé), and of some others whom, being more discreet than the Cardinal Archduke, I prefer not to name.

"Well," he went on, "one thing is clear: my cousin doesn't regard Montalto as *persona non grata*! So all right – Montalto will do!"

"So, Eminence, may I tell my friend San Sisto you're in favour of Montalto's candidacy?"

"Certainly."

"I thank you, Eminence."

After bowing low I turned and was making for the door when he said: "May I ask what *your* name is, my friend?"

Without batting an eyelid I replied: "I am Cardinal San Gregorio, Your Eminence, entirely at your service . . ."

I said it on the spur of the moment, and may God forgive me for the joke that was also a lie! But how could I say I was the Medici written down in black and white on his list of rejected candidates? Anyway, what did it matter? Ever since he'd entered the conclave the Cardinal Archduke had been mixing up all the names, and if he did happen to quote me no one would dare tell him there was no such person as Cardinal San Gregorio.

On the evening of April 23rd the original nucleus of Montalto's supporters met in my cell to consider how his candidacy was getting on. The position seemed very promising. Alessandrino's last cavalry charge had won over San Sisto, who had carried out his promise to consult the cardinals created by his uncle, and with excellent results. I reported on my conversation with the Cardinal Archduke, and how I'd secured the support of the Spanish faction. D'Este had won over two of the French cardinals, though he hadn't approached the third, a unregenerate supporter of the League. Santa Severina, "*il putto-papa*" as they called him now, had fluttered from group to group spreading the news that Montalto's chances were growing by the hour. The sound and solid Rusticucci had done even better, and gone to Farnese and asked him straight out if he'd vote for Montalto if the case arose.

Farnese's reaction had been both friendly and bitter.

"Eleven cardinals voted for me," he said. "Yes, you heard me – only eleven! Isn't that disgraceful, given who I am? But Montalto was one of them. Tell him I'll remember that. At least if Torrès doesn't arrive in the meanwhile."

This made us decide to act the following day, April 24th, although we could still only count on the votes of just less than half of the conclave. Even so a difficulty arose at the last minute: San Sisto came and said in his soft voice that he'd only vote for Montalto if the latter would adopt his name if he became Pope. I thought this extremely childish, but knowing how obstinate the weak-willed can be I decided not to object. I sent Rusticucci to Montalto to ask him, *primo* if, as Pope, he'd agree to be called Sisto, and *secundo* if he had any objection to our proclaiming him Pope the following day after Mass.

The answer was swift and resolute: "(1) Sisto I and Sisto II were both saints and martyrs in ancient Rome: I should be very glad to bear their name. (2) April 24th is a Wednesday, and Wednesday is a propitious day for me: it was on a Wednesday that I took religious orders and on a Wednesday that I became a cardinal."

Encouraged by this good omen, we decided to precipitate events the next day in chapel after Mass.

Unluckily, just as it was ending the arrival was announced of Cardinal de' Vercelli and a Spanish cardinal. Our group were in some dismay as the whole conclave flocked to the door to greet them. Would the Spanish faction take advantage of the confusion to proclaim Torrès Pope?

But as soon as we saw the new arrivals we heaved a sigh of relief. True, Vercelli was one of them, in the flesh – and plenty of it – but the Spanish cardinal was Madruccio, not Torrès. Madruccio, whom we scarcely knew, probably never understood why we seemed so glad to see him that day.

We went back into the chapel where, as was the custom, the master of ceremonies began to read out to the newcomers the bulls governing the election.

Though not actually obliged to, the other cardinals, out of politeness, attended this rather tedious ceremony. That was the moment we chose to act.

I nodded to Alessandrino and he went out, accompanied by San Sisto, who gave his group of cardinals a significant glance as he left. They joined him one by one. Then, as had been agreed, d'Este rose and went out of the chapel alone, closely observed by the Spanish faction. At regular intervals after that, Cherubi, Santa Severina, Rusticucci, Riario and Gustavillanio all went out, each taking with him the cardinals he had won over.

The cardinals who weren't in the secret didn't notice these departures, for the audience usually thinned out during the interminable reading of the bulls, which all of us had heard five or six times already.

We gathered in the royal hall, where the first thing we did was take a count. We had a pleasant surprise, for since the previous day our numbers had increased. We had a majority – a very small majority of two. And not all of us were equally determined: you only had to look at some people's faces to see their anxiety and uncertainty.

San Sisto, with his changeable nature, nearly spoiled everything again, saying he'd only vote for Montalto if the Cardinal Archduke came and told him in person that Montalto's election wouldn't offend Spain.

I took Santa Severina and Alessandrino aside and asked them to go back into the chapel: the first, who spoke some German, to fetch the Cardinal Archduke; the second to ask Farnese to join us.

Farnese arrived first, and understood in a twinkling what was the matter. As he was really neither for nor against, he decided to say nothing, and just looked contemptuously at all the cardinals who had failed to vote for him and were now proposing to vote for a former minder of pigs. On the other hand, great prince that he was, he thought it unworthy of his honour to refuse to support Montalto when Montalto had supported him.

Santa Severina had great difficulty first in rousing the Cardinal Archduke, who had fallen asleep listening to the bulls, and then in making him understand that we were waiting for him in the royal hall. At last he came, one hand on Santa Severina's shoulder. As soon as he saw us he swivelled his pale, astonished eyes around our gathering, saw me (though, thank God, without remembering the name I'd given him), and said to me: "What's this all about, Cardinal?"

Before I had time to answer, Alessandrino did so. "Your Eminence, we want to elect Cardinal Montalto Pope."

"Montalto!" said the Archduke, wide awake at last and throwing up his hands. Then again, in stentorian tones: "Ja, Montalto!"

Falling from Austrian lips, that was decisive. The last hesitations vanished, and it was with enthusiasm that our crowd set off in procession to the chapel, led by the Archduke, Farnese, San Sisto and Alessandrino. I stayed in the third rank, not wanting my hand in the election to be seen too clearly before it had succeeded.

When our large troop entered the chapel the master of ceremonies interrupted his reading in surprise, and the cardinals who'd stayed where they were and knew nothing of our machinations looked at us in petrified silence, some turning pale and others red. Then Alessandrino, San Sisto, Farnese and the Archduke advanced towards Montalto, and San Sisto said loudly: "Eminence, we have made you Pope, and I myself ask you to take the name of Sisto."

"I shall certainly do so," said Montalto.

He couldn't say any more, for his voice was drowned by cries of "Papa! Papa!" from his supporters, all crowding round him to take their turn and kiss him on the mouth, as is the custom.

Then Alessandrino turned to the cardinals who were still seated, gazed at them with his dark eyes, and said in a commanding, almost threatening voice: "Do you want to take part in a formal vote? Or will you join with us in electing him by acclamation?"

They stood up, some hastily, others more slowly, but in the end they all rose, cried "Papa! Papa!" and went to join their colleagues surrounding Montalto and singing his praises.

When I saw this I went over to the master of ceremonies, who was still standing open-mouthed on his rostrum, his hands tangled up in the bulls. I told him in a whisper what he had to say, for he was so taken aback he hadn't realised.

But though his mind was slow his voice was strong, and had no difficulty making itself heard above the cries of "Papa! Papa!" echoing round the chapel.

"Your Eminences, I see you have unanimously and by acclamation elected Pope the most reverend and illustrious Cardinal di Montalto. As soon as His Holiness has chosen the name he wishes to be known by as Pope, His Eminence Secretary of State Cardinal de' Medici will anounce it to the people."

There was a sudden silence, and the new Pope said, firmly and clearly: "I take the name of Sisto Quinto!"

His Excellency Armando Veniero, Venetian Ambassador in Rome

When the conclave was over and the cardinals, freed from their incarceration, returned with a sigh of relief to their marble palaces, I was overcome by a kind of retrospective terror when I learned we'd very nearly had a Spanish Pope. I literally trembled like a leaf at the thought. How could a Spanish Pope have stopped Philip II from seizing the rest of a peninsula of which he already owned more than half? Venice would have gone the same way as the Duchy of Milan, the Kingdom of Naples, and Sicily. And my own dear country would have lost its liberty, its merchant fleet and its flourishing trade all over the world, and instead groaned, like the Low Countries, beneath the yoke of Spain and the Austrian generals.

The end of a conclave is the beginning of indiscretions. It was as if as soon as the cardinals were back among their creature comforts they felt they could also relax and tell their secrets. I got to know of various things in this way. Some were of great political interest, and I shall keep those to myself. Others shed an ironical light on men and manners, and of these none amused me more than Cardinal Alessandrino's comment about Montalto, when he decided to support his candidacy: "Don't let's oppose the poor old man: we'll be the masters."

I wrote and told the Doge and senators of Venice about it, among other more serious matters, knowing how they like to amuse themselves sometimes at the expense of the Romans. And they were so delighted with Alessandrino's remark that throughout the whole five years that

Sixtus V's reign lasted, I couldn't appear in Venice — either to take the air on the Lagoon or to deliver a personal report to the Doge — without meeting a senator who laughed and said, "Well, Armando, how's the poor old man?"

As a matter of fact the "poor old man" was the master from the very first minute of his reign — a stern master, too, who made evil-doers tremble: the thief in his lair, the whore in her tavern and the bandit in his mountains, not to mention venal judges, priests who bought and sold preferment, dealers in indulgences, shady bankers, absentee bishops and nobles who gave outlaws asylum.

Even before he was crowned he instituted the death penalty for anyone found bearing firearms in the streets of Rome, whether by day or by night. And when, out of bravado, two young brothers belonging to the nobility went out carrying small arquebuses, he threw them in gaol and despite the pleas of the cardinals and all the most important families in Rome, had two sets of gallows put up on the Ponte Sant'Angelo and had the two culprits hanged side by side.

The results of this inflexibility were not slow to appear; I could observe them from my window, which overlooked the Tiber. During the reign of Gregory XIII not a day had gone by without my Venetian valet saying as he drew the curtains in the morning: "Another corpse floating down the river, Your Excellency! And another! And another! This city's a den of murderers!"

I don't know where the murderers went to after the accession of Sixtus V, but the fact is that although dead bodies didn't disappear from the Tiber altogether, they did become much rarer.

Soon after the advent of Sixtus V, Cardinal de' Medici told me of something that struck him as symptomatic of the new reign. One day, riding along a street in Rome in an open coach, he saw two respectably dressed men engaged in a fierce fight on the roadway. He stopped the coach, and on inquiring the reason for the brawl, was told that two of Cardinal San Sisto's servants had come to blows over some belle. Medici, who was such a misogynist he could hardly bear the sight of a woman, especially if she was beautiful, thought this a ridiculous reason for such a relentless battle. Taking advantage of a moment when the two men had paused for breath and were merely glaring at each other, he offered them ten piastres each to be reconciled with one another, or at least to stop fighting. His offer was rejected out of hand, and the fisticuffs began again.

Eventually one of the champions downed the other, pinned him to the ground with one knee, held him by the throat and drew his stiletto. The crowd gasped and held their breath, but the man suddenly lowered his arm, sheathed his weapon and said: "You can thank Sixtus V. If I weren't afraid of him I'd have slit your throat."

"If you'd thought of that sooner," said Medici, in whom the banker was never far from the surface, "you'd be ten piastres the better off."

But he stayed and listened to the comments of the people around him, which struck him as very significant. They all agreed with the man who'd spared his enemy's life. The Pope who'd had two young noblemen hanged for walking the streets with guns in their hands was not only feared but also respected. The people admired such swift and above all such even-handed justice.

Medici was one of the cardinals who'd exerted himself most to get Sixtus elected. But he was incapable of understanding a man of such calibre, and was therefore amazed by the vigour and rigour with which this great Pope took things in hand and briskly reformed the bad ways that had characterised both Church and State in the previous reign.

Medici was extremely witty and sharp, but his heart was arid and his senses inert, and he loved nothing and no one. He was equally indifferent to good and evil, regarding them as mere tools for the gaining of his purpose. And his only purpose was power – or power in its other form: money. He was quite unable to understand a man like Sixtus V, for whom the supreme throne was only a more effective means of correcting abuse and iniquity. At the age of over sixty-five, Sixtus was still the pure-hearted Franciscan who'd taken the habit at twenty with the firm resolve of making good triumph over evil wherever Providence pleased to place him.

Less than a week after the new Pope's accession, a servant came from Montegiordano with a note from Prince Orsini asking me to receive him. But, having learned that it was difficult for him to walk, I sent word to say I would call on him the same day at Montegiordano.

I was struck by the change in his appearance, and by how hard it was for him to move about.

344

After he'd offered me a drink, for it was the beginning of May and very hot, he said: "Armando, I'd like you to ask Sixtus V to grant me an audience."

"But Paolo," I replied, "you're a great prince, a great power in the State — why don't you ask yourself?"

"I want you to be present, Armando, and to guarantee my safety all the time I'm inside the Vatican."

"But why me particularly, Paolo?"

There was a shadow of a smile on his lips. "*Carissimo*, do you want me to ask Count d'Olivarès to go with me?"

"God forbid!," said I, smiling too. "To speak plainly, you want the backing and protection of the Venetian ambassador? Are you afraid that if you go into the Vatican you might not be able to get out again?"

"Yes," he said.

"I don't see why. Sixtus must have read della Pace's report, so how could he think you guilty of murdering his nephew?"

"That's not what I'm afraid of. But I took up arms against his predecessor, and he has some reason to regard me as a rebel. Especially as, despite quite an ominous order from him, I still haven't sent away the outlaws that live in my courtyard."

"Forgive me, *carissimo*, but isn't that somewhat rash?"

"I promised them my protection and feel rather responsible for them."

"They don't all deserve it."

"No doubt. But how can I turn them out unless I get some assurance they won't be thrown straight in gaol?"

"And you've asked the Pope for that assurance?"

"Yes, by letter. But he hasn't answered. And he can't be very pleased at my having taken advantage of the interregnum to remarry Vittoria."

I thought for a moment, then said: "I don't think your fears are really justified, Paolo. But if you still want me to go with you . . ."

"I do."

"Then I'll have to refer to Venice."

"But that will take days!"

And suddenly there was something so tragic in his eyes and voice that I wondered if he thought his days were now numbered. I tried to conceal my sadness by burying my nose in my cup and sipping at my wine.

"You're right," I said after a pause. "It will take a long time to refer to Venice. And I suppose, in this heat, you must be anxious to leave Rome and go and enjoy the cool and the shade with your wife in Bracciano. All right, then, Paolo — I agree! I'll ask the Holy Father to give us an audience, and I'll do it this very day."

I made my request to the Vatican on the morning of May 2nd, after my conversation with the Prince. And the same day, at five in the afternoon, a courier from the Vatican brought me the answer: the Holy Father would see me and Prince Paolo Giordano Orsini the following day, May 3rd, at ten in the morning.

I sent a footman to tell Paolo, and to say I'd call for him in my coach at nine o'clock on the 3rd. After his return from Bracciano the Prince's coach hadn't been able to go about in Rome without being stoned, so great was the popular resentment against him. True, the streets were quiet now, under the new dispensation, and there was no need to be afraid of stones. But who was going to stop the Romans, especially the women, from hurling an insult, or even a rotten apple, at the Prince as he went by?

So we went to the Vatican in my coach, with the windows shut and the curtains drawn. Paolo was pale. The slightest movement was painful for him, and he had to lean on my shoulder and that of his secretary in order to climb the stairs.

It wasn't a week since his coronation, but the new Pope's methods were already becoming established. Unlike his negligent predecessor, Sixtus V never put off a decision, and once it was made he never went back on it. When someone asked for an audience it was either granted or refused in forty-eight hours. If it was refused there was no point in insisting. If it was granted, the audience began exactly on time. And you were told by the chamberlain that it mustn't exceed the stated length.

Paolo began by offering the Pope his earnest and respectful felicitations on the "most lofty and august dignity to which he had just acceded". Then he added: "I come, Most Holy Father, to the leader of Christendom and to my sovereign in order to swear loyalty and obedience and, as the humblest of his servants and vassals, to put at his disposal all my forces and possessions . . ."

"Duke, that is more than I ask," said Sixtus.

This interruption made Orsini very uncomfortable. For a moment he was at a loss for words, the sweat standing out on his brow.

"Go on," said the Pope.

"The links that bind the house of Orsini to the sovereign of Rome," the Prince went on, as if reciting a lesson, "are too ancient and too well known to need rehearsing. I should just like to recall with gratitude that my lands at Bracciano were elevated into a duchy by your illustrious predecessor."

"And you demonstrated your gratitude," said the Pope caustically, "by fomenting an insurrection against him."

This blow was so sudden and direct that the Prince finally realised he must abandon formality and confront the Pope on the plane of fact.

"Most Holy Father," he said with some firmness, "I did not foment an insurrection. I joined in one that had been raised by the nobility in order to right a wrong. And as soon as that wrong was righted I put down the popular rising."

"True," said Sixtus. "But you had no authority to put right the injustice you refer to — you weren't related to the person who'd been imprisoned."

"But there was a link between us," said the Prince bravely. "The same accusation hung over us both, and charged us with a crime we hadn't committed."

"We'll come to your innocence later," said the Pope, glancing at his watch. "For the moment, make your request, and let it be brief."

"It is this," said the Prince, invigorated by the verbal duel. "When Gregory XIII died, certain theologians held that the ban on my remarrying contained in his *precetto* was no longer valid. I therefore took Vittoria Accoramboni as my wife for the second time. I humbly ask your Holiness to allow things to remain as they are."

"Here is my opinion on the matter," said Sixtus, giving the Prince a sharp look and speaking loudly and resolutely. "*Primo*, the theologians you refer to, some from conviction, some out of greed, gave an opinion which they now try to slide out of by saying it was extorted under duress. That is a specious excuse. If they didn't want to be constrained they could have refused to go to Montegiordano in the first place – the purpose of that meeting was all too obvious. *Secundo*, they had no authority whatsoever to offer an opinion in this matter, and I shall take no account of their deliberations."

I glanced at the Prince: he was swaying, and so pale I thought he was going to swoon. Unluckily I was too far away to prevent a fall that, with his bad leg, would be bound to do him great harm. I felt very sorry for him. The Pope's words seemed to sound the knell of all his hopes.

"As for the *precetto*," the Pope went on, "a distinction must be made between those who requested the dissolution of the marriage and those who agreed to it. The first were motivated by sordid considerations of inheritance, and the second harboured a grudge. I shall say no more on this point."

But if you ask me he'd said enough already! He hadn't named either of them, but he'd rapped both Medici and Gregory XIII over the knuckles. True, the latter was dead, and the former needed the Pope's help too badly to try to harm him. But the more I saw of Sixtus V the more I admired his character. He reminded me of my father who, when he was Doge of Venice — scarcely for a year, alas, before he died — skilfully alternated the subtlest diplomacy with the most brutal frankness, as the case required.

As for the Prince, the colour came back into his face and he was clearly encouraged by hearing his enemies so roughly handled.

"As for the innocence you proclaim yet again," said the Pope, "it has two faces. One face is light and the other dark."

"Dark, Your Holiness?" said the Prince indignantly.

"You shall tell me about all that in due course," interrupted Sixtus. "Meanwhile I'll concede one point: there's absolutely no proof that you were implicated in the murder of . . ."

He was probably going to say "my nephew" or "my unfortunate nephew", but instead he went on impassively: "Of Francesco Peretti. On that point the police report drawn up by poor della Pace implicitly exonerates you. And the evidence of the unfrocked monk whom you sent to me, and who made a full confession — probably much fuller than you expected — showed that the murder was planned with Machiavellian cunning by one of your relatives — a real gallows bird — in order to harm my . . ."

Again he checked himself and went on with an effort: "To harm Vittoria Peretti. That's the light side. Now let us consider the dark. It is

348

unfortunately beyond all doubt that the ruffian I've just mentioned would never have plotted to murder Peretti if he hadn't known of your fatal passion for Peretti's wife. For, to quote the Ten Commandments, you 'coveted your neighbour's wife', you wooed her with numerous letters, pursued her with ceaseless attentions, and finally prevailed on her weakness to obtain various guilty encounters, one at Santa Maria and others at the Villa Sorghini in Rome . . ."

Here Sixtus paused, his piercing eyes fixed on those of the Prince as if to give him a chance to reply. But it was a good half-minute before the Prince spoke, and that's long for a silence, especially one that follows precise accusations. Orsini looked at a loss. As he told me later, he realised then that the unfrocked monk had not only been Lodovico's go-between in the matter of Peretti's murder: before that he'd also spied on the Prince's own meetings with Vittoria. His evidence, of which the Prince had known only a part, turned out to be double-edged: it cleared him of the murder, but it convicted him of adultery.

"I haven't much time," said the Pope with another glance at his watch. "So I'll say this in conclusion. Prince, you are not guilty of Francesco Peretti's murder, but you are certainly indirectly responsible for it."

He left another short pause for the Prince to reply. But Orsini seemed stunned and incapable of uttering a sound. The theologians, Medici and Gregory XIII had all been hauled over the coals, and now it was his turn. And the rebuke was so severe it might have even worse consequences than the annulment of his second marriage.

"Prince," said the Pope loudly, enunciating every word, "I am not speaking to you as an enemy. I wish no harm to your property, your titles or your liberty, still less to your life. And since I consider it is the intention of the two spouses to give themselves to one another that constitutes the sacrament of marriage – and in this case that intention was undoubtedly present in both parties – I shall not issue a *precetto* annulling your second marriage. But I do require that, to use your own words, you shall be my loyal and obedient servant, and I shall see that you are. I've already ordered you to eject from Montegiordano those you sheltered there under the previous reign by a privilege I myself grant to no one. I repeat that order, and I require you to obey

349

it within twenty-four hours."

"Most Holy Father," said the Prince, trying to speak firmly, "I have written to you on this subject. It seems to me incompatible with my honour to hand these men over to the Bargello."

"Prince," thundered the Pope, with a terrible look, "it would certainly be incompatible with your honour to disobey your sovereign! Besides, don't worry — I'm capable of distinguishing between bandits and those who have merely been banished. The exiles are mostly respectable folk who for various reasons were unlucky enough to displease my predecessor. I shall examine each of their cases, and most will be amnestied. As for the bandits, if their crimes are proved they'll take their last look at the sky through a noose."

"Most Holy Father," said the Prince, bowing his head in submission, "it shall be as you wish."

"When?"

"Tomorrow, before noon."

"Good. One last word: I'm told you are having trouble with your leg. I advise you to go and take the waters at Albano, near Padua. Padua belongs to Venice, and because of the glorious services you have rendered the Most Serene Republic in the past, you'll be among friends there."

The Prince started. "Most Holy Father," he said, "how am I to understand what you say? As a banishment?"

"Not at all. As urgent advice that I expect to see followed. I don't hate you, Prince, but I do hate the disorder your passion has introduced into the State. And I'd like it to have time to fade out of people's memories."

He straightened up his powerful torso, placed his great hands flat on the arms of his chair and raised his heavy head. Then, with a look that conveyed as clearly as his words that he wanted neither thanks, protestations of devotion, nor respectful farewells, he said: "Prince, our interview is at an end."

Giuseppe Giacobbe, head of the Roman ghetto

In 1585, at the accession of the present great and noble Pope — truly inspired by the spirit of Adonai despite the fact that like all his countrymen he professes the Christian heresy – our people had for a quarter of a century been the subject of worse persecution than ever in the Papal States. In 1569 Pius V had even gone so far as to expel all Jews from his possessions, except those who lived in Rome and Ancona. And by an incredible refinement of cruelty he gave them only three months to leave, and threatened them with fines, confiscation of property and imprisonment if they didn't get out in time.

Such a bad example in such high places awoke the age-old hostility of the mob against us. Not even in Rome and Ancona, where we had permission to remain, were we free from the restrictions, insults, wrongs and humiliations that have always been our lot among the Gentiles.

Those of us unfortunate enough to be only the tenants of our houses found our rents doubled overnight. The land allowed us for our cemeteries was restricted. Our religious ceremonies were strictly forbidden. We had to wear yellow whenever we went outside the ghetto. Our taxes were increased. Jewish doctors – the best in Rome – could no longer enter Christian houses. All kinds of restrictions were imposed on our trade. In the special courts set up to hear our cases we were certain to lose if our adversary was a Christian.

Vexation became our daily bread. Butchers either refused to serve us or gave us pork instead of the beef we'd asked for. If we refused it they called the police. Worse still were the jokes: "What's the difference," they would ask in Rome, "between a Jewish dog and a Christian dog?" The answer was: "A Jewish dog is fatter, from eating all the pork his master is forced to buy."

Gregory XIII was no better disposed towards us that Pius V had been, but as he was very indolent by nature and didn't bother about anything, the special measures against us were less rigorously applied during his reign. As for the new Pope, I shall tell in due course of the strange circumstances in which I came to meet him.

It is typical of our nation that there should always be some Jews who want to be more Jewish than everyone else. And some of them, soon after the accession of the new Pope, decided to print and circulate the *Talmud*. That in itself was a perfectly worthy idea. The trouble was it needed permission from the Vatican.

I tried in vain to make them see how foolish and useless it would be even to try. How could the Vatican, which had forbidden the practice of our religion, authorise the publication of one of our holy books? When Michel de Montaigne came to Rome his *Essays* had been seized and censored, and there was nothing heretical about them!

But it was no good. The more I argued the more excited and enthusiastic the zealots became. In the end they almost accused me. "Be careful, Giacobbe!" they said. "You're so cautious you're in danger of becoming craven and losing your Jewish faith!"

So despite my protests and without my support they made their absurd request to the Vatican. Young Cardinal Santa Severina, who received the petition, called it "an incredible piece of audacity", and asked the new Pope to hand the petitioners over to the Inquisition.

I was horror-struck, and so was everyone in the ghetto. Stupid as the zealots were, they were still our brothers. And if they were burned at the stake there might well be a new outburst of popular persecution. Experience had proved that for every Jew who burned in public in the light of the flames, ten others were privately stabbed to death by fanatics in dark alleys.

The zealots themselves were terrified, and came to me with their tails between their legs, asking me to intercede for them with the Pope. It was a good opportunity to tell them off, and I took advantage of it.

"You poor fools, why did you have to take such risks when there was so little chance of success? We still have twenty or so copies left of the Talmud in the excellent Venice edition. And how many of us know enough Hebrew or Aramaic to read them? About ten rabbis and scholars! And with your request to publish a new edition, you've gone and given the Vatican the idea that we want to proselytise, when we don't want anything of the sort! That's the only reason why the Gentiles tolerate us. Otherwise we'd have gone the same way as the Lutherans long ago!"

Then came the tears and lamentations. "Giacobbe! Giacobbe! You're not going to abandon us to our fate? You're our leader!"

"A leader you've called a coward!" I replied. "And what am I supposed to do now? Go and confront the Pope and offer myself up as a scapegoat! Take on myself all the consequences of your stupidity! And we know very well this Pope used to be the Grand Inquisitor in Venice, and has been a member of the Holy Office all his life. Some hopes of *him* being merciful!"

At this the supplications burst forth louder than before. Everyone joined in: relatives, wives, children, cousins, neighbours, and why not babes at the breast while they were about it — all kicking up hell's delight with their moaning and groaning, tearing their hair and beards out, rending their garments (or at least pretending to), throwing themselves at my feet, grabbing at my hands and swearing eternal gratitude.

So then I did what I'd decided to do anyway, and what they deep down always knew I would, as I was their leader and had never let them down: I asked the Pope for an audience.

It was granted within forty-eight hours, though I was told that the Pope, instead of receiving me in public, would see me in private audience. I was to go in through a side entrance, which I did in fear and trembling, not knowing what fate awaited me inside this enemy fortress. For who was I, after all, lost in the labyrinth of this great palace where the very walls were hostile to me and my faith? Nothing but a little old Jew in a long yellow robe, a pepper and salt beard standing on end with fear, and a skull seething with anxiety beneath its little cap!

Sixtus V received me in a small and simple room where we were alone except for a Monsignore, quite a handsome fellow but presumably dumb, since he communicated with the Pope only by signs. "His Holiness", as the Gentiles call him, was sitting not on a throne but on an ordinary chair, with the Monsignore standing on his right.

"Sit on that stool, Giacobbe," said the Pope briskly, "and for goodness sake stop trembling! I'm not a monster who's going to eat you! I'm a man just like you! I feel cold when it snows, I'm hot in the dog days, and if I put my hand in a flame it burns! I suffer from the same diseases as you do, and I'm just as mortal! So just tell me your business quickly."

I told him about our zealots' request.

"Which *Talmud*?" he cried. "The Jerusalem *Talmud* or the Babylonian?"

"The Babylonian."

"But if I'm not mistaken that was published in 1520, by a Christian publisher in Venice?"

"Yes, but that edition is out of print, Most Holy Father."

"Ask the publisher or his descendants to reprint it then! If the

Venetian Republic allows you to do that, I have no objection. Only the ignorant think the *Talmud* contains passages that are anti-Christian. I go by the opinion of Reuchlin, a scholar who knew Hebrew and Aramaic and read both *Talmuds* carefully – he never found anything in them that might offend the faith of a Christian."

"If only His Eminence Cardinal Santa Severina saw it as you do, Most Holy Father!" I ventured to reply.

"It doesn't matter whether he does or not!" said Sixtus, exchanging a smile with the dumb Monsignore. "I've taken the matter out of his hands. And so that the Grand Inquisitor doesn't take it up, I've ordered the *Talmud* to be examined by the Congregation of the Index. Which is the same as saying I've asked a lot of blind men to read it, for not one of them knows Hebrew."

I was doubly delighted to hear this. First, because it dispelled my fears of fresh persecution, and secondly because the Pope's strategy of "giving the book to a lot of blind men to read" seemed to belong to Biblical tradition. From then on I had high hopes of a sovereign who concealed so much wit and humanity beneath his rough appearance. So much learning too, for unlike Santa Severina the Pope had read Reuchlin and was not taken in by the slanders about the *Talmud* invented by malice and spread by ignorance.

Nor were my hopes disappointed, for not long afterwards the Pope promulgated his bull *Christiana Pietas*, which greatly improved the status of the Jewish community in the Papal States. We were given the right to live in all the cities, and not only in Rome and Ancona as before. More extraordinary still, the bull granted us liberty of worship and the right to build synagogues and open new cemeteries. Our legal cases were to be tried in the ordinary courts instead of in special ones as hitherto. To our great relief, we no longer had to wear yellow robes: before, we'd had to do so not only when travelling outside the ghetto but also at fairs and markets, where they made us the target of all kinds of ill usage at the hands of both competitors and customers. Lastly, Jewish doctors – who'd introduced into current medical teaching, based on Galen and Hippocrates, not only traditional Jewish medicine but also the Arab medicine they'd learned in Andalusia – were given permission, long asked for but never before granted, to treat Christian patients.

This bull was supplemented by a *bando* or decree – drawn up by Secretary of State Rusticucci but prompted by Sixtus himself – which forbade the Pope's subjects, on pain of fine, to insult, humiliate, strike or spit on us. Two more provisions also lifted a great burden: landlords were forbidden to double their rents when leasing houses to Jews, and butchers were forbidden to sell us any other meat than the kind we asked for. Those who tried to ignore the *bando* and keep on with their former harassments could be reported by us to the Bargello and were immediately punished.

As ghetto folk joke about everything it became common, when anyone asked another how he was, to answer, "Well, you can see how thin my dog's getting!"

We rejoiced greatly at having our disabilities so much reduced, and the leaders of the ghetto met with me as their chairman to decide what kind of present we could give this enlightened Pope to show our gratitude.

As our race is very good at arguing and holding forth, the debate was both long and passionate, but finally it was concluded that the only gift the chief of the Christians could accept from us would be a richly decorated pectoral cross.

I had nothing to do with this decision, but as soon as it was arrived at my colleagues asked me to make the cross, with all the care and skill I bring to my craft. For unlike many others I not only sell but also design and make the jewellery I trade in. For a long time, to make them all the more eager, I wouldn't agree, and when I finally did I insisted, knowing how changeable my brethren can be, that the necessary money be got together before the work was started. Then the arguments began again, and looked like going on for ever. For each one wanted to contribute a share proportional to his income, and as the figure was always left very vague to evade the Roman taxes, it took a great struggle to establish who was really rich and – the same thing, really – who was as poor as he claimed to be. When after endless difficulties the collection was made, the result was paradoxical: stingy as the individual members of the ghetto were or seemed to be, the community as a whole was very generous. We'd collected the enormous sum of a hundred thousand piastres.

To protect myself from suspicion and slander I declined to keep the money at my house, or even to take charge of it. I arranged for five

355

treasurers to be elected, and they were to pay as and when necesssary for the gold and precious stones I would use in my work. Even so there was one person who had the impudence to say, in front of the whole council: "What about you, Giacobbe? Aren't you going to make a contribution?"

I glared at him.

"I'm contributing my labour and my skill!"

Unlike many others, I don't want to blow my own trumpet, so I shan't describe the cross I made with so much trouble. Suffice it to say that when I exhibited it in my shop window, everyone in the ghetto filed past to see it, fascinated by its beauty. So much so that old Rabbi Simone, who was with me in the back of the shop, shook his head and said: "Just like us Hebrews! Always ready to worship idols! Yesterday they made fun of the cross and called Christ 'the little gallows bird'" — a joke in very doubtful taste, in my opinion — "and today they admire it open-mouthed just because it's made of gold and studded with diamonds, rubies, sapphires and I don't know what! It wouldn't take much to make them worship it! To think I might have lived to see that, Giacobbe! — a cross worshipped like an idol, in a ghetto!"

When, having asked for and been granted an audience, I took the cross and presented it to the Pope, he was at the same time admiring and embarrassed.

"It's wonderful," he said, turning it over and over in his hands, which were slender and shapely, unlike his rugged countenance. "I'm glad to see there are artists in the Roman ghetto as good as any in Florence. And the cross is further sanctified by the kind feelings that inspired you and your brethren first in thinking of such a gift and then in actually making it. So I accept it with pleasure as a token of the loyalty and gratitude of my subjects in the ghetto. I mean to go on protecting them from the malice of fanatics: they are hardworking, inventive, peaceful, law-abiding citizens, and contribute greatly to the prosperity of Rome and the Papal States. But while I do accept your gift, Giacobbe, I must make it clear to you and your brethren that the leader of Christendom cannot wear a cross presented to him by subjects not themselves Christians. But it will remain in my family, and I shall bequeath it to my descendants."

Then he engaged me in the most friendly and easy conversation about the improvements he'd made in the status of the Jews. Referring to the wearing of the yellow robe, he said: "If I hadn't been afraid of shocking my Christian subjects and the Catholic hierarchy too much, I'd have abolished it altogether."

"Most Holy Father," said I, "you've already done a lot for us in exempting us from wearing it when travelling. That's a great relief, for it meant that all over Italy everyone thought they could charge us what they liked in inns and at tollgates, and even molest and rob us."

"Do you travel much, Giacobbe?"

"Twice a year. At the beginning of the summer and at Christmas I go to Brescia, Padua and Venice on business."

"Brescia? That's interesting!"

But he didn't say any more. After glancing at his watch, he dismissed me.

I reported this conversation to the ghetto, and was surprised to find the most fanatical among us rather cooler towards the Pope than before. On reading the bull *Christiana Pietas* more closely they'd discovered that three times a year they were to be summoned to church, where the word of the Christian God would be preached to them. Some of the more excitable said we shouldn't go. I could scarcely believe my ears when I heard such mad talk.

"You're a pack of hopeless idiots!" I said. "You suffer from the strange disease of never being satisfied! For twenty-five years you've had a terrible time under two bad Popes, and now you've got a good one you want to defy him! What does it matter if you have to sit in a Christian church and hear some parish priest talk nonsense about Christ? Are your souls going to be in danger just because your backsides are on benches worn out by generations of Gentiles? Are your Jewish arses better than Christian buttocks? Or is your faith in the God of Israel so fragile it collapses as soon as someone talks to you about Christ? Are you going to start worshipping Mary and the saints after half an hour of it? Do you know what? You are worthy descendants of those who clamoured for the death of Christ. Have you never thought that if he'd never been crucified no one would ever mention that gentle crank now? And that we wouldn't be branded as deicides?"

That caused a fine old row. Some of them yelled that Christ deserved to be killed because he'd attacked the law of Moses even though he claimed to be defending it. There was no end to their resentment: they were still railing at Christ for his teaching fifteen hundred years after his death!

Fortunately old Rabbi Simone intervened. He agreed with me, and said that those who disobeyed the summons to church would put the Jewish community in Rome in grave danger. He spoke in a sweet, quavering voice, looked at them all with black eyes still shining and youthful in a face more wrinkled than an old apple. When he'd finished, no one had anything more to say.

This fracas was still echoing in my ears a week later, when the Pope summoned me to the Vatican. I went in through the same side door as before and found the Pope sitting in the same small room, a little table on his left and the mute and motionless Monsignore (I knew now that his name was Rossellino) standing on his right. As usual, Sixtus cut short the formal exchange of greeting.

"Giacobbe," said he in his quick clear voice, "when are you thinking of going to the north this year?"

"In a fortnight's time, Most Holy Father."

"If you put your journey forward by a week I could give you an escort of ten of my Swiss Guard, going home on their annual leave – and I could entrust you with an errand."

"Most Holy Father," I said with a bow, "I should be very glad of the escort and very honoured by the errand."

"It won't take you far out of your way – if I remember rightly your business will be taking you to Brescia? I want you to take this box and a letter from me to the Duchess of Bracciano, who's at present staying on the shores of Lake Garda. And would it be possible for you to take along a Jewish doctor who's an expert at treating wounds?"

"Arquebus wounds, Most Holy Father?"

"No, wounds caused by arrows. But I suppose they're not all that different. The Duke of Bracciano was hit by an arrow a long time ago, and I'm told that the wound has been getting worse recently."

"My friend Doctor Isacco is very competent in that field. He studied at the medical school in Salerno, and has translated Ambroise Paré's book on wounds into Latin. His translation, with his own annotations, is used all over the world."

"And do you think you can get him to go with you?"

"I think so, Most Holy Father."

The Pope looked pleased, and made a sign to Rossellino. (I noticed that although the Monsignore was dumb and not deaf, the Pope often spoke to him in signs. I've been told he invented this language himself so that his attendant could make himself understood to him.) Rossellino immediately fetched a little silver casket that was standing on a table, and handed it to me, together with a sealed letter addressed to the Duchessa di Bracciano, Palazzo Sforza, Barbarano, Lago di Garda. When I'd taken my leave and was going out through the little door, I could tell by feeling the letter that it must contain the key to the casket.

My sons, my nephews and myself – eight of us in all – laid out some money on clothes for the journey, since it was to be made in such worthy company and to the gates of so great a prince. I also hired some good horses, and we hid a few stout pistols under their saddles: for Jews to carry them on their persons would have been considered too provocative. And we had to think of the return journey, when we'd be without our Swiss Guards. There were ten or so of them, and their sergeant presented me with a safe-conduct drawn up in my name in very complimentary terms and stamped with the Papal seal. I have kept this precious relic, thinking that if the persecution ever starts up again it might come in useful.★

The worthy Swiss were with us for a fortnight. They were much the same age as my sons, but they took up about twice the space and were about twice as broad. They were great big lads brought up in the fresh air and on the fresh milk of their Swiss mountains, with bodies used to hard work since childhood. Whereas we Jews grow up pale and packed together in urban ghettoes, forbidden to live in the country, let alone buy any land there. But to be fair I must point out that the placid countenances of the Swiss lacked the subtle spark to be seen in the shining eyes of my own boys.

When we got to Salò we were very disappointed not to be able to see the lake for mist, and the hostess at the inn where we took our midday meal told us there was no hope of its clearing. The mist was usual at this

★ The persecution did start up again several years later, under Pope Clement VIII.

359

time of the year, she said, and might last for a whole month.

As you go from Salò to Barbarano the space between the shore and the hills narrows: the slopes grow steeper and leave less space for the road. After less than thirty minutes' ride we saw to our right a building that from the hostess's description we took to be the Sforza palace. As we weren't sure, however, I went and knocked at the door of a monastery perched on the hillside on the other side of the road. Only the judas window opened in reply to my knock, and a Capuchin friar looked through at me suspiciously, as if sensing that I was some kind of black sheep. But when I'd shown him my safe-conduct and the Papal seal he relented and told me the building opposite was indeed the Sforza palace. I slipped him a small offering through the bars. Not because I wanted to but because he seemed to expect it and because like all our people I'm rather scared of priests. By way of thanks he was good enough to open his thin lips again – they were like the slit in a collecting box – to tell me Admiral Sforza had only finished building the palace eight years ago. I might have guessed as much: the stone was still quite white.

The safe-conduct and Papal seal worked the miracle at the palace too, but we had to wait while the servants fetched the majordomo, the only person who could order the drawbridge to be lowered. You could see the place had been built by an admiral. It looked much more like a fortress than a palazzo, with a long bare façade relieved only by a few narrow, heavily barred windows and a big square tower at either end. It was surrounded by a broad deep moat fed by water from the lake.

As soon as we'd been let in the majordomo told me I'd have to be patient, as the Prince and his wife had gone off in one of their galliasses to visit their friends in the castle at Sirmione, and wouldn't be back till late in the afternoon. Seeing my surprise that anyone was able to navigate in that mist, with visibility no more than a quarter of a mile, he explained that the sailors on the lake took their bearings from the sun, the faint outline of which could always just be glimpsed through the haze.

I've already mentioned the two great square towers at either end of the building, but it wasn't until I followed the majordomo into the courtyard that I understood the overall plan of the place. Behind each of the towers there was a wing stretching as far as the lake, and, by a curious arrangement, in between and parallel to the other two a third wing –

though I don't know if I should call it that, seeing it was in the middle — also reached from the main building down to the water, dividing the courtyard in two. This part of the palace had a gabled front and a balcony running along the first floor. The balcony, together with the two glass doors opening on to it and the three vaulted arcades supporting it at ground level, made up the only really elegant and imposing section of what was otherwise a rather uncouth building.

The three arcades opened on to a square expanse from which a short flight of steps led down to a little harbour. I could see a boat moored there, a little galliass of the same type as those that acquitted themselves so well against the Turks at the Battle of Lepanto, but much smaller. It had a space for the oarsmen, but instead of being left open this space was covered by a deck from which the sails could be manipulated.

I asked the majordomo if the vessel had been built here or brought from Venice. His reply was so long and confused that what with trying to listen to him, the fatigue of the journey, and the discomfort I felt from the mist and its musty smell, I came over quite faint. I sat down on the steps and almost swooned away.

Not quite, though, for I could feel that someone — I could tell it was Isacco from the smell of him — was loosening my ruff, patting me on the cheeks and trying to make me drink sugared water. At first it was hard to swallow, but soon I was drinking it greedily. I blinked but couldn't open my eyes, and I could hear Isacco saying in his fine bass voice, probably to one of my sons: "Don't worry. He's very strong. He'll live to be a hundred."

My vision was clearing, and the first thing I saw properly was a row of about six magnolia trees growing by the water's edge, to my right. They looked more like huge round bouquets than trees, with their white flowers delicately tinged with pink. I must have seen them as I entered the courtyard, but I couldn't have taken them in. Now however, in my weakness, with my mind almost as misty as the lake, my thoughts fixed upon them with a pleasure that seemed as if it would last for ever.

"What are you looking at, Giuseppe?" asked Isacco.

"The magnolias."

He looked surprised. "Yes, I see," he said. "They grow all round the lake."

But speaking was too tiring. How could I explain that two minutes ago I'd felt as if I were dying, and now, looking at these magnificent bouquets, I was being reborn?

"They are all the beauty in the world," I said with an effort.

Isacco guffawed.

"You're a poet, Giuseppe!" he said. Then he added, with a mixture of indulgence and affection: "But you have to be, to create such beautiful jewellery."

Meanwhile some servants had come up with trays of refreshments; the majordomo must have ordered them in the belief that I'd fainted from hunger.

I realised wryly that this was the first time a Gentile had ever been so *gentile* to me. It only needed Rusticucci to put a Christian kind of name on my safe-conduct, and the Pope to allow Jews to travel in ordinary clothes, for everyone to be friendly to me. Yet what's in a name, or in a coat? Isn't it always the same man underneath those fleeting rags?

Out of politeness to the majordomo I made a pretence of eating, but my sons and nephews and Isacco fell to as if their midday meal was just a distant memory. Isacco in particular was a hearty eater: in everything he showed an appetite for life that seemed to belie the unfailing, though cheerfully voiced, pessimism of his words.

"My lord and lady are approaching," said the majordomo.

Everyone turned towards the lake, but all we could see was the white mist that a couple of hundred yards away shrouded the whole landscape.

"I can't see anything," said I.

"If you listen, Signore, you'll hear the sound of the oars. The wind has dropped and they've abandoned the sails. It's the rowers who are bringing her in."

Yes, I could hear the regular beat of the oars, and even, on the backward stroke, the creak of the rowlocks. Then suddenly the galliass burst through the mist like a ghost ship, and began to emerge more clearly. Someone rapped out an order. The galliass seemed almost to halt, coasted gently forward for a moment, then veered in majestic silence into the little harbour. All the oars were shipped simultaneously, and the ship slid smoothly into its moorings alongside its twin.

The Duchess, followed by a maid, came lightly down the gangway.

But I saw that the Duke had to be helped ashore by two of his gentlemen, while the Duchess waited for him on the quay, smiling, but with her great blue eyes full of anxiety. It was the first time I'd seen this celebrated beauty, but although my mind had been prepared for it by many descriptions, I now realised they all fell far short of the truth. Behind her – and, as I afterwards saw, inseparable from her – was her maid. By contrast with the mistress's golden tresses, the maid was as dark as a daughter of Israel, with bright bold black eyes and an ample bosom that made me lower my eyes, for even at my age they are only too easily attracted by such charms.

The majordomo went over to the Prince and spoke to him *sotto voce* at some length, no doubt explaining who we were. He showed him my safe-conduct, while we stood some distance away in deferential attitudes, gazing respectfully at the Duke and looking out of the corner of our eye at the Duchess and her comely maid.

"Welcome, my friends," said the Prince, coming towards us, as we all made a low bow.

At a sign from the majordomo two servants brought a chair and placed it in front of the three arcades of the central building. The Duke seated himself, still with the aid of his two gentlemen, one of whom was very handsome and a darker replica of the Duchess. We knew he must be the famous twin brother, who one day in broad daylight stabbed Lord Recanati to death in an open coach in Rome. A chair was brought for the Duchess too, but she refused it and placed a little stool at the Prince's feet instead. Then she sat down gracefully, bringing her long mane of hair round into her lap. The maid sat on a step behind her, taking advantage of the fact that her mistress couldn't see her to dart bold looks at our party, not excluding me. Signor Marcello, noticing this, started up the steps where she'd perched herself and in passing dealt her a sly little kick on the thigh, which made her grimace but not cry out. Then he sat down nonchalantly a couple of steps higher up.

"Master jeweller," began the Duke. He didn't want to call me by my real name, which he knew very well from having commissioned jewellery from me for his first wife. Nor did he want to use the Christian appellation written on the safe-conduct (he may even have forgotten it). "Master jeweller, I'm surprised to see you so far from Rome, and curious as to the errand with which the Holy Father has charged you."

I told him about the letter and the casket, and about Isacco's having come with me.

"Master jeweller," said the Prince, a shade of sadness falling over his face, "pray give us what the Holy Father has sent. And you, Vittoria," he went on gently, "perhaps you will wish to retire to your apartments, the more easily to read the letter and examine the contents of the casket."

"As you wish, my lord," said the Duchess, rising.

Then I gave the Prince the casket and the letter, which he put into Vittoria's hands with a tender glance and a smile that vanished as soon as she'd gone up the steps, through the arcades and into the house, followed by her maid. As soon as they and their shimmering finery were gone – for the maid was scarcely less well dressed than the mistress – the courtyard seemed suddenly duller and colder.

"*Dottore*," the Prince said then, looking at Isacco gravely, "please don't be offended at what I'm going to say. But I'm mortally weary of doctors and medicine, and I fear the word 'mortally' is only too appropriate. Fourteen years ago, at the Battle of Lepanto, I was wounded in the thigh by an arrow, and the wound has troubled me almost ever since. I've consulted dozens and dozens of doctors, each more eminent than the last, but not only have I not been cured, but the thing has got worse and worse. Quite recently, at the request of my wife the Duchess, two famous scholars came specially from Venice to examine my wound. They began by wondering what to call it. If I understood them correctly, they thought it very important that it be called by the right name. They discussed it for an hour and then agreed to call it *lupa*, which is Latin for a female wolf. And when I asked them, 'Why "a female wolf"?', they said, 'Because it devours the flesh around it'! 'An ingenious name,' said I, 'but how does it help me? What treatment do you propose?' Then one of them said they'd have to bleed me morning and evening, and when I asked why he answered, 'When the water in a well is murky, you draw water out of it until it becomes clear: and the same with your blood, my lord. By bleeding you we draw the bad blood out of your body, and your wound will stop devouring you.'"

The Prince gave a bitter smile. He waited for Isacco to make some comment, but, as he said nothing, went on: "I agreed to be bled morning and evening, but after a week of this treatment I felt much weaker in myself and my wound wasn't any better. I concluded that the bleedings couldn't distinguish good blood from bad and were taking away the first and not the second. So I paid the physician and sent him back to Venice. But the second one was still there, and he was very pleased to see the first go. 'You're quite right, my lord,' he said. 'He's an ignoramus, not to say a quack. He just uses whatever cure is fashionable for every case. Whereas my own treatment is always adapted to the circumstances.'

"'And what is your treatment in these circumstances?'"

"'Apply a compress of raw meat to the wound every day. Then the *lupa* will have something else to eat and stop eating your leg.'"

"And did you try it?" asked Isacco, staring.

"I did, and the result was that after a week I was much worse. I deduced that the female wolf preferred my flesh to all other kinds of meat however appetising, and sent my Hippocrates packing. And you, *dottore*," he said, looking at Isacco with a mixture of mistrust and hope, "what remedies do you suggest?"

"My lord," answered Isacco, "I can't tell until I've examined the wound."

"Very well," said the Prince. "As soon as the Duchess has retired for the night I'll show it to you."

Isacco had been given a room in the palace next to mine, and as soon as I heard him come in from his consultation, at about eleven o'clock, I went in and asked him what had happened. He seemed in a very bad humour, and said sourly, keeping his deep and sonorous voice low: "The trouble is, the Prince has been dealing with ignoramuses whose medicine is merely a matter of words and based only on metaphors. Bad blood like the murky water in a well! A wound like a wolf devouring flesh!"

"But even in the ghetto there are doctors who argue like that . . ."

"I know, I know! — who better? But the poor man has undergone so many ludicrous treatments that now, when the right one is suggested to him, he won't agree to it."

"And what is the right one?"

"To cut the leg off before it's too late."

"And he won't agree?"

"He absolutely refuses," said Isacco angrily. "He says he'd rather die than live mutilated."

"Naturally!" I said. "Such a fine figure of a man! A hero! A prince! And in love, too!"

"What's that got to do with it?" said Isacco, who refused on principle to understand what he understood very well. "Would you agree to die rather than lose a leg?"

"I'm not married to the most beautiful woman in Rome."

"And what good would it do you if you were?" said Isacco, who was proud of his own fecundity and gave his wife a child a year, as well as putting the maids in the family way.

There was a pause.

"So what can be done for the Prince?" I asked.

"Apart from amputation?"

"Yes."

"Nothing."

"So the outcome is bound to be fatal?"

"Yes. The summer that's just beginning will be his last."

"Oh, Isacco," I said reproachfully, "what a dreadful thing to say!"

This was too much for him.

"To hell with your mawkishness, Giuseppe!" he roared. "Do you think I'm going to shed tears over him? He was born in a silver cradle with a golden rattle! He's had everything all his life: titles, wealth, fame, love! And now he's suffering the fate we all suffer. Gentile or Jew, we all come to it. No, don't say anything! Leave me now, Giuseppe, please — I'm tired. And I can't wait till tomorrow, when I can go away. I don't like this lake! I don't like the smell of it! And I don't like the mist here! They say this is a miniature paradise, and maybe it is — if you can see it! Nor do I like this palace. How can anyone sleep under a ceiling that high? These people want us to think they're five or six times taller than we are! I'll tell you what — I'll be glad to be back in my ghetto! And above all! above all! above all! I can't bear the kind of patient who turns up his nose at living! If he'd been through what we've been through in Rome since the days of Pius V, maybe he'd be a bit more eager to stay alive! And what use am I, I'd like to know, if the patient himself isn't determined to cling on to life for all he's worth?"

366

14

Paolo Giordano Orsini, Duke of Bracciano

I haven't got much longer to live. I hope I'll show some courage in the time I've got left – though in such circumstances courage is only another kind of vanity and doesn't change anything.

All my life I've known that one day it would have to end; but I never really believed it. At least, I only believed it half-heartedly, or perhaps I should say half-mindedly. And my first reaction, when death became certain, was to say to myself: "What? Is it really happening to me too? And so soon?"

It's easy to understand that sort of incredulity. How can a thinking being imagine his thinking might ever cease?

Thank God I'm neither a philosopher nor a theologian. But now I can't walk any more I have time to think. And it seems to me human beings go to a lot of trouble to believe in a life after death. Yet how can they either rejoice in Heaven or suffer in Hell if their bodies and minds no longer exist? Suppose I were damned: what would there be of me to burn if I hadn't got a body any more? And how would I know I was burning, when my skull would be empty?

Nothingness makes much more sense. We didn't exist before we were born, so why should we exist after we die?

I'll take care not to say all this to my chaplain. He's a good man, but rather silly. He's over seventy and still repeating what he learned when he was ten. He's sure it must be true because he's been saying it for sixty years.

I don't want to upset him. And I don't want him to refuse me absolution. I want to avoid worrying or scandalising the people around me. It's mainly for the sake of the people around them that people try to die according to the rules.

As regards heaven we're pretty well taken care of in the palazzo Sforza. Behind us there's a monastery full of Capuchins, and on the island facing us there's a monastery full of Franciscans. I've handed out the largesse they expected of me, and in return they've promised to pray for my recovery, or, if that fails, for my salvation. How can I doubt that their prayers will be answered!

That Jewish doctor was the first one to tell me the truth about my situation – a truth I knew already but had managed to hide from myself. He was also the first who seemed sincerely anxious for me to survive. He looked very disappointed when I refused to let my leg be amputated.

I've seen that sort of operation performed more than once at sea. It's a horrible butchery. Very few people survive it, and they are mere wrecks. Dragging themselves about on crutches, in pain for the rest of their lives from a limb that's not there any more! How could I inflict the sight of such degradation on Vittoria?

This morning I told her I was going to die. Up till now it had been understood between us that my illness was nothing serious. We each did our best to keep the myth going. She was better at it than I was, perhaps because she believed in it more.

When I told her, she turned pale. After a moment, tears rolled silently down her face. I was lying on the bed, and she came and lay down too, and took my hand. We lay there side by side like a couple of effigies on a tomb. Just as that thought occurred to me she said: "We look like two effigies on a tomb."

"That's just what I was thinking."

"I wish it were true, and that I could go with you."

"Even so," said I, "we'd be separated. How would we see each other without eyes? Touch each other without hands? Kiss without lips?"

"At least our souls would stay together."

I didn't answer, not wishing to undermine that belief if it comforted her. After a while I said: "Vittoria, what's your happiest memory? I mean since we've been together."

"Before that," she said gravely, "I've no happy memories. But with you everything has been so wonderful I can't choose."

She was silent a moment, then pressed my hand. "Perhaps the Villa Sorghini. Though I suffered terrible remorse because I was committing adultery. And because I couldn't confess — a single word and I'd have been locked up. I wept every evening. But the next morning, when I thought about our coming meeting, the chains fell from my heart and I felt happy and gay. As if I were dancing on the mountain tops."

"I often think of the Villa Sorghini, too. That white tent on the roof! Right in the middle of Rome, and yet so far away from everything! You could see the geraniums through the white curtains, and the shadows of the swifts passing over the awning above us. I can still hear their shrill cries mingled with our sighing."

Vittoria was silent, and when I turned my head to look at her I saw she was weeping again. I held her hand more tightly and said in a different tone of voice: "Vittoria, when it's over I'd like you to go and live in Padua. I've rented the Cavalli palace for you."

"Why Padua?" she asked, turning her immense blue eyes towards me, still shining with repressed tears.

"The Podestà of Padua is a friend of mine. He'll protect you."

"Shall I be in danger, then?"

"Yes, from the Medicis."

"But why?" she asked in astonishment.

"What else could motivate the Medicis except money?"

"What money? And what harm have I done them?"

"This afternoon two learned jurists are coming from Padua to draw up my will. I'm leaving all my property to Virginio, and to you, Vittoria, I'm bequeathing a large sum of money — enough for you to live in a suitable manner."

"If that legacy's going to make the Medicis hate me, Paolo, don't make it."

"Vittoria," I answered, "can I leave the Duchess of Bracciano in want? Your share, large though it is, is only a tenth of what I'm leaving Virginio. He's not being unfairly treated. It's only the Medicis' greed that will make them think so."

"Oh, don't leave me anything, Paolo!" she cried. "I've got the cross the Pope has just given me. I'll sell it and go back to Rome. I can live in the Rusticucci palace with my mother and Giulietta, under

369

my uncle's protection."

"My love, first of all you'll offend Sixtus V very much if you sell his cross. And secondly it would be very unwise of you to make yourself dependent on him. It's true he's very fond of you, but he manages his domestic affairs as he rules the State – with a rod of iron. Didn't you suffer enough at Santa Maria under his tyranny? My angel, that's not the kind of future I want for you. I want you to go and live in Padua and get the Podestà to prove my will. And when you've entered into possession of your legacy you can live free and independent and respected. In Rome, under the Pope's thumb, you'd never be anything but Francesco Peretti's widow. In Padua you'll be the widow of the Duke of Bracciano."

"Oh, Paolo!" she cried, "don't use the word 'widow'! I can't bear it! And please, don't worry on my account. Of course I'll do anything you want. My life without yours will be nothing to me."

That afternoon, in answer to my urgent message, Professors Panizoli and Menochio arrived from Padua. I closeted myself with these two gentlemen, together with Marcello and my majordomo, and dictated my last wishes for them to draw up in legal form. I left all my property both at Bracciano and at Montegiordano to my son Virginio; and to my wife Vittoria, Duchess of Bracciano, I left the sum of a hundred thousand piastres, together with the jewels I'd given her and the furniture, hangings and carpets I'd brought with me to the Sforza palace.

When the will had been drawn up it was signed and witnessed by the two professors, Marcello and my majordomo. At my request a second copy was made by the same scribe and signed by the same witnesses. One copy was to be taken by the two professors and given to the Podestà in Padua, and I gave the second to Marcello, knowing it would be safe in his brotherly hands.

All this cost me a great effort, and I felt tired when the jurists had gone, taking with them my thanks and a fee that surpassed their hopes. But I had to have a few more words with Marcello.

"*Carissimo*," I said, "you must take good care of Vittoria, especially immediately after my death. She has said she'd like to come with me."

"I heard her."

"Were you listening at the door?"

"I always listen at the door when Vittoria's concerned. The best way to be careful is to be well-informed. And you, my lord – do you think you're taking good care of her by making that will?"

"I'm providing for her future."

"You could provide for her future in other ways. For example, by giving her *da mano a mano* your collection of jewellery."

"I haven't got it any more. I pledged it when I left Rome, to pay my debts."

"To whom, my lord?"

"Giuseppe Giacobbe."

"Who's he?"

"The jeweller you saw here with the doctor who wanted to take off my leg."

"Is he so rich?"

"Not he himself, but the ghetto is."

"Hence this unfortunate will."

"Why 'unfortunate'?"

"Because it's as if you were giving the Medicis a loaded pistol."

"It is a loaded pistol, but I'm giving it to Vittoria."

"She won't know how to use it. She's too good, too generous. The Medicis will shoot first."

"They wouldn't do such a thing! Not in Padua, a city that belongs to Venice!"

"You're right, my lord. They won't do it. They'll get someone else to."

"Lodovico?"

"Who else? The Medicis themselves won't say anything or write anything down – they won't even see him. They'll just stay in the background and pull the strings."

"Well, get in before them! Kill him!"

"I've thought about that, but it's not so easy. He's the leader of a gang, and he's always surrounded by bandits. Oh, my lord, what on earth possessed you – paying your debts!"

"An Orsini always pays his debts."

"Except if his name's Lodovico. My lord, I don't know that you've done the right thing, renting a palace for Vittoria in Padua. She'd have been safer in Rome under her uncle's wing. Everyone's afraid of

371

his beak and his talons."

"In Padua she'll be protected by the Podestà."

"Not so closely. The Venetians are like the Medicis — they're merchants. Men of compromise, who don't mind compromising their consciences too."

"Oh, Marcello, you're making me wonder if I've done right! But if she went to Rome, Sixtus would leave her practically no freedom! What am I to think? What am I to do? How can I see into the future when I have so little future myself?"

Marcello Accoramboni

When the Jewish doctor left at the end of May, the Prince was sure he had only two or three weeks to live. But four more months went by without any further change. I mean without either improvement or appreciable deterioration. He had great reserves of energy, and although he was sometimes in great pain he looked like someone withstanding a siege and determined never to surrender.

Strangely enough, although he alluded almost every day to his approaching end, his remarks seemed somehow propitiatory, as if he were trying to disarm death by talking about it. For that reason, and not wanting to seem to take his references to the fatal issue seriously, I didn't mention our disagreement over his will.

Moreover, my own opinion on the matter had grown less clear-cut. On reflection, I thought the Padua suggestion, which I'd opposed, might after all be better than the Roman alternative, which I'd supported. The latter involved great risks for both Vittoria and myself. For her it might mean, at the worst, being sent to a convent to expiate her adultery. For me it could mean the scaffold for having killed Recanati. True, Gregory XIII had pardoned me for the murder, but I'd heard that Sixtus was reviewing his predecessor's "pardons" and sending people to the gallows every day who'd forgotten all about their crimes by now.

As the Prince's health remained stable the summer wasn't so bad as we'd feared, especially as we had three warm, sunny months without rain and practically without mist.

The Prince had made a little beach beside the harbour at the Sforza palace by dumping cartloads of sand half on the land and half in the water. He'd then had the area fenced in on three sides so that Vittoria could bathe there unseen. He liked to have himself carried down to the beach when Vittoria went swimming, clad in only her mane of hair. She was a good swimmer and went in the water alone, as Caterina, who thought cold water unhealthy, wouldn't so much as dip her toe in. As for me, I used to splash about in the lake in the morning, and wouldn't have wanted to spoil the Prince's pleasure by joining Vittoria in the afternoon. I just kept him company by the water's edge. We played draughts, but he spent most of the time watching Vittoria's splendid white body gleaming in the waves, her long hair streaming out behind. Behind us, where the Capuchins were, the sun would be going down. In front of us to the north-east, when the weather was clear, we could see the eternal snows of Mount Baldo, scarcely distinguishable from the little white clouds that floated by high in the sky and seemed so happy to be free. Looking up at them I realised for the first time why lakes, however beautiful, are so melancholy: it's because the water's imprisoned.

In the mornings Paolo and Vittoria went for a sail on one of the two galliasses. Although the Prince was lying down and there was a helmsman, he liked to give orders as in the days when he scoured the Adriatic for Barbary pirates: it gave him an illusion of action. I don't know if Vittoria enjoyed these cruises as much as he did, but she was glad to see him interested and amused. Since he'd been unable to walk she'd become more maternal towards him. While taking care not to overwhelm him with solicitude, she enveloped him in her affection.

I must say women are very good at coiling themselves round a man, either to stifle or to pamper him. They're like ivy – they've got little pads with which they cling on. Margherita Sorghini wrote to me every day after I left Rome, telling me how much she missed me. And to tell the truth, despite the comforts Caterina supplied me with, I missed her too.

I liked her mature charms. For me there was nothing to compare with a beauty whose beauty was fading. For her, love had become an art and a religion. She was consumed by a passion to please, and that in itself made her attractive. As soon as I wrote that I missed her, Margherita rushed here and rented a little house at Salò, on the shore of the lake. And after the midday meal, when Vittoria and Paolo had gone to their room for a siesta, I'd have my horse saddled and gallop to Salò to see Margherita and spend an hour with her.

One day I asked her: "What do you do with the rest of your day, my love?"

"I wait for you."

"Do you think I deserve so much love? After all, as the Pope rightly said when he was still only Montalto, there's not much to be said for me. I'm a liar, selfish, lazy, hard-hearted, and I exploit you ruthlessly."

"You're not hard-hearted. And I love you as you are."

"I've forbidden you to say you love me."

"All right — I don't love you," she said with a slow and ravishing smile.

I could feel the little ivy suckers sticking to me all over. At first it used to worry me, but in the end I decided it wasn't dangerous. I considered love to be an illusion born of desire and pleasure. Man, the only mammal with enough wit to make love whenever he chooses, couldn't help feeling some affection for the female concerned. And she naturally felt some affection too, because in most cases he protected and provided for her. And that was all there was to it.

But when I said this to Margherita she objected strongly, despite her anxiety not to displease me. "It may be true of what you feel for me, but it's certainly not true of what I feel for you! I . . ."

She just stopped herself in time, and, with the nimbleness I so much admire in women, skipped on to safer ground. "For example, you adore Vittoria."

I shrugged. "That's different. Vittoria is the same as myself."

Then I brushed her lips with a kiss, but she insisted on coming with me to the stable where my mare was waiting for me. I vaulted into the saddle, and her eyes sent me a kiss, and another when she came to the gate to watch me ride away.

I'd be glad to see her again the next day, but I was glad to leave her now. That kind of love is pretty burdensome. I told myself yet again as I rode home that the best way to be happy with a woman is not to live with her.

Living under the same roof as Caterina was becoming a problem. Of course she'd found out about Margherita being at Salò, and made scenes that I really didn't know how to deal with. If I scolded her she just laughed. If I beat her she complained that I didn't slap her nearly as hard or as often as *il mancino*. She actually liked being beaten: she liked bursting into tears, repenting, throwing herself at my feet, and begging me with heaving bosom to "rape and kill her". How can you control a woman who converts everything into pleasure, even her own chastisement?

Even while she grieved at the thought of losing the love of her life, Vittoria still managed to be concerned about other people. One day she said to me: "Why don't you love anyone, Marcello?"

I didn't answer, so she went on: "And why don't you do anything? A man ought to have an object in life."

I still didn't reply, but I thought, What sort of object? Love, perhaps? What a joke! Money? – which only enslaves those that serve it? Fame? – that empty echo? Ah, Vittoria, thought I, I wouldn't tell you so for anything in the world, but in ten years' time who will remember that the Prince fought so bravely at Lepanto? And in a hundred years' time, who will even remember Lepanto?

In November everything took a turn for the worse. The mist came back over the lake thicker than ever, only to be dispelled by a fierce east wind known in those parts as the *vinessa*. The *vinessa* brought with it cold and rain and storms. With incredible speed the lake, which a minute before had been quite calm, was suddenly whipped into foaming waves that smashed down the fences around the little beach and covered its sand with silt. The moorings of the galliasses had to be strengthened and the smaller vessels moved into the moat, where breakwaters were built to stop the water from the lake being hurled with too much force on to the palace. There was no more bathing or sailing. Soon it was impossible to stay out on the balcony because of the spray: although the harbour was protected in the east by a strong mole, the *vinessa* hurled water and foam over it right up as far as the house. At first, as the Prince enjoyed the spectacle of the storm, we used to watch it from the arcades. But after the tempest had been raging for some days he tired of it, probably looking back with regret to the days when he stood on the deck of his galley braving the squalls of the Adriatic.

The sun vanished behind a ceiling of black and grey clouds. When the storm abated the rain took over, falling in slanting gusts. Everything grew depressing and damp and started to go mouldy. The waters of the lake, so clear in summer, grew murky, with yellow streaks here and there. It smelled mustier than ever; almost nauseating. The *vinessa* blew all day, and made the tight-shut windows rattle all night.

After we had to retreat inside the house and light the fires, and the Prince was deprived of his excursions on the lake and the pleasure of watching Vittoria bathe, his health rapidly declined. Curiously enough, his appetite wasn't affected. He ate and drank as usual – that is, copiously and fast. According to Caterina, his siestas were as active as ever. But his mood had changed. He was more withdrawn, spoke little, and for quite long periods remained apathetic and languid. Sometimes his eyes would go dull, and only brightened up when they lit on Vittoria.

Never before had he gazed at her so much or so profoundly. It was as if her beauty had become the only thing that linked him to life. Yet even in his state of weakness and dependence he was never selfish, and he insisted on her resuming her daily rides alone, because the exercise did her good.

At her request I kept the Prince company while she was out riding. Most of the time, at least when opium brought some respite to his suffering, he drowsed or even slept, his head resting on his shoulder.

One day – it was November 12th, if I remember rightly – he suddenly awoke with a loud cry.

"Aziza! Aziza!"

Then he saw me there, became fully conscious again, and said hoarsely, like someone speaking after a long silence: "Marcello, do you remember Aziza?"

"Your little Moorish slave girl? The one who wore a stiletto in her belt? I never met her, but I know about her."

"Do you know what happened to her?"

"No, my lord."

"The night I freed Vittoria from Sant'Angelo and took her to Montegiordano, Aziza plunged her stiletto in her own heart."

"Out of jealousy?"

"No. She left a note telling me she was going not out of hatred and resentment, but because she was no longer of any use. That's what we all ought to do: go when we're no longer of any use."

I was inclined to agree with him, but I didn't say so. It was clear the

Prince had already considered suicide. Otherwise, why did he keep a loaded pistol on the table by his bed? If he hadn't yet decided to use it, that was no doubt because he knew all too well that suspicion would fall on Vittoria.

He went on quietly, his eyes half closed: "I've just been dreaming about Aziza. I was alone at night in dense forest, absolutely lost. I was dragging myself along on my bad leg. I was very thirsty and very worried. Then suddenly a path appeared in the middle of the trees, and along it came an open carriage drawn by four horses. Aziza was sitting in it in her best blue gown, wearing all her jewellery, just as she did on the day she killed herself.

"'Come on, get in!' she said. 'I'll give you a lift!'"

"She helped me in, because of my leg. I could feel her hand on my arm. It was strong, with fingers like steel that sank into my flesh. I wondered if this could be the little Aziza who used to melt in my arms?

"But the carriage was sweeping us along at a furious rate. The road opened through the trees in front of us and then closed behind us, cutting off all retreat. I could only see Aziza in fits and starts: her face was alternately lit up and in shadow, according to whether the moon was hidden by the trees. She turned to me and smiled. Her smile looked sweet and affectionate when she was in the shade, menacing when she was in the light. But I felt reassured by the thud of the horses' hooves and the tinkling of the bells on their harness.

"'Where are you taking me, Aziza?'

"'Look at the coachman and you'll see.'

"But there was no coachman, and I could no longer hear the hooves or the bells. The carriage sped on as fast as ever, but I couldn't see anything because we were enveloped in a thick mist. Then I guessed from the sound of the lapping of waves in front of us that we were now sailing over the lake, though there wasn't a breath of air to fill the sails, nor any beating of oars. I was alone on the galliass with Aziza, and as she kept looking at me with an enigmatic smile I asked again: 'Where are you taking me, Aziza?'

"'Look at the helmsman and you'll see!'

"I turned round, but there was no helmsman. The tiller was swinging idly back and forth. I made desperate efforts to get up and reach it, but I couldn't stand. And then I woke up . . . Give me something to drink, Marcello."

He had a drink. He was pale. He seemed exhausted at having talked for so long. But at that moment Vittoria came in from her ride – splendid, with tousled hair, bright eyes and rosy cheeks – and he made an effort and managed to smile, and even to exchange a few words with her. But he cut the conversation short.

"My love, why don't you go to your room and dress for the evening meal? I'll have a little sleep. But when you're ready, don't hesitate to wake me up to show me how beautiful you are."

He still had strength enough to smile, but as soon as she'd left the room he lost consciousness. I called the majordomo and between us we succeeded in getting a few drops of wine down him and reviving him. When he came to I had him carried upstairs to the first floor and laid on his bed. There he summoned up enough strength to forbid us to undress him: he didn't want to frighten Vittoria.

As the wind and rain had stopped, I went out through the glass door on to the balcony, just pushing the door to behind me. I took some deep breaths. The mist was back but the air was warm and still. In the ordinary way I liked the Prince's company, but in the long run the presence of death, an invisible third party, was beginning to get me down. I'd always thought my life wouldn't be a long one, and I wasn't all that interested in it anyway. But I'd just as soon live out what remained to me without that continual weight on my heart.

I stayed out there alone for a good half-hour. I tried to remember a Petrarch sonnet that Vittoria did her best to teach me when we were in our teens. I managed to conjure up a few bits here and there, and tried to fit them together. I got almost all of it except for one line, and I kept at it, pleased with what I'd done, vexed at what I couldn't do, and sure the missing parts were the best.

There wasn't a breath. Nor a sound. Not even, on the sunset lake, the beat of an oar. Then I heard a loud cry behind me. I turned and pushed open the door. Vittoria, in all her finery, was lying across the Prince's breast, shrieking like one run mad. One glance was enough. He was dead.

Though I loathe touching or being touched, I put my hand on Vittoria's shoulder. She shook me off fiercely. Then suddenly her piercing

378

cries ceased. She rose to her full height, dry-eyed, seized the loaded pistol from the table, and put it to her temple. I was quick enough to grab her wrist and turn the barrel aside. The gun went off and the bullet struck the ceiling, bringing down scraps of plaster that fell on the Prince's doublet, making a white patch on the black velvet. Vittoria stood there, her eyes blank, looking at the white patch on the black. I took the pistol out of her clenched hand, and after a moment she leaned her brow on my shoulder, put her arms around me, and wept. I was trembling from head to foot at the thought that I mightn't have been there, or might have acted a second too late. What would I have been without Vittoria? A creature half living, or half dead?

Giordano Baldoni, Majordomo to Prince Orsini

The very morning after my master's death the Duchess was good enough to say that if I had no other plans she'd be glad to keep me on in her service. I at once agreed to stay, not mentioning that in fact I'd intended to retire to my native city of Genoa and devote the rest of my life to my children. But seeing her so young and helpless and surrounded by dangers, with no family to defend her but her brother – the bravest of young men, certainly, but very inexperienced – I decided to remain in her employ at least until she entered into peaceful possession of her inheritance from the Prince.

Fearing she mightn't have enough money to pay and maintain all her late husband's soldiers, she wanted to dismiss most of them, but I prevailed on her to keep at least a score of the trustiest, most experienced and most noble among them, as behoved the dignity of her household. And I arranged for us to move to the Cavalli palace in Padua with the least possible delay.

To tell the truth, we'd have been safer in the Sforza palace, with its drawbridge and moats and towers, than in an urban mansion lacking in all such defences. It was difficult to tell in advance whether this lack would be counterbalanced by the fact that we'd be near the Podestà and the city officers. When we got to Padua and I went round the Cavalli palace, I found some of the ground-floor windows could easily be broken into, and decided at once to have bars put in them. But as it was getting on for Christmas, which the good folk of Padua start preparing for a fortnight beforehand, the work couldn't be put in hand immediately.

We hadn't been in Padua a week when the Duchess received a note from Lodovico Orsini, Count of Oppedo, asking to see her. Signor Marcello thought we should shut our door to him without even deigning to answer, but when I was consulted I advised replying politely and saying there was no point in such a meeting. The Duchess decided otherwise. In his note the Count had presented himself as the emissary of Prince Virginio, and she didn't want to offend the second Duke of Bracciano by refusing to receive him.

I must admit that Lodovico Orsini, bandit though he'd become, and murderer and gallows-bird, was very attractive. In face, figure and gait he bore some resemblance to the Prince, though the likeness was belied by the falseness of his expression. He was wearing an elegant doublet slashed with yellow, and had draped a corner of the skirt of his coat over his left arm, as our gallants do in Rome. He made his way across the audience chamber in the Cavalli palace holding his head as high as the Blessed Sacrament, and when he arrived in front of the Duchess swept her an apparently respectful bow. Then he began a funeral oration in praise of her late husband couched in terms designed to win her goodwill – and it succeeded in doing so, though to my mind his little speech was pure hypocrisy. You could tell by the contradiction between the warmth of his words and the coldness of his eyes.

But after purring and sheathing his claws for half an hour he finally showed them.

"Madam," he said, "my cousin the late Duke of Bracciano had some silver plate that belongs to me, and I should very much like to have it back."

The Duchess looked at me inquiringly.

"That is so, my lady," said I, "but the plate was the pledge for a debt which his lordship the Count contracted towards the Prince and which has never been repaid."

"As the Prince is dead," said the Count, "it's obvious that the debt is cancelled."

"It's not obvious at all," said Signor Marcello, entering the room.

Then he went on, neither greeting nor even looking at the Count: "The opposite is the case. As the debt has never been paid, it counts as a claim outstanding in favour of the Duke's heirs – in other words, of Prince Virginio and of yourself, Vittoria."

"Precisely," said Lodovico. "Prince Virginio has commissioned me to come and defend his interests, and here's a letter to prove it."

He held a letter out to the Duchess, who read it and passed it to her brother. He read it and passed it to me. In fact it was very vague, and didn't define at all clearly the powers delegated to the Count.

"Count Lodovico," said the Duchess, "this is what I've decided. I agree to give you your silver plate back without your repaying the debt. I do this out of pure courtesy, and because of the family bonds between you and my late husband."

"Vittoria, you don't owe the Count anything," said Signor Marcello curtly.

But his tone must have displeased the Duchess, for she said in a manner that brooked no reply: "My mind is made up."

"My lady," said I, "since the claim the plate represents pertains jointly to both you and Prince Virginio, if you hand it over to my lord the Count you must ask him for a receipt to cover you vis-à-vis Prince Virginio."

"A receipt!" cried the Count, going crimson with anger. "To ask a gentleman for a receipt as if he were a merchant!"

"It strikes me as quite natural," said the Duchess calmly. "And the plate will only be given back to you on that condition."

"Madam," said the Count through set teeth, "it's clear you grew up in a different world from mine. Otherwise you wouldn't talk of receipts. My word of honour would be enough for you."

"Vittoria," said the Lord Marcello with the utmost calm, "instead of being thanked for your excessive generosity you are being scorned and insulted. You've only to say the word and I'll put a couple of inches of steel in this boor's belly."

And for the first time I noticed that before joining us Marcello had taken care to buckle on his sword and dagger.

"It's you who are insulting me, you wretch!" cried the Count. "And you think you can do it with impunity! You know very well you're too basely born for me to cross swords with you!"

"You're quite right," Marcello drawled insolently. "I know. I know that rather than risk your own skin you usually prefer to hire some henchman to murder a man in the street."

At this allusion to the murder of the Duchess's first husband, the Count turned from red to white, and despite what he'd just said his hand went to the hilt of his sword.

"I am mistress here," said the Duchess firmly, "and I order this quarrel to cease at once. Marcello, please be quiet. And you, sir if you address another uncivil word to me I shall order my servants to show you out."

"Madam," said the Count, managing to make his low bow convey a touch of mockery, "I submit entirely to your wishes, and since you attach such importance to it I'll sign a receipt."

The impertinence in his bow and the feigned respect in his voice must have vexed the Duchess, for she said coldly: "Baldoni, please fetch the Count's plate."

Then, with the briefest of nods to the intruder, she began to walk towards the door.

"Madam," said the Count, the mockery scarcely concealed beneath the politeness, "I beg you won't deprive me so soon of your charming company. For as Prince Virginio's proxy I have other requests to make."

"Very well, sir. I will hear you," said the Duchess.

But she and the Lord Marcello retired to the other end of the room, leaving the Count the benefit of the bright fire burning in the hearth that damp, cold December afternoon. The Count used the pretext of warming his hands at the flames to turn his back on his hostess. The only person he had with him was a secretary, as I'd requested him to leave his escort at the palace gate.

I left the room to carry out the Duchess's order, and used the opportunity to take a few small precautions. I'd noticed that the Count's escort was armed, so I now armed our own soldiers and asked them to station themselves in a room adjoining the audience chamber. Then I returned to the latter with four sturdy footmen, whom I got to move a long table from beside the wall to the middle of the room. This was ostensibly in order to set out the plate, but my real intention was to divide the room in two, putting at least that obstacle between the potential adversaries. Then I had the famous plate brought in, and the footmen laid it out on the table. And though perhaps I oughtn't to say so, I was very sorry the Duchess had so easily handed it over to a bandit who wasn't even grateful. For the service was made up of beautiful pieces exquisitely chased, and it was worth a fortune.

"That's more like it, madam," said the Count.

This struck me as very meagre thanks for such a large present.

"And here's the receipt, my lord count," said I, holding it out across the table. "All you have to do is sign."

He took it as if absentmindedly, ignoring the goose quill I was proffering.

"Madam," he said, "Prince Virginio is very anxious that I should make an inventory of all the jewels that were in Prince Orsini's possession when he died."

"Have them brought, Baldoni," said the Duchess.

Despite its weight I fetched the casket myself. I handed the Duchess the key, and she opened it. One by one and not without emotion, she took out her dead husband's jewels and laid them out on the marble table-top.

"What? Is this all?" said the Count, raising one eyebrow. "There aren't very many! I've seen my cousin's collection with my own eyes, and it used to be one of the finest in Rome, comparable with those of Gregory XIII and Cardinal de' Medici!"

"The Prince," said I, "pledged his collection to pay his debts before he left Rome. What you see here are his personal jewels."

"He pledged his collection?" snarled the Count. "Strange that I should come to hear of it like this! Where's the proof?"

"Madam," said I, not looking at the Count, "the Prince's collection was pledged in the presence of lawyer Frasconi of Rome and two witnesses. The transaction was recorded in writing and signed, and the lawyer has kept a copy."

" You hear, sir?" said the Duchess.

"I hear, madam," said the Count, "but what I hear is very different from what I see. For instance, you are wearing a magnificent cross which looks surprised to be on your bosom, for as a present to you from the

Prince it ought to be on this table."

"It belongs to me personally!" cried the Duchess angrily. "It was a present from my uncle, Sixtus V!"

"What's to prove it?"

"My word proves it! And if that doesn't satisfy you, the letter that came with the gift!"

"In any case," said Marcello, "all the jewels the Prince gave his wife while he was alive are part of his bequest to her. It's down in black and white in his will."

"So there's a will!" exclaimed the Count, and this time his disappointment wasn't feigned.

But it lasted only a moment, and immediately afterwards his face resumed the mask of polite insolence that had so exasperated the Duchess from the outset.

"Madam," said he, "as Prince Virginio's proxy I must ask you to let me see the will."

"I don't see that it's necessary," said Marcello, without looking at him. "A copy will be sent to Prince Virginio as soon as the will's been proved by the Podestà."

But there again, rightly or wrongly — wrongly, in my opinion — the Duchess differed from her brother. It was probably because she wanted to show proper deference towards her late husband's son. But there I think she was being too scrupulous, whereas Prince Virginio, entrusting his interests to this unsavoury blusterer, was not being scrupulous enough. It would have been a pleasure for me too to put a couple of inches of steel in the impudent fellow's guts, if only my worthy mistress would have let me.

"Baldoni," she said, "please bring me the will."

Instead of leaving the room by door on the right I went out by the one on the left so that I could tell the soldiers in the next room to burst in with drawn swords if they heard me clap my hands. Those of them who were gentlemen not only wore swords but also carried small arquebuses. Their eyes flashed when I told them the Count had been insolent and threatening towards the Duchess. If the worst came to the worst she could certainly count on them. All her servants were very attached to her. They admired her for her beauty and loved her for the goodness of

384

her heart. I shared these feelings, but with a slight difference, for if I may say so with all possible respect, I considered she had two small faults: she was both naïve and obstinate. Because she was naïve she sometimes made unwise decisions, and because she was obstinate she stuck to them through thick and thin.

She provided with me with a striking example of this when I returned with the will. As I handed it to her I whispered: "Read it out yourself, madam – don't let him get his hands on it."

Marcello heard this warning, and repeated it into her other ear. But in vain.

"If the Count wants to read the will, Baldoni," she said, "let him read it. We have nothing to hide!"

So with a heavy heart I had to hand the precious document over to him across the table. Grabbing it and shamelessly sitting down, although the Duchess hadn't given him permission to, he started to read it, his nose growing longer with every page. I'd have been surprised the scoundrel took Prince Virginio's interests so much to heart if I hadn't realised he thought it in his own interests to defend them, partly because of promises the young Prince must have made him and partly because he expected the business would give him a chance to exercise his own natural talent for theft and plunder. Hadn't he already managed, by abusing the Duchess's generosity, to get her to hand over – and without a receipt! – the silver plate he'd pledged to us a year ago for fifty thousand piastres?

"Madam," he said at last, standing up. "There's a legal term here I don't understand. Please allow me to consult one of my men, who's a clerk."

And immediately, without waiting for the permission he'd asked for, he whispered something to his secretary and sent him off. When he'd been gone a few minutes I heard a great commotion inside the house, and a footman rushed in.

"Madam," he panted, "the Count's escort are forcing their way in here!"

"Good gracious!" said the Count with ironic calm. "Perhaps they think I'm in danger?"

"And so you may be, now," said Marcello, drawing his sword.

I clapped my hands and unsheathed too. Our soldiers burst in, sword in hand, and lined up behind the table where the plate and jewels lay. Those with arquebuses posted themselves between the ends of the table and the two side walls. All this took place in silence, but a few seconds later the Count's escort made a very tumultuous appearance. When they saw the soldiers, however, they halted, realising they had to do with professionals and that it was no use making threats they couldn't carry out.

As for the Count, he drew himself up to his full height and called out loudly: "Madam, I am convinced this will is false! — as false as your marriage, which Gregory XIII annulled! as false as the title of Duchess you trick yourself out in!"

And he whirled round and threw the will on the fire. Then, facing us again, he drew his sword and dagger. "Gentlemen," he said, turning towards his escort, "this plate and these jewels are mine. Take them away!"

"My lady duchess," said one of our gentlemen armed with an arquebus, "this fellow speaks too lightly. Will you allow me to put some lead in his brain?"

"No, sir," said the Duchess. "As for you, Count," she went on, "you may take the plate, since I was weak enough to give it to you. But you will not touch the jewels."

"Take no notice, gentlemen!" laughed the Count. "She's mad! 'Give' me my silver plate? She's only giving me what's my own! She's talking nonsense. Pay no attention!"

Two of the bandits put out their hands for the jewels. But they drew them back again quickly, covered with blood. Our men's swords made a formidable curtain over the jewels, but as they didn't attempt to defend the plate the bandits, as they fell back, took that with them.

"Count," said Marcello scathingly, "I propose a bargain. You and I will fight one another, and if you kill me you take the jewels."

"You'll do nothing of the sort, Marcello," said the Duchess, taking him by the arm. "My orders alone are to be obeyed here. Count," she went on, "my majordomo has sent for the Bargello, and I advise you to leave before he arrives."

"If you don't want to escape the fate of your brother Raimondo," added one of our gentlemen.

"I'll make you pay for that," said the Count to him with a scowl.

"Now, if you like," replied the gentleman.

But the Count and his bandits were already at the door, and he seemed in no hurry for a fair fight against an opponent as well-born as himself.

As soon as the last bandit had left the room I vaulted over the table, rushed to the fire and tried to retrieve the will with the tongs. I did manage to get it out, but it was half burned away, especially the part that contained the signatures. As the Duchess came up to me, gazing with horror at the shrivelled and blackened pages, I told her not to despair, as there was a copy. On the Prince's instructions the lawyers who drew it up had taken this copy from the Sforza palace to the Podestà in Padua.

Then the Duchess and Lord Marcello retired to a smaller room and asked me to bring them some wine. A lively discussion followed, and I heard Lord Marcello criticise the Duchess severely for the way she'd handled the affair. First of all, she should never have agreed to see Lodovico. Secondly, it was sheer folly to make him a present of the pledge we held. It would only encourage him to make further demands.

"There's no need for you to handle him with kid gloves, with all the things you know against him. Nor do you have to show Prince Virginio all that consideration, when he chooses an envoy like that to extort more than he has any right to."

It seemed to me the Duchess realised Marcello was right, but she resented his criticism and wouldn't let him go on.

However, she did follow the advice he gave her immediately afterwards.

When the Bargello of Padua arrived with his men a good hour after I'd sent for them – a prudent delay, showing he had no desire to confront the Count and his gang – the Duchess not only told him of her complaints against Lodovico; she also gave him a letter for the Podestà in which they were written down. And she wrote and immediately sent off a similar letter to her uncle, Sixtus V.

When the Podestà had read his letter he found himself in some difficulty: she'd started a hare that was a bit too big for him. Not knowing what to do, he passed the problem on to Venice, where they too procrastinated.

The Most Serene Republic knew all about Lodovico: the Pope had asked for his extradition on the very first day of his reign. But behind Lodovico there was Prince Virginio, and behind him the Medicis and the Grand Duchy of Tuscany. Venice was not keen on antagonising a power of that magnitude over a matter that didn't affect any of its own vital interests.

So instead of summoning Lodovico and ordering him and his gang to leave Padua immediately, all the Venetian authorities did was send courteous remonstrances through the Podestà. Lodovico listened politely and laughed up his sleeve. The Doge was making the same mistake as the Duchess, and handling the bandit with kid gloves. But the Doge didn't have the excuse of naïvety.

Ten days later, however, Venice received a letter from the Pope complaining vehemently about the way Lodovico had treated his niece. The Doge and the Senate then thought up a rough and ready solution. They placated the Pope by ratifying the will which the Duke of Bracciano had made in his wife's favour and of which the Podestà had a copy. But so as not to displease the Medicis they still didn't order Lodovico to decamp.

As to what happened after that, I'm not in a position to talk about it, as I had to go to Rome for my father's funeral and didn't get back to Padua till after Christmas.

Caterina Acquaviva

Everything that happened was my fault, all my fault, and it's my firm intention, as soon as I can, to go into a nunnery and spend the rest of my days in prayer and fasting to ask God's forgiveness. But if you want to know what I think, prayer and fasting won't do any good. Deep down in my heart I'll always be tortured by remorse. The only thing I'm sure of is that it will only end with my life. When I think of what I used to be like — so cheerful and merry and keen on the men — and of what I'm like now — weeping day and night, or else eating my heart out over my memories — I'm sure I shan't suffer any more than I do now even in hell, being consumed by the flames I've so richly deserved.

But first I have to go back a bit and explain how it all came about. You must forgive me if I have to stop every so often: whenever I think of the old days and how happy I was then – happier than I knew, poor fool that I was – I can't hold back my tears.

The treacherous way Lodovico burned the will and tried to get possession of the Prince's jewels by force had angered the Duchess and alarmed Marcello. From that time on, the Cavalli palace was closely guarded day and night, and so was the Signora herself, who whether she liked it or not, was always accompanied by a large armed escort whenever she left the house to go into the city. She and her brother had arguments about this every day. She was too good and too naïve to believe Lodovico would kill her if he got the chance.

"What?" she'd say. "You don't mean he'd murder me just to save Prince Virginio a hundred thousand piastres?"

"And for your jewels. You really oughtn't to go about wearing them!"

"I don't wear them out of vanity!"

That's what it is to be a great lady! If I said a thing like that, who'd take it seriously? If I wore her uncle's cross, with Christ's feet almost touching the top of my nice soft bosom, I'd burst with pride! As a matter of fact I actually tried it on one day when I was alone in front of the Signora's mirror.

"I don't wear them out of vanity," she repeated, "but because each one brings back a memory."

Yes, but not always a happy one. That cross, for instance, could have reminded her of the Duke's last days.

The arguments started up again worse than before in the middle of December, when the Podestà proved the will.

"Well," said she, "we've won! Lodovico can't do anything to me now!"

"Not legally – no," said Marcello. "But on the practical level he's still got daggers and guns. Your death would wipe out the will."

"Oh, Marcello!" she cried, "you're dramatising! Kill me here in Padua, a stone's throw away from the Podestà, who's so well-disposed towards me?"

"Not so well-disposed as to banish Lodovico from the city,"

"But supposing Lodovico did murder me," she said, laughing (the idea seemed so senseless to her), "wouldn't his obvious interest in my death point him out at once as the murderer?"

"Certainly! But it would have to be proved! And even if it was proved, and he was put to death, that wouldn't bring you back to life!"

A week later, to her amazement, the Signora received a letter from Lodovico asking to see her. I was there when she read it out to Marcello.

Prince Virginio was complaining that when his father left Rome he'd taken the best horses from his estate with him. Virginio now asked the Signora to give back some or all of them. According to the will the Signora inherited all the furniture, but he didn't think horses counted as furniture.

"And he calls me the Signora!" she said angrily. "He doesn't even given me my title! In his view my marriage is null and void! Well, he shan't get anything! Not one horse! — not even a mule!"

"Vittoria," said Marcello, "it's not at all certain the horses *can* be considered as furniture. It might be wise to give Lodovico at least a few of them to send to Prince Virginio."

"What!" she cried. "I can hardly believe my ears! Can it be you telling me this? You, who advised me not to give him his silver plate!"

"This is a different matter altogether! The plate was undoubtedly yours! But it's not certain the horses are! Besides, it would be unwise to let Lodovico go away empty-handed. That would make him lose face with Virginio, and a man of his temperament won't put up with that!"

"Let him lose his treacherous face!" she cried. "You've reproached me often enough for handling him with kid gloves. Now I've learned my lesson."

And she sat down and wrote an irate note to the Count in which she refused either to give him the horses or to see him. Marcello looked over her shoulder as she wrote.

"'Our first meeting,'" he read, "'was not such as to make me wish to repeat the experience.' Vittoria — you're not going to send him this! It's insulting! It's like waving a red rag at a bull — he'll be furious! Let me write to him — more politely!"

"Certainly not! I'm the one he's written to, and I'm the one who's going to reply!"

I agreed wholeheartedly with Marcello, but I took care not to say so! The Signora had always been rather quick-tempered, but after she was widowed she grew much worse. She flared up like tinder, and, once alight, was as difficult as tinder to put out. The fact was, the Prince's death had left a terrible void in her life. She missed him as a husband, as a companion, and also as a man. Poor Signor Peretti had a heart of gold, but that was about all. The Signora had absolutely blossomed with the Prince. I watched her from the time of the Villa Sorghini on: she was a different woman. Radiant! If I'm to believe what I'm told, the Prince was an extraordinary lover almost up till the day he died. I used to dream about him myself sometimes! Of course, every rose must have a thorn, and in the long run the Signora would have realised that the thorn in this case was that she herself couldn't have a child. Poor Peretti — to think how she and I used to blame him!

But what's the use of talking about the future? It's been blotted out now. I don't like to say it, but the fact is the Signora is losing her grip. She thinks her beauty has declined and her life is over. And it affects her temper. Mine's not what it was either, now that Marcello won't have anything more to do with me. So the Signora and I are both bundles of nerves! And since she's the mistress, the air's thick with "idiots" and "impudent chits" and even, occasionally, slaps! And the reconciliations, the cuddles and kisses, don't come as quickly as they used to! The worst of it is, it always ends in tears — she's always more or less on the brink of them, poor thing. But whose arms can she weep in now except mine? You can't see anyone unburdening themselves on Tarquinia's or Giulietta's bosom! After the Prince died they wrote and asked if they should come and stay with the Signora in Padua. But she flatly refused. And I think she was right!

It's my own fault about Marcello. I never stopped making scenes at the Sforza palace after I found out he was going to see Signora Sorghini at Salò every afternoon. I know you're not going to believe this, but it's the absolute truth: when I found out about it I was so beside myself with rage that if there'd been a dagger handy I'd have stabbed the wretch! As it was, he got a bit more of my tongue than he'd bargained for.

"How disgraceful! How disgusting! The old leech! Following you here just to cling on and suck your good red blood! And you let her! I must say you're not fussy! That old crone! Old enough to be your mother! All those wrinkles! Those varicose veins! Those sagging breasts!"

"Her figure's perfect, you stupid slut," said he, "and you can take this for not showing her more respect!"

And he threw himself on me, pushed me over, and beat me. I moaned and groaned, but it wasn't all suffering, because I managed to undo his aglet. So it wasn't too bad an arrangement; I'd insult his old woman, he'd beat me, and then he'd possess me. It was a habit that had its advantages. But in the end he tired of it. There's men for you! You think you've worked out a little system with them, and then they suddenly cut their moorings and sail away leaving you high and dry.

It was because of the break with Marcello that the Alfredo business started up. The wretch followed me round the streets of Padua and had the cheek to speak to me – me, a maid in a noble household! You can imagine how I'd have boxed his ears for him if I hadn't been feeling so humiliated and rejected! Especially as he wasn't much to look at, with his rugged phiz and tiny little eyes. His only attraction was his strength, and that hit you right in the eye. That neck and shoulders! Like a bull! In short, he was the sort of man who comes to seem good-looking if he gives you pleasure.

But I did repulse him the first time he came up to me. And the second time. But he sensed that the second refusal was less inflexible than the first, so he followed me to the church of the Eremitani and leaned against a pillar while I was praying. Being in Padua, I might have prayed to St Anthony and asked him to help me find my lost lover again, but I preferred to pray to the Virgin. She was more likely to understand a woman's sufferings. I asked her to touch Marcello's stony heart and make it soften towards me.

But all the time, behind my back, I could feel Alfredo's presence and the warmth it generated. And when I'd finished praying I let him speak to me.

He told me his name and said he was squire to a great nobleman, but he spoke very poor Italian, mixed up with Venetian dialect. At first I found him ridiculous, but as he was speaking he got hold of my left wrist and squeezed it, and after that I forgot his faults. Later on, I shan't say where, I let him do as he wished – and as I wished too. So that's what happened with Alfredo. It's not something to be proud of, and if it were to do all over again I'd rather cut both my legs off.

392

Meanwhile life went on at the Cavalli palace, and the soldiers still kept a close watch on the Signora, indoors and out. Majordomo Baldoni saw to that. He'd been with the Prince longer than any other officer: everyone respected him, and when he gave an order they jumped to it.

After his rebuff over the horses Count Lodovico was expected to issue more threats and even offer more violence, but nothing happened. He even bowed quite respectfully to the Signora once when he passed her at a distance in the street. Even Marcello was beginning to feel reassured. Then the majordomo left us to go to his father's funeral in Rome, and discipline grew rather slack among both the servants and the soldiers. The more so as it would soon be Christmas, and a festive atmosphere already reigned in Padua.

There was great relief in the Cavalli palace when on the morning of December 24th the Bargello himself came and told us that Lodovico and his band of outlaws had left Padua in the early hours for Venice, to take part in the magnificent celebrations for which Christmas provided a pretext in the Republic.

"Are you sure they've gone, Signor Bargello?" asked Marcello.

"Quite sure. And don't worry – it wasn't a false exit. I had them followed and they really took the road to Venice. What's more, I've doubled the night guard at the Venice gate so that I'll be warned immediately if they come back during the night. So you can rest easy, over the holidays at least."

After the Bargello had gone the news spread among our soldiers, and the most senior man among them came and asked the Signora if in the circumstances they might go to the Podestà's ball that evening – they'd all been invited a week ago. They were delighted when the Signora, ignoring Marcello's advice, agreed. They'd led a rather austere life since they'd been in Padua. But it was arranged that they should be back in time to escort her to early morning Mass at the church of the Eremitani: the Signora didn't want to attend midnight Mass because it would be very crowded. Probably very noisy too, as the wine had been flowing freely since nightfall.

The men begged Marcello to go with them to the Podestà's ball, but he refused, preferring to spend Christmas Eve with his sister. I was very glad about this at first. Even though he wouldn't speak to me any more,

393

I'd at least have the pleasure of seeing him. They sent for musicians, who played and sang Christmas songs for part of the evening. As Marcello and the Signora had dressed up just to spend the evening alone at the palace, I did the same. And Marcello deigned to pay me a little compliment on my gown, apparently forgetting he'd seen his sister wearing it a year ago. I was overjoyed at this, and, fool that I am, my imagination immediately ran away with me and I saw myself back in his arms again. And why not? That night, when the Signora had gone to bed . . . But my happiness was short-lived. At about eleven o'clock a courier brought Marcello a note.

"It's from Margherita," he said. "She hasn't been able to go to the Podestà's ball – she's in bed, not well, and she wants me to call in and see her. I don't know if I shall, though. My place this Christmas Eve is with you, Vittoria."

"Oh, no, do go, Marcello," the Signora said, without a moment's hesitation. "Margherita must feel very lonely here in a strange city amid all the rejoicings. As for me, I'm rather tired, and I shan't sit up any longer."

The wretch didn't need telling twice! He buckled on sword and dagger, stuck a couple of pistols in his belt, and set off as fast as he could, accompanied by two servants, also armed. You'd have thought he couldn't wait to get to that bloodsucker's bedside. She was supposed to be ill but no doubt she was waiting for him all painted and titivated. Oh, I'd have stabbed the pair of them if some devil had been able to fly me to them! And the worst of it was, I had to put a good face on it all the time it took to undress the Signora and brush her interminable hair.

Then I retired to my room, where I undressed and put on my nightgown, trying not to cry. The fact that I wanted to made me even more furious. The sight of my empty bed was unbearable, so I paced up and down with clenched fists, grinding my teeth and railing at the two wretches whose embraces I couldn't help imagining.

I was just going to draw my curtains when a stone hit one of the window-panes, though not hard enough to break it. Thinking it was some drunk playing games, I opened the casement to tell him off. But when I leaned out I recognised Alfredo standing there, lit up by the bright moonlight and looking up at me.

"Let me in, Caterina," he said. "I've brought you a Christmas present."

"How can I let you in?" said I. "There's a porter on duty, and he'll never open the door even if I beg him! He's got strict orders not to!"

"Yes, but there's a little ground floor window that's not barred! I can get in through there if you'll let me."

"Certainly not! What would the Signora say if she knew?"

"But she won't know! I'll only stay long enough to give you this pretty ring and a hug."

"Ring?" I cried. "What sort of ring?"

"A gold ring with a sapphire and some little diamonds! I spent all my savings on it!"

I was touched by the ring and by his kind thought, not to mention his broad shoulders and bull-like neck. *Santa Madonna*, I was really going to get my own back! I was going to put another man in the bed where Marcello had lorded it.

Still in my nightgown, I went down and opened the window. It was no easy matter, for inside there was a heavy wooden shutter that I had to use both hands to unhook. Then I had to draw back a couple of bolts, and that was difficult too: the window was in a little scullery where nobody ever went, and the bolts had rusted.

Finally I opened up and Alfredo was through in a flash, out of the moonlight into the dark.

"Come in," said I, "we can't stay here!"

"What?" he whispered. "Don't you want to see your present?"

"Come on, Alfredo! I can look at it in my room – there's a candle there!"

"It shines so bright," he said with a laugh, "you won't need a candle!"

And, pretending to rummage in his doublet with his left hand, he gave me such a terrible blow on the back of the neck with his right that I fell to the ground at his feet.

It must have been some time later when I came to. I had a gag in my mouth and my hands were tied behind my back with a cord. Alfredo had got hold of the end of it, and after a moment I could feel him pulling me to my feet.

"So far so good, my beauty!" said he. "I've stabbed the porter and opened the door, and my friends are all inside! Now march, you strumpet! The best part of the show is going to take place on the first floor, and I don't want to miss it."

And pushing me along with the flat of his hand, he drove me up the stairs in front of him, jerking me back by the cord if I went too fast.

He was overtaken on the way up by two soldiers, one wearing a hood and the other a mask. Both were carrying bloodstained daggers.

"What are you doing with this slut still alive?" asked the man in the mask. "We've killed all our lot. You know our orders."

"This is my little sweetheart," laughed Alfredo. "She let me in, and she's going to stay alive a little bit longer than the others. I'm saving her up till last."

The other two laughed and bounded up the stairs ahead of us. They must have been very young, judging by the rate they moved. I didn't know why they still had their daggers in their hands – from what they said they didn't need them any more. Perhaps they wanted to show them off to their friends still covered in blood.

I went on up the stairs, but I was still half stunned. My mind was numb. I wasn't even afraid. I just registered everything as if it didn't concern me.

When we reached the landing we found about thirty masked soldiers all crowding round to get into the Signora's room. Alfredo, cursing and swearing, pushed me in front of him and forced a way through the mob, who were more impressed by me than by his oaths. "What's this slut doing alive?" some kept chanting, while others grabbed at my breasts. None of them pitied me for the fate that awaited me. I could see that as far as they were concerned I was as good as dead. They were only surprised at my brief stay of execution. They reeked of wine and sweat and leather. I could breathe better when Alfredo pushed me out in front. But in front there was just a small circle of them, and in the middle stood the Signora in her sky-blue night-gown, her long hair hanging down to the ground. In front of her was the prie-dieu from which she'd probably just risen, interrupted at her evening prayers. She held herself upright and dignified despite her scanty attire. Facing her was a tall gentleman in a mask.

"Madam," he hissed, "I'm sorry to disturb you at your prayers, but thanks to us you're going to rise up from this prie-dieu straight to heaven."

The taunt didn't ruffle the Signora's calm. Casting her great blue eyes over the thirty or so soldiers crowding round her, some of them even standing on her bed to get a better view, she said: "Do you really need so many men to kill a defenceless woman?"

The gentleman made no reply, either because he couldn't think of one or perhaps because he felt a pang of shame.

"And you, sir – who are you?" went on the Signora. "And what harm have I done you?"

"My name will mean nothing to you, madam," said he. "But as you're not going to be in a position to repeat it, I may tell you I am Count Paganello. And it's not me you've wronged, but my friend Count Lodovico Orsini."

"I haven't wronged the Count," she declared firmly. "I've only defended my legitimate interests."

"Maybe, madam. But we've talked long enough," said Paganello. "The time has come to act."

And he strode forward, seized the neck of her shift and ripped it down to the waist. As her breasts were revealed the soldiers let out a gasp of satisfaction, as if at some fair-ground show.

As Paganello stepped back to contemplate his handiwork, the Signora clutched the torn material over her bosom with both hands, looked at him with flashing eyes, and said, almost in a tone of command: "Kill me if you must, but I will not die unclothed."

Her look and tone must have had some effect on Paganello, for instead of tearing off more of her clothes as both he and the soldiers no doubt would have liked, he drew his dagger as if he was now in a hurry to get the business over and done with.

The Signora saw this and demanded: "First let me have a confessor!"

"I'm the only confessor here!" said a Franciscan friar with his hood pulled down over his face.

"Father!" cried the Signora, starting towards him in a burst of hope.

But the Franciscan moved forward into the circle and put back his hood. It was Count Lodovico.

"You?" cried the Signora in horror. "Well, let's have done with it, then!" she said imperiously. "Kill me and spare me both your presence and your words!"

"But I could still spare your life, Signora," said Lodovico. "On one condition."

"It's bound to be ignoble, coming from you," said the Signora haughtily. "I don't wish to hear it."

"You shall, anyway. You have to choose between death and me."

"Then I don't choose you."

"Comrades," said Lodovico, turning to the soldiers, "you've heard what she says. Of her own free will the Signora chooses death."

But the soldiers remained silent. If you ask me, they were beginning to admire my mistress's courage. Lodovico must have sensed this too, and realised the debate wasn't going his way. He went over to Vittoria and started tearing her night-gown off strip by strip. She offered no resistance: she just looked at him with scorn. When she was naked she pulled her long hair around in front of her body.

Lodovico drew his dagger.

"Help me, Paganello," he said hoarsely.

Paganello knew what was expected of him and drew the Signora's hair behind her back. Then Lodovico put his hand round her waist, imprisoning her left arm, and drew her to him, immobilising her right arm against his shoulder. He plunged his dagger below her left breast, but only half-way, turning the blade back and forth in the wound and asking if he was giving her pleasure. The Signora groaned, her eyes half-closed. As her groans grew fainter, Lodovico drove the dagger in to the hilt and cried: "This time, madam, at least, I touch your heart!"

The Signora turned her head towards him, opened her eyes wide, and murmured before she expired: "*Nel nome di Gesù, vi perdono!*"*

Baldassare Tondini, *Podestà of Padua*

Shortly before midnight on Christmas Eve 1585 a girl in a nightdress covered with blood came and banged on the Bargello's door. She told him the Duchess of Bracciano had just been murdered together with all her household, except her brother Marcello Accoramboni and two servants, who were all three at the house of Margherita Sorghini.

* In Jesus's name, I forgive you.

The girl said she was Caterina Acquaviva, aged twenty-eight, and had been in the Duchess's service for ten years.

As she seemed very agitated, weeping and crying and expressing herself in a confused manner, and as she accused Count Lodovico Orsini of the murders, whereas we knew he'd left that very morning with all his doubtful crew for Venice, the Bargello thought at first she was deranged. But seeing that her gown was covered in blood and her wrists were bruised and bore traces of having been bound, as she alleged, the Bargello decided to take a dozen or so men and go and see what had happened.

He saw that it was as Caterina Acquaviva had said, and sent word to me discreetly as I was presiding over the ball I give every Christmas Eve in the town hall. I went to the scene at once, and was appalled at the audacity of the massacre. It had been perpetrated only a gunshot away from my own house, and against a person of very high rank – one, what's more, whom His Holiness Pope Sixtus V regarded as his niece. Without even waiting to refer the matter to Venice, I ordered the Bargello to carry out an inquiry with the utmost speed, sparing no one.

On the second floor of the Cavalli palace the Bargello identified the corpse of Alfredo Colombani, squire to Count Lodovico. Caterina Acquaviva declared that after forcing her to watch her mistress's murder he took her up to her own room on the second floor, untied her hands, undressed her, then attacked and tried to rape her. Meanwhile, she managed to unfasten the dagger he wore, Italian fashion, behind his back, and drove it with all her might into his left shoulder-blade. He let out a shriek and tried to strangle her, but she stuck her fingers in his eyes, arched herself up on the bed and threw him on to the floor. Then she plucked the dagger out of the wound and stabbed him again and again all over his body – "like a fury", was her expression. She said she did it partly to avenge her mistress and partly because Alfredo had said he'd stab her as soon as he'd had his way with her.

According to her he got into the house through the window of a scullery on the ground floor, took her by surprise and overpowered her, then stabbed the porter and let in the rest of the intruders.

Asked why the window was open, she said she didn't know. The Bargello was unable to clear up the point. When Caterina was asked why the bandits had killed all the maids except her, she said Alfredo had probably taken a fancy to her, which was why he'd told his friends he was "saving her up till last". This struck us as plausible enough, as the witness was a comely wench and, though rather common, might pass for pretty in certain circles.

After a systematic search of the house it became clear that the bandits had carried off all the jewellery – the late Prince's as well as that belonging to the Duchess, including a splendid gold pectoral cross set with precious stones, given her by her uncle, Pope Sixtus.

Various indications showed there'd been a large number of intruders, and we guessed that Count Lodovico and his crew might have returned to Padua during the night. So we checked the city gates, and found to our surprise that while the guard at the Venice gate were awake and alert, those at the southern gate were still fast asleep after drinking wine that had been tampered with. When my people examined the ground around the southern gate, and in particular the road leading to Stra, they saw that the verges had been trampled, suggesting that a considerable number of horses had been left there during the night.

The still fresh hoof-marks and the stupor of the guards spoke for themselves. The Bargello sent an experienced spy to look around in Stra, and he reported that Lodovico and his gang had been feasting in a well-known inn there since the previous evening. It's only a few leagues from Stra to Padua: a good horse could cover the distance twice in a night.

But it didn't escape either the Bargello or myself that while the presumptions against Lodovico were strong, the evidence was weak. It consisted solely of the evidence of one witness, which Lodovico could easily challenge by saying, "How could the crazy girl have seen us in Padua when we were feasting in Stra?"

So we decided to lie low and let it be understood that our inquiry had come to nothing. Count Lodovico no doubt had friends with their ear to the ground in Padua, and when they told him he wasn't under suspicion he'd probably return to the Contarini palace, which he'd rented for three months. But we had to make sure neither Caterina Acquaviva nor Marcello Accoramboni gave the game away. The Bargello, who was a widower, was kind enough to take the girl into his service, and he impressed it on her that she must hold her tongue. As for Marcello, he was in no state to talk. When he saw his sister's corpse he tried to stab himself in the heart, but the leather doublet he was wearing against the cold deflected the blade, and he only gave himself a deep gash. But it was serious enough to keep him in bed at Signora Sorghini's house with a high fever.

Our plan worked perfectly. Count Lodovico was back in Padua two days later, more arrogant than ever and flaunting his Roman nobility. This didn't impress the citizens of the Most Serene Republic, though, either in Venice or in Padua.

His palace and his comings and goings, were kept under constant surveillance day and night. We thus discovered: *primo*, that he was short of money and behind with his rent; *secundo*, that he'd had dealings with Giuseppe Giacobbe, a master jeweller who visited Padua two or three times a year. Even before we summoned him, Giacobbe asked the Bargello for a private interview. The Bargello told me of this, and instead of seeing him at the Corte we told him to come to the Bargello's own house at ten o'clock at night. He turned up with three of his sons and three of his nephews, who seemed to hold him in great respect and waited for him without saying a word in the ante-room. If only my own children were as well-behaved as those Jews!

Giuseppe Giacobbe began by showing me his Roman passport, signed by Cardinal Secretary of State Rusticucci. We realised from the Christian name attributed to him in this document that despite his religion he enjoyed the protection of the present Pope. What followed confirmed it. Giacobbe told us that to thank the Holy Father for the measures he'd taken in favour of the Jewish community in Rome, the ghetto had commissioned him to make a valuable pectoral cross. The Pope had accepted the gift, but said that as he couldn't wear it himself he would keep it in his family. And a few weeks later he'd asked Giacobbe to take it to his niece, the Duchess of Bracciano, in the Sforza palace on Lake Garda. But to Giacobbe's surprise, Count Lodovico had that very morning given him the cross as a pledge for a loan of twenty thousand ducats. The Count didn't know, of course, that he, Giacobbe, had made the cross himself and knew all about its history.

Then the jeweller brought out from among his robes the same cross that the Bargello and I had admired on the Duchess's bosom when she first came to Padua. He laid it carefully on the table, and we all gazed at it for a while in silence. You'd need to have had a heart of stone not to marvel at its beauty, and at the same time not to be moved by the tragic end of the woman who had worn it. We sent someone to wake Caterina Acquaviva, to see if she recognised the cross and could testify that it really had belonged to her mistress. The maid appeared at last, still only half awake and less than half dressed. As soon as she saw the cross she cried, "My God! My God! My poor mistress!", and burst into sobs. The Bargello considered this proof enough, and sent her back to bed in a kindly manner. By the way he looked at her as she left the room I concluded it wasn't just out of kindness that he'd taken her in.

Then Giacobbe produced a document signed by Lodovico Orsini, Count of Oppedo, and declaring that he'd given a pectoral cross belonging to him (there followed a detailed description of the article) to Giuseppe Giacobbe, jeweller, as pledge for a loan of twenty thousand ducats. Giacobbe was prepared to give us this document in exchange for a written promise, signed by me, that the city of Padua would return the twenty thousand ducats to him should Count Lodovico be unable to do so. I wrote out and signed the required paper and let Giacobbe go, promising at his request that I wouldn't act against the Count until he'd left the city. Which he and his sons and nephews did at dawn the next day.

I then had all the city gates closed, and summoned Count Lodovico to appear in court. He came with all his gang, and when our men tried to keep out all of them but him they forced their way in, practically under our very noses. The whole forty or so, all armed, were separated from me and the other judges only by the dais and the long bench behind which we sat.

I whispered to the Bargello to get together all the men he could find and post them in the room behind me, but not to intervene unless I gave two strokes with my gavel. I did wonder, however, what kind of resistance our brave fellows could put up against such determined scoundrels, and I decided that in the circumstances I'd question the Count as unprovocatively as possible.

He was extremely arrogant from the outset, and before I'd opened my mouth declared it was outrageous for one of his rank to be subjected to interrogation. It was an intolerable affront to treat him as a suspect,

402

almost as the accused, in a matter that was nothing to do with him.

"But, Signor Conte," said I in the mildest of voices, "you're not appearing as the accused – only as a witness. For example, I'd like to know what your squire Alfredo Colombani was doing in the Cavalli palace at the time of the massacre?"

"From what I've heard he was having an affair with a maid in the palace. That's why he didn't come with us to Venice."

"Have you ever seen this maid, Signor Conte?"

"No."

"She claims to have seen you, and Count Paganello, in the Cavalli palace on the night of the massacre."

"She's crazy."

"Perhaps. I've been told that you and your friends, instead of going to Venice, stopped and feasted that night in an inn at Stra, not far from Padua."

"That's right. Is that a crime?"

"Not all all, Signor Conte. I've also been informed that the Duchess of Bracciano's pectoral cross has been seen in the hands of a Jewish jeweller. Do you know anything about it?"

"Absolutely nothing."

"That's a pity, because the Jewish jeweller has run away, and we're looking for him."

"I hope you find him."

"Thank you, Signor Conte. That's all. As you see, it wasn't much. You and your friends are free to withdraw."

"Am I free to leave the city?"

"Not yet, Signor Conte. The gates have been shut on orders from Venice, and they can't be opened without further instructions from there."

"Can I at least send a courier to take this letter to Prince Virginio Orsini in Florence?"

"Yes, Signor Conte, on condition that you tell me what it says."

"Here it is," said he scornfully, giving it to one of his men to pass to me.

I read it carefully. It was so completely innocuous it aroused my suspicions.

"Signor Conte," I said "please write down the name of your courier and I'll give orders for him to be let through."

He complied, and as soon as he'd gone I sent the Bargello to give our men two very precise orders: first, to let the courier through; second, to stop him a league outside the city and search both him and his horse. Him from head to foot, and the horse from its mane to its hind hooves, not forgetting the saddle.

The search, which the Bargello decided to supervise personally, produced the results I'd hoped for. The letter I'd read was found in the courier's doublet – but in his right boot there was another, briefer but not nearly so harmless.

"To Lord Virginio Orsini.
Most illustrious lord,
I have carried out that which we agreed upon. I've been under some suspicion, but have outwitted the Podestà and am now regarded as the most gallant gentleman in the world.
    I did the job myself. Send me men and money. I'm destitute.
    Your devoted servant and cousin,

Lodovico Orsini"

"I did the job myself." And he was boasting about it, the wretch! The more I studied the letter the more I was struck by Lodovico's baseness and stupidity. Why did he have to write it at all when he knew he was under suspicion? And he'd only reinforced that suspicion by saying he knew about Alfredo's affair with a maid in the palace. And the poor fool preened himself on having got the better of the Podestà!

Armed with this irrefutable evidence I gave orders for the militia to surround the Contarini palace and cover it with all the artillery we possessed. Then I sent a courier to Venice with a copy of the incriminating letter. At seven the next evening the most illustrious Avogador Bragadina arrived from the Republic with orders to capture all the miscreants, dead or alive.

As those besieged inside the palace refused to capitulate, we used the cannon, the walls collapsed, and Lodovico had to surrender.

He did so in his own peculiar way – in other words, like a bad actor striving for effect. He appeared alone in the doorway of the ruined palace, sombrely dressed, with a dagger at his side and the skirt of his coat thrown elegantly over his arm.

He was brought to the town hall, and while they were waiting for me to arrive they took away his dagger. I found him leaning nonchalantly against a pillar, trimming his nails with a small pair of scissors. When he saw me he dropped this affected pose. He put the scissors away in his doublet, gave me a bow proportioned to my importance, apologised politely for putting me to so much trouble, and asked me to have him put somewhere appropriate to his rank. He later declared himself dissatisfied with the cell I'd given him. Then he asked for writing materials and wrote a long letter to the Venetian Republic requesting, as a count, a prince and an Orsini, that he might be spared the indignity of public torture. His wish was granted. He was strangled in his cell in accordance with all the legal forms, and with a cord of red silk.

In his last moments he acted with studied bravado. You'd have thought he was wearing a mask and buskins and performing on a stage. You felt like tearing the mask off to see if there was anything behind it. Probably a terrified little boy afraid to die.

His air of haughty self-assurance wavered only for a second. I'd asked Marcello Accoramboni if he wanted to be present at the execution of his sister's murderer, and to my great surprise, ill though he was, he said he did. He arrived leaning on the shoulders of two servants and looking pale and wan, just as Count Lodovico was condescendingly pretending to fit in with the executioner's requirements.

"Is this right, sir? Am I in the right position for you?"

I asked Accoramboni if he had anything to say to the condemned man.

"Yes," he whispered.

And fixing his feverish eyes on the Count he said in a weak but audible voice: "Signor Conte, I regard you as the most odious little vermin God ever allowed to crawl over the face of the earth. But as my sister forgave you, I forgive you too."

The Count turned pale and opened his mouth to speak, but changed his mind. Probably he didn't want to detract from the decorum of his end. Then he turned to the executioner and said with an affable smile: "I am ready, sir."

The executioner put the red cord round his neck, and as he was tightening it Lodovico murmured "Gesù, Gesù, Gesù". He'd probably thought it up beforehand to lend some dignity to his exit, though he'd been so bad a Christian his whole life long.

The cord broke, but he had already fainted, and the executioner was able to apply another one without his regaining consciousness. When the Bargello rebuked the executioner for twisting the tourniquet too fast, the man said: "I'm sorry, Signor Bargello, but I wanted to get it over with — him and his airs and graces!"

With three exceptions, Lodovico's thirty-four men were put to various kinds of torture. The judges decided on this, against my wishes, to satisfy the mob.

About half of the ruffians had already been dispatched when the executioner went and asked the Bargello for two days' rest.

"Rest?" said the Bargello. "What for?"

"Forgive me if I offend you, Signor Bargello," said the man, hanging his head, "but I'm tired of all the blood. So are the people. They booed me yesterday."

So the judges met and decided to make do with hanging the rest. But it took them a long time to make up their minds, and while they were still deliberating one of the condemned men, majordomo Filenfi, managed to prove that he couldn't have taken part in the massacre at the Cavalli palace because he was in Venice that night on business for his master. His reprieve arrived as he was standing on the scaffold with the noose round his neck.

I'd like to say a word about the two survivors: Marcello Accoramboni and Caterina Acquaviva. .

Marcello became quite a changed man after he'd recovered from his wound. He renounced his aristocratic pretensions, gave up wearing sword and dagger, and married Margherita Sorghini. He performed his religious duties devoutly and regularly. And — something he'd never done before — he worked. With a loan from his wife he followed in his grandfather's footsteps and set up a majolica factory in Padua. As there were no competitors here he prospered, and soon became one of our leading citizens. But there's still something rather strange about him that makes him less popular than his virtues and perseverance deserve. He's very taciturn, his eyes are blank, and he never smiles.

As for Caterina Acquaviva, when she first started to live in the Bargello's house she used to talk quite seriously of going into a convent, though this surprised everyone as she didn't seem at all that kind of person. But the Bargello must have been very persuasive, for she remained in his service. Gossips predicted she'd bring dishonour into his house, but they were wrong. She looked after the place well and was an exemplary mother to their children.

The cross that the Pope had given his niece was given back to him at his own request. He paid Giuseppe Giacobbe back out of his own pocket for the twenty thousand ducats he'd lent Count Lodovico with the cross as security. Some people in Rome said the Pope was being almost too honest, considering the person in question was only a Jew. But others, including myself, think Sixtus was right. If the head of Christendom doesn't set a good example, who will?

Not only in Venice and Rome but throughout all Italy I was thought to have handled the inquiry into this unfortunate affair with skill and prudence. But in Padua itself, and even in the city council, some people criticised me for not having banished Lodovico after he'd burned the will. I soon reduced these mischief-makers to silence by reading out a copy of the letter I'd sent to Venice the day after that incident, asking for Lodovico to be banished. I also read out the reply, in which Venice rejected my request, for perfectly valid reasons which it's unnecessary to go into here. When the same trouble-makers then criticised Venice, I ordered them to hold their tongues, and my firmness on this occasion was universally applauded.

My term as chief magistrate of Padua expires in three months' time, but I don't think I'll have any trouble being re-elected. I don't know whether to be glad or sorry: much as I appreciate the esteem my fellow-citizens so loyally demonstrate, I do sometimes get rather weary of the burdens of power.

To return to the unfortunate affair with which we have been concerned, it teaches some lessons that might be regarded as salutary if they themselves weren't so remarkably ambiguous.

The legacy by which Prince Orsini meant to assure his young wife's future cost her her life. Count Lodovico, whose crime aimed at gaining favour and money from Prince Virginio, got only death for his pains – and that less than a week after slaying an innocent young woman whom he despised because she wasn't of noble birth. But what does the word "noble" mean, applied to a creature as base as the Count?

If "justice was done" as regards Lodovico, one can't help regretting that the same justice was so negligent when it came to Prince Virginio, who was obviously shown by Lodovico's secret letter to be his accomplice and the instigator of the murder. Even if the Venetian Republic had taken the right decision and summoned the young Prince (then only sixteen) to appear in its courts, would it have had the power to make him do so, given that he was living in another sovereign state and was the nephew of the Grand Duke of Tuscany?

What happened immediately after the Duchess's death is no less a matter for astonishment to a perspicacious observer.

When dawn broke after the massacre at the Cavalli palace, Vittoria's naked corpse was displayed on a table in the church of the Eremitani, and the mob flocked to see it. Her youth and beauty, together with her reputation for kindness and piety, called forth their tears. One witness said some of them gnashed their teeth. They all cried out for vengeance. So many people came to see her that the Bargello had to send some of his men to organise a queue. Then everyone could file past to contemplate, admire and pity her – and to pity Padua too for having lost the most beautiful woman in Italy.

At about eleven o'clock the priest in charge of the Eremitani, shocked by this pagan adoration, brought a black cloth embroidered with gold to cover the Duchess's nakedness. But the people snatched it from him, practically accusing him of sacrilege. The priest and the adepts of this new religion started to argue so heatedly that the Bargello's men had to intervene and impose a compromise. The Duchess's body wouldn't be covered up, but for decency's sake it would be wrapped in her long golden hair. And it was expressly forbidden for anyone to cut off a lock of it as they went by, as some had secretly managed to do before.

It then got about that the Duchess, as she was dying, had forgiven her murderer. And she was thenceforward regarded as a saint. But instead of supplanting, this only supplemented the worship of her beauty. One woman in the queue genuflected when she reached the body, then made the sign of the cross and kissed the dead feet. All those who came after did the same.

The poor priest was very upset. Not daring to confront so determined a crowd himself, he came to see me, and with tears running down his face implored me to put a stop to this scandal.

I went to the Eremitani and saw that the Duchess had indeed become the object of a fervent half pagan, half Christian cult. It was obvious that it would cause great offence if anyone approached her without genuflecting and kissing her feet, so, not wishing either to acquiesce in the ritual or to arouse the hatred of the crowd, I kept well away. I decided the best thing to do was wait till it was dark and then have the body removed on the pretext of having it embalmed.

After that I lost no time in giving it decent burial, but a few days later there were new developments. The victim's mother, Tarquinia Accoramboni, wrote to me for permission to take her daughter's body back to Rome. Despite all my precautions to keep the letter secret, a rumour leaked out and masses of people crowded round the town hall declaring in the most vehement terms that the Duchess's own grave must stay in Padua.

I reassured them, quaking inwardly lest Sixtus V add his demand to that of Signora Accoramboni. If he did I'd have to refer it to Venice, and the decision would be out of my hands. But fortunately the Pope didn't intervene, and with the support of Marcello, who, once he'd decided to go on living, wanted to settle in our city, I was able to refuse the mother's request.

So the people of Padua still have Vittoria's grave, and faithfully every spring they deck it with flowers. Perhaps their children will remember her tragic story. But their grandchildren? And their grandchildren's children? One day the grave will be forgotten. And yet another day will come when even the lovely Vittoria's name will have vanished from the stone that shelters her dust.